C0-BEJ-319

Order this book online at www.trafford.com
or email orders@trafford.com

Most Trafford titles are also available at major online book retailers.

Note for Librarians: A cataloguing record for this book is available from Library and Archives Canada at www.collectionscanada.ca/amicus/index-e.html

Printed in Victoria, BC, Canada.

ISBN: 978-1-4251-8843-6 (Soft)

Trafford rev. 12/30/2009

www.trafford.com

North America & international
toll-free: 1 888 232 4444 (USA & Canada)
phone: 250 383 6864 • fax: 812 355 4082 • email: info@trafford.com

Dedicated to God to whom this would not exist without and to everyone who has supported me along the way.

A Starless Sky

Paige Agnew

Prologue

And then you feel it. You can feel the ground moving beneath you and everything around you quickly falling to the ground. The world is crumbling into nothing and all you can do stand still and watch the earthquake consume everything that you once knew and loved. But then you open your eyes and see that everything is at ease. And it's so surreal that as the war and the earthquake go on in your head, everyone and everything else around you is completely fine. Then you realize that life has been moving on without you as time stands still in your head. You realize that somehow you have to start moving with time...with life.

Part I

We cannot banish dangers but we can banish fears. We must not demean life by standing in awe of death.

— David Sarnoff

1. Dean's Creek

She was gone. Without my permission or consent, just gone. Forever. I couldn't bring myself to go to the funeral. It wasn't because I was afraid of the hurt I'd feel or because I didn't want closure. I already had my closure. I never really liked funerals. Not only did dead bodies freak me out but I didn't need closure with a dead body in a casket.

"Sweetie, you have to go."

In response I just moaned underneath my covers and waited patiently for my mother to leave my room in peace.

"Come on honey. You'll regret it later if you don't go. I don't want you to have to live with that."

She sat at the foot my bed rubbing my back gently. I shifted in my covers away from her and groaned yet another time.

"Pumpkin, it's not just about closure. It's about remembering."

In the seventeen years I'd known my mother, she had never run out of ways to relate me to some type of food. Every so often she would actually speak my name, but most of the time, Kahlen had been replaced by sugar, honey, sweetie, pumpkin, cupcake... etc.

I sighed as I removed the covers from over my head and looked my mom in the eyes. "Mom, just please," I cupped my hands together and gave my best puppy dog look. "Please just let it be."

She sighed as she hugged me tightly. "I don't mean to pressure you sweetie-pie. I just worry about you sometimes. That's all."

My mother released her tight grasp around my back and stood up off of my bed. She walked slowly on her way out the door as if she were fighting herself with all her might not to say more.

"Mom, wait," I said quickly. She turned around, hopeful that I had changed my mind. "Tell Ms. Bryant I'm sorry that I couldn't be there today."

She nodded understandingly before leaving my room.

I plopped my head down on my pillow hard, almost hoping that it would hurt. I stared up at my ceiling, trying as hard as I could to make some sense of the crazy world I had been thrown so viciously in. It had been exactly one week, three days, ten hours, fifty-two minutes, and I'm not sure how many seconds since I was convinced my life was slowly crumbling into nothing. I closed my eyes as tight as I could and tried to imagine myself some place happy. No matter how tightly I closed my eyes all I saw was the darkness my eyelids were providing.

I heard the familiar sound of the old engine on my Chevy pulling out of the driveway and slowly out of sight. I figured they would take my car just to make sure I wouldn't sneak off anywhere. When the sound had completely faded, I jumped out of my bed, slipped on a pair of ripped jeans and a sweatshirt before opening my window and stepping outside onto the sturdy tree. Although no one was home and I could have easily walked out the front door, I liked the tree outside my window better. Step by step I inched from the tree to the soft grass below my feet.

I took the same route I had been taking. I went

behind my house, over my neighbor's fence, down the street, and across the bridge all the way to what had become my *new* best friend, Dean's Creek. Surprisingly no one had wondered why it was called Dean's Creek, no one except me. Three days ago, I made up my own little story of the reason for the name. Dean was some bored guy who made a wooden sign with red letters painted on that said, **DEAN'S CREEK** to add some excitement to his boring life. It was pretty much a stupid and unoriginally boring story but my imagination was lacking these days because I had so many other things to worry about.

I stared into the rippling water oblivious to the rest of the world. The creek had officially become my new thinking place. It was almost serene in a way. The slow rhythmic sound of the rippling water was calming in a way and the warm April sun balanced out evenly with the cool breezes that made my skin tingle every so often. It felt like *mine*. It was undisturbed, peaceful, and whatever else *I* wanted it to be. I felt like I had gained control over something in my life, and if that something just happened to be a creek that was actually some guy named Dean…then so be it.

The creek was bigger than other creeks. It almost seemed like a tiny river going through the forest. It looked like if anyone got into the water it would at least go above the waist. Because the creek was abandoned, the grass was overgrown with dead wood lying around in some places, but it never took away from the creek's beauty.

It was times like these that I wished I wore a watch or at least remembered to bring my cell phone. But then again, I guess it didn't matter whether I remembered my cell phone or not because I'd lost it. It's not the first time I'd lost my cell phone and it probably wouldn't be the last. I had no idea how much time had gone by as I stared into space but I knew that if my mom arrived at home and found me gone, she was likely to call the police and have a full investigation and search underway.

I slipped my feet from out of the lukewarm water and put my purple flip flops back on. I lay back against the grass and took in the beautiful sunset slowly fading in the sky. Everything seemed to be fading these days. I felt like I was losing touch with life altogether. I was holding onto a thin string but not for myself, but those around me. It seemed like I should cry. It only felt like the appropriate thing to do with a situation like this— but I couldn't. After that night my eyes were eternally dry and everyone around me had classified me as a freak because of it. They all expected me to be completely distraught and crying loud sobs all the time. But what was the point? Tears wouldn't bring her *back*. Believe me if they could, I wouldn't stop crying even if took a lifetime— but they wouldn't. So therefore, it made it pointless.

I stood up off the grass, not bothering to wipe off any grass or dirt that may have been stuck to my butt and ran as fast as I could back to my house, back over the bridge, back down the street, and over my neighbor's fence, all the way to the tall tree leading to my window. My old black Chevy was back in the driveway and a pang of fear automatically struck my heart like a drum.

"Crap," I mumbled underneath my breath. I climbed back up the tree, into my open window, and back into my room. All had appeared to be fine in my house. There were no police, or the FBI, or a huge mob of investigators and search dogs. I looked over at my clock and my parents' and I had only been gone for an hour. I knew the funeral couldn't have been over with already. I sighed knowing my mom was probably worried about me and had come home early, dragging my dad along with her.

I walked out of my room and over to the staircase. I couldn't see my parents but I could hear their voices from the kitchen.

"I'm just concerned, Bill. What if this isn't just a stage with her?" I heard my mom ask.

"It's not like she doesn't have the right to act this way. Her best friend just *died*. Give her time."

Her best friend just died. The words sounded surreal to me. *Best friend? Whose?* Those were the questions that crossed my mind. But the answers to those questions crossed my heart and left scratches as they went.

"I know. I do. It's just... I care about her so much and she's been through a lot this past week. Sooner or later it's going to hit her, and it's going to hit her hard. But when it does...I just want to make sure I'm there to hold and comfort her," I started to hear sniffling and crying from my mom. "We could have lost her. That could have been *our* daughter in the casket today. The same questions keep popping up in my head, "why *not* her? Why was *her* life saved?" The sobs were getting louder. "I don't know why and I'll never know why. I don't know what to do with myself these days. I don't want to take any moment of our time together for granted."

"Life's way too short to take anything at all for granted," I heard my father say. I assumed he was hugging my mom right now to comfort her and her cries.

"One of us should go check up on her and make sure she's okay," she said before blowing her nose. I could picture my dad nodding compassionately.

My mood had just been completely switched to raw anger. I was not some fragile child who needed to be checked upon every five minutes. I was not going through a *stage*. I was being myself and if that was too much for my parents to handle, then they, along with the rest of the world, were just going to have to deal.

I heard my dad's heavy footsteps coming up the stairs and I quickly ran over to the white chair in front of my mirror before sitting down like I was busy doing something. As the footsteps came closer, I fumbled around in my jewelry box for a pair of earrings. The pair I finally grabbed weren't even matching but my dad wasn't exactly one to pay attention to detail anyway.

When he arrived at my open door, he gave a pointless knock as to announce his presence and I stayed focused at my mirror putting on my silver hoop earring on my right ear slowly.

"Hey dad," I said unusually cheerful. After I finished the right earring, I picked up a blue dangling one.

"Hey Kido," he said just as fake happily as I had. Unlike my mom, my dad had replaced a simple, Kahlen, with Kido. "You do realize that you're putting on two different earrings right?"

Geez. It seemed like lately everyone and everything's senses had been heightened. Since when did my dad notice what earrings I put on? "Yeah I do. I was just trying to see which one would look better with my outfit," Each time I lied I surprised myself with how believable it was.

"Well my vote goes for the silver," he said nonchalantly. I kept my mouth closed to suppress the irritated sigh I wanted to unleash. There was an awkward silence as my dad struggled with the right words to say. "But anyways, Kido, I came up here to check up on you. Your mother has been worrying herself to death about you lately." I couldn't help but notice how he winced a little at one word in particular.

I just rolled my eyes in response.

"She cares...that's all," he said as began to walk out of my room. Once he got out of the door he stopped and turned. "You said outfit..." He scanned my ripped jeans and sweatshirt assuming that's not what I meant by outfit. "Are you going somewhere?"

Crap.

"Uh...um... yeah. I am. I thought about it and I'm going to go stop by the funeral for the last little bit of it." I wanted to bang my head against the wall several times for my stupid lie.

My dad raised his eyebrows up at me surprised. "Oh, well I'll go tell your mother. We'll drive you."

"Dad, no. I'd rather drive myself if you don't mind." I cleared my throat, realizing that my voice was shaking a little bit. All he did was give that famous, compassionate nod he did so well before leaving my room and heading back down the stairs.

By the time I had gotten to the funeral, they were already carrying out the casket to go to the burial. I could have easily gotten out of the car and followed everyone to the burial but now I had an excuse. I could tell my parents that by the time I gotten there, they were already leaving and I didn't know what cemetery they were going to. It wasn't the best lie, but my parents wouldn't pry too much considering they had been walking on egg shells around me lately.

As I sat at the red light, I had a choice. I could turn left onto Main Street and pull into the church parking lot, or I could keep going straight towards Dean's Creek. My conscience pulled me left but my choice no longer existed. I was in the wrong lane and the red light had changed to green so I was forced to go straight.

I looked over at the church and saw them all standing there in the parking lot. There were at least twenty people from school crying their eyes out and I was positive that half of them didn't even know her. It was amazing to me how some people would do anything they could to turn the attention back to themselves. Instead of having people focus on the reason why they attended the funeral in the first place, they would cry their eyes out so other people would spend their time comforting them instead.

I took my foot off the brake and stepped forward on the gas.

I parked the car on the street before getting out and being blinded by the unusually hot April sun. I slammed the door hard and walked around the winding creek all the way to the front. I realized that anyone that might see me would think I was absolutely insane. I was in a black dress and black heels wandering around in an old abandoned creek. With the next step I took, my right heel sunk into the dirt. My body lost balance and I fell down hard to the ground before starting to roll down the steep hill towards the water quickly.

My body rolled and rolled and then finally hit something hard that felt like a leg. I was so stunned by everything that had just happened that I didn't have time to think, stop, or scream. I was breathing hard as I laid flat on the ground and not only had my dress flown up about five inches above my thighs, but I also realized I had lost another heel in the process.

"You know, I may not know a whole lot about heels but I'm pretty sure that walking on the grass isn't such a good idea." My rescuer extended his arm and held out his hand.

"Thanks for the tip," I mumbled.

I looked up at his upside down body feeling a little

dazed and disoriented. I stood up by myself, ignoring his hand then smoothed out my dress and made sure my messy bun was still intact.

"I'm Kennley." He offered a hand shake.

I chuckled a little to myself. *Kennley?* What kind of a name was Kennley? The image of a Ken Barbie doll kept popping up in my mind. Once again, I ignored his hand and walked away from him towards the creek to sit down on the grass and stick my feet in the lukewarm water. Who was this so called *Kennley* anyhow and what was he doing at my Creek. No one ever came here. The creek was practically abandoned but I liked it that way. I loved the tall tree that created the perfect amount of shade and the long, winding creek that disappeared in the forest. He felt like an intruder and I couldn't help but be rude to him. He seemed nice and maybe a little overly friendly, but I didn't care. I wasn't looking for any new friends or acquaintances. I was looking for some place peaceful and that place had just been robbed from me.

"What are you doing here?" I asked staring at my reflection in the creek. I wanted my words to sound more curious than accusatory but they didn't come out that way.

Kennley walked over to sit next to me but I immediately scooted away from him. "I'm sorry. I didn't think I needed a reason be here. Next time I'll call you first to get your blessing."

I rolled my eyes. Even though I could feel him staring at me I ignored it. His cell phone began to ring to *Barbie Girl* and he looked at his phone before swearing underneath his breath.

"Well… um…," Kennley paused like he was about to say my name, but then realized he didn't know it. "I'm guessing your name is Dean since you seem to own this Creek. So Dean, it's been nice bumping into you today, but I gotta run. Oh, and by the way, I'm pretty sure my little sister changed my ring-tone."

He quickly stood up and left and part of me wanted to say goodbye to him but instead I just ignored him completely. I picked up my scattered heels, got into my car, and left because I didn't want to stay at the creek. It didn't feel like mine anymore.

By the time I made it back to my car, I realized I was being stupid. I couldn't go home just yet, I had made up my mind not to go back to the creek, and the funeral wasn't even an option, so where else was I going to go? I sat in my car trying to come up with a plan but I barely had five bucks on me so I was considering going to McDonald's. My thoughts were all distracted when I saw Kennley speed walking across the street and dodging cars while he was talking on his cell phone. He looked like he was unusually angry. Although I didn't know what his usual behavior was, he seemed much too friendly and jovial to have a look like that on his face. He screamed something I couldn't hear— partly because my window was up— before he slammed the phone shut, and took off in a fully fledged sprint down the street. I pushed aside my curiosity, turned the key in the ignition, and pulled off down the street to the closest McDonald's.

I was learning to accept adapt to the world I had been thrown so viciously in. The past was well... the past. As for the future, that was a mystery. But as for the present...the present held power. The present could be whatever I wanted it to be... And that alone created my future. I had never felt so powerful and yet so weak in all my life.

2. Pity

"I'm fine!" I sat up in the hard, cold, hospital bed. "Really I am. Look, not a scratch on me," I said in a calmer tone.

"I know honey. But the doctor said that they want you to stay overnight just to make sure you really *are* okay." My mom put her hand on the back of my neck and ran her fingers through my dark, sandy brown hair.

I crossed my arms and slammed my head down hard onto the pillow. Pain shot through my head and neck but I tried not to wince. If I showed any signs of hurt, there was no way I was ever going to get out of this horribly boring place. The TV only got ten channels and the bland white walls were driving me away from my sanity along with that recognizable *hospital* smell.

"But I *am* okay. I just want to go home to my nice, warm, comfy bed," I whined.

I heard frantic footsteps and yelling from down the hall. A nurse was screaming for a doctor. I immediately sat up in my bed and winced just a tiny bit. My dad walked over to the door and into the hall. He looked away quickly from the hallway and looked at me first, then my mom with absolute fear written all over his slightly wrinkled face. Almost like a chain reaction, my mom looked out the door and turned back with the same look he had had.

"What is it? What's happening?" I asked softly. Neither

one of them answered. "What's going on?" I had already thrown the covers off of me and had started walking to the door. Neither one of them tried to stop me.

I felt my heart dive to my stomach as the realization sunk into my head. There was a crowd of nurses, people and doctors watching in awe as they got her onto the stretcher quickly and moved her into the elevator.

"Everyone clear out! Move! We need to get her to the ER stat!" One of the doctors yelled.

Almost involuntarily, I screamed at the top of my lungs, "No!" as I ran to the elevator doors and watched them shut in front my face.

I sat up quickly in my desk at the back of the room and wiped the little bit of drool away from the corners of my mouth. Many sets of wide eyes were looking back at me, studying every little movement I made. I looked around the room confused and then immediately realized what had happened. I had fallen asleep during a test that just happened to be ten percent of my grade. In the crowd of wide, wondering eyes, I found a pair that seemed faintly upset.

"Kaitlyn, see me after class please," Mr. Simmons ordered.

I nodded once, a little disoriented, before beginning to focus on my slightly wet with drool test. I grabbed my pencil and began to circle the letter A when the bell rang. I sighed and started to put all of my things into my backpack. As soon as everyone had filed out of the classroom, Mr. Simmons closed the door and went to the back of the room where I was still putting my stuff into my backpack slowly.

"Kaitlyn, I know you've been going through a hard time and—,"

"It's *Kahlen*," I corrected him. It was simply amazing

how no one could ever seem to get my name right. I've been called everything from Katie to Karina.

"Kahlen," he corrected while searching for the right words to say. "Why don't you come in early tomorrow to take the test?"

I really didn't like Mr. Simmons. All the girls at school thought that he was the next best thing since Matt Damon which left me as an outcast for not thinking about guys my dad's age.

I studied his face for a moment. Pity had spread across his forehead all the way down to his chin. This face wasn't unfamiliar. It was the same face I had seen on mostly everyone lately. Everywhere I went that face would follow. I felt like Mary but I was *trying* to lose my little lamb whose fleece was white as snow.

Looking at Mr. Simmons reminded me of my mom's face this morning. When she woke me up, she was pleading with me to stay home for one more day. She sat at the foot of my bed like she always did and rubbed her hand in little circles around my back.

"Sweetie-pie, maybe it's too soon to go back. I don't want you unfocused at school." She had looked at the dark circles underneath my eyes. "Honey, I know you didn't get much sleep last night. I thought I heard you scream last night. Were you having a nightmare?" Ridiculous pity had shadowed her face.

"No," I had lied. "I think I was having a dream that I got to meet Johnny Depp and Orlando Bloom."

She pondered over my lie for a second before cracking a little grin. "Well... I guess that is scream worthy." Her smile faded. "But when I heard you scream, I went to go check on you just to make sure you were alright. You seemed fine, but you were snoring like your father." She winced in disgust.

"I was not!" I objected.

She shrugged and stood up off of the bed. "Just think about it okay? One more day of rest wouldn't kill you,"

"Mom, I've been gone for a week already. I don't want to get too behind."

She nodded, gave up her fight, and left my room in silence.

Mr. Simmons stood up from the desk he was sitting on top of and started to walk back to the front of the room.

"Tomorrow. Seven-thirty," he said. Showing up tomorrow was no longer an option.

"No," I said quietly.

"Excuse me?" he asked turning around to face me.

"No. It was my fault, my mistake. I shouldn't have fallen asleep. I have no excuse."

"But you *do* have an excuse."

I blocked my mind from the excuse he had implied and tried to focus on the situation at hand. Mr. Simmons face had now turned to confusion. -"Just give me the zero... well unless I got number one correct." I gestured towards my wet-with-drool test with "A" circled for number one.

He gestured for me to hand him my test and once I gave it to him, he looked at it for a moment before handing it back to me.

"Number one is C. So tomorrow...Seven-thirty," he repeated.

"No," I said again, but louder this time. "I know your policy on making up tests. You're only doing this because of pity." I picked up my backpack and swung it over my shoulder. "And I don't need yours... or anybody else's *pity*." I practically spat the word.

I was happy he didn't try to stop me as I walked out the classroom and into the loud hallway packed with students. I walked to my nearby locker and opened it in record time, dropped my backpack down on the ground, and shoved the contents of it into it. Usually I kept my locker neat and tidy but I was in no mood to carefully stack my books into it nicely.

I tuned out all of the voices around me except for one. Bradley Robinson. His voice was impossible to tune out or ignore. He was a tall six foot one with bright red hair and blue eyes. "Here we are, 5123." He gestured towards the locker one down from mine. "It has good locale too. The boys' bathroom is to your left, drinking fountain to your right, and the vending machine is straight ahead." He stopped talking and I heard his footsteps walk closer to me. "Oh, and not to mention the absolutely lovely and beautiful Kahlen Thomas—also to your right."

I gave him a tiny smile. There was no doubt Bradley would be Bradley. "Talking to yourself again Bradley?" I asked.

He leaned against the locker next to me with a smug look on his face. "No." He put his arm around my shoulders and turned me around to face the opposite direction. "Actually, I was talking to your new locker neighbor…" He stopped his sentence short, staring confused because there was no one behind him. He looked right, then left, searching for my new locker neighbor but saw nothing. Bradley sighed with relief when he found my neighbor hiding around the corner. He grabbed his arm and dragged him over to me.

"Kahlen, meet—,"

"Dean," my neighbor said. I couldn't decipher his emotion because his face was completely blank.

"It's *Kahlen*," I said as a knee-jerk reaction.

Bradley was standing in between us and looked at us both in confusion. "Who's *Dean*?" he asked.

Neither of us bothered to answer him. After a moment of silence, he brushed off his curiosity. "Well anyways, let's get your things in your locker so we can head to lunch. We've already missed a good five minutes," he continued.

Kennley was a rugged kind of handsome. His green eyes were like headlights and his biceps big. It was so weird that his green eyes were in so much contrast with his dark brown hair, but somehow… it matched perfectly. I must have looked like an idiot standing there, trying to figure out the mystery of it all. I forbid my eyes from wandering to his muscular chest and still I just stood there like an idiot, looking at him not saying a word.

"I have an idea," Kennley broke the prolonged silence. "How about you head off to lunch without me, and Kahlen and I will meet you there?" he offered.

Bradley looked like he was about to disagree but then changed his mind. "Well… it is fish stick day. I guess I can't pass up that." He smiled at us and then walked away.

As soon as Bradley was out of sight, Kennley let out a deep sigh and said to himself, "Finally." He looked down at a piece of paper he held in his hands with his combination on it and opened his locker with ease before starting to pull all of his things out of his backpack. "How do you stand that kid? It's already fifth hour and I've barely seen one corner of the school. He talked about the importance of the Gerald R. Ford statue by the wall for an hour then he showed me the trophy case and explained each one of the big wins the trophies represented. If I had to spend one more minute— let alone a whole lunch period with him…"

he trailed off, easily disturbed by the thought. One by one he stuck his books in his locker and then looked at me, slamming his locker closed. "Well I'm done. Let's head off to lunch."

I ignored him in silent shock. It was *him*... the guy that stole my creek. Was he trying to steal my school too? Well if he wanted the school he could take it, I wasn't too fond of it anyhow. As for the creek, I wasn't going to give that one up without a fight.

"Excuse me?" I broke my silence. I hadn't said more than one sentence to him yet he was under the impression we were friends.

"Well... I need someone to show me where the cafeteria is." His green eyes were staring at me intensely. It was like he could see into my soul and I had to admit it scared me somewhat. "If we don't go soon, he's gonna come looking for me."

I still stood there in silence, half ignoring him. I wasn't even really sure why I was acting the way I was. But then again, was it so bad that I wanted more than anything to be left alone? I was still in the wrong. What really had Kennley done to me? He showed up at a creek I was claiming as mine? I was torn between actually giving this Kennley a chance or to continue acting as I was.

He sighed. "Listen, I don't know what I did to personally piss you off but I'm sorry. I'm sorry I stopped you from rolling into a whole bunch of water and I'm sorry that I thought to myself, 'wow, that girl is beautifully out of my league but it's worth a shot to try and start a conversation with her'," he said as he picked his backpack off the ground and swung it around his shoulder.

When he started to walk away I grimaced before finally speaking. "I'm sorry!" I yelled after him. I paused for a moment and I wasn't exactly sure why or where I was going with this. "Yesterday, I wasn't having the best of days, even though that's still no excuse. I'm stubborn and set in my own ways. Sometimes it takes a little while for someone to finally knock me off my high horse and back to reality where I belong." I surrendered to the beautiful eyes. "You just caught me off guard yesterday," I sighed. "That's all. And plus... today hasn't been all that grand either. I just willingly got a zero on a test that's ten percent of my grade and might potentially fail another test next hour. The list could go on and on but I think I'll stop now considering I'm babbling and I'm probably just as bad as Bradley." I let out a huge sigh trying to catch my breath.

Kennley laughed at me, still keeping his incredible eye contact. "So does this mean were going to lunch?" he chuckled.

I started to walk, leading the way to the cafeteria and we walked in silence for a little while until he broke it.

"Can I ask you something?" he said.

"Sure," I said hesitantly.

"Why did you leave the funeral early?"

I stared at him incredulously and at least one million questions were running through my head. "I wasn't at the funeral,"

"Well...I just thought that because you were wearing a black dress and shoes, plus the creek isn't that far off from a church that just happened to have a funeral going on...,"

I was quiet for a moment trying to decide how much information to give on the matter. "You're not completely wrong," I admitted. "I was kind of planning on going but things changed."

"Why did they change?" He asked.

I sighed. "You ask a lot of questions don't you?"

He grinned and shrugged. "Just part of my charm."

"Yeah, well... curiosity *killed* the cat." I joked.-

"Ah... yes. But satisfaction brought him back."

I started to laugh and the sound was almost foreign to me. It felt as if I hadn't laughed in ages and soon he started to laugh too even though his laughter seemed to be more directed at me than what he had said. After our laughter died out the silence returned briefly.

"Can I ask *you* a question?" I asked.

"Knock yourself out," he shrugged.

"Where did you take off to yesterday? I saw you running and yelling at someone on your cell phone. You were practically frantic... You seemed really upset."

He dropped his eye contact and stared into the now empty lunch room. I wanted to apologize and take back the question but I didn't...I was too curious to take anything back. I still had the image of the panic written all over his face and it was practically frightening so with interest on the matter, I instead waited patiently for his answer.

"Great. We missed lunch," he said irritated.

I stared into the empty room with amazement. Had that much time really gone by? I hadn't even heard the bell ring or seen anyone going to class. It took me a minute to respond because I was too flustered by the fact that I had just spent about fifteen minutes talking to a stranger I was supposed to be aggravated at.

"Not everyone feels like Bradley. Its fish stick day... there wasn't a lot to miss." Then the realization sunk down into my head. I was missing class right now... a *test* right now. "Crap!" I nearly shouted. "I'm missing my test, I'm missing class, I'll get a detention if I show up late, and if I don't show up at all I'll get a Saturday detention not to mention being grounded for eternity by my parents, and—," I was silenced by Kennley extending both of his muscular arms, putting them on my shoulders and stared into my eyes... into my soul. For some reason I felt like he could see right through me even though I hardly knew him.

"You know... I think I've got a plan," he grinned.

I must have been really desperate to go along with Kennley's plan, but I wasn't complaining. We had walked to the school office to discuss some things. I kept asking him where were we going and what were we doing but he just kept repeating, *"Patience is the key."* It seemed like something out of a fortune cookie *and that alone had my head distant in other thoughts.* When he got to the office he told me to sit down and wait while he talked to the vice principal.

He came back out of the office only fifteen minutes later with a smile on his face. "It's all settled."

"Are you kidding me?" I asked in disbelief. "How on earth did you—",

"I worked my charm that's all. I told Mr. What's-his-butt that Bradley Robinson ditched me and I needed another guide for the rest of the day. And for that lucky guide of my choosing, he or she will get to miss the rest of their classes for the day to show me around the school. But I have some different plans in mind."

Poor Bradley, I thought. He was probably going to get in trouble for so-called *ditching* Kennley.

"Like..." I asked.

"Well I was thinking that my guide and I... whoever he or she might be— could go get something to eat because for some odd reason I missed lunch. Of course no one would know my guide and I...whoever he or she might be— could ditch. And then my guide... whoever he or she—,"

"Okay! Enough!" I extended my arm and put my hand on his chest to make him stop talking. "I get it, I understand." I removed my hand from his muscular chest quickly. Although he did not seem to mind, I couldn't stop the sheepish grin from sliding on to my face and my cheeks from blushing.

We walked out the school and to Kennley's car and I looked at it in amazement. It was a beautifully gorgeous, dark blue BMW.

"Dean, Eddie— Eddie, Dean," he said introducing me to his car.

"Eddie?" I asked.

"I don't know... he just looks like an Eddie don't you think? I got him as a gift not too long ago."

"Yes. I can definitely see how this inanimate object deserves the name Eddie."

"Inanimate object? That is so condescending... patronizing even." Although it sounded like mock horror, he looked serious like I had actually hurt his car's feelings.

He walked over on my side of the door and opened it for me.

"Thanks," I said surprised. "So...why did you get Eddie as a gift?" I wished my parents would get me a car like this as a gift although it was very unlikely.

"Good behavior," he said. "I was being rewarded."

It was almost as beautiful on the inside as it was on the out. It looked like it was brand new. As we pulled out of the school parking lot, I didn't bother asking where we were going because the truth was... I didn't care. I didn't care where we were going or the fact that I was in the car with almost a complete stranger. It felt so good and I wasn't thinking about everything that had happened over the last couple of weeks. I wasn't fighting any emotions...I was just living in the moment, in the present. It was powerful... and that felt good. Mostly, it was strange that I was talking with Kennley like I had known him for years instead of for minutes.

I let down the window and let the wind blow through my hair. It was a scorching, hot day so any little bit of breeze felt wonderful against my warm skin. We eventually pulled into the parking lot of Ice Cream Central. We walked in and ordered. I got a double scoop of cookie dough while Kennley devoured his triple scoop of vanilla ice cream. I found vanilla ice cream boring compared to all the other many options out there.

"Can't beat the classics," he explained to me when I asked him why he ordered just vanilla.

I was so confused. Part of me was saying that I should feel kind of weird or at least guilty for ditching school and hanging out with someone whose last name I didn't even know. But the other half was telling me to relax and enjoy the moment. So I did. Kennley sat silently eating his ice cream at the booth across from me. I sat there and studied him. I studied every movement he made and that beautiful shape to his face. I couldn't put my finger on it, but it felt as if I'd known him for a lifetime. It didn't feel as if I'd just met him yesterday and then more officially today. I felt so unusually comfortable around him.

"It was so funny. The dude is jumping on the trampoline right? And he's totally being a show off, performing for us all the different tricks he can do then—" He paused to laugh at his memory. "Then he tries to do this trick he calls a Wampo."

"A Wampo?" I asked.

"I have no idea why he calls it a Wampo, but never mind that. So anyway, he flies in the air and does this back flip with twist-spin-thingy, and then BAM!"

I jumped back in my seat.

"He lands the Wampo but goes flying off the trampoline into a tree! He ended up with a mild concussion, broken leg, and arm. Funniest thing I've ever seen."

"Wow. That sounds...pretty awful," I said imagining the amount of pain the "dude" had went through.

"Awful? Well I guess that's one person's opinion. I for one thought it was hilarious."

I stared at him incredulously.

"You know..." he explained. "I read once in a dictionary that it's other peoples' discomfort that causes laughing."

I responded with a shrug. "Well I guess that's one person's opinion," I said repeating his previous words.

"So... what's the funniest thing you've ever seen?" he asked.

I froze.

I guess I had underestimated how much time had gone by again. School must have been out been out because Marissa Harrison and her friends whose names I was not aware of walked into Ice Cream Central.

Marissa Harrison bothered me. Everything about her... *bothered* me. I had absolutely no idea what it was about her exactly that made me want crawl out of my skin and get as far away from her as possible...but it did. I just couldn't put my finger on it. It wasn't that she was rude and mean, or that she was gorgeous in every way possible, or even that she would always call me—

"KAY!" she yelled from across the room as she ran over to me as fast as her sparkly silver heels would let her. Her arms were extended out to me for a hug and it took every fiber of my being to get out of the booth and hug her back…just to be polite. Her long and wavy dark brownish red hair smothered my face. I was always somewhat envious of that hair of hers. It was the dark kind of red that looked like it had to have been fake but you could tell it was natural. It matched perfectly against her pale skin.

"Hey Marissa," I said with fake enthusiasm.

She still didn't let go of her hold around me. "I didn't know you were back today. I thought that you might be out for another week or so… you know… all things considered."

I slipped my way out of her grasp and stood there motionless. I suddenly remembered what it was exactly that I didn't like about Marissa Harrison…

I took a deep breath. How did that song go again? *Raindrops on roses and whiskers on kittens, bright copper kettles and warm woolen mittens…I simply remember my favorite things and then I don't feel so bad.* I replayed the song from *The Sound of Music* over and over again in my head but I still couldn't tune her out.

"If I were you, I don't know what I'd do with myself," she continued.

It's been so hard moving on without her. I still can't get over what happened. It's so completely heartbreaking. I feel like I'm watching a movie or I'm dreaming. I mean as much as *I* miss her… then you must be—,"-

Marissa had no idea how much this topic hurt in the pit of my stomach. My stomach twisted and turned in my body and I could feel the color of my skin fading.

"I don't feel so good," I announced before sprinting out of the doors and onto the sidewalk. I rested my hands on my knees and inhaled deep breaths.

FOCUS. FOCUS. FOCUS! Get it together Kahlen.

Come on. Get it together! The screams inside my head weren't helping.

Cream colored ponies and crisp apple strudels
Doorbells and sleigh bells and schnitzel with noodles
Wild geese that fly with the moon on their wings
These are a few of my favorite things

"Kahlen?"

I didn't have to turn around to know who it was. I stood up straight and took my hands off of my knees, at least trying to pretend like I wasn't having an anxiety attack...or whatever you wanted to call this little episode.

"Listen, I—," he started to say.

"I'll walk." I didn't want to hear what he had to say. In the short time I had been standing out here, I was sure that Marissa had filled Kennley in on all the happenings lately. You know... all things considered.

"What?"

"I'll walk," I repeated. "The school is only a couple of blocks away. I need to get my car and drive home because I'm sure my parents are probably wondering where I am by now. If I'm not there soon, the FBI could be involved."

"What kind of guy would I be if I let you walk?" he asked.

"Someone who knows what's good for him," I said as I started to walk off.

After I was about two minutes into walking, the clouds darkened and each raindrop sounded like bullets hitting the cement. My hair was beginning to become completely drenched along with my clothes. I had been walking for ten minutes now and I wished I wasn't so stubborn. Why had I not gone back with Kennley? Why had I fooled myself into believing the school was only a couple of blocks away, when in actuality, it took us ten minutes to get from the school to ICC with a car. But in the back of my head, I knew exactly why. Pity. I was guessing that Kennley had found out and he was probably somewhere feeling sorry for me. Then that face would start to arrive, the same face that followed me everywhere, the face that was on my mom, on Mr. Simmons, on Marissa, and now on Kennley.

"DEAN!"

I looked over onto the street to see Kennley yelling at me from his car named Eddie.

"You know, you should really stop calling me that!" I yelled over the pouring rain. It was so loud I could barely hear my own thoughts.

"Would you stop being so stubborn and let me drive you back?" he yelled.

I thought about it for a second. I could continue walking in the pouring rain, eventually get my car and get home extremely late, or I could let him drive me, and I could just get home a little late instead of pushing the luck I didn't have with my parents.

I walked over to Eddie and got into it, slamming the door behind me.

"Easy," Kennley warned.

His phone began to ring to Barbie Girl and I still couldn't help but smile at what he had said was his sister's doing. He ignored his phone and let it ring.

"Aren't you going to answer that?" I asked.

"No." The light in his eyes had vanished and they seemed much darker than before.

I thought about the day of the funeral when I had gone to Dean's Creek. The same questions crossed my mind that still went unanswered. Why had he left in such a hurry? Why did he take off running down the street? Who was he yelling at on the phone?

"Why not?"

"Because," he paused. "It's dangerous to drive—especially in weather like this, and talk on the phone." The light returned to his eyes just a tiny bit but then he sighed as if he was annoyed.

"What?" I demanded.

He paused, hesitant, "You're getting the seat wet."

"Well there's nothing I can do about that now unless you'd like me to take my clothes off," I said annoyed.

I saw him grin a little bit out of the corner of my eye. "There I go again…" he said. "…Personally pissing you off."

I sighed. "I'm not—," I started to explain myself but then stopped. "Just drive Kennley."

The car ride was silent from that point on.

When I eventually got home, there were no police, not including my dad who happened to be a police officer. My parents, of course, interrogated me with questions about where I had been, so I told them the truth. Well… part of the truth.

"I went to ICC," I explained.

"Honey, what's ICC?" My mom asked.

"I think that's what the kids are calling Ice Cream Central these days, dear." My dad told her and he was obviously proud of himself for knowing the answer.

"Well, I'm really tired from today, so I'm just gonna head up to bed early." I turned away from the couch my parents were sitting on and towards the stairs.

"Wait Kido!" My dad called after me.

I turned back around to face him. "Yes dad?"

My mom nudged my dad gently. I could tell it wasn't something I wasn't supposed to see. So I pretended I didn't but waited patiently for my dad to answer.

"Never mind." He fought the words out.

I walked quickly up the stairs and took my usual

spot out of sight from anyone downstairs and waited patiently for my parents to begin discussing me.

"This is getting ridiculous," My dad practically spat and his tone scared me a little. "I can understand grieving but there is no need to baby her like this."

There was a long silence so I was guessing my mom had nothing to say in return.

"First, we get a call from her teacher about her falling asleep in class, she has a bad attitude most of the time, and then she comes home three hours late soaking wet—,"

"Well it's raining outside," My mom defended me. "What else did you expect?"

"Are you telling me she got that wet from getting out of the car and walking into the house?" It was obviously a rhetorical question. "Lisa, why are you babying her? I miss Emma as much as anyone else but there are only so many times you can use the Emma excuse. Her behavior is starting to get out of hand. What if she needs help?"

I moved away from the staircase and into my room, slamming the door behind me, and then locking it.

Help? What did he mean help? Like professional help? A therapist? I shuddered at the thought. I pondered over every word my dad had said— each like a little needle poking at my mind but I didn't try to think of something else. I didn't try to block the pain, but there was still one word...one name I wasn't willing to think. There was only so much one person could take in two weeks, let alone one day.

I fell back onto my bed and drowned myself in music. My ears were filled with Natasha Bedingfield's *Pocket Full of Sunshine*.

Take me away: A secret place.
A sweet escape: Take me away.
Take me away to better days.
Take me away: A higher place.

3. Barriers

I had never had a hangover in my life, but when I woke up this morning, I believe I came remarkably close. My head pounded and I even felt somewhat nauseous. My body was telling me to stay home and rest but as stubborn as I was, I refused to listen. I had already missed too much school for one more day in bed to be justified. Everything that had happened yesterday felt like a dream. I was still a little unsure of the reality of it all. It seemed like yesterday didn't fit along with the other puzzle pieces of my life. Then again, some other things that happened didn't seem fair or fit either. I had trouble convincing myself that I had skipped school with the new guy in town I hadn't even known. Kennley was so welcoming and friendly that I felt as if I were the new guy instead of him. He seemed so confident of himself and his actions. It was confusing in a way that it was in so much contrast to myself. I unwillingly pushed the covers from me to the edge of my bed and stood up onto the floor. I stepped onto my wet clothes that were lying onto the ground which took me by surprise.

It wasn't a dream.

I wasn't exactly sure if I wanted it to be a dream or not but it was time to face the truth. My life was changing. The Kahlen I had known a couple of weeks ago was like a snake in the process of shedding its skin. I could feel it. I could feel the war raging inside my head on whether to push out or take in the new.

I heard a knock at my door and there was no doubt in my mind that on the other side of the door would be my mom standing, waiting patiently.

"Sweetie, are you hungry? I made you breakfast."

"What?" I practically cut her off.

For as long as I'd known my mother, I wasn't sure if breakfast had even been in her vocabulary, especially if the words "*made you*" were in front of it. Needless to say, she had never been much of cook. That was usually my father's department. She had always meant well, but after the great fire of '99, my dad and I didn't let her get near the stove, no matter what her intentions were. It just wasn't safe. We didn't leave anything to chance.

"Honey, it's just cereal. Calm down. I swear you and your father grow more alike each day. I grabbed the milk out of the refrigerator and he about had a heart attack and *died*." She recoiled at her last word and a silence followed.

I remembered it like it was yesterday. Trauma just doesn't go away that easily. It was thanksgiving in 1999. My family decided to have a huge thanksgiving dinner at our house that year and my mom decided to go all out. Every other day it seemed like she was at Barnes& Nobles buying cook books. Instead of trying something simple and easy like chocolate chip cookies, she wanted to impress us with her cooking skills (or lack thereof) by making a chocolate chip cheesecake from scratch. Knowing that my mom would need assistance, I volunteered for the safety of the household.

"Combine crumbs and butter, press onto bottom of nine-inch springform pan. Bake at 350°F for ten minutes."

I had read the directions to her as she frantically moved around the kitchen looking for ingredients.

She was mumbling something to herself while practically turning in circles around the kitchen. I laughed to myself before turning around and grabbing the butter off the counter behind the bag of chocolate chips. I handed the stick of butter to her and watched the stress loosen from her face as she de-aged about ten or more years.

"Thank you, Cupcake. I don't know what I would do without you." She kissed the top of my head.

I left out of the room and by the time I had come back, I was helping my mom put out the fire while my dad was calling the fire department. My mom had explained to us how her jacket had hooked onto the stove and turned it on but she hadn't noticed. And unfortunately... a towel had been lying on the stove too. I wouldn't have believed that story if it had been anyone else but my mom; only she had that amount of bad luck.

In the end, Thanksgiving was ruined, along with our entire kitchen.

I grimaced at the memory.

"Just leave the cereal on the floor, I'm not dressed yet." Lying was almost becoming a sport for me. With practice, I grew better and better.

"Oh please. Sweetie, there's nothing you've got that I haven't got...or seen." She started to turn the knob.

I gasped in fear but it didn't open. The knob twisted again.

"Why is your door locked?" She asked.

"For mothers who can't understand privacy, because I'm hiding my meth lab, and oh, because I'm actually *changing*," I said a little annoyed.

"Okay, okay fine. I can take a hint."

I heard her footsteps go unhappily down the stairs which made me think if there had been an ulterior motive behind her bringing me breakfast. I pondered over it a second but then decided to deal with it when the time came.

I opened my bedroom door and saw the cereal lying on the floor, the blue bowl standing out against the white carpet. I picked up the bowl and started to walk back into my room.

"Kido, I thought you said you were changing."

I jumped and the milk in my cereal spilled out making a mess on the floor. It was amazing how my dad could just pop out of nowhere. It felt like a trap. I felt like a mouse that just wanted some cheese and had fallen for the trap. There was no way I could lie and say I was changing considering I was still in the pajamas I had gone to bed in last night.

He chuckled a little to himself. "I didn't mean to scare you. I just wanted to talk to you. I can see that your mother tried that and failed."

The time had come.

I sighed. "Dad, I can't talk right now. I need to go into school early to take the test."

He opened his mouth like he was about to object.

"Or would you rather have me fail the test?" I asked.

He was silent for a moment. "Fine...but come straight home Kido,"

I was surprised by how easily he had given up. As soon as he was gone from my room, I shoved the bowl of cereal down my throat while I blasted my radio to drown out all other sound. I dressed quickly, not really caring about how I looked. I tied my hair into a messy bun, put on black sandals and blue sweatpants, not really caring how I looked for school. I grabbed my backpack off my chair and closed my door behind me. As much as I wanted to climb out of my window so I wouldn't have to deal with my parents on the way out the door, I knew I had to.

When I got downstairs my mom only gave me a kiss on the cheek before saying, "Have a nice day at school, Honey."

I got in my car and waited for the engine to roar to life. There was absolutely no way I was actually going to school early to take the test and I still had and forty-five minutes to kill, so I made the short drive to the creek. It was a particularly cool day so the breeze going past the water gave me chills. I lied back against the cool and damp grass from the rain last night and let out a huge sigh.

I didn't even know why I so disappointed. Was I really expecting him to just *be* here? Why did I want him here anyhow? No. No. I didn't want him here. I didn't want to even talk to him anymore. I refused to see that face on him.

My brain wouldn't stop battling against itself.

"Oh come on Kahlen... he is cute. Give him a chance."

I stopped breathing. Everything around me stopped. The voice was familiar. *Too* familiar. I fought myself on saying the name. But the walls were being broken... slowly brick by brick...The barriers were being broken.

"Emma?" It was barely a whisper.

There was no answer. Of course there was no answer. I was going insane. Slowly but surely I was going completely insane!

I stood up from the grass, disoriented, and stumbled my way to my car. I pulled open the door and slammed it behind me hard. I winced and put my hands to my head. My headache had returned and I sat that way until the pain eased a little before driving to school.

I pushed this morning behind me as I pulled open my locker. A CD and two notes fell out of it. I picked up one of the notes and read it:

Hey Kay!!!

Hope you don't mind, I asked the main office if I could have your locker combo so I could put the CD in.

~ Marissa

I made a disgusted sound at the last word. I crumbled the note in my hand and threw it in a nearby trashcan. Of course the office would give her my combo because innocent Marissa would never do something wrong. Her pureness disgusted me.

"You know… you should really recycle that."

I didn't have to turn around to know who was behind me. I sighed and ignore him.

"No, really, I'm serious. Its people like you who are cause of global warming," he continued.

"I'm not really in the mood today Bradley."

He sighed too. "Yeah, neither am I, actually. I was just trying to do my job as a member of the Earth Club—,"

"Well if it really bothers you *that* much why don't *you* dig in the trash and get the stupid note so *you* can recycle it yourself?"

He didn't respond. I looked over and saw his face drop just the tiniest bit.

I sighed again and my eyes dropped shamefully to the ground. "I'm sorry Bradley. Things just aren't really going well for me right now."

I stood up on my tippy toes to try and grab my English book stacked at the top of my locker. I wondered how I had gotten it up there in the first place.

"Exhibit A," I muttered to myself. "Can nothing go right?"

Bradley walked over and grabbed my book for me. Of course he could reach it, considering his height.

"Thanks," I smiled weakly.

There was silence between us for a long minute.

"So um... do you want to talk about it?" he asked.

I thought about how to respond to Bradley without hurting his feelings but kept coming up short.

His smiled a little to himself. "Bad mood. Got it," he said nodding as he started to walk off but then turned back to me. "You haven't seen Kennley have you? I haven't seen him since yesterday before lunch. I'm starting to get nervous that he went and robbed a bank or something," he joked but remained unsmiling.

"Or something," I shrugged.

As Bradley started to walk away I grabbed the CD and shoved it into my backpack, then I took the other note (probably something else from Marissa), and shoved into my pocket.

The day dragged on at an impossibly slow rate. I felt like I was going through a montage of my own life. By the time lunch came, I was still a little nauseous and didn't feel like eating. I sat in the library like I always did instead and studied. I was fighting my heavy eyelids from falling down over my eyes. I gave up so I slammed my science book shut and sat for a while, trying to figure out what I should do. I didn't like sitting in silence. As much I liked being alone, I hated the silence... or mostly, not doing anything. When I was by myself with nothing to do... all I could do was *think*. I didn't like thinking much these days, I was more into doing. I guess the thinking part wasn't that bad, mostly, what I was thinking *of*. It was amazing to me about how much something could emotionally hurt you. I never knew emotional pain could hurt so much more than any kind of physical pain. There are things you can do to lessen the pain from cuts and breaks, and sores... but for emotional, there was only two healers but only one efficient: Not dealing, and time.

My headache was coming back. I tried to stop thinking. I tried to focus on something different, something happy, but I kept coming up blank. I was desperate so I grabbed Marissa's second note from my pocket and unfolded it quickly... but it wasn't her handwriting which I knew oh too well.

Hey um... Dean, Kay, or Kahlen... which ever you prefer. We never finished our conversation last night. If you want to continue it, meet me at YOUR creek (you seemed kind of territorial) around 3:30... I'll understand if you don't show up,
~ Kennley

I sat there in shock for a while before I realized that the bell had rung and lunch was over. The whole rest of the day was a long blur. I wasn't exactly sure what I would be doing, or where I would be going today at three-thirty, but now I was definitely considering my options.

"Oh come on Kahlen... he is cute. Give him a chance," The same words kept replaying painfully in my head.

When that last bell finally rung, I practically sprinted to my car and ran home. I greeted my mom quickly before going up the stairs and throwing off my sweatpants and replacing them with a pair of dark jeans. I put on a blue tank top and a black zip up hoodie. I felt silly and foolish that I felt I needed to change to go meet some boy I hardly knew. Then realization hit me like a meteor falling from the sky. The talk...

This morning my dad had asked me to come straight home to talk with me and I shuddered at the thought. I shoved my cell phone into my pocket and opened my window as far as it would go. I climbed down onto the tree and made my way to the soft grass, step by step. I took the same route I had been taking. I went behind my house, over my neighbor's fence, down the street, and across the bridge all the way to Dean's Creek.

I made my way to the abandoned creek and stopped behind my perfect shade tree. I saw Kennley already sitting there, waiting for me, or so it seemed like. From what I could see, he had that same intense look I had seen on him once before as he was talking on his cell phone.

"Yeah, don't worry. I'll be there." He paused listening to the person on the other line talk. "I *will*." He paused again. "Yeah, well Ross is an idiot. You can pass that message along for me. The sooner everyone else realizes that the better." His voice was growing more annoyed. "Don't worry. I got it. Eight O'clock." He slammed his phone shut and sighed heavily.

I stood behind the tree motionless. I mulled over when would be the appropriate time to move from behind the tree without it looking like I was eavesdropping. I shifted my weight and I felt a branch snap from underneath my foot. Typical.

Kennley turned around quickly, almost startled, and then let out a sigh of relief when he saw it was me.

Busted.

"Hey." My voice cracked.

He smiled at me and ran his fingers through his dark brown hair. I watched his arm as it flexed before he put it back down.

"Hey," he greeted me.

We both stood there a minute like mindless dummies looking into space.

"So... how much of that did you hear?" He didn't sound worried, just curious.

"Enough to know that Ross is supposedly an idiot."

He smiled. "Oh, it's not supposedly... he is definitely an idiot. He's the one I was talking about that went flying off the trampoline."

"Ahh... the inventor of the Wampo." I winced a little at the thought of a mild concussion, broken leg, and arm.

"Good. So you do remember."

I was shocked at how easily a conversation could flow between the two of us. It didn't seem right to feel this comfortable with someone I hardly knew. But I knew this friendship wouldn't last long. Soon I would see that slight cock of the head a tiny frown and pout. I would see that stupid face that would ruin everything.

I walked over and sat down next to him. I grinned at the thought that less than two days ago we were sitting in this exact place except everything was so much different. I took off my black hoodie, then my shoes, and placed my feet in the water.

"Why do you like this place so much anyway?" he asked.

I thought a long while before I answered. I was torn between telling the truth, half of the truth, or no truth at all.

"Because," I said. I was still undecided.

Kennley chuckled. "That's not an answer, Dean."

I grimaced at my acquired nickname. "Kay. Len. It's not as hard most people seem to think it is. But besides that... why did you want me to come here anyways?"

"Oh, you are terrible!"

I looked at him confused.

"If you want to distract me from the fact that you didn't answer my question, you don't retort by asking another question," he continued.

"And how exactly am I suppose to *retort*?" I asked.

"You did it again! You don't ask another question. It just makes the distraction too obvious. But...I'll lend you some of my abundant wisdom. The perfect distraction is to show a little skin." He lifted up his shirt a little to reveal his abs before he put it back down.

I couldn't stop my cheeks from burning red. My jaw dropped and I put my hands to my face.

"See? Perfect distraction."

I dropped my hands from my face and watched as he took of his shoes and put his feet in the water next to mind.

"So are you ready to answer my question yet? Why do you like this place so much?"

"Because...," I sighed. "It's the only place that I don't have any memories of her. It's my own place where I can go and get away without tagging any bad emotions with me. It's like... an escape."

"Her...as in Emma?" he asked hesitantly.

All the doubt in my mind that Marissa hadn't clarified things was gone now. I studied his face. There was no tilt, or frown, or pout... just him listening to me intently. I waited for the pain to start... The familiar pain with the twist in my stomach like someone just punched me and knocked all the air out, leaving me gasping. But it didn't hurt so much this time.

"Yeah, her." I stared off into space at the rippling waters. "So why did you want me to come here?" I asked again changing the subject.

I was still staring out into space but out of the corner

off my eye I saw Kennley's bare chest. All he was wearing was his khaki shorts. Before I could even blink he was in the water. My jaw dropped in awe.

"Are you out of your *mind*?!"

Kennley smiled. "See, here's the thing Dean, I was never *in*."

I was up on my feet now just staring at him incredulously.

"Anyone who goes to such great lengths to avoid a question obviously has something to hide."

"Perceptive, but no." He sloshed around in the water. "I put that note in your locker because I wanted to talk to you—."

"And I can see how doing that at school can be so much of a burden. You know... with showing up and all," I said referring to his absence at school today.

"Hey! I was at school... I just didn't stay there for long. It tends to get somewhat monotonous. But anyway... what I was saying before I got so rudely interrupted was that I wanted to talk to you about last night. You kind of freaked out all of a sudden and then you took off. I was worried about you. Then you were angry with me out of nowhere. Serious mood swings. I was so confused."

"I do not have mood swings!"

"So then what's your excuse for yesterday's little episode?" he asked.

"That was *hardly* an episode."

My new cell phone vibrated in my pocket. I still hadn't found the one I had recently lost. Of course my mom had decided it was an absolute necessity that I get a new one right away. Because, in her words, "*contact between us in mandatory*". I pulled it out and saw that I had a new text message:

Hey Kay!! Did you get my note and CD?!

I sighed and didn't respond. I looked at my phone to see the time. It was four already.

"Crap." I muttered. I grabbed my hoodie and put it back on.

"You do realize the art of distraction is to take off... not put on?" Kennley said.

I ignored him. "I have to go. I'm sorry."

"No, it's okay. I wouldn't want the FBI involved," he joked.

"Exactly." I smiled before I started to walk away.

"Hey Cinderella!" he called after me. I looked back over my shoulder and he was getting out of the creek with the water dripping off his half naked body. My eyes drifted to his hands where he was holding my shoes. "You forgot these." He held them up.

'Thanks." I walked over and took the shoes out of his hands. "But Cinderella lost one shoe, not two.

"You know Kahlen... people who pay attention to one color, miss the beauty of the whole rainbow."

"What's that suppose to—," Before I could even finish my sentence I heard a splash in the water.

When I climbed back through my window out of breath from running, I heard music coming from downstairs. I walked down the stairs to see my parents sitting on the couch watching a slide show. I stood there in awe.

A picture of Emma and I flashed across the screen. We were both in our new bikinis we had bought over the summer. The ocean was behind us as we posed for the camera. Before I could say anything, the picture slid off the screen and went to the next which left me speechless. Emma was lying down on the ground against the grass in her backyard. She had her tongue sticking outside her mouth while holding up two fingers in the peace sign. I remembered taking the picture. In the next one, she didn't look like she could be any more than four years olds with frosting all over her tiny face and hands. The next picture was of our middle school graduation. Emma was standing next to me in her lime green dress with a light blue band at the waist. I tried not to smile at the fact that my black dress with pink polka dots had a big brown stain in the back from me sitting down on someone's chocolate cake. The next picture was of Emma and her rather large black lab, Macy.

Before I knew it, hot liquid was streaming down from my eyes uncontrollably. I hadn't cried since that night and my sudden tears had taken me by surprise now. My mom turned around startled to see me standing behind the couch.

"Turn it off," was all I could manage to get out.

"Sweetie—,"

"Please. Turn it off now." My voice was a little louder.

They both sat motionless on the couch looking at my now red eyes. I grabbed the remote off of the couch and the screen with Emma doing a cartwheel went blank. I got the disc out of the DVD player and I immediately realized it was the CD Marissa had given to me. I turned away from the TV back to my parents waiting for them to explain.

"Honey, I found it in your backpack and—,"

"Why were you in *my* backpack?!" I yelled.

"Kido, calm down. Just sit down and we'll explain everything," my dad said quietly.

I ignored him and glared at my mom.

"I was concerned about you, Honey. I just wanted to make sure you weren't..."

"What? Doing drugs, having sex, failing school, going to commit suicide, or maybe being a prostitute that stands out on corners at the bad part of town? What lack of trust is it that you have in me this time?"

"Kahlen! You do not talk to your mother that way!" my dad yelled and I flinched. The only time my dad called me Kahlen was... well... never. "Sit down! Now!"

I sat and wiped the tears from my eyes.

"Your mother and I are worried about you. We're sick of your constant lies, sneaking out your window and having the neighbors calling about you hopping over their fence, and the school calling about you skipping school and sleeping through tests."

"Hun, you haven't been dealing," my mother added. "It's not healthy and... we think you might need some *extra* help. We've already talked to your principal and she was having the same concerns. She suggested Mrs. Kraft, the school counselor."

"There is no way I am—,"

"You're meeting with her tomorrow. End of story..."

I didn't hear what else he was saying as his voice just trailed off in my head. I walked away in the middle of his sentence, threw the stupid CD down on the hardwood floor, and smashed it underneath my feet. I stomped my way up the stairs and slammed my bedroom door behind me with all of my might. It felt like the walls were spinning and the ground was shaking. The brick wall inside my head was shattering to pieces. Would the raging war ever end?

I opened my window and climbed out. I didn't care if I was going to get in trouble. I didn't care if the stupid neighbors were going to tell on me. I ran all the way to the creek with tears streaming down my eyes. I could feel it. It was all the conformation I needed that my life was indeed over. I was so angry and so frustrated and so...*sad*.

When I got to the creek, I felt stupid for coming there.

I should have known Kennley would still be there. He was out of the water and lying on the ground and I wanted to run back but he had already seen me. He saw my red face and the tears streaming from my eyes. We both didn't say anything for a second. As confused as he looked, he didn't bother asking me any questions. He stood up and walked over to my frozen body. I commanded my tears to stop but they didn't listen. They only fell harder, followed by tiny sobs. Before I could say or do anything, he was hugging me tightly, burying me in his chest and slowly…I hugged him back.

4. Aftershock

I felt awful. When my head wasn't whirling, it was pounding. When my stomach didn't ache, it was nauseous. Being sick definitely sucked and no matter how much I tried to convince my parents that I was sick, neither one of them had believed me.

"You're going to see Mrs. Kraft today. End of story," my dad kept repeating.

Obviously he thought that my sickness was a little coincidental considering I had a meeting with the school counselor today. I had almost gotten my mom to give in and let me stay home, but my dad swayed her harder. I had decided to wait patiently for my mom to return to work. Once she did, nothing would be so easy going anymore. The house would turn back into chaos and she wouldn't be that easy to sway.

This morning it wasn't my alarm that woke me up, it was my cell phone. I got up angrily and groggily out of the bed to see who had dared to disturb me at six in the morning. I looked at my phone and saw that I had a text message:

Dean, if you can, meet me at your creek at seven.

As much as I didn't want it to, my heart fluttered with joy. I was still a little embarrassed from the last time I had seen Kennley. I was a complete wreck in front of him. I had even soaked his shirt with my tears. As much as I didn't want to admit it, part of me was happy I had gone back to the creek. It was still so strange that I could feel so completely comfortable with this guy that I barely knew, and yet so uncomfortable around the world that had surrounded me for years.

I ignored my pounding head and went through my normal routine quickly. I showered, brushed my teeth, got dressed, and ate breakfast before grabbing the car keys and starting to head out the door.

"Where are you going?" my mom asked. "It's just barely seven."

I decided it wouldn't kill me to be honest. "I'm going to Dean's Creek. It's only a couple of blocks away from here," I said curtly.

"...*Why?*"

"I like going there to think." I didn't give her time to respond. I slammed the front door behind me. I was still a little upset at my parents.

I took a different way to the creek this time so my parents wouldn't be getting any calls from the stupid, tattletale neighbors. When I got there, Kennley hadn't beaten me there like before. I lay down on the ground against my perfect tree and waited...and waited... and still waited. I was beginning to get restless. *Where was he*, I thought. My curiosity was beginning to turn into anger. Why did I care anyway? It's not like we were actually friends...Just acquaintances that could coexist at a creek. Nevertheless there was no excuse for being stood up, especially when he was the one who had asked me here in the first place. Every minute felt like a lifetime as the seconds ticked away. I took out my phone, convinced that a major amount of time had gone by. It was seven-thirty, two minutes later than the time I had looked at it before.

"Where is he?" I said to myself.

I heard a loud engine roaring to a stop and the music in the car was blasting to the point of being obnoxious.

I saw Kennley step out of the black SUV and as soon as he shut the door the car sped off leaving Kennley's hair blowing in the wind.

I sat up a little straighter as he walked towards me. I could feel the embarrassment all over again. I hoped he wouldn't make any references to the night before.

He plopped down beside me. "Hey," he greeted me but then he frowned. "Oh, you don't look so good."

I put my hand to my face a little self-consciously, wondering if it was still green or pale. "Yeah, well I don't feel so grand either," I snapped.

"No, I mean you look unhappy, and somewhat *meaner* than usual."

"Thanks," I rolled my eyes.

"Don't worry. Deep down I know you're just an old softy," he chuckled.

I didn't.

I hoped by "old softy" he didn't mean "old weepy".

He sighed. "Okay. I am completely serious now. What's up?"

"Well...where do I begin?" I said. "My parents want me to see a counselor, I'm sick, and oh, because I've been sitting here for a half an hour and I don't get so much as a simple apology."

He sighed again and looked away from me, out into space. "I wanted to be here sooner but I couldn't. Trust me, I tried to."

"Hmph. Funny. That still doesn't sound like an apology." I was far beyond irritated.

He paused for a second and thought to himself. It was easy to tell when Kennley was in deep thought. It was kind of funny actually. His forehead would wrinkle just the tiniest bit. He'd press his lips together and narrow his eyes but he never looked angry, just lost in a world I couldn't see.

"I'm sorry," he said simply, but his face was serious. "One thing you have to know, Kahlen, is that I let people down. Some way or another I can be a disappointment." In an instant his face brightened again and was less serious. "But I always find a way to make up for it. That, I can promise you." After a minute of silence he came back from his invisible world to planet Earth. "So… you got any ideas?"

"Ideas?"

"Ideas for me making it up to you. You know, a favor, maybe even a wish."

"Hmm… I don't know. Are there any limitations to my favor/wish?" I said. I tried to keep my voice even because I didn't want to make forgiving him that easy.

"No, Not exactly. I mean, it has to be within reason. Of course…I'm not afraid of a challenge if that's what you're getting at."

I chuckled. "Not yet."

Later when I got to school and walked reluctantly into the Mrs. Kraft's office, it was a fairly small room but well decorated. The green and blue walls brightened up the otherwise dark room with only one tiny window where you could see the hallway outside. I examined the two pictures sitting on her desk in a medium sized, dark purple frame. One picture was of a baby boy who couldn't be more than two, and another one of a little girl who looked about five. I had to admit they were two very cute little kids. Soon a woman with long curly brown hair walked in and sat down in the chair behind her desk before swiveling it around to face me.

"So… Kay-," She stopped her sentence short to look down at the clipboard she held in her hands. "Kassey-,"

"It's Kahlen," I sighed.

"Oh, I'm sorry. That's how they had your name written on my folder." She smiled slightly and placed her clipboard behind her.

"Figures," I muttered underneath my breath.

I tried my best to keep my voice at least somewhat friendly, but it just kept coming out indifferent. I didn't want to be here. I didn't *need* to be here as far as I was concerned.

"So... *Kahlen*, how are you doing?"

...And the questions began. I knew that the whole forty-five minutes would be filled with me swatting away questions with an invisible stick.

"Not so good," I said curtly.

"May I ask why?"

"I'm sick. I think I have a fever or the flu or something like that," I said nonchalantly.

She frowned a little bit sympathetically. "Well, then why are you at school if you're not feeling well?"

For a second, she actually seemed sincere. "My parents forced me. They didn't believe I was sick. You know... the whole kid who fakes sick so they don't have to go to school bit."

Mrs. Kraft swiveled back around to her clipboard and grabbed a pen off her desk. She started to scribble down some notes quickly and then turned back to me.

"So... why are you sick? Any reason in particular?

I shrugged. "Maybe it's because I was walking in the rain for a while. I might have caught something..."

My sentence trailed off. I thought about on the way back to school how Kennley had asked me the same question. I had given him the same answer I had Mrs. Kraft.

"Unlikely," he had stated earlier. "Once a pathogen enters your body, you go into the incubation stage and those don't usually last longer than about 2 days. So unless you have bacterial meningitis or something, you didn't get sick a couple of days ago."

My eyes had widened in shock. Maybe it was time I started paying attention in health class.

"And what would happen exactly if I had bacterial meningitis?" I had asked him.

"Oh... well... you'd probably be dead by now."

I snapped back into the present with Mrs. Kraft asking me something I wasn't paying attention to.

"May I ask why?"

I was learning that she used that phrase often when she asked a question...and yes, it was annoying.

I thought back to that night that seemed like weeks ago. The reason why I had been walking out in the rain in the first place... "It is a really long story." I expected her to respond with something like, *"well, I have time"*, like most people do when you feed them the, *"it's a long story"*, line. "So... if we're finished with this interrogation, can I leave now?"

She sighed. "Kahlen, I know this is probably the last thing you want to hear from me, but I understand. I'm sure many people are trying to understand what you're going through and you may think they always fall short... that it's inconceivable that anyone could feel the same amount of pain that you have. But it's not the case. Lots of us have experienced loss in our lives and some of us haven't, but will. The longer you live, it just becomes inevitable. About 7 years ago I lost my 2 year-old son, Noah." She said the last word almost as a whisper.

I stared at her blankly for a minute. I pictured everything that must have gone on and all the hurt she must of felt. I pictured little Noah taking his first steps and smiling like he was in the picture on her desk.

Then, I saw it. I saw him vanish away in my head quickly. It was slightly disturbing and I gasped a little bit. My mother had always told me that a parent's worst fear was losing their child and it was awful that Mrs. Kraft had lost hers so soon. Kids are supposed to bury parents, not the other way around.

"I'm sorry," It was two words but they were filled with the most emotions out of any of the other half sincere words I had said before.

She smiled at me gratefully. "I'm sorry as well... for your loss. The weird thing about death is that it's not the actual *death* of the person that hurts the most. Death *is* just a word. But it's the meaning behind it that causes people to shudder at the thought. It's not death that's the terribly awful part of it. It's the aftershock of it all. All the things that follow after it is what leaves that big gaping hole inside. The day that Noah died was the earthquake. It was the moment that I thought my life was pretty much over. But after a couple of days once the shock had died down, that's when the pain really set in. You have no idea how much you're hurting until you start living your life *without* them." She shook her head to herself, lost in her own words. "But um... Let's talk about something else. Friends...family... they're supportive right?"

I sighed heavily. "To my parents, I'm a wreck, and to my friends... well, I don't think I really have any." When I really thought about it, I didn't really have any other friends. Emma had sadly been my one and only friend. Not because I couldn't make any others, I was just satisfied with her.

"You don't have any friends?" she asked unbelievingly.

I shook my head no. "I have one, kind of... a new friend, but besides that, no. I always had Emma so I never really bothered making new ones." Saying her name out loud was new, but it was something I was trying out.

"Tell me about this new friend. Who is she?" She looked at me intently waiting on my response.

I had to ponder over my answer for a bit because I wasn't sure how much I wanted to reveal. This whole therapy thing was all new and it felt so odd to open up to someone I didn't even know. "Well *he*... is very—," I struggled for the right word. "...Interesting. The complete opposite of me."

"How so?"

"He just sees things differently than most people. It's like I see a mountain and he sees the Grand Canyon. He's very honest and sure of himself." I was amazed at how easily the words came out.

"And you're not?"

"Sometimes."

She turned around again and scribbled something else down.

"So... Kahlen, if you're not ready to discuss this, then that's fine. I understand, but what exactly happened that night?" She was very careful with her words trying not to over step her boundaries.

I knew exactly what she meant. I thought a while about answering her question. No one had really bothered asking me that. Of course the doctors and my parents did, but I lied and told them it was all a big blur and of course they left the subject alone...considering. But it was somewhat of a blur, or at least most pieces of it were. It was like the memories were in my head somewhere but I just couldn't get to them.

She took my silence as a response. "It's okay," she said gently. "Anyways, how do you like school?

"I don't." I hated it actually. I hated the way the days

all blurred in together and dragged on in a way I didn't believe was even possible.

"May I ask why?"

I shrugged. "Because everything is just so rote."

"That's understandable," she said as she nodded.

"The only thing that isn't rote in my life is Kennley." I said the words and then immediately recoiled at them. What was I doing? I was beginning to feel comfortable with Mrs. Kraft. During the whole session, I had only given information when asked, not on my own. Half of my brain was telling me to push her away, but I didn't. I fought back against my better judgment.

"Your new friend?" she asked.

I nodded. "He's just so unpredictable. It's always new with him. Never boring. We just sort of clicked from the start." I thought about the first time I met Kennley and then smiled. "Okay... maybe not from the start... more like the day after that."

More scribbling. She turned around and wrote down some more notes and I really wanted to ask her what she was writing but I knew it would just come out snappy and rude.

"Okay. Let's move back to your parents. What are they like?"

I sighed heavily. The one thing I didn't want to think about right now was my parents. As Kennley would say, they had personally pissed me off. "My mom is quiet, soft spoken, always concerned or worried. My dad is sort of the spokesperson."

More scribbling. It was starting to drive me insane.

"Do you mind telling me about Emma?"

I waited for the pain to start...That usual twisting in my stomach. And it did, but it didn't hurt as much. "She was... amazing. To me she was almost a little hippie-ish. She was always so optimistic and insightful.

She was incredibly open-minded and made me feel like such a pessimist most of the time. She was loud, outspoken, and painfully friendly. Some days she was punk, others bohemian. Whatever phase she was going through there was always some touch of Emma lurking beneath it," I ranted.

"How long had you two been friends?" she asked, still very carefully.

"I don't know… a while. Since about when her family moved here when we were in sixth grade."

She swiveled around again. I assumed she was going to do more scribbling but instead she looked at the time on her computer screen.

"Perhaps another story for another time." She smiled and stood up as she gestured for me to do so as well. "Well Kahlen, I'll see you this time next week."

I smiled. "Sounds like a plan."

I walked out of her office and down the long narrow hallway to my locker. I wasn't surprised to see Kennley leaning against his locker skipping class.

"So, how was it?" he asked.

I grinned reluctantly. "It wasn't *excruciating*."

5. Games

"Favorite color," he said.

"Don't have one," I said. "You?"

"Dark Blue."

"Ah...well I just happen to be wearing dark blue." I pushed up the sleeves on my hoodie.

"I know," he winked at me. "Favorite movie."

His wink was breath-taking. It took me a moment to answer because I had to recollect my clouded and cluttered thoughts. "I don't know. I don't think I have any."

"Do you have a favorite *anything*?"

"I don't have a favorite movie but I have favorite types of movies."

"Such as..."

"I love comedies. I like movies that are action packed, but not too action packed. I hate horror films because they make me make a fool out of myself. I'm the kind of person that will cut off your circulation during scary movies. I'll scream the whole way through and it's downright embarrassing. I have a soft spot for the *Sound Of Music* but mostly I like a lot of superhero movies like *Spiderman*, *Iron Man*, *Batman*... pretty much anything that ends with a "man"."

He chuckled at my response. "Favorite superhero... And don't say you don't have one because that's just unethical."

I had to think about it for a second. "Spiderman."

He rolled his eyes. "Are you serious? The dude can climb up walls because he got bitten by a spider. I could have come up with something better than that."

"Oh yeah, well what's your favorite?"

"Batman," he answered quickly. "He's the only superhero that doesn't have powers. It shows you what our world could accomplish with a little brain power... Oh, and because his theme song is awesome."

I shook my head in disapproval. "Batman... dun nuh nuh nuh nuh nuh nuh nuh Batman," I said flatly. "I could have come up with something better than that."

He sighed heavily before moving on. "Worst ex-boyfriend."

"I thought we were doing favorites?"

He sighed. "We have done everything from favorite slow songs to favorite flower...it's time to move onto least favorites."

I didn't have a worst ex-boyfriend. I didn't have any ex-boyfriends.

"I don't have one," I answered.

"Oh come on. You've had to have one that was—,"

"I don't have *any* ex-boyfriends."

He seemed surprise.

I was trying not to be self conscious but I couldn't help it. Why was he so surprised? Did he expect me to have had many boyfriends by now?

"Does that shock you?" I asked truly curious.

"No." He paused. "It just seems like someone like you would have had caught someone's eye by now."

I wasn't sure if I was supposed to take that as I compliment. I looked over at him but he was staring out into the water just as I had been.

"Yeah well I haven't really been looking. Life's complicated enough without throwing another ball in to juggle."

He turned to look at me. I could see his expression changing just the slightest bit. "You're such a mystery." There was a little frustration behind his voice. "Every time I see you it's like I get another little piece to the puzzle."

I chuckled. I would never consider myself as mysterious. "Only as long as you like mysteries."

"As long as they're not too hard to figure out," he added.

"So are you saying you like them *easy*?"

"Are we still talking about puzzles here?" he asked.

"I don't know," I said. "Are we?"

He pulled a bag of candy out of his pocket, poured some candy into his hand and then put it into his mouth. He handed the bag to me and I reluctantly poured the little candy pieces into my hand before putting them into my mouth. My eyes widened and watered. My lips puckered out and my tongue hated me for what I had just put in my mouth. I turned around and spat them out. I couldn't take it anymore.

Kennley was laughing hysterically.

"What is *that*?!" I yelled.

He couldn't answer. He was on the ground rolling around laughing and tears were streaming ridiculously from his eyes. I hit him but he didn't seem to notice so I hit him harder.

"Oh, if you could have seen your face... That was definitely a Kodak Moment." He sat up as his laughter very slowly died out. "Besides... didn't anyone ever tell you, don't take candy from strangers?"

"You're not a stranger," I said.

"Not anymore I'm not."

I smiled to myself. I remembered when he still was a stranger. If I was willing to get into a car with him and skip school, I probably would have been willing to take the candy...but he had offered ice cream instead.

I snatched the bag out of his hand and examined it. It was called, Lip Puckers. Around the bag it said, Sourness to the Extreme! I had never even heard of these before but they were by far the sourest thing I ever tasted in my life.

"How could you eat a handful of these and not even flinch?" I asked.

"I don't know. They're just not really sour to me. They are about as harmless as gummy bears."

I lied back on the grass. "Yeah...Gummy bears with machine guns."

He lied back on the grass too and smiled. "... Wimp."

"Whatever," I said quickly.

We laid there in silence for a while, just looking up into the sky. It was becoming a routine with us for the last week or so that had gone by. We'd both meet at the creek early before school and my mom was always suspicious of me leaving early but I always gave her the same story. I told her that I liked coming here to think. And it was the truth. I did like coming here to think but lately I also liked the creek for other reasons...

It was easy being with Kennley. Although we really didn't have anything in common, it never hindered our conversations. I felt like I could be myself around him and I didn't have to pretend to be in a good mood or act like everything was okay. Kennley was the one person in my world that didn't have that stupid pity face on when I was around him so it was easy to enjoy his company.

Our hands brushed against each other for the tiniest moment and we both shifted awkwardly away from each other. I almost wished I wouldn't have moved my hand away but then shook off those thoughts quickly. Kennley was very attractive, I'd give him that. But we were friends and I didn't want to ruin that with my foolish thoughts.

"Would you rather...drink a bottle of ketchup or shave your head," he asked, breaking our silence.

"What?"

"Answer the question," he demanded as his green eyes looked over at me.

"I can't answer a question like that. It's ridiculous!"

I thought about drinking a bottle of ketchup and I could have thrown up just from the thought. It was disgusting but would I rather shave my head? I could always wear a wig I figured.

"Neither," I finally answered.

Kennley sat there looking at me, waiting for a real answer.

"The ketchup I guess," I sighed.

He grimaced. "I'd shave my head in a heartbeat," he said, running his fingers through his dark brown hair.

"And you're also a boy. Hair isn't as important to you." I tried to think of two really bad situations. "Would you rather be eaten by an angry shark, or be electrocuted to death?"

"Why do I have to die?"

I shrugged. The object of the game was to come up with two equally horrible options and death seemed pretty awful...Although it wouldn't be awful for him, only the people he was leaving behind. I patiently waited for him to answer.

"This game is stupid. Let's play a different one."

"Nope," I said quickly as I grinned. "You have to answer the question."

He was silent for a moment thinking about his

answer. I thought about my answer in the mean time but I couldn't decide between the two.

"How about instead you get to ask me any question you want and I promise to answer one hundred percent truthfully."

He was being difficult but it was tempting... It was extremely tempting, but what would I ask him? I sadly couldn't think of anything.

"No," I said simply. "Answer the question."

He didn't say anything as he thought and it was taking him a long time to make up his mind.

I took off my shoes and put my feet in the water but winced when the water was colder than usual. I dealt with the cold and kicked my feet in the water, making splashing sounds.

"The shark," he finally said. "I think it would be faster that way."

I tried not laugh at him. He looked so serious and I couldn't believe he had put so much thought into a hypothetical question.

I just nodded. It did made sense though.

"Would you rather-?" he started.

"No. This game is so finished." It was silly that the game was so difficult considering it was all hypothetical...so why should it matter? But in the back of my mind I still grimaced at the thought of drinking a whole bottle of Ketchup.

"Fine. Let's play random." He put his feet in the water and splashed some at me.

I gasped but I shouldn't have been surprised. I splashed some water with my foot up at him. After a while of us acting like little kids I asked, "What's random?"

"It's easy," he explained. "Each person has to say something completely random. When I say a word, you can't say another word that is in the same category, it can't even start with the same letter. You have ten seconds to answer before you lose, and it can't be anything around you because then it's not random. If you break any of these rules you lose," he said everything like a game show host and I just rolled my eyes.

"Okay. It sounds simple enough."

"Aluminum foil," he said.

"Ham."

"Nope. You lose," he grinned.

"What? Why?" I asked confused.

"People wrap ham in aluminum foil. They are related therefore making it not random."

I sighed rolling my eyes at him. "Dental floss."

"Pickle juice."

"Puppies."

"Digital camera."

"Chocolate chip cookies."

"Butterflies."

"Golf."

"Earwax."

Crap. I was running out of things to say. I looked around me for something to give me ideas but the obvious moving of my eyes gave me away. I knew I should have been sneakier.

"Looking around for something to say will lose you the game, Dean," he busted me. "Ten, nine, eight, seven, six, five, four-,"

"Apple sauce," I said quickly.

I waited for his response but it didn't come. I took advantage of the moment to think of more random words. After a while I realized that almost ten seconds had gone by.

"We're gonna be late."

"Ten seconds." We had each spoken at the same time.

"No. Look at the time," he urged.

I grabbed my new cell phone out of my pocket and looked at the time. It was twelve minutes until the first bell.

"That's not good," I said panicked.

I shoved the cell phone back into my pocket and zipped up my backpack before swinging it around my shoulders.

"This isn't over Kahlen," he warned. "Let's just say it's a deuce for now." He smiled at me gently as he walked over to his car named Eddie and I just shook my head to myself, trying to wrap my head around him.

I flew to my car and went far beyond the speed limit to school.

6. Dr. Jekyll and Mr. Hyde

It was official. My mother had completely lost her mind. I watched her frantically search through all of her papers. I found it hard to try not to smile. Watching my mother work was better than television or even a movie. It was a complete transformation between my nice, sweet, quiet mom to someone I barely recognized. Like a kitten trying to be a tiger; it was pretty entertaining.

"Honey, what do you think of this aqua blue and this pea green? Which do you think will go well with this lavender?" She kept throwing paint samples at me. "Or... what about this creamy yellow?" She threw it over to me and the little rectangular card landed in my cereal.

"I think that you should stop throwing samples into my food... and at me!"

She looked up and me quickly and then at my cereal and reached over her pile of papers, into my cereal before grabbing the creamy yellow card and carelessly shaking the dripping milk on it onto the floor.

My jaw dropped and I tried to stifle my laughter but it wasn't working.

"Are you laughing at this? You think this is funny?" She looked at me completely serious and stern which just made my laughter worse.

"I have to have these designs ready in two weeks for the entire house!" she said. I just laughed harder.

"Are you even listening to me? The entire house!" she repeated.

I snatched the royal blue sample out of her right hand and threw it on the ground. She looked like she was ready to slap me.

"Relax," I got hold of her shoulders and shook them.

My mom was an interior designer. She had started her own business called Thomas Design Corporations about a year and a half ago. It was actually pretty impressive that she started it all by herself and that was one thing about my mom that I admired. When she put her mind to something, I pity the fool that would try *to* stop her.

She sighed. "It's easy for you to say. All you have to worry about is school and... well nothing else."

I hadn't realized how much I missed this side of my mom, the crazy, hectic side. I only saw this side of her for only half of the year. Because she was her own boss, she decided how her schedule went. Most of the time her employees would take the clients and she would just do the supervising and throw in some suggestions every now again. But times like these, she would take the bull by the horns and do the project herself.

"Ha! I've got plenty to worry about. Don't even get me started on my list," I said. "...But ignoring that for the time being...Look at you! You're an absolute mess!"

I wasn't sure if she had even *looked* at a brush this morning let alone used one. She was wearing a black pants suit, but her pants were unbuttoned and she was wearing two different earrings.

"Did you even sleep last night?" I asked looking at the dark bags underneath her eyes.

She hesitated before answering. "Honey, adults need less sleep than teenagers."

I rolled my eyes. I got up out of my chair at the kitchen table and poured my mostly uneaten cereal into the sink.

My mom looked down at her watch and practically flew out of her chair. "Oh no. No, no, no! I have to be at the office in five minutes."

She grabbed all of her color samples and I tried my best to keep a straight face but it wasn't working. There was a light pink color sample stuck onto her butt and another on her back. My eyes began to water and the tears started streaming. I held my breath hoping to keep from laughing. I could feel my face turning red and I gave in. A loud bellowing laugh erupted from my stomach to my mouth. I was bent over on the kitchen counter to keep from falling onto the ground. My mom turned around confused.

"You know what… I don't even *want* to know." She turned around, grabbed her purse, and left out the door. Once she was gone the laughter died out. I heard her start the car up and then the garage open. I looked out the window waiting to see her car speed off down the road but it didn't. I looked over on the table to see her big bag, which she preferred to carry instead of a brief case, sitting on the counter with fancy designs, tile and wallpaper samples, and of course the paint samples stuffed into the bag, practically overflowing. I heard the clicking of high heels coming toward the door. The door flew open. She grabbed her bag off the table without even shooting me a glance. Before she left she yelled back to me something I could barely understand.

"Don't for-…I'll see-… I mean it-… three o'clock!" The door slammed behind her and watched as she drove off.

I had forgotten up until now that I had to be at T.D. Co. (my abbreviated name for Thomas Design) today to work until five. This was my usual summer job. I did everything that my mom needed and wanted me to do. I was her own little personal assistant that didn't get paid half as much as someone who was non-family might.

"What a way to spend a Saturday," I muttered to myself.

"What was that Kido?"

My breath caught abruptly, clearly startled. It was so unnecessary and pathetic. Was I really that jumpy? Still breathing harder than I should, I turned around to see my dad standing there almost as panicked as me. Then he cracked a smile.

"Why do you always do that?" I yelled at him still panting.

"I never try. You're just so unusually jumpy…that's not my fault."

I didn't respond, still trying to catch my breath. It was getting to be downright embarrassing.

"I came down here to tell you that I'm leaving to go fishing with Greg. I should be back around eight or nine tonight."

"Okay," I said and my breathing was finally calm.

"Oh, and another thing, could you pass that message along? I don't think your mother really wants to talk to me right now."

My face twisted in confusion. "What did you do?"

He sighed. "I made the mistake of mentioning something to her about her hair. Oh, and I told her that pea green looked more like puke green."

"Figures."

"Yeah well I'll see you later Kido." I watched him as he made his way into the garage.

It was official. I was pathetic. I was stuck at my house alone on a Saturday and the only thing that I had to look forward to was working. Truly pathetic.

I thought about hanging out somewhere with a few friends like regular teenagers did but sadly I didn't have any. I found myself getting desperate when thoughts of Marissa Harrison came to mind as a last resort. I couldn't help but shudder at the thought…I wasn't that desperate. Then I thought about Kennley…it only made sense that if he could call, or rather text me, then I should be able to do that too. But hanging outside of school or even Dean's Creek was a big step. It was the kind of thing that said, *hey we're friends, let's make it official.* I wasn't quite sure if I was ready for that just yet. Against my better judgment, I pulled my phone out of my pocket and laid it on the counter where it stared at me menacingly. Finally as the minutes passed of making my lists of pros and cons, I slowly reached for the phone, still hesitant, then gasped, startled, and almost flew out of my chair. Thunder roared angrily through the sky and once again, I was left catching my breath.

Looking out the window I smiled a little to myself thinking about my father's plans for tonight. "So much for fishing..."

I looked back down at the kitchen counter and my phone was still lying there… so conspicuously. It was driving me crazy.

"*Call him.*"

I stopped breathing. I knew I was being stupid. I knew it wasn't actually her I was hearing. It was evident that it was my own subconscious but I couldn't help but react. I really wanted my sub-conscious to shut up.

"*Admit it…you like him,*" she said again.

Did I like Kennley? I thought about all the time we had spent together in a short amount of time. Was the time we spent together less friend-like than I had thought. I thought about that day when he hugged me and how good it felt. I cleared my head shaking all of these thoughts off. It was nonsense. We were just friends.

"*You like him*," she said.

But would it be so wrong if I really did like Kennley? Would the world cease at an instant? I couldn't remember the last time I had a crush on someone. There was never really anyone that ever caught my eye. I had stupid middle school crushes but never anything in high school.

I grabbed my phone quickly and flipped it open. I knew I didn't have his phone number but some way or another he had gotten mine. I looked at my text messages and scrolled down until I found his. His number was there at the top of the screen. I slammed my phone shut because I was a wimp and I couldn't do it. *It's no big deal*, I told myself but it wasn't working. I was the biggest wimp. I felt so stupid now as I thought about how I was wasting so much of my time just considering calling a boy.

Then the light bulb went off in my head. It was raining; I couldn't go to Dean's Creek. So there was no need to call Kennley. Problem solved. But what if we went to someplace else like the mall or maybe to a movie, any place that was indoors?

I sat there staring at my phone having hundreds of debates going on in my head before I grabbed my phone again, dialed the number, and waited as each ring created suspense.

"Hello?" he answered after the third ring.

But it wasn't Kennley. I had no idea who it was. I

hung up. I looked at the number I had just called, and the number that was displayed above his text message. They matched perfectly. I didn't try calling again. I was too scared to try.

"Louisa?!"

I flinched back by the abrupt call.

"Where is my coffee? I *swear* I just laid it down here a second ago," my mom said, only a little bit calmer this time.

I looked around my mom's office observing every little detail. It had been a while since the last time I had been here.

"Ma'am, its right behind you," A very shaky Louisa said.

She turned around and her eyes got very wide with surprise. "Oh, well it is isn't it?" She picked up the cup and turned around back to Louisa. "Thank you. I don't know what I do without you..." She trailed off. Before she had finished her sentence she was already on the hunt for something else.

I was thankful that my mom hadn't showed up at work the way she left the house this morning. As soon as she got to work she called to yell at me for not telling her she looked like a train wreck. I tried to explain to her that I had tried this morning but then I heard a something hit the ground and crash. The line went dead.

"Sweetie?"

I stood up straighter against the wall and tried to look alert.

"Have you seen my teal paint sample?"

I shook my head no and she sighed.

"You know mom... you should get one of those big

ring thingies with all the paint samples on them. I bet it would make things a lot easier."

She stopped looking for the paint sample and looked up at me. "Ugh! I hate those things! Why would you even suggest that?"

Until now I have forgotten about my mom's superstitions. The last time she had bothered to get the ring thingy, she said it brought her bad luck. It rained for a week straight, then one of the people she hired to put in the hard wood floor fell down and twisted his ankle, and then finally, the couple that had come to T.D. Co. in the first place, out of nowhere decided to move to California.

"Oh don't tell me you're still superstitious? It was a bad week. You can't blame that on a ring of paint samples."

"I am *not* superstitious. I just don't like those things." She shuddered. "At all." I watched her roll her eyes.-

"Okay Mr. *Hyde*, I'm gonna get a snack from the lounge. I feel like I haven't eaten in ages."

I sped out of the room before she could protest. As soon as I got outside the door I stopped, closed my eyes, and took a deep breath. *In just two weeks this will all be over*, I thought, just *two more weeks*. When my mom was working on a project it was like a mini-pregnancy. She had mood-swings and craving and pretty much drove us all insane. But in the end, once she was all finished, things would go back to normal.

I walked past the receptionist desk and then down the hall. I was looking for signs or maybe stairs leading to the basement. I walked back past the receptionist desk and figured I must have looked like a moron.

"Need some help?" said an unusually perky voice.

I looked over my right shoulder to see the receptionist who looked about twenty-three with short, spiky blond hair that just barely dusted her shoulders. As she leaned over the desk, her necklace with a heart at the bottom spilled out from underneath her shirt.

"Um... no. I think I'm good," I lied.

I quickly searched again for signs... any signs.

"Are you sure? Cause you look sorta lost to me."

"Yep. I'm sure."

"Okay. But if you just told me what you were looking for I'm sure I could—,"

"Cece!" another voice said curtly. "She said she's fine! Leave her alone."

I hadn't even seen another person sitting next to the blond. The other receptionist was a brunette with long wavy hair who seemed somewhat annoyed.

"*Sorrr-rrry* if I was trying to do my job by actually *helping* someone instead of sitting there as motionless as a brick doing Sudoku!"

I started to walk off.

"So um... where are you going?" Cece asked.

I turned back around. "I was trying to find the lounge but—,"

The brunette interrupted me. "Oh, that's easy. Go down the hall, third door to your left leads to the stairs. Once you get down there you can't miss it unless you're a blind monkey."

"Thanks—,"

"Hey, while you're down there could you bring up like two of those chewy granola bars? The chocolate chip kind?" Cece asked.

The brunette hit her arm.

"Owwwwahh!" Cece turned around and hit the brunette back.

"We had our lunch break like an hour ago and you ate that massive Whopper. You can't be hungry."

"Oh for Oprah Winfrey's sake, would you mind your own business and finish your stupid Sudoku?"

I started to walk away again although Cece had other plans…"Wait!" she yelled.

Was there no way she was going to let me leave?

"I'm sorry. We're being rude," she continued. "I'm Cece, and grumpy over here is my younger sister Laura."

Laura shot Cece a look.

"I'm Kahlen—,"

"No way! No way!" She slapped the top of her desk. "Oh my gosh, you're boss's daughter aren't you?"

"Yes I'm—,"

"I have heard so much about you—,"

Laura hit her again. "Stop interrupting and let her finish a sentence every once in a while."

Cece ignored her. "So… anyways, you're Kahlen Thomas and you're…sixteen? No. Seventeen. And you're a junior." She held out her fingers counting how many things she was saying. "Ugh! There's something I'm missing. No wait! I've got it! Boss told me something about one of your friends… but I can't remember exactly what it was."

The usual twist in my stomach began as I stood there motionless.

"Oh I know," Cece continued. "She said that she used to work with Mrs. Harrison. Isn't that one of your friend's moms?"

I shrugged although I knew the answer.

"No… maybe there was something else I'm missing. Was it— Hello, you've reached Thomas Designs." She automatically switched to a professional voice.

She held up a finger and mouthed one second.

Laura leaned over Cece and said, "Take my advice, leave while you can."

But it was already too late.

"Tuesday at nine, got it. You have a good day Ma'am." Cece hung up the phone.

"Holy mother of pie! This lady's house is 1800 square feet! Isn't that like really big?" She announced.

"I think so..." I answered.

My stomach started to growl and I remembered that the only thing I had eaten today was a bowl of cereal and I hadn't really had much of that.

"So um... you got a boyfriend BD?" She asked.

BD? I knew I must have looked confused. I have been called a lot of wrong names but this was one was a little odder than the others.

"You know... BD... Boss's daughter. I'm no good with names so I always give people nicknames with Laura as an exception. She's kind of hard to forget."

"Because she's your sister," I added.

"No," she said flatly. "Because she's so annoying."

Laura shot her a look.

"Chillax man. I'm only kidding."

I started to walk away again. I had gotten farther than all the other times... at least five steps.

"Wait!" she called and once again I stopped midstride before turning around on my heels to face her. "I was asking you about your boyfriend. A girl as pretty as you has to have a boyfriend. Or are you single and just beating them away with a stick?"

"Um...neither?" It wasn't meant to come out as question.

She made a big O with her mouth but the O faded after a second when I started to hear a *tap, tap, tap. Tap, tap, tap. Tap, tap, tap.*

"Lauuuu-ra! For the love of French fries do you mind? I am trying to have a conversation here without listening to you getting out your frustration with a stupid pencil."

There was no response except another, *Tap, tap, tap*. Then another, *Tap, tap, tap*. Then finally, *TAP, TAP, TAPP*!

"She always does this," Cece explained. "Whenever she gets stuck on a Sudoku puzzle the tapping begins because and so does my loss of sanity!" Finally as Laura continued to ignore her sister's frustration, Cece snapped. "Ugh! I cannot work under these conditions anymore!" She stood up from her seat and desk before walking over to me. "I'll walk with you over to the lounge."

Before I had time to react she already had her arm linked with mine and we were halfway down the hall. I heard Laura say something about having "poor boundaries" as we walked away.

I sighed softly. Cece was energetic enough for the both of us and just being around her was making me feel like I just ran a mile. I was absolutely exhausted by her overfriendliness. Cece opened the door to the stairs and I practically jumped out of my shoes when I saw my mom standing behind it.

"Why are you *so* jumpy lately?" my mom asked.

I didn't answer.

"But anyway, honey, I was looking for you in the lounge. I've pretty much finished up here and I was wondering if you had any plans tonight. If not, I wanted to go out to dinner. I wanted to hang out... just us girls. You know, since the rain cleared up your father probably still went fishing."

I didn't answer. For some reason I just stood there in my own little world as my mom babbled on. I looked behind my right shoulder and out the window. The rain had cleared up pretty nicely. Maybe Dean's Creek was still an option. Maybe this time instead of calling and possibly getting the wrong person I could text him and—

A hand waved in front of my face. "So, do you have any plans tonight?" my mom asked.

I sighed. "Free as a bird."

So this was my Saturday; working most of the day and then ending with dinner with my mom. Lame was an extreme understatement. We made our mostly silent ride to the restaurant my mom had decided on. I watched as the stress left my mother's face when we walked in to the restaurant, Rocco's, which was a pretty popular place for kids at my school. You'd think that if one job could make someone so stressed they'd hate it instead of love it. The job was "her passion" as my mom had told me many times before. I nodded like I understood but I really didn't.

The restaurant was packed with waiters and waitresses scrambling all over the place. I sighed. I would have just been happy with Burger King. After a wait of fifteen impatient minutes, we were finally seated and as soon as our menus were handed to us and our drinks were served, my mother didn't waste any time starting a conversation.

"So honey, did you do anything interesting today while I was gone?"

I shook my head no.

"Nothing at all?" she asked surprised. "You didn't hang out with any of your friends or anything?"

Ugh! *Friends*. I tried not to make a face. The topic of friends was beginning to be a sore subject with me. I took a sip of my soda and shook my head no again.

"So do you have plans for tonight?"

I put my glass back down on the table hard. "Why does it matter mom?"

I was beginning to get annoyed. We hadn't even ordered our food yet and she was already hounding me with questions.

"I was just concerned that's all."

I rolled my eyes. She was always "just concerned". You'd swear I was the biggest problem child to ever walk the earth. I had yet to do anything completely earth shattering.

"Yes. I know you're *just* concerned. I figured that out earlier this week when I was stuck in counseling." I took another big sip of my soda and slurped louder than usual just to drown out her words.

She ignored my jab. "Do you have any plans for tomorrow? Maybe you could go the mall with Marissa."

I slammed my glass back down. "Oh you have got to be kidding me?!"

"Why? What's wrong with Marissa?"

But could I really be mad are her for suggesting it? I had almost been so desperate as to consider it earlier. I didn't feel like getting into it with her so I keep it short and said, "Nothing."

"Then I don't see what the problem is. I don't get it."

I tried to ignore her and tune her out but it wasn't working. She just kept bugging me and wouldn't leave the subject alone. "That's just it mom, you don't get it."

"Well then why don't you help me get it? You never tell me anything about your life. I have every reason to be concerned. I have no idea what is ever going on with you."

It amazed me how she sounded so calm talking to me but yet her words could come out otherwise. I picked up my glass and realized that it was almost empty. I drank the last of it and slammed it down hard again.

"What happened to the nice, quiet, understanding mother I knew last week? I don't need yet another person prodding into my life." I tried not to raise my voice but it wasn't easy. "What does it matter if I'm hanging out with friends tonight anyway? You're the one who invited me here in the first place."

The waiter came over to our table looking down at his notepad and scribbling down something.

"Hello, I'm your waiter for today. What can I start you two ladies to start off with?"

I gasped... and so did the very familiar waiter. He obviously had not been paying attention to who was sitting at our table because when he put his notepad away from his face, it turned as red as a tomato.

I didn't say anything. I pretended as if I had never seen him before in my life.

"Well if it isn't—," he started to say.

I looked quickly at the first thing that popped out to me on the menu.

"Chicken tenders! Well if it isn't chicken tenders. Yum! I haven't had these in a while." I didn't even *like* chicken tenders! I could feel my mom's glare stinging my forehead. I had always made a big deal about the food I didn't like. Whenever she'd cook, she would practically have to make a whole other meal in the process because I was so picky. Once for a whole year I only ate macaroni and cheese.

I didn't bother looking up from the table. I folded the menu and handed it to the waiter without looking up. I knew Kennley was looking at me hesitant and confused. I still didn't look up. I grabbed my empty glass and tipped it into my mouth. I got a tiny drop of water that was the melted ice.

"Can I get you a refill?" he asked.

I wasn't paying attention to what he had said. Rapid thoughts were speeding across my mind like lightening.

"Sweetie?" My mom said after a second. "Do you want a refill?"

"No, I'm good. Thanks," I said quickly.

"So um... Miss, what can I get you?" Kennley asked my mother.

She tapped her finger against her chin for a second before answering. "I'll have the grilled chicken with broccoli and cheddar mashed potatoes.

She folded her menu and handed it to him slowly while narrowing her eyes suspiciously.

"Okay ladies. I'll get your food to you as fast as I can. If you need anything feel free to ask."

I knew he was directly talking to me with his last sentence. My jaw clenched. As soon as I heard his footsteps walking away, I looked up from the table relieved.

"Do you know him?" she asked.

"What?" I said quickly. "Um no...no maybe. I think I've seen him school around." I winced. "No, I mean around school. Yeah that's what I meant to say. But besides that I don't know him. Nope. Not at all. Whatsoever." I had to stop to catch my breath.

"Me thinks thou doth protest too much."

I rolled my eyes.

"Honey, so is that maybe your... boyfriend—,"

I didn't know it was possible for my eyes to grow so wide.

"*Do you want him to be your boyfriend?*" She said.

"Whoa... what? No! Why would you think that?" Crap. Maybe I was protesting too much.

"I don't know. You've seemed a lot *happier* lately and then I overheard you talking to Cece for a second today and I thought maybe..."

"Mom, no. Like I said, he's just some kid that I've seen around school. Nothing more. I'm not even friends with him let alone have any feelings for him."

It couldn't have been worse timing. Kennley walked up to the table and made an effort to look me in the eyes. Not breaking eye contact, he leaned slowly across the table and set the glass of coke down on my coaster. He didn't look happy and I wanted to bury my face in my hands. I knew my cheeks had to be totally red.

"I didn't ask for this." I said quietly.

"I know," he muttered before leaving.

I watched my mother raise an eyebrow but she didn't say a word.

I took the straw from my empty glass and put it into my glass of coke. I closed my eyes and tried to relax but before I knew it I was drinking melted ice. It was embarrassing that I had chugged down two glasses in less than fifteen minutes.

By the time Kennley had made his way back to our table with the food, my bladder was about to implode.

"I have to go the bathroom," I told my mom.

"Figures," she said. "It was only a matter of time..."

I didn't hear what all else she had said. I zoomed past Kennley almost making him drop the food on my way to the bathroom. When I finally came out, my mom was sitting waiting patiently for me.

"You're waiter friend and non-boyfriend said to tell you that 'he gets it'... whatever that means."

I didn't waste time being confused. I dug into my food to keep my mouth as full as possible to prevent any conversation with my mom. I had no idea why I was acting the way I was. It was completely unnecessary… or was it? I could feel the battle in my mind starting again. I could hear the swords clashing against each other and the bullets firing.

"So sweetie, Ms. Bryant called today."

I froze and dropped the chicken tender to the plate. Ms. Bryant was Emma's mother of course.

"What did she want?" My mouth was still full with the disgusting food I was forcing myself to eat. I swallowed as much as I could before speaking.

"Well… she said that she was ready to clean out Emma's room and she wanted you to stop by. She thought some of the stuff in there you might want or it might be yours."

After a second, I said, "Oh."

"She said that she was going to do it sometime next week."

No one said anything else until a different waiter came and picked up our empty plates and told us to have a nice evening.

"Do you think you can come to the office tomorrow?"

"Free as a bird," I repeated. But I didn't feel free. There was this big, invisible burden tied to my back but I couldn't figure out why. "But only as long as you can remain Dr. Jekyll," I joked.

When we finally got home I was no longer the only person who was jumpy… We opened the door my dad was standing on the other side about to hang up his coat.

"Gah!" my parents both screamed at the same time. I started to laugh. Finally I wasn't the only one who was so anxious to the point it was getting ridiculous.

The coat my dad had held in his hand was now on the floor. His hand was on his heart trying to catch his breath. His was in his uniform... which probably contributed to why my mom had screamed. She hated that he was a policeman. No, not hated... despised, detested, loathed, and reviled that he was a policeman. Whenever he was working she was always worried sick. After two years ago when a local policeman and also one of my dad's friends, Greg, had gotten shot and almost died, being a policeman had become utterly abhorrent.

"Bill, I thought you were going fishing?" she was still catching her breath. I could hear the strain in her voice trying to keep calm.

"Now Lisa, don't get upset." He had heard the strain in her voice too. "About two hours into fishing I got a call from the station. There are some suspicions about some drug dealings over on Jefferson Street. Greg and I went to go check out the area and we didn't see anything. I just got back about five minutes ago."

My mom relaxed a little. "Well you could have called to tell me."

My dad sighed. He unbuttoned his shirt a tiny bit to show his bullet proof vest underneath. "Lisa... I'm not going down without a fight," he said simply. My mom smiled. I figured she could be content with that for now.

I walked into the kitchen to find something to eat. At the restaurant I couldn't force the rest of my chicken tenders down so I was still hungry. I was making myself a bowl of cereal when I heard the TV...

"...Sources are saying Britney Spears was not driving the car during the time of the accident, but the charges still may not be dropped. Now back to you Linda."

"Thanks Bob. Now with our lasted story, Police are suspicious of a potential drug bust downtown. Although nothing has been proven yet they will be investigating until further notice."

I walked into the front room where my parents were sitting watching the TV. I saw my dad flash across the screen briefly; he was walking downtown with some others. Maybe this whole thing was more serious than I had thought.

I walked up the stairs to my bedroom and put on my pajamas. I turned on my radio as loud as it would go and drowned myself in the music. My eyelids were getting heavier and heavier. I turned my lights off, turned the music down, and snuggled myself underneath my covers. Then it hit me.

"He gets it?"

7. Alone

Cece was very... interesting. The strange thing was that it wasn't her behavior that was weird, it was the fact that I was getting used to it. Hearing her say things like, "for the love of Maroon 5", and other things like, "for beef jerky sake", and especially, "Holy vaca," didn't make my eyes squint and an eyebrow raise anymore... although that last one did tickle me a little. I know it was a little stereotypical to think that her high voice and behavior matched perfectly with her blonde hair, but I did and I wasn't ready to take it back. I was beginning to find that having conversations with Cece and Laura could be pretty entertaining. Their constant bickering was never a bore although I wondered if it was the same for them. Today, the debate topic was about Johnny Depp: Creepy, or not?

"He is nawt creepy Laura how could you say that?" her jaw dropped.

"Do you need to watch *Secret Window* again for proof?"

She had a good point. Secret Window was a creepy movie about a writer (Johnny Depp) whose wife had cheated on him and then divorced him. Six months later the writer then comes in contact with a man named John Shooter who claims the writer stole his story. He threatens the writer and even kills his dog to show he means business. But then it gets creepier... The writer's ex-wife and her new husband show up at his home and Johnny Depp kills them both! It turns out he was actually insane. John Shooter was himself! His name was Shooter because it meant *shoot her*, as in his ex-wife...Very strange.

"Oh come on! Every actor or actress is entitled to at least one bad or weird movie. Think about Mariah Carey and *Glitter*, she bounced back didn't she?!"

She had a good point.

"How many times has the guy changed his hair style? And don't even get me started on *Charlie and the Chocolate Factory*! He looked like some kind of pale pedophile! That's two bad movies. He's over the limit."

Cece was outraged. "Oh my glitterbugs!"

Okay... that one I cracked a smile at. Maybe I wasn't completely used to her phrases.

"You're just mad because of *Pirates of the Caribbean* when you thought Orlando Bloom was hot but you didn't like Keira Knightly," she continued.

"Whoa! There are so many things wrong with that sentence. First of all, I did not like some grubby pirate and Keira Knightly has nothing to do with Johnny Depp and his creepiness," Laura retorted.

"Well!" Cece thought for a moment. "It made sense in my head when I said it!"

"I'm sure it did!" During this whole fight she hadn't looked up from her Sudoku once.

And that's where the fight ended. The whole time I stood around the corner watching and listening, going unseen by both of them.

I sat there in my seat in art class thinking about the famous phrases while being bored. I looked over at the empty seat next to me and sighed hoping I wouldn't feel the twist in my stomach.

Art was completely pointless now. I wasn't even good at art. I could hardly draw a stick figure. There was only one reason why I had decided to take art in the first place, and now that reason was just an empty seat beside me. I sighed again. She had been the one that was good at art. Heck, she had been the one who was good at everything. Whenever I would mock her about it, she gave the same reply, "Perseverance is the key". Then I'd say, "Yeah... well do you mind making a copy?" I smiled to myself and repressed a sigh. I looked up from the table and it took me a second to realize that someone was standing in front of me waving her hands in my face.

"Uh... um you, can I borrow a piece of sketching paper? I'm all out."

Um... you... how flattering. She didn't even know my name. Then again, I hadn't known hers either.

I tore out a piece of paper out of my notebook and handed it to her.

"Thanks!" She flashed me a quick smile. I just nodded.

I tried not to groan. I knew that smile. Anyone that could flash a smile like that so quickly had to be a cheerleader. I was trying to build up a tolerance for cheerleaders and I was almost getting there. I really had nothing against them personally; the only thing I didn't like was how perky they were... all the time. It killed me. It was like they had ten pounds of caffeine in their systems that refused to go away...or at least in my school it was like that. They were like the energizer bunny. Every bit of it slowly killed me.

I sighed again but it was cut short.

"Why does she keep *doing* that?" I heard someone behind me ask. I hadn't realized how loud my sighs were.

"I don't know, but give her a break. Her best friend did die. Show a little sympathy," the second girl said.

"Oh please," groaned the first girl. "She acts like she's the only one that's hurting. Emma was friends with practically the whole school, even the lower-classmen. I'm sure lots of people are hurting. I know I was and still am."

"Yeah, she was really nice. That explains why she could put up with such a—," the third girl said. She sounded like the person that had asked for the piece of paper.

They were very few times in my life that I had been called a female dog but this time was enough to make me want to turn around and slap her until she begged for mercy… then grab my piece of paper back! I gasped. What had I even done to get this type of reputation? I barely even talked to anyone at the school.

"—I heard that she totally fell asleep during Mr. Simmons' test and he let her off the hook, but then little miss-too-good-for-anybody refused."

I balled up my fist trying to restrain myself from turning around and giving them a piece of my mind.

"Well… she's not too good for *everyone*…" the second girl said. She was making "everyone" seem like such a dirty word.

"Ahh… right. That's true. I heard her and the hot new guy ditched. They are so disgusting together. They obviously like each other," the first girl said.

How was all of this around school? Were people so bored with their lives that they had to talk about mine?

The third girl sighed. "He is hot isn't he? He's like a Brad Pitt kind of rugged mixed in with Matthew McCaunaghey kind of muscles, and Orlando Bloom and Matt Damon kind of mysteriousness."

That was some list she had compiled.

"Oh and don't forget those piercing eyes like Zac Efron ... except green," added the first girl. "She so doesn't deserve him. I heard he was like asking people for her phone number. I don't even know what he sees in her."

As far as I was concerned he didn't *see* anything in me...Or at least not in that way. We were friends, although I wasn't exactly sure how friendly we were at the whole restaurant episode...

The third girl sighed. "She's pretty," she said flatly.

It was hard to be flattered considering everything else they had said about me.

"Yeah, she's like a Jessica Alba and Taylor Swift kind of pretty. What a waste," said the second girl.

My jaw just dropped and I couldn't believe this was really happening. There were all sitting behind me in their little group talking about me like I wasn't even here. Were people so rude as to so blatantly talk behind my back... literally! They were at least five feet away from me, six tops.

"Excuse me." It was a new voice. "Do you guys mind shoving your rude jealousy where the sun don't shine so I can focus on the art project please?"

I turned around to see who was talking, not that I knew any of them by name.

"Oh and another thing," the girl continued. "Maybe you all should try getting your own lives instead of bashing on someone else's that you probably know nothing about. And besides, if anything's a waste it's teenage minds believing every rumor they hear."

I was in awe, but I wasn't the only one. The three girls turned back around and saw me looking at them. That's what really got them and their cheeks flushed and I couldn't help but smile slightly.

I turned back around and focused on drawing the shadow of an apple.

"Well what do you know?" the third girl murmured. "Little miss-too-good-for-anybody cracked a smile..."

My mouth and my throat were dry. I wanted to say something. I wanted to tell them all they were wrong. I wanted to say everything the girl who had stood up for me had said. But I couldn't.

"*Can't or won't?*" she said.

I wanted to tell her to shut up... to get out of my head. But how can you tell your subconscious to shut up?

I was pathetic...so incredibly pathetic that it was eating me up inside. I had never felt so useless in all my life. Life isn't supposed to be rote. It's not about surviving day-to-day and that was hitting me and hitting me hard.

As much as I didn't want to show weakness I said, "Ms. Moore, can I go to the bathroom?"

Before she had even said yes I was half way out the door. I ran to my locker and started grabbing all my books for homework. I thought about ditching but my parents would be furious if they found out. So I was going to do the responsible thing. I was going to the office and tell my mom that I really and truly didn't feel good and that I wanted to go home. Book after book I shoved it into my backpack and then zipped it up quickly. When I slammed my locker closed, I saw Kennley standing on the other side leaning against his locker. I jumped back startled. I must have looked like a deer in headlights.

"You know... being incredibly anxious is a sign of a high stress level," he said flatly.

I could tell he was angry and I knew I must have hurt him. I wanted to apologize and explain everything that had happened to him, but unthinkingly I didn't. I didn't say anything. I just stood there with my mouth wide open trying to catch my breath. I didn't even know what to say to him. How could I explain why I acted the way I had at the restaurant? I barely knew why I had acted that way. First of all, it was embarrassing enough being with my mom on a Saturday night; second, I knew what my parents would think of Kennley. They wouldn't approve of how much time he actually *spent* at school during the school day. I had acted stupidly. I knew I had. But what did "he get"?

My throat was still dry. I tried to speak but nothing would come out. I managed to give him a weak smile before grabbing my backpack off the floor and walking away.

"Fine!" he yelled after me. "But I thought you were different. I thought you were smarter than to believe rumors. The least you could have done was ask me," he said angrily

I had no idea what he was talking about. Before I could ponder over anything, the bell rang and everyone began filing out of their classrooms. I saw everyone from art class come walking in between the gap between Kennley and I. I couldn't even see his face anymore. All I could see were the three girls from art waving flirtatiously at him.

"Ugh..." the second girl groaned, obviously annoyed. "I bet she just asked to go to the bathroom so they could meet up and talk here. Besides, I heard that he called Marissa Harrison," the second girl said.

"Yeah, better Marissa than what's her name."

The tears began to well up in my eyes. I darted for the bathroom and I tried to pull myself together but it was a futile attempt. The water leaked from my eyes, ran down my cheeks, and into my hands. I wasn't crying over those stupid girls though. I was crying over something else... something more important. As I sat in the bathroom stall crying, I was thankful that I was alone. But then it hit me... I was alone. All alone. The tears fell harder. I missed her so much. My stomach was twisting and contorting so I was afraid I might barf...even though if I did I would have a legitimate excuse for going home sick. It kept twisting with pain and I couldn't calm it anymore.

I flushed the toilet and wiped off my mouth. I looked in my backpack and was thankful that I had some gum to get rid of the disgusting taste. I rinsed my face off in the sink hoping it would reduce the puffy redness of my eyes. It didn't work so I gave up and walked out of the bathroom. Kennley was taking his slow time going to class and I wasn't surprised. I tried to comb my hair with my fingers so that it could cover up the side of my face. Unfortunately, Kennley saw me anyway.

"Kahlen?" he asked.

I kept walking but this time faster.

"Kahlen?" he called my name again. I could hear his footsteps coming towards me. Before I knew it, he had gotten hold of my shoulder and turned me around.

"What?" I practically yelled. The tears began to spill again.

He seemed taken aback as the tears streamed.

"Ar-are you okay?" he let go of my shoulder.

I wiped the tears away from my face with my hand and avoided looking at him.

"Okay..." he said slowly. "Never mind, stupid question. Listen, I know I'm probably the last person you want to talk to right now...,"

He was wrong. If anything he was the only person I wanted to talk to. But my mouth was still dry if not drier from crying.

"But things do get better, I promise. Maybe we could go somewhere and talk about it," he continued.

How could he know? How could he possibly understand anything I was going through? As wrong as it was to think that way, I did. I knew he was trying to help and understand but it just made me madder. I was so angry. I was angry at the world, angry at God, angry at myself. Something clicked in my mind and it went into automatic defence mood.

"Will you at least talk to me?" he pleaded. "Let me explain before you make up your mind."I cleared my throat and it burned. I knew he was trying his best to reach out to me but I didn't want him to. I didn't want to get close to another person just for them to end up hurting me. I was fine. Everything was just fine.

"No!" I yanked my shoulder away from his hold. "I don't even know what you're talking about. I haven't heard any rumors, Kennley!"

He paused for a second. "What?" he finally said.

By the time he had finished his sentence I had already started power walking away from him. I knew what I was doing. I knew I was purposefully pushing him away, but it felt like I couldn't stop.

"Kahlen, wait!" he ran after me.

"Just leave me alone okay?" The tears were finally stopping. "Leave me alone," I repeated.

I didn't give him a chance to say anything. I took one last glance at him as I walked away.

"*They're wrong Kahlen*," she said. "*It's more like Channing Tatum meets Ashton Kutcher*."

Adjacent to the main office was the guidance office. I saw through the tiny window Marissa Harrison sitting down in a chair, her eyes just as red as mine. A wave of curiosity washed over me. Because I was looking on the other side of the hall, I ran right into the door of the main office. My already red cheeks burned redder. I could see a secretary sitting behind her desk trying to stifle her laughter.

I walked up to the desk and said, "I need to make a phone call please."

I convinced my mom that I was well enough to drive myself home and I signed myself out at the office. I had kept myself together until I got outside the school doors. Then the tears started to pour again. They wouldn't stop. Even when I tried to stop them they just kept going and going. When I got to my car in the parking lot, I fell over the top of it and let my tears wash it. I didn't know how I was going to drive with my vision being blurred like it was. So I waited for the tears to stop. I shut my eyes to stop them but had only stalled them. *Come on Kahlen, get yourself together,* I told myself. *Get yourself together.*

I abruptly opened the car door and slammed it behind me. I put the key in the ignition and turned it hard. The old car roared to life and I pulled out of the parking lot and onto the street. My vision was still blurry but I didn't care. When I finally got home, I locked myself away in my bedroom. It was all hitting me. Usually when I was upset I went to her, when I wanted to hang out, I went to her, for anything and everything, I went to *her*. Now who did I go to? I went to my radio and blasted it.

I lied down on my bed and the tears finally began to stop as I looked up at my ceiling. It was awful how life could change in less than a second. In less than one second your whole world can start spinning in the opposite direction. It amazed me how life could be so predictable. Everything was planned out. Nothing changed. Out of nowhere babies couldn't start being born at four months instead of nine. It's to be expected that the sky wouldn't turn brown overnight. Most things in life are predictable and yet life could be so unpredictable whether we want it to or not. Sometimes life can be as unpredictable as we want it to be and others... a meteor could fly out of the sky and knock you on the head and it takes years just to contemplate what actually happened. I had been hit by one huge meteor. Before I knew it, my eyes were beginning to close. I was completely knocked out.

I pushed him away. Only one thing mattered to me at the moment. I watched as the elevator doors closed behind my face. He grabbed my arm again and tried to put me back into my hospital room but I wouldn't budge. I must have looked insane laying there on my knees hysterical. *Everything is going to be okay*, I told myself. It had to be. It was something programmed into all teenagers brains. It was the illusion of invincibility. We all thought the same. We believed that no matter how big a mess we had gotten ourselves into that everything would work out in the end. Such an evil illusion it was.

He tugged again but this time he grabbed both arms. Although he was twenty some years older than me, my father was still stronger. My mom was at his side bringing me back into my room. My head was still hurting to the point that it was ridiculous but I didn't complain. I could barely even think about the pain at the moment. All I could think about was her. I knew that everything would work out in the end, the illusion was so real, but deep down I still worried. I waited anxiously for someone, anyone, to tell me what was going on but no one did. My mom sat at my hospital bed with me trying to comfort my sobs by rubbing circles on my back gently. I could see the tears brimming in her eyes, even my dad looked a little torn.

After an hour of impatient waiting, the doctor came into my room and I already knew. As much as I didn't want to know, I did. He didn't even have to say anything. He knew that and I knew that. He explained everything that had happened and what had gone wrong. It felt like a never ending rollercoaster ride. Usually in roller coasters there is only one really big drop and the rest are smaller in comparison. But the drops kept coming and so did my heart into my stomach. Then after a while, I got used to drops. I could feel my heart still dropping, but it was becoming somewhat numb. The tears had stopped and my eyes felt eternally dry. The illusion had completely disappeared leaving a void in its place. It felt like all these years I thought the grass was green and then just found out it was actually purple.

"I um… I uh," the doctor started to say,

I wanted to scream for him to spit it out, but I held my tongue.

"I don't know how to say this but—,"

I rose up so quickly from my bed and almost fell out of it. My room was dark. My radio had been turned off and the only light I had in my room was the moonlit sky and red neon numbers on my alarm clock.

"No, no, no, no, no!" I whispered quickly.

How could I have possibly slept that long? It was three in the morning which I suppose was no surprise. My parents would always complain to me about how when I was a baby I would wake up at three on the dot crying. I'd always roll my eyes. It's not like it was my fault. I couldn't be held responsible for something I didn't even remember. That trait of my mine had continued throughout all of my life. If I woke up in the middle of the night it would always be at three, three o one tops.

I was one step away from being frantic. I had school work to do, I had missed the new episode of *American Idol*, and I hadn't even eaten in over ten hours. I got up out of my bed and tip toed my way down the stairs. I opened the refrigerator first and slammed the door closed in frustration.

"How come we never have anything to eat here?" I mumbled to myself.

I opened the cabinet door and pulled out a big bag of potato chips. I brought the bag with me up the stairs to my bedroom and sat there for a second realizing I wasn't at the very least sleepy. Then the light bulb flickered in my head. I opened my window as high as it would go and climbed down the tree one handed with the bag of potato chips in the other hand. I strolled down the street slowly taking my time. It was amazing how peaceful everything was at night and the silence was relaxing. When I had finally gotten to Dean's Creek, the bag of chips was half way empty. I felt like such a pig… and yet I shoved another handful in my mouth.

I sat down on the ground and laid the chips next to me before putting my head to the ground and looking up into the sky. I squinted trying to see if I could find more than six stars in the sky. I had seen pictures of what a sky full of stars looked like but had never seen it firsthand. When my dad would go fishing he would always try to convince my mother and me to come with him but we wouldn't budge. We just weren't outdoorsy people. He told me how beautiful the star filled sky looked but I would always pass on going. Every now and again he would always ask just to be polite. He knew what my answer would be but that didn't stop him. I always appreciated him asking me if I wanted to go anyway.

An airplane flew by and shook the ground beneath me. I could hear the engines of cars driving by, and annoying crickets cricketing. The silence my neighborhood had provided had left, but overall it was still peaceful. I liked it. I liked the way the moon reflected on the water and how the grass moved very gently in the breeze. It was the perfect temperature, chilly yet warm. I could hear the water moving down the creek and winding into the woods and it calmed me. It calmed my rapid heartbeat and all the thoughts running across my head.

The beauty of the creek never ceased to have its impact on me. I loved the way the sun's light reflected on the grass in the daytime or how the trees' shadows moved among it. The sound of the wind drifting past the leaves and my hair was like magic. I felt like the V.I.P. guest who had the front row seat of nature's beauty taking its course. The way the warmth from the sun heated my skin and the way a cool breeze caused goose bumps to rise on my arm. It never ceased. The only difference was that now it was nighttime and impossibly lovelier than before.

8. Memories

"Honey, are you sure you don't want a ride? I'm on my way over to the office right now and dropping you off wouldn't be a problem."

I sighed. "For the last time mom, I'm fine. I can drive myself."

She opened her mouth to protest but I held up a finger. "I'll tell Ms. Bryant that if she took out part of the wall in the kitchen leading to the front room that it would create more openness to the main level."

She smiled satisfied. I knew that was really the only reason she had wanted to go in the first place to lend her interior designing knowledge. I only had one more week of this interior decorating madness and then it would be over.

I threw my tote bag over my shoulder and headed out the door. I knew this would be hard but I had to do it. All the drive there I was prepping myself on what was to come. I imagined her room that I knew by heart in my head over and over again and I imagined Ms. Bryant in my head. She had never really been the perfect mother. Then again, who really was? But she was only a mother when it was convenient and a lousy best friend the rest of the time. As a single mom, she did a good job of providing but beyond that it seemed like she was just kind of… there. Nothing more. Emma never was ever reprimanded for her behavior. The most talking those two did was a random and awkward sex talk that Emma had told me about. She didn't even call her *mom*. She called her by her name, Julie, because "mom" made her feel old. Heaven forbid she actually *act* her age. Most of the time I loved being there during their moments—their *good* moments that is. I remember when Emma would call me and tell me to get over to her house ASAP because Julie had decided to go on a shopping spree, the sky's the limit, or when they'd decided to have a movie marathon with stacks and stacks of pizza.

I'd always wondered about Emma's dad. She never talked about him much. I knew that they moved here after his death. I didn't know how he died but I knew that he and Ms. Bryant had been divorced before it happened. I was respectful and never brought it up although I still wondered.

Julie wasn't the single mom looking for love who would have a new boyfriend every month. She was the single mom looking for love that had a new boyfriend every once in a blue moon. I remember that blue moon about a year and a half ago. Emma was happy that she was happy and didn't have a problem with the new boyfriend Roger, except that he was thirty-one. Julie was forty-two. After a couple of months, Roger said that he couldn't take his family being angry with him anymore for dating an older woman. I wish I could have seen the look on Julie's face when he fed her that line. She slapped him, came home, practically scared Emma and I to death with her hysterical crying and we all gained five pounds from ice cream and chocolate.

"I don't need a man. I already have two, Ben and Jerry," she had said.

All of these memories were flooding back into my mind and I hadn't even reached the house yet. When I finally got to the house— the same small blue house engraved into my mind, I sat for a while in my car before going in.

"*Tell Julie I said hi,*" she said.

I got out of the car and walked slowly up the house. I took in a deep breath and let it out before grabbing the door handle and twisting it to open. Julie never locked the door. The door opened and I stepped inside. The place was a mess. I was surprised that I didn't see mice and roaches running around. Dirty and clean clothes were spread all over the floor. The milk was sitting out on the kitchen table. Bowls of half eaten instant oatmeal were stacked up against the couch and the place reeked. An empty beer bottle rolled to my foot and I kicked it away. I tried to keep from breathing out of my nose and only out of my mouth.

"Hello?" I called. "Ms. Bryant... Julie? Are you here?"

No one answered. I looked around for Macy, Emma's black lab. I called her name but she didn't answer.

I headed towards the upstairs to Emma's bedroom. "Julie?" I called.

Still no reply.

My eyes automatically locked on the door furthest down the hallway. The white door splattered with paint of every color. I could see the memories and flashbacks in my mind of when we had first painted the door...

"Help me," Emma had said that say so many years ago. I couldn't help but notice that she happened to be surrounded by many paint buckets.

My eyes narrowed and knowing Emma she probably had something crazy planned. "What...why?"

She sighed heavily. "You ask too many questions. Besides, you don't ask, you *do*."

"That sounds like something out of a fortune cookie," I mumbled.

She bent down to pick up one of the buckets with a sigh. "Are you going to help me, or not?"

Wordlessly I helped her bring all the many cans of paint up the stairs and I couldn't help but wonder if I would have been better off at home instead of helping with what I was assuming would be a tiring paint project. We stood at the top of the stairs looking down the long hallway at Emma's bedroom door.

"Look at it," she said as if the point she was trying to make was so obvious.

"Look at what?"

"My door," she answered quickly. "Look at my door!" When my brows furrowed she continued annoyed. "It's so...*white*. So plain and so...*ordinary*!" She cocked her head to the side to examine it from a different angle.

"But then why do we need so many different colors and don't we need paint brushes or something?" I asked.

She rolled her eyes before walking on ahead of me. "Would you stop with all the questions?"

"But—,"

She put a finger to my mouth abruptly. "Kahlen Thomas, I swear if you ask another question I'm going to slap you." She dropped the finger from my mouth slowly and then turned back to the vague task at hand. I followed her to the door where we dropped off the paint buckets that were stacked at the door although it took about two more trips down the stairs to get all the rest of the cans.

"Geez," I had said dropping the last heavy paint bucket. "Where did you even get all of this?" As soon as the words came out of my mouth I grimaced.

"No, it's okay," she said. "I'll let that one slide...for

now. But to answer your unnecessary question, I have connections."

"What connec—," I stopped my sentence short.

She shot me a look then continued to open the paint lids. She opened the orange one, submerged her hand in the bucket, drew it back, and flung all the paint at the door. Then she put her hand to the door and moved it around. I watched as her handprint smeared.

"Well are you just going to stand there?" she asked me.

Emma was being unusually bossy today. I knew something had to be up. I suspected something with Julie.

"I'll be back, I'm gonna go to the bathroom," She said.

As she walked to the bathroom a note fell out of her pocket and dropped to the ground. As soon as I heard the bathroom door shut I ran to the note and picked it up. I knew this was in invasion of privacy and that I shouldn't snoop... But was it really snooping if it just fell to the floor? I opened the folded note and read it quickly:

Emma,

Gone to Chicago for a couple of days. I'll bring you back something. You know where the money jar is if you need anything. Why don't you and Kahlen order a pizza or something? No parties please.

-Julie

What kind of mother takes off, doesn't say when exactly she'll be back, and makes it up by giving permission to order a pizza? Someone like Emma didn't deserve Julie and vice versa.

Emma came back and I quickly shoved the note

in my pocket. I stuck my hand down in pink paint but instead of flinging it at the door, I flung it at Emma.

She gasped and her jaw stayed there, dropped. "What was that for?" she asked shocked.

I smiled. "You don't ask, you *do*." I flung more paint.

She flung the blue paint at me and I retorted with the green. Before we knew it we both had multicolored hair and clothes.

We both lay on the floor next to each other trying to catch our breaths.

"Mission accomplished soldier," Emma said.

I looked over at her confused. She pointed to the door and it along with the wall and the floor had almost been completely covered with splattered paint.

I sighed. "Mission accomplished."

"Julie?" I called again, now snapping back into the present.

She still didn't answer. I opened Emma's door before walking into her room and felt like I had just been hit with a ton of bricks. I didn't know what I had been thinking in coming here or how I ever thought I could handle this. Her bed was messy. It looked like she had just gotten out it… like she had just been there this morning. Her room smelled like her too. It was that same Victoria's Secret perfume that she always wore. Clothes were thrown on the floor like they always were because of Emma's lack of organizational skills. It was all coming together… this room hadn't been touched. I blinked back my tears and started to shut the door behind me. A little nose poked through the door and scared me. It was Macy, Emma's black lab. I dropped down to my knees and hugged her. I thought about how much she must have missed Emma. Julie wasn't very fond of dogs so Macy must have been lacking in the attention she was getting lately. I shut the door behind Macy and patted her head gently.

Every time I was in her room I would always check to see the differences. She was always moving or changing something, even if it meant moving her bed to the other side of the room. She had pictures all over the walls and the door and of course the room was bursting with color, I wouldn't expect anything less. I looked over and saw a photo on her door of her and her ex-boyfriend, Dylan. I remembered when Dylan first officially became her ex when we were fourteen...

I remembered I had gotten a text from Emma to come over right away. I begged my mom to drive me over there until she finally did. She had only been gone for three weeks at summer camp but it felt like three years. I was so lonely without her. For most of the time I just moped around my house with my head hung low.

When we pulled up to her house I practically jumped out of the car, not even saying goodbye to my mother, and ran to Emma who was sitting on the porch swing with her face turned away from mine.

"Hey," I greeted her, "So I've decided that no matter how much I hate the outdoors I'm going to summer camp with you. I can't stand another three weeks without you," I sounded so pathetic but it was all true. "So tell me all about—,"

I was interrupted by her sobs. She turned her body around to face me and I saw her red eyes and tears streaming down her face.

"Dylan and I broke up," she cried.

I grabbed her into a tight hug. "What a jerk! How could he dump someone as gorgeous and smart as you? He doesn't know what he's missing. Anyone as stupid as him doesn't deserve you anyway!"

I had heard many stories about Dylan. I got all the details from me and Emma's late night phone calls. I was surprised by Emma's sneakiness because cell phones weren't allowed at camp and lights went out at ten. I had enough pictures to make a scrapbook from all the images she'd sent me on her cell phone.

"Kahlen no. Dylan didn't dump me. I dumped him!" Her voice cracked.

"Oh wow. Well um... why are you so upset?" I already knew the answer. Emma was too painfully nice to break someone's heart.

"He looked like he was about to cry," she sobbed.

"Why did you break up with him? You two seemed so perfect for each other,"

"We were!" she said in between her sobs. "B-b-but he always wore his pants a little low like most guys do and for five days he wore the same boxers,"

I grimaced, "Are you sure he didn't just have a lot of the same kind?"

She shook her head no. "Not unless they all had a tiny hole in them in the same place. It was disgusting and as much as I tried not to notice, it really bothered me. Then I couldn't take it anymore. After lunch I pulled him aside and told him that we were over. But then when he asked me why I just stood there and staring at him. I couldn't tell him it was because of the frequency of his underwear changing! So I told him it was because after camp we'd go back to our separate cities and I couldn't do long distance." Her tears were finally stopping. "He looked so hurt. Then I burst into tears and he was the one comforting me. How ironic. It made me feel even worse. I had stopped crying on the bus ride home but when I went on my computer and checked my e-mail and saw a picture of the two of us that I sent to myself and the waterworks started again."

"That's some story," I said wiping a tear off of her cheeks with my finger. "I heard that when boys get older they really do have better hygiene."

She sniffled, "I sure hope so."

Standing in the middle of Emma's room, now in the present, I didn't want to touch anything or move it. Leaving the room the way it was felt like she was still here somehow. Like she wasn't gone and that she really had been sleeping in her bed this morning.

Then something popped out to me. It was her golden locket shaped as a heart. I had always wanted to know what was inside of it but she never told me which only made me more curious. I picked up the locket and held it in my hands moving it back and forth between them. I heard footsteps coming and I quickly shoved the locket into my pocket.

The door opened and Julie walked in and Macy barked repeatedly. Julie looked awful as I had suspected. Her silky and thick, long blond hair was in a tangled mess. Her shirt was on backwards and her sweatpants were inside out. The perfume smelling room now smelled somewhat tainted and I realized that smell was Julie. God only knows the last time she bathed herself but my guess was sometime around a couple of weeks ago.

"Kahlen... Kahlen Thomas..." She slurred her words. "Well what do you know? You can show up to help clean out her room but you can't come to a measly funeral. What a shame. Shame... Shame... *Shame*." She wagged her finger in front of my face. "How dare you. You were supposed to be her friend. Her *best* friend. How could you just not show up? Your mom and dad showed up... but you..." She stumbled as she took another step towards me. "Everyone knows I'm an awful mother. Heck! *I* know I'm an awful mother. But at the end of the day, I knew Emma had soooomeone," She pointed her finger at me. "And the— and then you don't even show. Some friendship *there*."

It couldn't be more obvious that she was drunk. I had seen her a bit tipsy before but never like this. Even though she didn't know what she was saying she still meant it. A drunken girl's actions are a sober girl's desires. Her words hurt.

I had to think fast. I knew I couldn't leave her here and there was no way I was touching anything in Emma's room. It was fine the way it was. So I grabbed Julie's arm and started to pull her with me towards the stairs.

She yanked her arm back. "L-let *go* of me!"

I had no idea where my assertiveness was coming from but I grabbed her arm again and began to pull her down the stairs.

"No. You're coming with me."

She whined and complained all the way to my car. Thankfully she threw up right before she got into the car. It was disgusting. I felt nauseous myself. I put her in the backseat and put on her seat belt. She was like a two year old.

I speeded my way to my mom's office and yelled at Julie to stay in the car. When I ran inside and threw open my mom's door, she was busy as usual in her regular *Hyde* form. She looked up at me somewhat franticly because I had startled her.

"Sweetie—,"

"Mom!" I said trying to catch my breath from running. "Mom!" I tried again but I couldn't breathe. Was I really that out of shape?

"What—,"

"It's Julie. She is really drunk. She can barely walk. And the house is a complete mess and–" I managed to get out.

"Louisa!" she yelled, "Hold all of my calls!"

My mom and I both darted back out of the door to my car. I looked in the backseat window and didn't see anyone. She couldn't have gone far very quickly. I looked around the parking lot but I didn't see her.

"She was here a second ago I swear,"

My mom just sighed, "She still is," She flung the door open and lying on the floor was a passed out Julie.

I gasped as my mom tried to get her up on the seat.

"Her pulse is slowing. I think she's passed out." My mom said, "Call nine-one-one now!" She yelled and I searched my pockets for my cell phone and felt nothing.

"Oh no, I must have left it at home," I said quickly.

"Go get Cece or Laura to call and hurry."

I ran as fast as I possibly could but I felt incredibly slow.

"*Hurry Kahlen*," she said.

Step after step I pushed myself to go faster as I ran to the building. I ran into the desk and my knee ached but I didn't care.

Cece smiled at me then frowned when I didn't smile back.

"Call—" I panted and but tried to take deep breaths, "Nine-one-one now!"

Cece and Laura just looked at me shocked and although neither of them knew how to act in the middle of a crisis, I however had more than enough experience. I reached over the desk and grabbed the phone and dialed myself. It wasn't the first time I had called nine-one-one...

"Ohhhhh my gosh. Ohhhhh my gosh. Oh. My. Gosh!" I had said.

"Would you stop saying that?" Emma said.

"Sorry if I am slightly freaking out here when there just so happens to be a knife *through* your *hand*!" I screamed.

I had no idea how she was acting so calmly. Her own blood was dropping down to the ground in a puddle. If I were hurt I would have been so shocked I probability would have fainted by now.

"Doesn't that hurt?!"

"Not really. It's actually kind of numb."

"That's understandable considering all of the nerve cells in your hand are probably *shattered*!" I yelled.

"Would you stop screaming and call someone for help?" she asked.

I took a deep breath. "Right. Nine-one-one. Gotcha."

One moment I had been sitting on the couch watching TV and the next I was in an ambulance. I wasn't even exactly sure how she had gotten the big knife through her hand in the first place. She had told me that she was cutting up some watermelon, slipped, the knife went down with her, and went through her hand. It was all pretty gruesome and to this day I was still fighting to get the horrific image from being imprinted in my mind.

After an hour or two my mom called to tell me that Julie would be fine. She told me that she had to have her stomach pumped and that they were both staying the night. I didn't understand my mom's relationship with

Julie. She wouldn't even call her Julie in front of me, it was always Ms. Bryant. She'd complain to me about her poor parenting skills and how much she couldn't stand her and then the next moment the two were off to have lunch. It was so beyond confusing but I had learned to stay out of my mom and Julie's friendship.

I sighed and fell back on my bed but something didn't feel right. There was a lump in my side and I reached into my pocket and pulled out the golden heart shaped locket. I tried to open it but it wouldn't budge. I thought about all the times I had tried to find out what was inside the locket and failed.

Spring break of this year our whole junior class had put together beach day. We spent the whole day at the beach, with adult chaperones of course, and then we'd have a huge bon fire at night. Emma and I lay on our beach towels staring out into the ocean. Marissa had been annoyingly sitting with us earlier. Half of the time I felt like I had to share Emma with her. During the summers when Emma was away at camp, no longer attending but a counselor there, Marissa would be there with her. It was Emma's way of replacing me over the summer.

"Look at David. He is so hot..."

I tried not to laugh. Emma had an obsession with boys whose names started with a D but she wasn't quite aware of it.

I watched as David ran down the beach staring up into the air waiting for something. A football flew through the air towards David's direction and then hit right smack in the center of his face. He fell down and landed in the sand. Everyone around us laughed except for Emma. I was laughing so hard tears were streaming down my face.

"... And yet soo stupid," she continued. "Why did God do this? Why would He make guys so irresistible and yet so brainless?"

"They have brains, just not in the right places." I said.

Emma laughed.

"I want love. I want that amazing high school sweetheart and then that earth shattering break up."

"That doesn't even make sense. Who wants a break up?" I flipped the page of my magazine and readjusted my sunglasses.

"Not to be cynical, but we all know a high school relationship's odds of working out are slim. But I still want it. I want to find someone that I can grow old with... someone who I can end up sitting on our porch watching our grandkids playing in the yard while sharing a piece pie."

"Pie?" I asked.

"Yeah! Don't you want to find someone who wants to share your piece of pie?"

I rolled my eyes. She was being downright ridiculous. "Who needs love or *pie* anyway... or at least not right now. Boys complicate things."

"True. But sometimes complications are good. Exhibit A... look at Danny's tan. I'm gonna go talk to him."

"Wait," I threw down my magazine and grabbed her arm. "You can't just leave me here alone."

I knew I was being pathetic. There were a whole bunch of people around us... a whole bunch of people in our class that I didn't know and that I didn't want to know.

She sighed. "Well Danny's talking to Ryan. Why don't you come be my wing man?"

I shook my head no quickly. "I have a no boys

policy right now." Emma's eyes widen at me with mock suspicion. "And no I am not a lesbian. Don't even go there. I'm just not looking for a relationship. I don't need love."

"Kahlen, life without love is like a starless sky."

I sighed heavily. "I knew it. I knew you couldn't go five minutes without saying something that sounds like it came out of a fortune cookie. And besides, I have love. I have you and my family and that's all I need.

"Not that kind of love. That's the kind of love you're born with. You have no control over that. And yeah, I love you but that kind of love isn't as unique either. People can't be completely happy alone forever. Men and women were meant to be together and besides, I think you're afraid to try."

"To try what?" I asked quickly.

"Love," she said slowly. "A relationship. Anything that involves taking a risk. The cautious never live you know."

"Fortune cookie," I whispered to her.

She ignored me. "All I'm saying is that you can't be satisfied with the moon forever. You need stars, Kahlen."

I was getting sick of this conversation. "Is that Janette walking over to Danny?" I said to distract her.

In an instant she was already over by Danny tossing her hair behind her shoulder. I saw something gold in the sand shaped as a heart. I walked over, picked it up, and examined it. I fought myself on opening it. I did the right thing. I called Emma and she waved me off. I walked closer to her and held the locket up so it was dangling out of my hand. I called her name again. This time she turned around and ran back to me. I had forgotten how fast she was...but of course she was the track star. She grabbed the locket out of my hand.

"It must have fallen off of you or something," I said.

"Thanks," she said. "I need to get this thing fixed. I think the clasp is broken."

"What's inside of it anyway?" I asked nonchalantly even though my curiosity was burning inside.

"Nothing." She said quickly. "It's just not important okay."

I had no idea why she was getting defensive. I knew I should have stopped but I didn't.

"Well it obviously is important because I can't think of a day that you haven't worn it."

"Geez Kahlen. Can't you understand privacy? Don't you have anything of yours that just... *yours*?"

She didn't give me time to respond. Before I could even blink she was back talking to Danny.

9. Giving In

I sighed. Beside all the previous drama I was stuck at home by myself on a Saturday. I didn't even have my dad for company. He was out on Jefferson Street again looking for anything suspicious. I was waiting for someone to come and put a "lame" stamp on my forehead. Again the same options popped up in my head. I wasn't calling Marissa and I wasn't calling Kennley. The only difference was that Marissa was probably willing to talk to me and Kennley wasn't. For the whole rest of the week at school things had been... interesting between us. He wouldn't even look my direction. The only communication we had was the angry slamming of our lockers before heading off in our different directions. I hadn't gone to the creek anymore in fear of seeing him. I knew I was being stupid but I didn't care. I had told Kennley to leave me alone and he had decided to obey my wishes. But did that mean things had to be so cold between us?

I kept doing it. As much as I tried to stop myself I couldn't. I was pushing him away more everyday and I hated myself for it. I was even pushing Mrs. Kraft away. I gave one word answers to her questions and acted like I despised this every second I sat in her office.

"So... anything interesting happen with you and your new friend?" Mrs. Kraft asked.

"Nope," I said the slowly so the P made a popping noise.

"Have your grades been doing okay?"

"Don't have a clue," I said quickly.

She seemed taken aback. We sat for a minute in silence. I knew she had nothing to say and neither did I.

"Is something bothering you Kahlen?"

"Nope," I lied.

"Are you sure?" she seemed concerned.

"Yup." The P popped.

"Kahlen if you don't want to be here you can always go back to class. No one is stopping you. And besides, if you're just going to waste my time then there is no point in me putting in the time and energy to be here." Her voice was suddenly stern.

I didn't know much about counselors but I was pretty sure it wasn't very professional-like to tell your client that they are wasting your time... no matter how true it was.

I sat up in my seat and uncrossed my arms. "The only reason I'm here is because my parents and my parents alone. So sorry if I can't pretend like I want to sit here and discuss my so-called issues," I said coldly.

"*Stop it Kahlen*," she said.

"You know everything here is confidential. Everything you say is only between me and you." Her voice was softer. "Please tell me what's bothering you."

I hesitated. "My life," I answered.

"What about your life exactly?"

"The fact that I have no friends, or that I miss her so much I have stomach aches, and me. I'm not too fond of myself these days."

"Well why not?"

I thought about my answer for a moment trying to get all of my jumbled thoughts together in my mind. "It's like there's this other side of me I can't control."

Well that sounded stupid. I was making it sound like I was the incredible hulk. "I push. I push people away constantly and then finally when I'm alone and I've pushed off everyone I can, I just kind of look back and think, 'man, I really suck'."

She smiled slightly. "Why do you think you push?"

She already knew the answer she just wanted me to say it out loud. I knew what she was doing and I didn't want to comply. "I don't know," I said in a whiny voice.

Her smile grew bigger. "Oh yes you do."

She couldn't tell me what I know and what I didn't know.

"Oh *no* I don't."

"Kahlen," She prodded. "Could the reason possibly be because you're scared?"

I responded with silence.

"It's like your mind's way of protecting itself," she continued.

She sighed looking at her watch. "Well it looks like you've got five minutes before the bell. So I'll let you go."

She stood up and hit her desk with her elbow. A whole bunch of folders went sliding off of it.

"I'll get them." I said bending down.

"No it's okay. I've got them."

I was already on the ground gathering them up. The papers had slid out of one of the folders. On top of it, it said, Marissa Harrison. My eyes widened in surprise when I saw some notes about Emma. I shoved the papers in the folder quickly and handed the pile to Mrs. Kraft. I could see she was worried I had seen something I shouldn't have. I smiled innocently, grabbed my stuff and left.

I decided to go to my locker before going to my

next class. Of course Kennley was there also at his locker skipping class; I wondered how many classes he actually went to. Wouldn't his parents be called? Shouldn't he have enough detentions to drown in? When I finished getting my stuff I slammed my locker and he slammed his back. That was our conversation for the day, the question was, how long would it last?

I walked into the cafeteria and scanned it quickly for Kennley. As much as I didn't want to see him…I wanted to see him. I wanted this whole little feud thing to be over between the two of us but at the same time I knew I was nowhere near close to going up to him to apologize.

I grinned a little to myself. Of *course* he wasn't here. School had never been much of a priority from him, let alone a necessity.

A small, hesitant, but friendly voice came from behind me.

"Um… you can sit with me, if you want."

Jenny Wilkins was small and somewhat timid. Her short black hair shaped her face perfectly and matched against her caramel skin. She was sitting at a small table behind me alone and her eyes were wide looking into mine waiting for my response. Jenny was the same girl that had stood up for me when those three she-devils attacked me in art. I just found out who she was two hours ago in art. She had taken it upon herself to make the empty seat next to me not so empty anymore. We didn't say much to each other. She introduced herself to me so I was inclined to do the same.

"Sure." I said indifferent. As much as I didn't want to give Jenny the wrong idea that we were actually friends, I couldn't help but smile back into those brown eyes. "Thanks." I said my voice a little higher this time.

I had to admit that it was a little awkward sitting at lunch not eating anything across from someone engrossed in their peanut butter and jelly sandwich.

"Want some?" she offered. She dumped out all the contents of her brown paper bag. Out spilled a pink bottle of Crystal Light, a green apple, a small zip lock bag of goldfish, and the other half of her sandwich.

"No thanks. For some reason, I'm not really hungry much these days."

She nodded and took another bite from her sandwich.

"So, um… about *these* days; how have you been dealing?"

My eyes grew wide. I didn't know tiny little Jenny Wilkins had it in her to ask that question. It had taken me by surprise. Jenny must have noticed this too.

"I'm sorry," she was looking down at the table now avoiding eye contact. "I'm just curious that's all. I didn't mean to pry. You don't have to answer."

I studied her face. She wasn't lying. There were no traces of pity on her face, just shame and honest curiosity.

We sat there looking at each other in silence while I thought of a reply. "One step at a time you know… baby steps." I sighed. In actuality, I was still pushing myself to take that first step.

"I understand," she said moving onto her apple.

I was incredulous. I had a hard time believing that anyone could understand how I felt, how I feel.

"About a year ago my dog Lucy died."

I kept my face emotion-less. I didn't want to hurt her feelings even though really I was thinking how on earth the loss of a pet could relate to the loss of a best friend.

"I know it may sound weird, but Lucy was my best

friend. You must think I'm crazy but it's true. I had Lucy since I was two. She was all I had ever known. She was a black and white, medium sized border collie. She'd sleep on my feet at night and keep them warm, and whenever I was sad she'd somehow know when to come lay next to me to put her head gently on my lap."

I imagined this in my head. Lucy was becoming more real to me.

"I loved her more than I knew my heart could bare."

Her eyes were distant as she relived her own story over again.

"Then *that day*, I came home and my mom broke the news to me. Lucy was old, it was her heart. It gave out. I was so…so *angry*! It made sense, though. Feeling anger is easier that pain. I completely trashed my room in a matter of minutes. And then it happened. "

She paused to take a bite of her apple.

What happened? I wanted to ask, but I made myself be patient.

I waited as she chewed and then swallowed. "In the mist of throwing my stuff around, my legs and my arms fell limp. They gave out on me. The tears began to burst out like a rushing waterfall. The only difference was that this time I hadn't tried to stop them."

I sat there across from her becoming as lost in her story as she was. Everything she was saying made so much sense to me.

"It's so strange how something can hurt so badly and it's not related to anything physical! That first month was the hardest though. I thought I was seeing and hearing Lucy sometimes and yet at same time I didn't want anything to do with her. The pain was getting so bad that I didn't want to wake up in the morning just to relive another day of hurt. I hid pictures and any other tangible evidence of her. The rest I did the best I could to hide in my mind. Then it was like the light bulb finally flickered to life." She took another bite from her apple leaving me to hang in suspense. "It was the perfect distraction. A puppy. You would think school would be enough of a distraction but it's impossible with everyone pouting around you and wanting to comfort you with a hug. It's all constant reminders of what you're trying to be distracted from. But I know everyone always means well."

I shook my head in disbelief. I was starting to think that everyone in the world couldn't understand that sometimes instead of being comforted some people just want to be left alone.

"Why would you want a puppy right after your dog died?" I interrupted her.

She chuckled a little as if the answer was obvious. "Think about it Kahlen. Do you know how much *work* puppies are? It's a lifetime distraction and plus, I was lonely without Lucy. So I begged my parents for one and when that didn't work I begged God. And wah-la!" she said like a magician.

"The next day my mom picked me up from school, threw the newspaper on my lap where she had circled some breeders' names. We had to drive way out in the country to the breeders but it was worth it. That night we came back with a tiny little Jack Russell Terrier named Mira, which is only fitting. Mira was and is my own personal miracle. She saved me from myself." Jenny started to bust out into laughter which was confusing. "But don't go out and buy yourself a puppy! Like I said, they are a lot of work!" she managed to get between her giggles. "Just today only she chewed up my dad's shoes and part of the carpet. Mira's wild. She about drives me insane half of the time. She's a hand-full alright, and completely and totally different from Lucy." Her laughter died out and her face was serious again. "Even though it's been over a year now, just a couple of months ago I had an epiphany. All that time I had spent blocking out every memory and anything else that reminded me of her had worked. I had tried to remember what exactly she looked like I couldn't get it just right. I found all of my hidden pictures but the image didn't seem like it did her justice. Memories fade, whether we want them to or not. And sometimes it's best just to remember while you can, even through the pain, because it does eventually go away. Not completely. There's still a scar, it just doesn't hurt as much. Sometimes I wish it still did, so it would seem like some of her was still here."

The bell rang and everyone in the cafeteria hurried off to their classes all of them trying to fit through the same door at once.

"Geez, I'm sorry. I monopolized the whole conversation, didn't I?" Jenny stood up and I watched as her frail body glided to the trashcans.

"No, its fine." I assured her. "I never really have that much to say anyway." I grabbed my backpack off the floor and started to walk away.

"Kahlen!" Jenny called after me. I turned around to face her. "You know... when life knocks you down to your knees, you're in the perfect position to pray!"

There was a little twist in my stomach. What she said sounded like a fortune cookie. I nodded and continued to leave. My family and I were Christians but I had never found myself pursuing my faith quite as much as they had. I considered Jenny's words through all of science. Her story was intriguing and I thought of all the possibly endless ways to apply her wisdom to my life. I went by her timeline. The first month was almost over and I was ready to move on to the second: My own personal miracle. It was time for new beginnings. But first I needed a distraction.

The final bell rang and I hurried off to my locker and then to my car. It was just my luck that Marissa's car happened to be parked next to me in the junior lot and that we were both walking to our cars at the same time.

"Hey Kay!" She squealed as she pulled me into a hug. "Oh it seems like it's been forever since I last talked to you. We really need to catch up sometime."

All I could manage to get out was, "Yeah, sure."

"Good. Maybe this weekend then?"

I reluctantly nodded.

"So how are things going between you and Kennley?" she asked.

I was slightly confused. "Um... what do you mean?"

"Well... aren't you two sort of got a thing going on or something?"

"Not really. I haven't even talked to him in days."

She seemed really surprised. "Wow. I could have sworn you two were going out. I'm usually right about these types of things." I shrugged my shoulders. "Sorry."

"Do you at least have feelings for him?" she asked.

I didn't answer right away.

"...I mean like that day at ICC it seemed like a date that I was interrupting... sorry about that by the way. And then he called me to get your number. He even went through the trouble to get my number by calling Bradley first and he doesn't even like Bradley... then again not too many people do. I think it's that whole talking too much thing he does." She continued.

I had always wondered how he gotten my number in the first place but then I'd always forgot to ask him.

"I—I didn't know that." I said stunned.

"And plus it was that way he looked at you, you know?"

But I didn't know.

"Not exactly. Kennley and I were just friends."

"Were?" She asked.

"Yeah we're not exactly on speaking terms at the moment." I had no idea why I was telling her any of this.

She cocked her head to the side. "That's so sad."

I shrugged.

"I've never been wrong about these things. And then the way you seemed so relaxed around him. Everything just seemed so natural between you two. There was serious potential."

I started to walk faster towards my car. I wanted this never-ending conversation to end.

"Help me figure this out some. Why aren't you guys talking now?" she asked.

I sighed. "It's nothing. It's stupid and petty stuff that's all."

Before I even finished talking she had a bright smile on her face. I was missing something; that was evident. But what?

"I knew it!" she practically screamed. "I am never wrong about these things. I'm not trying to be cocky, but it's the truth."

I was utterly confused.

"That's so cute… fighting over something *stupid* and *petty* like most couples do and then make up. You two will make up. I can feel it," she squealed.

We were to our cars now. Marissa started to step in her car.

"Marissa, I think you have it wrong—,"

She slammed her car door shut and waved goodbye at me before she took off.

The only thing more pathetic than constantly lying to other people was lying to yourself. I had been lying to myself for a while and I was sick of it. I had to admit it. I missed Kennley. I missed talking to him and hanging out with him at the creek. The creek didn't even feel the same anymore. It felt like something was missing which was ironic considering the same something that was missing was at first an intruder. I thought about all the time we had spent together over the past weeks. There was something different about when I was with him and when I wasn't. With him I wasn't alone. I didn't feel sad every second. I wasn't thinking about all the bad things in my life that left me with nightmares and counseling. With Kennley I was distracted. He was my puppy. My distraction.

It was like I was having an epiphany…I liked Kennley. I gulped. I was just making this realization now but I wondered how long I had really liked him. It was so insane. I hadn't liked a guy since middle school. By like I don't mean thinking, "oh that guy is really cute. I like talking to him…blah, blah, blah." Those are crushes. Everyone has crushes…but really truly liking someone was different. Kennley felt like a necessity in my life. I needed him.

I had been staring into space at the spot where Marissa's car was parked. I snapped back into reality and jumped into my car. I needed to think. I had to find him. I couldn't wait for the weekend to be over for Monday. I had to be impulsive. If I thought about it for too long I would talk myself out of it.

Where could I find Kennley? Chances were he wasn't still at school. I didn't know where he lived. When I really thought about it... I didn't know much about him, but I didn't care. Maybe he was at the creek.

I started up my car and drove past the speed limit to the creek. I practically jumped out of my car and ran over to it. I didn't see him. My heart was beating out of my chest. I couldn't wait until later to talk to him. By then I would have chickened out. I had to find him today.

I whipped out my cell phone so fast it almost went flying out of my hands which were now shaking.

I waited as the phone rang... and rang... and rang.

"Hello?"

It wasn't Kennley that answered. Maybe it was the wrong phone number. I fought myself on hanging up the phone. So I sat there not saying anything considering my options.

"Hellooo?" Whoever it was that was on the phone was getting more annoyed.

"Hi. Um...by any chance is Kennley there?" My voice was shaking.

"No. He's working." Click.

Whoever it was hung up on me! I ran back to my car and drove to the restaurant my mom and I had gone to that night. The rain had started to pour down hard. I was starting to get tired of spring and all the random rain showers we were having. The restaurant was all the way across town so it was taking me a while to get there. I could feel it. I was losing my nerve. What was I thinking anyway? I couldn't do this.

"*Yes you can*," she said.

It was getting to the point that could barely see the road ahead of me because of the rain but I didn't slow down.

When I finally got there I sprinted inside but still managed to get somewhat soaked.

"Hi and welcome to Rocco's. Is it just you today?" Someone asked me but I wasn't paying attention. I was scanning through the whole restaurant looking for Kennley.

"Um... no. Actually I was just looking for someone. Is Kennley here?"

The woman seemed very surprised for a moment and then answered. "Yes. But I think he just went on his break."

I sighed. "Okay. Thank you."

"If you would like I could tell him you stopped by."

"Uh... no thank you."

I had officially given up. Marissa was wrong. She wasn't always right. No one could be right all the time. We all had our slip ups. I walked out back to my car not caring how wet I was getting. I looked down at the ground as I walked watching the rain as it hit the ground. Then I ran into something hard.

"Ouch," I said looking up.

I screamed. I hadn't been really jumpy today but I was now. My heart was beating uncontrollably as I looked at him. I had run into Kennley in the parking lot and suddenly all the adrenaline was back pumping through my blood and I felt nauseous and dizzy.

I can't do this. I can't do this. I cannot do this!

"I thought you said you were sick of lying to yourself," she said.

"I am!" I answered out loud.

"Am... what?" Kennley said.

My cheeks blushed. I took a deep breath. "I know you hate me and all but before you say anything just hear me out. I just want to get something out in the open," I said quickly.

I waited for a second trying to build up some nerve.

"We don't make sense... you and me," I said.

"How so—,"

I put my finger to his lips to shut him up.

"Sorry." He muttered beneath my finger

"I mean... I barely know you and yet... here we are... Time after time again. People just don't become friends so quickly," I realized I was pacing back and forth next to him as I was talking.

I was talking so fast that I had to stop a second and catch my breath.

"Well if—," he started to say.

"... And I'm sorry for everything. I miss talking to you and seeing you are the creek. And I shouldn't have treated you the way I did when I was with my mom and I'm sorry... again. I know I already said that but I'm saying it again. I'm sorry," I continued.

"Well..." he started. I could tell he was stopping to see if I was going to stop him again. "I don't hate you. And to me... we make perfect sense. You're one of the few things in my life that do—,"

"Wait," I stopped pacing. "One more thing...Do you like pie? I said thinking about that day on the beach.

"Well, I don't know. What kind?" he yelled over the rain.

"Um... let's just say apple. Do you like apple pie?" I was feeling so stupid in asking this and I knew I was partially stalling from the point I was really getting to.

I was sick of being scared. I wanted pie. I wanted stars. I wanted him.

"*You don't ask Kahlen. You do.*"

"Yes... but—,"

I kissed him. It wasn't like the kiss I had gotten in seventh grade when we stupidly played spin-the-bottle. It was a real kiss and I couldn't believe I was doing it. His lips were warm against mine and nothing around me mattered anymore. I didn't care that it was raining cows and horses or that is was in the middle of a parking lot. The kiss seemed short but it felt like it had lasted forever...maybe it was because it was so long overdue.

Kennley pulled away and chuckled. "Are you *high*?"

I was hyperventilating and shaking. "Actually I'm not sure. What does it feel like because I'm really anxious and shaky and I can't stop babbling no matter how much I try and I do feel a little light headed and—,"

His lips met mine and my hands stopped shaking. My heart beat slowed but my mind still raced. It was taking my body a second to actually realize what was happening. I had no idea things could change so drastically in one month... some things good, and some things bad. Really and terribly bad. I was ready to take that first step. I was ready for new beginnings.

Part II

What we call the beginning is often the end. And to make a beginning is to make an end. The end is where we start from.

-T.S. Eliot

10. Family Fun Night

Before I knew it, Friday had snuck up on me. I couldn't believe the week was almost over. For some reason I had been extremely sleepy lately. It felt like I had slept the week away. I stayed in my bed hitting the snooze button on my alarm clock every five minutes. My only motivation for getting out of the bed was Kennley. I knew he would be waiting for me at the creek and I didn't want to stand him up. I reluctantly pushed the covers off me and got out of my bed. I slowly got dressed and went through the rest of my daily routine and I fought myself on going back to bed. It didn't even make sense to be this tired. I was so sick of school. I wanted it to be over so badly. I only had a little less than one month of school left and I didn't know if I could make it. I was sick of studying for tests and staying up late doing homework and then things would only get worse once exams rolled around. I walked downstairs and ate my breakfast quietly.

"Honey, are you excited for tonight?" my mom asked.

"Tonight?" I asked confused. My mouth was still full of cereal.

"Don't tell me you forgot Kido."

I didn't say anything. I just looked at them both confused.

"Pumpkin, it's the second Friday of the month."

I searched through my brain for the meaning for

this. I couldn't think of any importance of the second Friday of the month except... oh crap! Friday family fun night. I hated family fun night with a deep passion. Usually I dragged Emma to these things so I wouldn't completely die of boredom. I repressed a sigh. It was times like these that I wished I wasn't an only child. My parents were far too focused on me most of the time. The only time they weren't was when they were at work. I almost wished my mom was still on a project at work. My cup was running over with attention and I wished someone else was here to take half of it away from me.

On family fun nights we did everything from going to the movies to playing long monotonous games of monopoly. I wanted to break down in sobs. The last thing I wanted to do was have a nice bonding night of family fun. I remembered the last fun night. We played charades for two hours straight, but tonight would be different. I would have to face family fun night by myself.

"Family fun night," I said flatly through my teeth.

"Yup," my dad smiled.

He was always so competitive. One time we spent an entire hour arguing about the rules of checkers. I was just as stubborn as him so I couldn't back down from a challenge.

"So honey, make sure you don't make any plans for after school okay?"

I nodded. The only plan I really had in mind was getting a gun to put myself out of my misery. After breakfast I grabbed my stuff and was about to head out the door.

"Going to the creek again to *think*?" she asked and the suspicion in her voice was clear and evident.

"Yeah," I said curtly.

I knew she was apprehensive of my *thinking.* I knew she thought I was lying to her but I wasn't. The creek was an excellent place to think. I just wasn't going to be thinking alone...

"Could you hold on a second though? I wanted to talk to you before you left."

I dropped my backpack to the floor and slowly sat back down at the table. I knew it. I knew there wasn't much longer I could hide Kennley away from my parents. I had to give them some credit. They weren't completely oblivious to the happenings of my life. I had been busy most nights with him when he wasn't working. My mom would always ask me who was I doing things with and the conversation always went the same:

"So what friend were you out with tonight?" she would ask.

"You don't know them, mom."

"Well what's their name?

"What does it matter if you don't know them?" I would start to get defensive.

"Because I want to get to know them and I figured their name was a good place to start."

I would sigh. "Mom, it's been a really long day and I'm exhausted. Can we talk about this later?"

"Sweetie, I just want to be in your life. I think sometimes as teenagers you guys forget how you got here in the first place."

Then finally I would say goodnight before sprinting up the stairs.

She cleared her throat. "I was talking to Ms. Bryant the other day and well... I'm not going to tell you all of what she said but she wants you to stop by when you can. She said she wants to talk to you." She continued.

I thought about the last time I had seen Julie. She was passed out in my car. My mom had been over a lot at her house since. She said that she had been doing better. I was still kind of angry with Julie. I was mad at her for practically drinking herself into a coma. I had years of anger that had been built up because of the kind of mother she was. I was mad that the house was a complete mess and that poor Macy was stuck there with her.

"Well... do you know what about?" I asked.

"I have a good idea but I don't know for sure."

"Did she say when she wanted me to stop by?"

She shook her head no. "No, just to make it around there whenever you can."

I nodded, grabbed my stuff and headed out the door.

"Work!" I yelled.

It roared to life for a second before dying out again. I was so frustrated I was at the edge of tears. I was stuck at the parking lot at school because my stupid old truck wouldn't move. I wished my parents hadn't given me hand-me-downs. I didn't want their old car, I wanted a new car. I was seventeen. Soon I would be leaving off to college and I was hoping as a graduation present a new car might be involved.

"C'mon!"

It still wouldn't budge. I slammed my fist on the steering wheel and the car honked. I put my head in my hands and sighed. I should have known that today wouldn't have been a good day. It was Friday....The second Friday of the month to be exact.

There was a knock at my window. It scared me at

first when I saw Bradley standing there taller than the car itself. I wasn't sure if it was possible, but his red hair was redder than usual. It had been a while since I had actually had a conversation with him. We had our usual friendly wave to each other when we crossed paths in the hallway... always friendlier to him than me.

I opened the door and stepped out of my stupid car.

"Having some trouble?" he asked.

I sighed heavily. "Unfortunately." I kicked one of the tires hard until I hurt my toes. "I don't understand. It was going fine this morning!" I kicked it again but with my other foot.

Bradley was just looking at me amused. "Well I do a lot of work with cars because my dad's a mechanic. If you bring it by sometime maybe I could look at it.

"I might just take you up on that." I lied. Besides, Bradley looked far too scrawny to be a mechanic. I narrowed my eyes at the car and sighed again.

I thought that the conversation between Bradley and I was over but he was still standing there rocking back and forth on the balls of his feet.

"Soo..." he said. "Are you and Kennley still going strong? It's been three weeks since *the incident*. Twenty one days... it's almost a month now." His tone was casual.

I had no idea why the whole school cared about something that was none of their business. I knew it wouldn't even matter if Kennley weren't the new guy... but he was and that just *fascinated* people.

Marissa cornered me last week to tell me about how all the girls were jealous of me. I was so bemused as to why. When I asked her what she had said, "We've pretty much been going to school with the same boys since preschool. Finally someone new gets thrown into the pack and you snatch him up before any one of us even gets a second glance."

I just stood there staring at him. There was no doubt Bradley would be Bradley. What he referred to as the 'incident' was the parking lot scene. Unfortunately some people from our grade were at the Rocco's that night sitting by the window. They had seen everything that had happened in the middle of the rain. My cheeks still turned a little pink just thinking about it. Anyone that had ears to listen knew about all that had gone down… I was already well aware of everyone's misconceptions of me and Kennley's relationship before three weeks ago but I was almost positive that many of my classmates had bets on whether those misconceptions were true or not. They were all like piranhas waiting for someone to dangle the bait in front of them. I still wasn't sure why it had mattered to them in the first place and I hated that it did. So did Kennley… but for different reasons.

I hated PDA… public display of affection, at school. I didn't want to be the bait for the hungry piranhas. I knew that if Kennley and I so much as touched the chatter would begin. Kennley and I touching at all was already awkward. It was weird at first switching from friends to in a relationship but after awhile I realized that nothing had really changed. I could hear the buzzing in the halls as we walked to our classes. It confused me though. Kennley and I always headed in the same direction for our first class so we'd always walk together. We did that before as friends and we did it still now. But now there was constant buzzing as we walked by and it drove me insane. They were like bees! Maybe they always were but I hadn't noticed before the three she-devils in art and Marissa opened my eyes.

He was still standing there patiently waiting for my response.

I got a mischievous thought in my head at that moment. If the people wanted bait...I'd give them bait. "No. We broke up a couple of days ago actually," I lied.

His eyes widen for a second before he shrugged. "I heard the third week is always the hardest."

"Maybe."

I wondered how much longer would I be stuck in the parking lot talking to Bradley... or worse, he could offer me a ride home. I fought myself on kicking the stupid car again.

I pulled my cell phone out of my pocket. "Well I better call my parents so I can get a ride home so I'll see you later Bradley," I said quickly. I knew that at that moment he would offer me a ride so I thought quickly. I pretended to dial and put my phone to my ear. "Mom?" I said to the invisible person on the other line. "Yeah." I paused. I couldn't believe Bradley was still standing there. "But I'm going to need a ride home because the car broke down." I paused. He was still there! "I don't know. It just won't start." I prayed that my cell phone wouldn't start ringing like it always did in the movies. Why was he still standing there? "Okay so you'll be here soon?" I paused. "Yep. Great. Bye." I pretended to hang up my phone.

He was finally starting to walk away. "Yeah, well I see you tomorrow, Kahlen."

I appreciated that he was one of the few people to actually call me by my name. You would have thought that two easy syllables were the hardest thing to pronounce. Kay. Len. I think it's the H that throws people off.

"Oh and I'm sorry about you and Kennley," he said although there was a tiny bit of a smile on his face.

I frowned and nodded trying to look really torn up

about it. "Things just weren't working out between us," I said loudly hoping other people in the parking lot would hear.

Once he was gone I turned back to my stupid car and smiled. I figured the buzzing would continue for a couple more days and then die out. If there was no more Ken-len— Jenny had said combining our names—then there would be no more stupid gossip and rumors about us. I laughed quietly at my brilliance.

"So um...*who* didn't things work out for?" Kennley was standing right next to me. I hadn't even heard his footsteps coming at all.

Of course I screamed and my heart raced. I was lost catching my breath. "Someone. Is going. To be responsible. For me being. In the hospital. With a heart attack. Someday." I panted. He was just as bad as my father...always coming out of nowhere.

He wasn't smiling the way he usually did when he scared me half to death. I wondered how long he had been there while I was talking to Bradley.

"Is there something I should know?" he asked still looking unhappy.

When I finally caught my breath I said, "Relax. I just told Bradley that hoping he would leave me alone."

His expression slowly lightened up. "I can't stand that kid. I think the only reason he started to walk away was because I gave him a look. I must have scared him off," he said somewhat proud of himself.

"Be nice. He's not that bad...all of the time."

He shook his head. "Ugh, I remember that first day of school when I was stuck with him. I found myself scanning the halls for a weapon I could use to shut him up or do something where I didn't have to be bothered with him anymore," he seemed truly agitated.

"I've known him for a while. He can have his good

moments." I wasn't sure if it was a lie or the truth. I couldn't think of any good moments but I was sure they were there somewhere...maybe.

"And he's obviously fond of you. If you'd pay attention half the time he's not even looking at your eyes."

I rolled my eyes but Kennley face was serious still looking out in the distance towards Bradley. "You should have heard him when he was showing me my locker. Right as he saw you he started going on about how hot you were and that I was lucky my locker was one down from yours. He even went on to talk about the caramel-ness of your hair."

I ran my fingers through my hair and held it to my face. I had never really realized it before but it was a dark caramel kind of color.

"I couldn't take it anymore. When I heard him talking to you I thought it was my chance to escape," he paused for a second. "But luckily I didn't."

I knew he was referring to all that happened later that day. I smiled. Kennley started to walk towards me, closing in the tiny space between us but I backed away. "As of right now we are broken up." I reminded him and threw in a tiny wink. I knew Bradley was still watching because Kennley was looking past my head and down the parking lot. His eyes narrowed.

"Will you do me a favor and move to the right about two steps," he said still agitated. I was confused but I moved over as asked. I was now in between my car and the car next to it so I was out of view.

"What—,"

"I swear that stupid pervert was staring at your butt," he said still looking off into the distance.

I rolled my eyes again and sighed. I doubted that Bradley had any feeling for me. It seemed like most of the time when I talked to him he was staring at my eyes.

"Do you look at my eyes?" I asked. I finally got his attention back to me instead of off in the distance.

"You have beautiful big brown eyes. Of course I do…" he looked back off into the distance at Bradley. "…Sometimes…but that's irrelevant," he added.

This was all ridiculous. Boys are so much different from girls—which is a good thing— but some things just don't make sense. It seems like guys can see things that girls can't. It must be that Y chromosome. Then again… guys are completely oblivious to girl world.

"I'll be back in a second," he said to me. He started to walk away.

"No." I grabbed his arm. "He might be slightly suspicious as to why you care so much considering I just told him we broke up."

He sighed.

"And besides…do I smell a tiny bit of jealously?" I asked.

He seemed immediately repulsed. "At what?! That lovely shade of red on his head?"

I could see I was getting nowhere with this. "Okay maybe *jealous* was the wrong word to use. Would *hostile* be better?"

He didn't respond. I still had my hand on his arm and pulled him back over to me. He was still tense. "Listen, I seriously doubt he has any feeling for me but the next time I'm talking to him, if I catch his staring at me inappropriately I'll put a stop to it," I said but he was still a little tense. "I promise," I assured him.

"I never said anything about him having feelings for you. I'm sure he's gotten other things from you…"

I gasped and slapped his arm. He chuckled a little. "But I don't think *feelings* are on the list." He finished.

I decided to drop it. I didn't think there was any getting through to him. I held up my hair to my face again. I had always thought it was a sandy kind of brown but looking at it now...it was sort of a really dark caramel-ish brown kind of color. I was almost fascinated.

I leaned back on my rusty, good-for-nothing hunk of metal some might call a car. "Can you give me a ride home?" I changed the topic. "Or do you have to work?" I asked.

He shook his head no. "Nope, I don't. But what's wrong with your car."

I had the urge to kick my poor excuse for a car again. When Kennley saw the look I shot towards the car he chuckled before wrapping his arm around me. "Don't worry. I can give you a ride."

It took me a good three seconds before I realized everyone in the parking lot was looking at us and I slid out of his grasp. His only response was an irritated sigh that I tried to ignore.

We walked over to his car all the way down the parking lot. It was a coincidence that it was by Bradley's who for some reason was just standing there. He looked like he was waiting for something.

Kennley sighed. "Fantastic," he muttered.

He was starting to walk towards the passenger's side of the car to open the door for me. I looked at him and shook my head.

"What?" he said. "I would have done this before too... because I'm a true gentleman." He wasn't even looking at me as he was talking. He was looking at Bradley. The whole thing was beginning to get ridiculous. He opened the door for me still looking at Bradley and then shut it. As he walked to his side he still kept his eye contact with Bradley. From what I could see out the window, Bradley didn't look phased. He was staring at him right back just as intensely. He was leaning against his car with his arms folded across his chest. I knew Bradley still hadn't forgiven Kennley for lying to the principal by telling him that he had ditched him that first day.

Kennley was taking his slow time getting into the car. He looked like he was about to say something but I reached across to the steering wheel and pressed the horn. Neither of them were as jumpy as me so of course they didn't even flinch. Kennley finally got into the car and let down the windows.

Bradley looked over across Kennley and said, "Kahlen, I thought your mom was picking you up?"

Kennley stuck his head out the window. "I don't really think that's any of your business."

I pushed Kennley's head out of the way so I could talk to Bradley. I knew Kennley would only make things so much worse than they had to be. "She just called me and told me she couldn't after all. But luckily Kennley was walking by and he offered me a ride." I explained. I surprised myself. I was a good liar…not that it was something to be proud of.

He nodded. "Oh and Kahlen… just watch who you fall for because—,"

Kennley turned the key in the ignition and it roared beautifully unlike my hunk of metal which was more like snoring. I never realized how much I hated my car until it broke down on me now. I couldn't hear the rest of what Bradley said but I was beginning to believe Kennley…but only a little bit.

We pulled out of the parking lot and onto the street. "I bet he actually believes you. He thinks we're broken up…which is just *perfect*. I bet he's going to ask you out too," he said.

"What happened to he 'doesn't have feelings for me'?" I asked confused.

"Many a guy has asked a girl out, feeling being put aside. Lovey-dovey crap isn't exactly what they're looking for."

I was being to have my doubts about him not being jealous. "What would it matter if he asked me out anyhow? It's not like I'd say yes."

"I know *that*. It's just the fact that he's doing it to get to me is the problem."

I could see his body tensing again. "Candy corn." I said changing the subject.

He looked at me confused.

"Ten, nine, eight, seven—,"

He smiled looking back at the road. "Bouncy ball."

I smiled too. Kennley wasn't the only one good at distractions.

In between our game I showed him the way to my house. When we finally got there I was full of relief when I didn't see my mom's car in the driveway. I knew it was only a matter of time before she found out about Kennley and I wasn't sure how she or my dad would react. I couldn't think of a lot of reasons why they would be upset besides me hiding it from them. But besides that, it was my inner pessimist that told me things would go badly.

I was about to get out of the car when Kennley said, "So...can I get a tour of the house?"

I stared at him for a long second. I knew that if I told him no he would only pout like a five year old about it and find some way to convince me to say yes...he always was good with that. Besides, we never did get to spend any alone time together except for the creek... five minutes inside my house alone couldn't hurt. It wasn't like we were going to do anything... "Fine."

I stepped out onto the street while he parked the car. I told him to park it on the other side of the street so when my parents got home they wouldn't be suspicious. When we got inside I saw a note on the kitchen counter that said:

> Gone to the store. I'll be back in an hour or so
>
> ~ Mom

I turned around and Kennley was no longer behind me. I saw him in the front room looking around at all of our cheesy family photos. I walked into the front room and watched as he observed.

He turned around to face me. "Your house is very well...*decorated*."

I laughed. "Yeah well my mom is an interior designer. She's kind of obsessed with that sort of thing. She's always constantly changing things in here."

I remember just last week she wanted to redecorate my room but I refused.

I felt like a tour guide as I led him through the house. He was silent as I showed him everything... except when we got to my room which I decided to save for last. I put myself in his place and pretended like I was seeing everything for the first time. It was a little messy which was good. It meant that I wasn't a neat freak but I wasn't a slob either. The blue and purple walls were girly but not too girly like pink.

Something in my closet caught his eye and he walked over to it. I followed closely behind him. He reached in and pulled out my ballet slippers. He didn't say anything; he just held them out in my face waiting for me to explain. I could tell he was fighting a smile.

"I was six. I was going through a phase." I grabbed the shoes and tossed them back into the closet.

He reached back into the closet again and pulled out my guitar. "You play?"

"I can...but I don't."

He went over to my bed and plopped down. He seemed awfully comfy in a room that wasn't even his. "Why not?" he asked.

Guitar playing was a sore subject in my family. My mom had forced me into an instrument when I was ten. I liked playing the guitar at first although it was really tricky. I practiced constantly until it wasn't as frustrating. Then I started to get sick of it. I had lessons two times a week and I cringed at the thought of recitals. I was somewhat shy at that age so I hated the idea. I remembered it perfectly. After Melinda Wright played Beethoven on the piano I was next. I ran to the bathroom while my parents waited anxiously for me to appear on the stage. I never showed. I heard them calling my name...pronouncing it wrong, while I was in the bathroom. I couldn't push myself to leave. I remembered the pregnant woman in the bathroom with me giving me strange looks as I paced back and forth. My mom was so mad at me when I told her I was quitting.

I shrugged. "I don't know. I guess it stopped being for fun. I could see my mom's little dream cloud. I knew she thought I had potential and she was considering me playing more instruments but I didn't want it...not anymore anyways. So I quit. I haven't touched that thing since."

I put the strap around my neck and held the guitar in my hands. It felt good to have it there...almost like it belonged.

"Play me something," he said.

I put the guitar back into my closet quickly. "No way!" I was almost positive that if I did play something from him it would be awful. I hadn't played in years. "The guitar thing was just another phase. I'm sure there's a leotard in there somewhere from my gymnastics days."

"Am *I* just a phase?" he asked hesitantly after a second, creating sound in our silence.

He threw me off guard. I had to think for a while before answering. Was he just a phase? "You never think something's a phase going into it."

He didn't seem satisfied with my answer. "Do you think I *will* be?"

In the three weeks we had been going out I had wondered how long would it last? It was that pessimist lurking inside of me.

"I don't know," I said honestly. "But I hope not."

And I didn't want him be a phase. I didn't want any of things in my closet to be phases. I wanted to do something and stick to it for once. But then again I wasn't sad that they were phases now.

He seemed happy with that. He was still lying comfortably on my bed. He patted the area next to him with his hand.

"Don't even *think* about it," I said quickly.

"Relax," he laughed. "I was just offering to share the space."

"How incredibly generous of you," I mumbled sarcastically

He grinned. "*I* thought so."

I just stood there staring at him and rolled my eyes.

"Oh come on. It's not like it could be considered PDA here. We're in your room," he argued. He patted the bed with his hand again. "I promise you I won't bite."

I knew how Kennley felt about the situation at school. Whenever he'd come within a foot of me I'd back away. He'd always mutter to me, "I don't understand why I can't touch my own girlfriend."

I sighed and gave in. I walked over to the bed and lied down next to him. He shifted closer to me so I was cradled in his chest. I was so comfortable I could have gone to sleep. We both didn't say anything just lying there in the silence with the only sound being our beating hearts, my heart beating faster than his.

Usually when I was with Kennley I didn't think about Emma. But I did now. I remembered sitting with Emma and neither of us saying anything... Conversations without a sound. It still hurt. Deep down in the pit of my stomach it hurt. I was beginning to get used to her not being here. As more time went by she was becoming a distant memory. I could see it in my future. I could picture ten years from now thinking about the girl I used to know that died. Then twenty years from now when I would never think about her at all. She wouldn't constantly be in my mind...it would be as if she never existed.

All of a sudden the tears were falling down from my cheek. It didn't take long before Kennley noticed. He didn't say anything. He just pulled me tighter against him but I pulled away. I sat up on the bed and wiped away the silent tears from my cheek. I begged myself to get it together but I didn't want to. I wanted to hurt. As masochistic as it was, I wanted to feel the pain of the twist in my stomach. I didn't want to grow old one day and forget about her. If I was hurting, I wasn't forgetting.

Kennley sat up too. "If you want to talk about it—,"

I shook my head now refusing to look his direction. This was the third time I had cried in front of him and I knew eventually he would get sick of my little episodes. It was so completely embarrassing.

"I'm sorry," I whispered still not looking at him. I couldn't think of anything else to say.

I felt his warm hand on my shoulder. "You have nothing to apologize for," he said simply.

The silence returned as I stared out my window looking at the blue sky and clouds. I still didn't want to look at Kennley. I was utterly embarrassed. He was still right beside me lost in his own world as I was in mine.

It amazed me how so much could change in such little time. I heard the front door and I was off of my bed in a millisecond. It had to have been my mom back from the store. How would this look? My boyfriend and I in my room alone...in my house alone! Not that my parents knew he was my boyfriend which would make it all the more worse. I had to think quickly. I heard footsteps coming up the stairs and my heart nearly beat out of my chest. I looked at Kennley who also looked panicked. The light bulb flickered to life in my head.

"Go out my window," I whispered.

"Kahlen, we're on the second floor!" his whisper screamed.

"I know that. But there's a tree outside my window. It's sturdy, and big, and really easy to climb down. I do it all the time, now go!"

He took a second to grin. "*You* sneak out of the house?" he seemed fairly amused...almost proud.

"Occasionally, now go!"

He walked quickly to the window and opened it. I could hear the footsteps getting closer. As soon as Kennley was out of my room and onto the tree I gently shut it hoping it wouldn't make a sound.

I couldn't just be standing in the middle of my room looking like a deer in headlights. I had to be acting like I was doing something. I did the first thing that came to my mind. I went to my closet and grabbed my guitar and the pick sitting on the shelf. I sat on the bed with it.

I heard my doorknob twist and then my door open. My mom was on the other side and she looked shocked.

"Y-you're playing your guitar?" she asked surprised.

I could see her dream cloud again. "Yeah. It's been a while. I missed it a little bit."

"Well I'll let you continue then." She stared at me for a moment looking in amazement. I repressed a sigh. "Your father should be home any moment. I just brought some stuff to cook for dinner and then after that we'll start family fun night." She walked out and closed my bedroom door behind her.

As soon as I heard her footsteps going down the stairs and I ran to my window. I didn't see Kennley anywhere but I saw his car still parked on the other side of the street. I was a little worried...panicked actually. I realized that I had to play my guitar because if my mom didn't hear anything she would wonder if I was lying. I placed my fingers in their right positions and began to play.

I was rusty but not half as bad as I thought I would be. I still remembered everything. It was like riding a bike except a little wobbly. I heard a car and I wasn't sure if it was Kennley pulling off or my dad pulling in. I went to my window again. Crap. It was my dad... and Kennley's car was still parked across the street. I gasped.

There was no way any good could from this. I heard the front door open doorsteps and I stopped breathing.

"Sweetie, could you come down here please?" my mom called from downstairs.

I had never had a panic attack but I was pretty sure I was having one now. I ran down the stairs and almost forgot how to walk when I saw Kennley standing there next to my dad by the door. I was beginning to feel so dizzy that I was afraid I was going to faint. I took a deep breath in and out. Kennley looked just as surprised as me. I wasn't sure of what to say. All I knew was that everything was about to go downhill.

"*Pessimist*," she said.

"Your friend said he wanted to talk to you." My dad said slowly emphasizing every word, standing in his uniform.

I stood there at the bottom of the stairs as stiff as a brick. I think I learned in health if someone is going into shock you elevate their feet twelve inches off the ground...

"Yeah," I said finally. "Okay." I walked over to Kennley. "I'll be back in a second."

He followed me out the door and I shut it behind us. We walked around to the side of the house where my parents couldn't see us talking.

All I could manage to get out was, "What the heck!"

"Your dad's a *cop*?!" he asked, horrified.

"What happened?!" I asked. I had to pace to calm myself down.

"Well um...I was walking to my car down the driveway and then your dad pulls in and comes out looking like he's about to arrest me. I didn't even know he was your dad. Then he asked me what I was doing here and then I just told him I needed to talk to you." He was talking quickly.

I stopped pacing. "Okay...well maybe this isn't as bad as I thought it was. But we need a story. What did you want to talk to me about?"

We both stood there thinking. "Maybe you could tell them the truth."

My eyes almost popped out of my head. "You want

me to tell my parents that I had you sneak out of room but we had bad *timing*?!"

"No. I mean tell them the truth about *us*."

My immediate reaction was to object but I thought about it for a second. Maybe it wasn't such a bad idea. Why was I so afraid in the first place? They had no reason to disapprove of Kennley. I started to pace again.

"*You can do this*," she said.

"Okay," I said. Kennley looked surprised at my answer. "I'll tell them and you can just go home."

"Are you sure because I can go with you and—,"

"No," I interrupted him. "You've already caused enough trouble."

He grinned. "Well I happen to think trouble makers are a necessity. Without people like me, who would you have to spice things up?" I refused to admit he had a point. "Kennley go home." I was fighting a smile.

He leaned in to kiss me but when his face was only inches from mine...

"Honey, could you come in here please?"

I backed away and he sighed like he always did. I waved goodbye to him and walked back to the front of the house and through the door. Soon I heard his car pull away.

When I got inside I wanted to dart upstairs to my room but both of my parents were sitting there waiting for me to explain. So of course I lied. "I forgot my cell phone in his car and he drove back to give it to me."

My mom sighed heavily. "Are you saying that you almost lost another cell phone? If you lose this one you'll have to by another one with your own money."

I grimaced. Maybe it wasn't best to make up a lie about forgetting my cell phone. Every now and again I would still wonder where I had lost my old one.

"But I guess that's nice of him… but why was it in his car?" my mom asked.

I grinned briefly. I wondered if I could convince them to get me a new car. "Yeah well about that… when I got in my car to drive home today it wouldn't start. I was stuck at school with no ride home. Kennley just so happened to be walking by and offered me a ride."

"That stupid truck," My dad muttered. "It was only a matter of time before it finally gave out." He seemed just as frustrated as I had been.

"Kennley?" my mom said. I expected her to make some remark about his name like most people did. "Isn't he the same kid at the Rocco's that one day?"

I tried my best not to sigh. "Yes," I said slowly. I started to make a break for the stairs. I was chickening out. Why did they have to know about Kennley anyway? I wondered if Kennley's parents knew about me. I could see freedom. It was so close. I started up the stairs.

"No," My dad said. "Lisa, I know you wanted to wait until she told us but this is just *ridiculous*."

I took another step up the stairs. "Kido get back here."

I slumped back down the stairs and into the room with my parents. I had to tell them. There was no more backing out. "Okay um… guys I need to tell you something."

My mom took a deep breath in and out like she was preparing for bad news.

"Kennley and I…" I cleared my throat. "Are in a relationship." It felt like someone had lifted a yacht off my chest.

My mom gave a sigh of relief. "Oh thank God," she said.

"See I told you," my dad said.

I just stood there confused looking at them both.

My mom looked at me and smiled. "So that's *it*?"

I nodded still puzzled.

"Well we knew *that*. It's not like it was a secret. We already figured that with you leaving to the creek every morning, suddenly you were busy every weekend, and then you never deemed it necessary to share who you were out with." She was laughing now. "Sweetie, I may not be the brightest bulb in the auditorium but I'm not stupid."

My knees felt weak. They had known the whole time and I was maybe one the stupidest people to walk the earth. I had been sneaking around for nothing. "W-well then what did you think I was about to tell you?" I was still confused.

My dad sighed. "You mother was under the misconception that you were possibly...expecting."

I all about fell to the floor I was laughing so hard. I was practically having hysterics. My stomach was aching from my laughter. How could my mom possibly think I was pregnant? It was ludicrous, insane, outlandish, and whimsical, anything but something close to reality. I was somewhat insulted that she would even think that. Did she really think I was so irresponsible as to get myself pregnant at seventeen? I still had one more year of high school and I wasn't going to go through it as a new mother.

"How could you possibly think I was pregnant?! Do you not know me at all?" I was wiping the tears away from my laughter.

She hit my father. "Well in my *defense* I hadn't made up my mind yet. I just threw the idea out there. It was only a moment of doubt that's all."

I started laughing again. "During that moment of doubt were you drinking hard liquid?"

My dad started laughing too although my mom

wasn't. I was still laughing all the way up the stairs. When I was at the top of the stairs I waited at my usual spot for my parents to start talking about me. I waited... and I waited. But they didn't. I was about to turn around and go back into my bedroom when I finally heard them.

"Did you hear that?" My dad said.

"Hear what?"

"She was laughing," he said. I could hear the smile in his voice.

"She was, wasn't she? I haven't heard her laugh in a while," she said. "Or at least not like that."

"As much as I hate to admit it I think it might be that *Kennley* of hers. As much as I don't like that kid, I think he makes her happy."

"He seems like a nice boy," my mom said in his defense.

"I never said he wasn't...But I know what goes through a teenage boy's mind. That alone puts him on my list," he said. "Ha! And you should have seen his face when I got out of the car in my uniform. Poor kid looked like he was about to pee in his pants. I only wish I would have had my gun on me. That really would have got him."

"Be nice," my mom warned. "Anyone that's responsible for her laughing like that again is alright by me."

They were both silent for awhile. "So... what are we going to do about that car of hers?" my dad asked. "I almost going to be sad to see it go...we had a lot of *good* times in that car."

I grimaced. It was the price I paid for eavesdropping. I went into my room and tried not to be completely repulsed by what I had just heard my dad say. I blocked out all images that were being forced into my head.

It's like if someone says "don't picture a purple cow". You automatically picture a purple cow in your head whether you want to or not.

My guitar was still lying on my bed looking like it was waiting for me. I truly did miss it. I picked it up in my hands and started to play again. I started playing around with all the chords until eventually I was forming my own song.

It was my father's turn to decide what we were doing and we ended up in a dark theater watching a movie that made me feel like I was getting stupider each second. There are different types of comedies. They are the funny, the stupid-funny, and the funny-stupid. The funny movies are the really good regular kind of comedies. The funny-stupid are the movies that are stupid but have actual comedy in them besides laughing at the unoriginal things like someone tripping or a pie flying into their face. The stupid-funny movies are the movies that try to be funny-stupid but always come up short. With this kind you end up watching a movie questioning the sanity of the people who made it. That's what I was doing next to my dad who seemed to be enjoying it. My mother was on the other side of him looking as annoyed as I was. I remembered now why we never let my dad pick what to do for family fun night.

"I'm going to go get something from the concessions." I whispered to my parents before leaving out of the theater. I hated leaving in the middle of movies. I never wanted to miss a second... but I didn't mind so much with this movie. I took my slow time walking out of the theater and to the concessions. I even went to the bathroom first to delay going back. All I brought was a candy bar, and then I decided to sit in the lobby and finish eating it.

I was finally about to go back into the theatre when I saw Kennley walking into the lobby. But he wasn't alone. There was a girl with long blond hair next to him. I watched as she playfully pushed him to the side and he pushed her back. I tried to steady my heartbeat and not jump to conclusions but it was hard not to. The blond was beautiful. Even from twenty yards away I was mesmerized by those deep blue eyes of hers. My heart started to beat faster. I wanted to go over there. I wanted to say something... anything. How could he? How could he do this to me?

"He wouldn't," she said.

I could have sworn there was a fan nearby because it looked like her long hair was blowing in the nonexistent wind. I hated her already.

"Excuse me." It sounded like her voice was miles away. "Excuse me...can I get by?"

I realized the voice was coming from in front of me. It was a woman with a little boy standing beside her. I was standing in everyone's way and I was causing a traffic jam. Not paying much attention to her I moved out of her way still keeping my eyes on Kennley. I watched as he and the evil blond got their tickets. It looked like she was paying for her own though so that was a good sign right? I couldn't take any longer of this. It felt like at any moment I was going to implode. They walked towards the lobby and now were only ten yards away from me. The blond tossed her hair over her shoulder. With each step she took she looked like she was a model going down the runway. Ugh... I was disgusted with myself. I couldn't be jealous of some relationship ruin-er...A borderline home-wrecker. She grabbed his arm and wrapped hers around it. I waited for Kennley to shake it off but he didn't. He and the blond sat down on one of the couches in the lobby and she released his arm. She seemed to be sitting a little closely to him. Kennley scooted away a little bit and I smiled. They were close enough that I could almost hear what they were saying. I moved a little closer but still stayed in the shadows where I couldn't be seen.

"You're so stupid," Kennley laughed.

She hit his arm. "I am not. I swear everyone is failing that class this year. So having a D- is considered good. It's because Mr. Morley hates everyone…I think he just needs to find himself a girlfriend." She started laughing too. "Just the other day Karen was bold enough to tell him that to his face during class. It was so funny, I was crying."

Kennley laughed too. "I bet it was. I wish I could have seen his face. It was probably classic. And besides… the only reason Karen told him off was because her straight A's got flushed down the toilet."

She smiled. "True." She sighed, "Kennley I miss you. I miss you so much. I wish you could come back."

Come back to what? Her?

He sighed too. "Yeah, so do I sometimes. But things aren't so bad. I'm happy I'm there."

"I can't remember the last time we talked like this," she said.

I wanted to get a pair of scissors and chop off all of her hair. It was killing me standing here watching it all.

"Neither can I."

"I wonder why it's been so long," she said, her voice sad.

"I can think of a couple of reasons." His voice was suddenly rough like there was some hidden aggression.

"Don't worry about that," she encouraged.

By *that* did she mean me?

"Speaking of them, where are they? We're going to miss the movie."

"Well...we could always go into the movie right now and I could text them and tell them where we're sitting," she suggested.

"I don't know, Hannah. I don't think that's such a good idea."

I hated *Hannah*. I wanted to hate Kennley, but I didn't.

My vision of Kennley and Hannah was blocked. "Um...excuse me Ma'am but may I help you with something?" An employee asked me. He was smiling at me in an unusual kind of way.

"No thank you," I said quickly. I tried to look past him but he moved in front of me. Why wasn't he leaving? He looked like he couldn't have been more than a year or so older than me. He was leaning against the wall in front of me, running his hand through his shaggy blond hair.

"Are you waiting for someone or something?" he asked.

"Yeah, sure," I was struggling to see past him.

"So um...what's your name?"

"Kahlen," I said slowly. I had no idea why I even answered him. I just wanted him to go away.

"Ah...Kahlen. That's a pretty name." He said my name again. "*Kahlen*."

He was talking a little loudly. I was afraid Kennley might hear. I tried to ignore him and look past him. I still couldn't see anything.

"So *Kahlen*..." he said. I hated the way he was saying my name. He was making it sound like such a dirty word. "...If you're still here a half an hour from now I could probably sneak you into a movie if you wanted or get you free tokens for the arcade room."

For a split second I could see past him but I didn't see Kennley anywhere. He must have gone into the theater with *Hannah*. I hated that name.

I wondered if I told him that I would meet him a half an hour from now would he go away. So I turned to him and smiled my best flirty smile. "That sounds great. So I'll see you a half an hour from now then," I lied.

Now that Kennley was gone I had no reason to still stand in the corner so I turned so I could walk back into the theater. I felt something tug on my wrist and pull me back. It was the employee's hand.

"Don't go yet. Maybe you could stay and talk." He was still holding onto my wrist. I tried to shake his hand off but he wouldn't let go. It was ridiculous.

"Let go of me," I snapped.

He let go slowly putting his hand in mine and then releasing it. I was considering slapping him like they did in the movies but all those thoughts vanished when I realized I was wrong. He hadn't left to the theater with what's-her-name. I about jumped out of my skin when Kennley was standing next to me with the blond not too far behind.

The theater employee ignored him. "So what movie are you seeing?"

I was beginning to get annoyed. But I wasn't sure who was more annoying, I read his name tag on his vest, Sean, or Hannah.

Kennley walked closer to me and said, "The-none-of-your-business movie."

Sean turned to Kennley. "I'm sorry Sir, may I help you with something?" he said in his professional voice.

"Yes. Actually you can go—,"

"Didn't think so..." Sean turned to me. "But anyways if you're hungry I could get you a discount on something if you wanted."

I wasn't paying attention to Sean or Kennley. I was looking at Hannah fighting away all of my homicidal thoughts. I hated her.

"Don't you have to be somewhere standing outside a theater holding a trash can for when people come out of the movie?" Kennley asked.

Hannah sighed. "...and you could cut the tension with a knife." She sounded bored.

I wanted to cut something with a knife but it wasn't the tension.

Kennley took a step closer to me and put his arm around me.

Hannah sighed again. "...like a dog marking his territory," she mumbled.

I glowered at her and moved away from Kennley's arm. I was so angry... it was only a matter of time before I would explode.

"Do you know this guy?" Sean asked. "If he's causing you any trouble I could have him thrown out of the theater." He said looking at Kennley.

He narrowed his eyes. "Is that a threat? Because I'm pretty sure I could talk to your manager about you hitting on random girls instead of doing your job."

Just then a little boy carrying a jumbo thing of popcorn dropped it and the popcorn was spread all over the floor.

Kennley chuckled. "Duty calls."

Sean gave up. He walked away unhappily but yelled back to me, "Kahlen...I'll see you in half an hour. We'll meet here," he winked.

Kennley cursed at him underneath his breath. It was just him and I...and *Hannah* standing against the corner. The blond was right. You could cut the tension with a knife. None of us were saying anything. I could feel Kennley staring at me intensely and I was giving the same look to Hannah who hadn't really seemed to notice.

Hannah sighed...yet again. I hated her. "You know...I really don't want to miss this movie sooo I'm just going to go in and wait for everyone. And besides...it seems like you two have some *issues* you need to work out." She walked away.

I had never been so happy for someone to leave in all my life. Kennley hadn't even looked at Hannah as she left. He was still staring at me. I could tell he was angry. But he wasn't the only one. I wouldn't even look at him. I didn't want to. I was so mad at him and yet I knew that if I had one look at him that would all go away. I wouldn't be mad anymore. I would be sad. I would crumble and the tears would fall. I would be feeling sad for myself instead of yelling at him. I still couldn't believe he would do this to me.

"*He wouldn't*," she said.

"Why were you talking to that loser?" he said slowly. I could tell he was trying to sound calm but it wasn't working. I knew he was angry.

I still didn't look at him. I crossed my arms over my chest. "I can talk to whoever I want to talk to," I snapped.

He seemed taken aback. "Well then would you talk to me?"

"I'm not so sure I want to."

It was almost like I could hear the click in his head. "Oh don't tell me you think that I would do that."

I raised my eyebrow a tiny bit.

"How could you think that, Kahlen? I thought you of all people would know me better than that. I would *never* do that to you...or *anyone* else for that matter," he continued.

I still didn't look at him. I knew I was just being

stubborn now but I was also ashamed. Why would I be so quick to think the worst?

"*Pessimist*," she said.

"Why would you think I would want to talk to Sean? He came up to me. I just wanted him to go away."

Kennley looked away from me. "He wasn't staring at your eyes either," he mumbled. "And what exactly are you doing thirty minutes from now?"

I was still looking straight ahead. I refused to look at him.-

"Will you at least look at me?" he pleaded.

I didn't budge so he moved in front of me and grabbed my shoulders. I was forced to look at him and my will crumbled. I couldn't be mad at him…not that I had any reason to.

"Hannah is just a friend. We were meeting up here with a couple more friends…one of which happens to be her boyfriend. I would never do that to you. I would rather be eaten by a shark or electrocuted to death before I would do that."

As much as I didn't want to smile…I did. I hated that he made me do that. He must have taken my smile as me surrendering because suddenly I was in his arms and he was hugging me. I remembered the first time I had hugged him in what seemed like forever ago at the creek. I smiled to myself. We weren't friends anymore but things hadn't really changed between us. Maybe they were always like this and I hadn't taken the time to notice.

He let go of me and was looking over my head. I turned around to see what he was looking at. I figured it was the friends he was meeting up with.

"So what movie are you seeing?" he asked.

I sighed. "Something my dad picked out."

"Ah…the cop."

"Don't let him intimidate you. That's what he wants to do."

I saw a small group of people start walking towards Kennley and me.

"Yeah well…Kahlen, I'll see you tomorrow morning okay?" he said walking away from me.

I nodded but he wasn't even looking at me anymore. He was walking over to his friends that I didn't know. His friends were walking towards me until he turned them around in the opposite direction. I wondered if there was a reason he hadn't introduced us.

I stood there against the wall and watched as he walked off until I couldn't see him anymore. I didn't want to go back to the stupid-funny movie I was being forced to watch. I had been gone for a while and I knew my mom was probably worried. I lingered by the wall for a second until I saw Sean coming across the lobby and over to me. I rolled my eyes and walked quickly back to the movie theater so I wouldn't have to talk to him. The blackness of the theater was overwhelming at first and it took me a second to realize where I had been sitting. I saw my mom way in the back and my dad sitting beside her laughing with a mouth full of popcorn. I walked slowly to my seat and sat down.

"I don't blame you," my mom said. "But if I were you I wouldn't have come back. Next time I decide to let your father chose what we do …stop me."

"One step ahead on you."

11. Friends

"I still can't believe you would think that," he said for the billionth time.

He would find some way to bring whatever I said back to the movie theater. I felt like I deserved it a little bit but I was hoping we could move on.

"How many times do I have to say I'm sorry?" I pleaded.

He rolled over on the grass so he was on his elbow facing me.

"It's not an apology I'm looking for. I'm just insulted that's all."

I sighed. "Well you seemed a little irritated that I was with Sean. Why was that? Were you jumping to conclusions...because if so that would be *insulting?*" I challenged. I remembered how agitated he had looked last night.

"Oh... you two are on a first name basis?"

"I read his name tag," I explained. "You still haven't answered my question."

He rolled back over so he was on his back. I looked over at him and he was staring up into the sky. I didn't say anything as I waited patiently for his response. I smiled a little bit. I knew he was struggling on how to answer.

"I heard someone say Kahlen and I didn't know if it was you or not but I was curious and wanted to see. So I started to walk over by him and I saw you smiling and talking about meeting him later...what was I supposed to think?"

I grimaced. He had bad timing. The last thing I wanted to do was meet him later. "Well...what if I knew him and we were friends. Then you would have been jumping to conclusions like I had, making it even. And besides...I was telling him I'd meet him later because I wanted him to leave me alone. But then when I tried to leave he grabbed me and pulled me back so I couldn't."

He grimaced. "Let's talk about something else. I'm sick of reliving last night."

Finally, I thought. "So...um, how do you know the guys you were out with last night? I don't think they're people from school so I haven't seen them around."

I didn't really know anyone at school so the only way I knew that they didn't go to our school was because of the conversation I was eavesdropping on...but I didn't want to admit to spying.

Kennley sighed. "Whatever happened to moving on to something else?"

"Oh you are terrible!" I said. He looked at me confused. "If you want to distract me from the fact that you didn't answer my question you don't retort with another question." I said remembering one of our past conversations.

He turned to me and grinned. "Well I could always show a little skin...or *you* could if you'd like."

I smiled. "But then why would I be trying to distract you? You're supposed to be the one distracting me."

He shrugged. "Just thought I throw it out there. *I* have no objection to it myself."

"Of course you don't." I rolled my eyes. "And you're usually better at the art of the distracting than you are now. Why don't you want to answer the question?"

I was truly curious. It seemed like he always avoided my questions but I was used to the ways he would try to distract me now.

I could see it. I could picture him and Hannah in my head. Although I didn't have the same amount of hatred for her as I did before she still wasn't high on my list. Even though Kennley said she had a boyfriend it seemed like they had been together once. I could feel it. The curiosity just kept burning inside of me until it was unbearable. I ended up having to bite my tongue to keep myself for saying anything.

"They're from my old school at Crest Moore High just outside of town," he answered.

I waited for him to say more but he didn't. I was still curious. I wondered why he didn't want to answer. It was like he was hiding something.

"Why did you leave Crest Moore to come here towards the end of the school year?" I asked. I had always wondered that but never asked. It seemed like it would be extremely difficult catching up on a semester full of stuff especially when you hardly showed. I could do nothing but wait in silence as he thought. I could see his body tensing and he seemed uncomfortable. I felt like I was crossing some kind of invisible line…like I was moving out of no-man's land and into the enemy's territory. Something in the back of my head was yelling, "Retreat! Retreat!" but I didn't listen. If satisfaction really did bring back the curious cat back-, then maybe there was still hope. I couldn't take it anymore. I was going to combust at any second.

"You know…you're silence only makes me think your hiding something." I tried to sound calm but I could hear the edge in my voice.

He smiled half-heartedly. "Well what if I am."

I didn't respond right away waiting for him to say

more. I could feel the blood pumping through my veins all the way to my toes. The only reasons I could think of why someone would leave to a different school towards the end of the school year were if they were being bullied and they absolutely hated it, or...if they were in trouble.

I sighed. "Then I'd wish you wouldn't. Half of the time I consider myself to be open-minded. It's not like I'd judge you about anything." I tried really, really hard to keep my voice steady.

He laughed quietly. "Yeah well after last night, I'm not so sure about you and you're judging skills."

I repressed a sigh. It amazed me how he could find some way back to the same topic every time. "Please Kennley, you're killing me. Just answer the question." My face was completely serious.

I tried to focus on something else besides my pounding head. I looked around the creek trying to concentrate on the beauty around me that I knew by heart...but it wasn't working. The silence was making it worse. I looked at Kennley and didn't take my eyes off him. He turned and looked at me and our eyes stayed locked. It was like we were having a staring contest. I refused to lose. There was a slight smile on his face as we looked at each other. I was still amazed at the contrast between his hair and his eyes. It didn't seem right. It didn't seem like it fit and yet...it fit perfectly. His eyes didn't match his hair or the tone of his skin but... somehow it did.

The staring contest continued on and I waited for him to finally stop driving me away from my sanity with his suspense. He sighed. "I didn't transfer from Crest Moore Kahlen, I was expelled." He spoke slowly still not breaking his eye contact with me. I could see he was waiting for some sort of reaction to show on my face but I kept it the same…emotionless. I wasn't completely surprised that he had gotten expelled. It seemed like anyone would if they skipped class all of the time. "Hannah and the other people I was with are just some friends from Crest Moore."

I couldn't hold my poker face for much longer. It was silly but even at the mention of her name my blood would start to boil.

Kennley must have realized this too. "Although most of the time Hannah's not with us…she has a way of getting under people's skin sometimes. But Ross insisted on bringing her."

I remembered Ross…The inventor of the Wampo and someone that was supposedly an idiot. I assumed that he was also Hannah's boyfriend.

Kennley bringing up Hannah made me realize something. He was trying to distract me again and I had almost missed it. "Why were you expelled?" I asked keeping my voice calm. It was obvious that he didn't want to answer which scared me a little bit.

He sighed heavily. "There was a rumor going around that our teacher, Mr. Morley, had made our big chapter test early and had it in one of the file cabinets in the back of his room. Some friends and I found the key and one day after school we snuck into his room and found the tests. We took pictures of it on our cameras and then put them back. Everything was going as planned except for the person we had on watch decided to take a little break. Mr. Morley came back into the room and everyone else had realized before I had. I was left in the room looking completely guilty and alone." He lost the staring contest and looked away from me. It looked like it was killing him telling me this. "It was an incredibly stupid thing to do but I wasn't really even the one doing anything. I was just standing around as the rest of them frantically looked through all of the file cabinets. I was just kind of there in the background. But anyway, the principal told me that I was in serious trouble which I just rolled my eyes to. He told me that he'd let me off with some Saturday detentions if I gave him a list of everyone else that had been in on it. But I couldn't do it. I couldn't rat everyone else out. But I also didn't know the consequences of refusing to tell the principal who was involved. I kept my mouth shut and he kicked me out. He expelled me the next day."

I pondered over all of it and tried to keep an open-mind just like I had promised. And I did. I looked at all the positive things for once.

He looked over at me. "Say something."

A tiny grin spread across my face. "Kennley you got expelled for sneaking into a teacher's room trying to cheat. You didn't steal a car or kill anyone." The new optimistic Kahlen was scaring me.

He raised an eyebrow. "So you have no thoughts on the matter at all?" he asked surprised.

I thought about it for a second. "I have a question... The same people that snuck in with you...are they the same people you were with last night?"

He nodded slowly. "Why?"

"I don't know...it just seems very forgiving on your part. I don't know how they could possibly be your friends if they were all willing to let you take the blame for something they all did. It just doesn't seem very loyal."

"It's not like I wasn't pissed about it," he explained, suddenly defensive. "I just accepted it and moved on."

I didn't understand how he could accept something like that. It wasn't something I could move on from. It seemed like friends like those weren't worth keeping. I didn't want to upset Kennley by showing the disapproval in my voice. Who was I to judge his friends? But something inside of me was still curious about something.

"Do your friends...your family, do they know about me?" I asked.

He smiled. "My little sister Carrie is possibly the nosiest person on the face of the earth. Everyone that has ears to listen to the little *brat* knows."

I smiled thinking back to his cell phone ringing to Barbie Girl. "Is that a bad thing?"

"People knowing? No. Carrie's nosiness? Definitely yes."

"I'm pretty sure it's every little sister's job to irritate their older siblings to death."

"Well Carrie's different. She treats making my life harder than it has to be like a part-time job. It would be full time but she has kindergarten to go to."

"If everyone knows then why didn't you introduce me?" I asked. I thought about how his friends starting walking towards us and he walked off having his friends go off in a different direction. Now the questions were pouring out of me. "I don't understand why you couldn't just tell me you were expelled in the first place without the distractions. Do you think I'm so much of a goody two shoes that I'd break up with you because of it or something?" I asked.

"Geez...cool it with the questions. I can only answer one at a time."

So I kept my mouth shut and waited for him to answer.

"Dean, you break out in a sweat at the thought of being one minute late for school...you have your goody two shoes moments," he said.

I grimaced at my acquired nickname. "No one would

break up over that. The fact that you assume that of me is *insulting*." I chuckled quietly. "Is that why you didn't introduce me to your friends?"

He sighed. "I just don't think they're your kind of people."

"Well why not?" I asked.

He was hesitant. "They're just not, Kahlen, okay?" He was getting defensive again.

This time when my brain yelled, 'Retreat! Retreat!' I listened.

"Yeah…okay." I said softly.

We laid in silence with our faces still only inches from each other. We were both looking up into the sky watching the clouds move across it.

I sighed. "We'd better get to school." But I didn't want to move. I felt like I could spend eternity here just looking into the sky.

Kennley sighed too. "You're right." He reluctantly stood up and extended his hand out to me. I put my hand in his and he pulled me up. We walked to his car since he was the one driving me to school. My mom offered to drive me but of course I declined. She wasn't too thrilled about someone she hardly knew driving me anywhere though. I thought it was better not to mention my ditching school and going to ICC with him last month after knowing him for barely over a day. My dad told me that my stupid car was being towed back home today and I was hoping that my parents wouldn't try to get it fixed. The sooner they realized that the stupid car was a useless hunk of metal the better. Besides…I didn't mind riding with Kennley.

"Kahlen…something has been brought to my attention recently." Mrs. Kraft handed me some papers.

I looked at the papers and it took me a second

to realize it was my progress report for the quarter. I winced. My grades were awful. I was failing English, I had a C in Spanish, a D+ in science, and all of my classes were C's except for math which surprised me. I would have thought math would be my worst subject. I was happy my parents never asked about my grades because if they had seen this I would be grounded for life. I would never see daylight again. I looked up from the papers and back at Mrs. Kraft. Her incredibly curly hair was pulled tightly into a bun.

"Your teachers have told me that you don't pay attention in class...that most of the time you look like you're lost in your own world. They're concerned about you and so am I. Did you know you were doing this badly?" she asked.

"I knew my grades weren't spectacular but I didn't know it had gotten this bad. It's kind of hard to care about school when you have so many other things on your mind."

"I understand, Kahlen, but you have to keep the balance. I know most of the time adults underestimate how hard being a teenager can be and it doesn't seem fair when life throws obstacles in front of your way to only make it harder...but you still have to try. You have to keep the balance."

I didn't want balance. As much as I knew I should, I didn't care about school. I didn't even look at my tests when teachers gave them back to me. I felt off balance but not because of school. I couldn't wait for the school year to be over. I wanted summer *almost* more than I wanted anything else in the world. I missed staying up late during the week and waking up at noon. I missed when the only worry in my life was getting sun burn. I missed my old life that felt robbed from me.

"Do you realize that final exams are coming up? You

have to do well on these. You don't have a choice. This is your junior year. Think about college. You need to take this seriously," she continued.

I hadn't realized that exams were so close. She was right. I did need to focus. As much as I didn't want to find balance I didn't have a choice. The rest of our session was a blur. I was lost in my own daydreams.

I walked into the lunch room and I saw Jenny sitting in our usual spot. I had reluctantly opened up to Jenny, but I didn't regret it. Ever since that day when she had invited me to sit next to her it had become a tradition. I sat down across from her and she greeted me with a smile. She had also started sitting by me in art everyday which at first took me by surprise. She had made the empty seat next to me not so empty anymore. At first I didn't know how to react, but then she was so nice and welcoming that I couldn't be mad at her for taking Emma's seat. It was impossible. We usually sat in silence at art and lunch and I liked it that way. I liked that Jenny understood the beauty of golden silence. But our usual silence had been ruined. I watched as Marissa walked through the cafeteria doors and I didn't think much of it until she sauntered her way over to Jenny and me and asked if she could sit with us. I didn't say anything hoping that Jenny would say no. But of course she didn't because she was too nice for that. Marissa sat down beside Jenny and explained how she had gotten switched to our lunch.

Marissa was so…perky. I think that's why I didn't like her. She was a perfectly good friend but I couldn't take it. I couldn't take how she was always so overjoyed about everything. It seemed like nothing went wrong in her life and it didn't seem fair. I thought about the only time I hadn't seen her happy…when she was in the guidance office crying. In the back of mind I had wondered about it and it only grew worse when Mrs. Kraft's folder had fallen off the table that one day.

"So Kay, anything new with you and Kennley?"

I tried my best not to give her a dirty look. As much as Marissa bugged me half of the time, she didn't deserve my anger. I should have known that Marissa wouldn't have been any different. People I didn't even know where coming up to me and asking if the rumors were true. I was so sick of it. It was none of their business and yet they were positive it was. It was like they felt entitled to know. I didn't roll my eyes, I didn't sigh...I just looked down avoiding eye contact with her.

She reached across the table and put her hand over mine. I looked up immediately shocked.

"I'm sorry. That was so insensitive of me. I wasn't sure if it was true or not that you and Kennley broke up...but I guess the rumor was true. You don't have to talk about it if you don't want to," she said sliding her hand back onto her lap.

I fought back a tiny bit of a grin. I didn't know that telling Bradley would plant the seed. I figured a few people might know...but not too many.

Strangely, I didn't want to lie to Marissa so I just smiled sadly. Jenny looked at me confused. I figured she would be. Although most of the time Jenny and I spent time together in silence, for a couple of minutes of each day I would give her the daily scoop on Kennley and I. I had to tell someone something or else I would explode. Jenny would always listen intently and give her input on things and I appreciated that. For a little bit today I was telling her about the conversation Kennley and I had at the creek earlier. She didn't seem shocked about Kennley's expulsion.

She had said, "He doesn't look like a typical bad

boy…but it's lurking somewhere beneath there. That's probably why everyone is so interested in him. He's somewhat mysterious in a way…it's hard to explain. But everyone loves a good bad boy."

When Marissa wasn't looking I looked at Jenny and shook my head no quickly. She nodded saying she understood.

"I saw the stupidest movie yesterday night," Marissa started a new topic.

I had a feeling I knew what she was talking about. I didn't remember or care what the movie was called but suddenly she had my attention.

"I saw a stupid movie last night too…but I don't remember what it's called. I missed half it though."

She laughed. "I wish I would have missed half of it. Some of my friends wanted to see it and they dragged me along with them. I almost died."

I laughed too. "Are we talking about that movie…the one with the stupid dork—,"

"That tried to make the hockey team to impress the hottest girl in school…" she said.

"Yeah…it was awful. I had to leave and do some math problems so I could figure out if the stupidity melted my brain or not."

I gasped. What was I doing? Was this some type of bonding between me and Marissa? Were we joking around and laughing? Had we found common ground? I shuddered a little. I didn't want a friendship implied more than it already was. I wondered was Marissa as bad as I had made her out to be.

"Well I was stuck with my friends who enjoyed it thoroughly. At least you were with Kennley…"

I didn't say anything hoping she'd take my silence as a signal that the conversation was over.

"…Oh I'm sorry. You probably weren't with Kennley…

considering. I'm so sorry. Well maybe you could tell me why you broke up. Maybe I could help. I feel somewhat responsible. I kept preaching to you about this budding relationship."

I sighed and Jenny cracked a tiny smile. I could tell she was enjoying my lie. I remembered what it was about Marissa that I didn't like. She was so nosy but somehow she was polite and nice about it. It drove me insane. "Marissa…we haven't broken up. I just lied about that to Bradley so he'd leave me alone and I thought that maybe it would stop some of the gossip about us."

Her eyes widened. "Oh," she said slowly. "Well I guess that makes sense. I could try to keep some of the gossip down if you'd like."

I nodded. "I'd like that…a lot.

She smiled. "Good."

I smiled too and then stopped quickly. I had Kennley and Jenny. I could be happy with *just* them.

By the time school was over I didn't feel like waiting for Kennley at our lockers. I was so sick of school…I didn't want to spend another second of my time trapped in that horrid building. I started to walk to Kennley's car without him. I saw Bradley standing in the parking lot. It's not like Bradley had any friends to talk to so I wondered why he was just always there…standing… waiting for something. I ignored him and walked past him quickly and soon after I heard footsteps coming after me.

"Kahlen!" he yelled.

I ignored him and walked faster.

"Hey Kahlen!" he said again. "Wait up."

I couldn't pretend like I didn't hear him anymore. I stopped abruptly and turned around. He was still running to catch up with me so we almost ran into each other. I stood and waited for him to say something but he didn't. He just stood there staring at me.

"Hey," he finally said, catching his breath.

"Um...hey." There was something about talking to Bradley that automatically put me in a bad mood. He still didn't say anything. "Did you *want* something Bradley?" I tried to keep my voice friendly.

"Yeah I was just wondering about that whole car situation of yours."

I almost asked him, "what about it." But I stopped myself. I didn't want to do anything to prolong the conversation.

"Well speaking of that whole car situation, I have to go meet Kennley. He's driving me home, so bye," I said quickly. I started to walk off and he grabbed my wrist just as that stupid guy Sean had. I had no idea what had gotten into Bradley lately. It was like he was the same person but intensified somehow. He was driving me crazy recently.

"I thought you and Kennley are broken up. Isn't it a little weird with him giving you rides and all?" he let go of my wrist.

"Not really. We're friends...just like we were before. It was sort of a mutual break up so nothing is awkward," I explained. Bradley didn't respond right away so I took advantage of the silence. "But like I was saying Bradley...I really have to go, sorry. I talk to you later though."

Later as in our ten year high school reunion...

I continued to walk at the same rapid pace towards Kennley's car. If I was walking any faster I would be running. There was someone standing against his car and at first I thought it was Kennley until I realized this person was taller and his brown hair was shaggy. My pace automatically slowed. I didn't recognize the person but they seemed familiar somehow. I couldn't put my finger on it but I had seen him before.

"Hi..." I said once I reached the car. The mystery person who wasn't facing me turned around quickly as if I'd startled him. I was a little pleased that I wasn't the only jumpy person around. "Who are you...?" I asked.

I knew that this person wasn't someone that went to our school. Although I didn't know many people, I knew faces.

"I'm Ben," he said. "And you're... oh, don't tell me I know this." He put his hand to his face. "Don't tell me... you're... Katherine."

I shook my head no. "I'm Kahlen." I was so very confused.

"Ugh. I so knew that. It was like on the tip on my tongue but I just couldn't—,"

I still hadn't known where I'd seen him before. "How do you know me?"

His jaw dropped and he looked disgusted. "Well," he snorted, annoyed. "Some friend...I figured he might at least mention me or something. All these years..." he trailed off.

"Excuse me?" I asked.

"Never? He's never mentioned me before...well that's verging on rude. Plain old disrespectful. Does the term best friend mean nothing to that kid? I swear sometimes he can be so..." He pretended to strangle an invisible neck in his hands.

"Kennley?" I asked confused.

"You look extremely *puzzled*," he said mostly to himself. "I always do that. I always go off practically having a conversation with myself and no one has the slightest idea of what I'm talking about. You must think I'm insane. You know absolutely nothing about me... not that it's your fault. I hardly know anything about you but I know enough." He took a deep breath. "I'm doing it again aren't I…that whole talking to myself you being confused thing?"

I nodded slowly.

"Okay well I'm Kennley's friend…but I guess in his eyes there is a very *loose* interpretation of the word. Kennley's said some things about you to us. Don't worry, they've all been good. Oh and I saw you last night at the movie theater. I thought we were finally going to meet the famous Kahlen—um…last name starts with a T or something like that— but then Kennley turned us in the opposite direction. Again…in his eyes, very loose interpretation of the word friend. What has it been, like two years now? Yup, I think that's it. No maybe it's three. I don't know."

I stood there trying to decipher all of what he just said.

"You go to Crest Moore?" I asked.

"Did he tell you that…you mean he mentioned something about me? Well that's a surprise."

"Not really, he was talking about how he used to go there. I just assumed—,"

"He told you that," he asked shocked. "Geez, you must really like him. I mean with all the stuff he's did and all." He paused for a moment. "Wow."

I looked around for Kennley. I saw him walking out of the school building finally but he was still pretty far away.

"Yeah he told me why he got expelled." I said.

Ben started laughing. "Wait, that's it? That's all he told you?"

I was confused again. I nodded.

"Oh, never mind. Well um…he's probably going to be pissed at me then. Can you do me a favor…when

Kennley gets over here; the only thing we said to each other was introducing ourselves."

I didn't respond. I narrowed my eyes but not in anger...in true confusion. I looked over my shoulder and saw that Kennley was getting closer.

"Um...actually, you know what? I'm just going to leave. I know how he can get. So can you tell him that Ross wants him to swing by later tonight?"

Before I could answer or even figure out what was going on, Ben was gone and Kennley was next to me. Kennley swore as Ben pulled out of the lot. Ben's face looked panicked.

I tried to think of something to say, anything to say but I couldn't form the words. I felt like I had been so confused to the point of incoherency.

Kennley unlocked the car door and opened in for me. I sat down it wasn't long before he had sat down too. I waited for him to volunteer some information but he didn't. He hadn't even said so much as a casual, "hi" or "hey".

"Ben wanted me to tell you that Ross wants you to stop by tonight," I said slowly. Kennley didn't say anything. "How come you never mentioned him? He seemed quite disturbed that I had never heard of him before?"

"Some things in my life I like to keep separate from others." He shrugged. "Did Ben say anything else to you?"

"I only caught about half of it. He kind of rambled on a lot. It was hard to understand."

"It's like a whole other language. It takes some time getting used to it," he explained.

I didn't say much the whole ride. I was trying to sort out everything that had happened. I was thinking so hard that my head was starting to hurt.

When we finally got to my house he said, "Well I gotta get to work so I'll talk to you later." He quickly kissed me goodbye.

I got out of the car and walked around the side to my driveway. I wanted nothing more than to go in my house and take something for my head. I could feel it. One day I was going to combust. There was only so much one mind could handle. I wanted answers but I was somewhat afraid to ask. Whenever I would begin to get the nerve, I would hear it in my head, "Retreat! Retreat!"

12. Confessions

I sat at the table enjoying my cereal. No one ever made the whole big breakfast with eggs, bacon, and sausage. On most days my mom was the one with the most time to cook but there was no way we were letting her get by the stove. I could sometimes but I was too lazy and my dad was too busy. So I was satisfied with just cereal.

My dad's heavy footsteps clunked down the stairs. He looked like he was in a rush as he fastened his buttons while trying to shove a granola bar down his throat.

"Geez dad, don't those people at work ever give you a break?"

He chewed and swallowed before answering. "I wish they could, but not with a generation like yours. What is it with your generation these days anyhow? Whatever happened to spending your days outside with bell bottom jeans, tie dyed shirts, and rallying for peace not war?"

I laughed. "Well for one, it's not the seventies and two, did you ever think that it's not my generation that's the problem, that it's the parents of my generation's lack of parenting skills?"

He paused for a second finishing the buttons on his shirt. "Hmm," he grunted. "Touché." He grabbed his jacket off the coat rack. "I'll see you later, Kido."

He shut the door behind him and it wasn't long

before I heard his car pulling off down the street. I was alone again. I didn't mind being alone, but I didn't like the silence. My mom was off running errands, my dad was now on his way to work, and I was stuck at home yet again on a Saturday. I was beginning to hate Saturdays. Kennley had asked me to meet him later at the creek but that was at least ten or more hours from now. I hated the silence. In the silence I wasn't distracted by anything. My mind was forced to wander and go to places I didn't want it to go. I couldn't take much more of it so I brought my unfinished cereal up stairs to my bedroom and set it down on my desk. I had been playing my guitar lately which surprised me. I was kind of rusty at first for not playing in seven years. But my guitar felt good in my hands. It felt like it belonged.

I began to strum a couple of chords, the same ones I had been and I realized it sounded pretty nice. Every now and again I'd add more to it and whether I was trying to or not, I was making my own song. It was the perfect cure for the silence. I loved music anyhow. I considered making words to the song but what about? I had never been much of a writer and I know that everyone says, "write what you know". But what did I know? As I scanned my mind there was only one thing that I really and truly knew about. I wouldn't even force my mind to go there though. So I kept playing. I sang the melody to what I was playing and it seemed to fit. They weren't exactly words, but they worked.

La La La
La De Dah, Dah Dah Dah
La De Dah, Dah Dah Dah
La De Dah, Dah Dah Dah Ah.

I sang it over and over again as I played the melody. I hadn't sung in a while. Something most people, as in everyone, didn't know about me was that I liked singing. It wasn't exactly something I advertised. I knew I wasn't the best singer in the world but in my eyes I thought I had a pretty nice voice, though that could mean nothing. Lots of people are positive that they are the next Mariah Carey and just embarrass themselves. I've watched many a person's dreams be shattered on the *American Idol* auditions.

I had no idea how long I had been playing but it all came to a stop once I heard my mom pulling into the driveway. I had already gotten her excited enough that I had been playing my guitar again. I didn't want to hear anymore comments from her about it. It wasn't long before I heard her footsteps coming up the stairs and I sprinted to my closet to put the guitar away. She busted through my door with a bright smile on her face. Of course knocking first would have been too much to ask. That smile looked like it was planted eternally on her face. She was practically glowing.

"Guess what?" She beamed.

Her smile was contagious. "What?"

"The house I did for the Berlin's last month really paid off. They liked it so much that they recommended us to all of their friends. And they have a *lot* of friends. One of her friends is starting a new company and wanted us to decorate the whole building, another one is having their house renovated, and another wanted us to do their nursery for their new baby boy! Work is pouring in Kahlen!"

I gasped. She never called me Kahlen. This was big.

"I hadn't realized how much I missed the office. We are going to be so busy. I'm so excited…so we," She grabbed my arm and started to pull me out the door. "… Are going to go celebrate! We're going to the mall. The sky is the limit. We are going to come home with so many new clothes you'll have to throw out your clothes to make room for a new wardrobe."

I smiled. I didn't know if my eyes could get any wider. "Am I being punk'd or something?" I asked while she continued to drag me.

"Punk'd? What's that? Honestly honey, I don't have time to keep up with today's slang and besides time's a wasting."

I shook my arm free. I didn't have on shoes, I was in my pajamas, I hadn't showered, and my hair was a mess. "Mom, look at me. We can't go just this second. Give me twenty minutes or more. I haven't even showered."

She sighed. "Pumpkin, you showered last night. I don't think your body needs to be bathed every five hours. So get dressed. You've got fifteen minutes."

I ran back into my room and got dressed quickly. My mom was already in the car waiting for me impatiently.

"So which mall is the biggest? It's been a long time since I've went shopping."

I had to think about it for a second. It had been a long time for me too. "The one across town." I finally answered. "It is by far the biggest by a long shot."

She turned the key in the ignition. "Oh you mean the one close by Crest Moore?" she asked.

"Yeah," I answered softly.

Crest Moore had been a sore subject between me and Kennley lately. I knew there was more he was hiding from me which drove me insane but whenever I tried to talk about it he would either get defensive or he'd find some way to change the subject. After a couple of days had went by of him getting mad at me for asking, I just stopped. He had me scared to bring it up now because I didn't want to make him mad. I could feel it. We were on the brink of a fight. Sooner or later one of us would have to give in and I wasn't sure who that would be.

The other day I had asked him, "So why did Ben come all the way out to our school just to deliver a tiny message like that. Hasn't he heard of cell phones?" I had tried to make my voice as nonchalant as possible.

Kennley sighed his infamous sigh. "Just forget about Ben, it was nothing."

"But—,"

He had kissed me interrupting my sentence and I knew this was only a distraction on his part. When I pulled away abruptly trying to remember what I was about to say to him he just looked irritated. He seemed so tense and now I was longing for the Kennley I had known before.

"What?" he asked.

It wasn't like we were at school or anything...we were completely alone in the middle of the creek. Then I had looked into his green eyes and surrendered, completely diverted from the fight we were so close to having.

I rolled my eyes now thinking about how Kennley would always get his way and distraction was the key.

I slowly reached to change the radio station expecting my mom to stop me but she didn't. She definitely wasn't Jekyll today. She was more of a nice Hyde.

When we finally got to the mall my mom bought a whole bunch of unnecessary things...which I guess was the point of our frivolous shopping. She even bought me two cell phone cases. She said she was sick of me putting my cell phone in my pocket and then losing it. I knew she would never let me losing my cell phone thing go. We even bought some goofy hats and cow girl boots. It was the perfect distraction I needed. It surprised me how much money we were spending on all of this stupid stuff but my mom didn't seem to care. I thought about Julie and Emma and how we used to go shopping like this... But it was different then. Then, it would be to make up for Julie's guilty conscience but now here with my mom it was nothing like that. It was pure fun and somewhat irresponsibility. I knew we should probably be saving this money, invest it, but I didn't complain. It wasn't my decision. The only thing I wanted to complain about was the heavy shopping bags I had been dragging around.

"Ugh, I think they should have baskets for malls to put all of your shopping bags in." My mom said setting all her bags down for a second.

"Amen to that...but it would take away the whole mall ambiance if people were pushing around baskets with their toddlers in there too like it's a grocery store. It would throw off everything."

She sighed. "True. How about I go put all of these in the car and I'll meet you in the food court in a couple of minutes?"

"Sounds good." I handed her my bags. I only had two but she had five. "But can you carry all of these bags?"

She snorted. "This is nothing. Try carrying a crying baby, the diaper bag, the pacifier that you kept dropping out of your mouth, your blanket that you wouldn't sleep without, and trying to talk on the phone all at the same time. I think I can handle seven bags."

My parents seemed particularly bitter about my baby days. It was no wonder they didn't have any more children.

My mom headed off in one direction and I headed off

in the other towards the food court. I knew I was going to have an almost near impossible time trying to decide what I wanted to eat. I was surrounded by every kind of food I could think of. Whenever I would think about this mall I would mostly think about the food court. It was humungous. There was even a merry-go-round in the center of it. The only thing it was missing was a Ferris wheel...okay maybe it wasn't that humungous. I had narrowed down my choices to Chinese food and Subway. I hadn't had Chinese in a while but the thought of a Subway Melt sandwich was mouth watering. So I did what any outstanding genius would do.

"Eenie meenie miny mo, one of you has got to go, I still don't know so please don't fret, I still haven't even chose one yet. I need to decide so I'm using this rhyme, and I have made up my mind at this time." I moved my finger back and forth and it landed on Chinese food. I think I secretly wanted that more anyhow.

"*You always were a poet but didn't know it,*" she said.

I remembered me and Emma making up our different version to Eenie Meenie Miny Mo when we were twelve. I sighed. Could I go anywhere where there weren't constant reminders of things I didn't want to think about?

Behind the merry-go-around there was gorgeous blond that of course was Hannah. I should have known better than to suggest a mall that was right outside of Crest Moore. She was a good distance away from me so I figured we wouldn't bump into each other. Not that it would matter any how because I would just pretend like I had never seen her before in my life. It's wasn't like we were friends or anything, I hadn't even said one word to her. I saw that she wasn't alone. She was holding hands with a tall guy with short brown spiky hair. I had never seen the guy before so I figured it wasn't Ross. I didn't know who Ross was specifically but it wasn't one of the guys I had seen at the theater that night. I wondered if Hannah was still with Ross or not…or if she really was a borderline home-wrecker, a cheater.

I ignored it and continued walking towards the Chinese food. The smell of shrimp fried rice filled my lungs. I got my food and sat at a table. It wasn't long before I saw my mom coming back. It had taken her longer than it should have I suddenly knew why. Her hands weren't empty.

I gasped. My mother had a problem. She couldn't so much as walk past a couple of stores without buying something. She was in the early stages of shopaholicism. She was holding a Victoria's Secret bag and sat down with me still smiling the way she had when she had first busted through my bedroom door.

"Guess what I got?" she sang.

I grimaced…Victoria's Secret was known for its lingerie after all.

She noticed my look and rolled her eyes. She dug through her bag and set a box on the table. "They don't just sell lingerie and other underwear you know. They have their makeup and perfume section along with a clothing section too."

I opened the box and it had perfume in it. It was called Honey Suckle breeze. I sprayed it once and sniffed the air. It smelled pretty good. It wasn't how I thought it would smell. It smelled sweet, yet floral and fruity.

"Doesn't that smell amazing?" she asked.

"How is it fruity and floral at the same time?" I sprayed again and sniffed. This time it smelled a little bit more like honey…but still floral and fruity.

"And I got one for you too. There was a sale," she continued as she put the perfume back in the box and into her bag.

"Mom, aren't you going to eat?" My mouth was still full so I wasn't sure if she could understand what I was saying.

"Sweetie, I'm too jazzed to be eating right now. Do you realize what this could do for our company? The only thing I'm sad about is that I won't have very much time to spend with you. I'm going to be really busy and I'm going to need all the help I can get."

I laughed. I couldn't believe my mom used a word like, *jazzed*. "Well summer is rapidly approaching so you'll have my help."

She smiled. "Yeah, that's what you say now. I know how you teenagers are. You're committed now until the last minute when one of your friends or Kennley wants to hang out with you then what?"

I rolled my eyes. I didn't want to talk about Kennley. I was so frustrated with everything concerning him.

"So how are things going with you two?"

I tried not to sigh, roll my eyes, or grimace. I hated when people asked me this.

"Okay I guess."

"You guess?"

I didn't care anymore so I sighed. Leave it to my mother to analyze every word I said. I didn't respond. I thought about those Twix candy bar commercials where they'd shove a Twix into their mouth to buy them some time. I shoved a whole bunch of my food into my mouth. I didn't want to discuss Kennley. He had officially made it to the things I didn't want to talk about list. My mom understood and dropped it. That's what I liked and didn't like about my mom...she was perceptive.

Kennley had asked me to meet him at the creek at 9:30. Despite my better judgment, I told my mom where I was going. She didn't hound me with questions which I was thankful for. I headed off to the creek but I took the long way. I didn't go through the neighbor's yard but instead walked all the way around the corner then down the street to the Dean's Creek. I was in no hurry to get there. I wanted answers and I didn't know how much longer I could go on pretending like everything was alright between us.

I saw Kennley sitting on the grass lying down beside the perfect shade tree.

I gasped silently. It felt like someone had just thrown a rock at my head. Today was our one month anniversary…well actually it was yesterday. I wondered if Kennley would make a big deal out of it or if I was supposed to. My mind began to race. I was hoping Kennley would know me better than to think I would make a big deal out of it. It was one month, thirty-one days, big whoop…

I walked over to him and sat down.

"Perfect," he smiled.

"What—,"

"Look." He pointed beyond the trees into the sky.

I saw the sun setting through the branches of the trees. It was beautiful. The sky was mixed with blues, and purples, oranges, and pinks. I realized why I had to be here at exactly 9:30…to see the sun set.

"You're always telling me about how beautiful this place is at night. I thought I'd go one step farther and show you the sunset."

I smiled. I hated how he did that…how he made me forget about everything I was mad or sad about.

"It's beautiful." That was all I could manage to say.

I had seen many sunsets but never one like this.

The little bit of the sun I could see through the trees was reflecting on the water. There wasn't a cloud left in the sky…all I could see was bright shades of colors.

"Well I figured it was only fitting…beautiful girl, beautiful sunset…"

I smiled. He pulled me closer to him. "You smell… different." He immediately noticed my expression change and then started to laugh. "I don't mean a *bad* different, I just mean different. Usually your hair smells like vanilla but today it smells like honey, only somewhat fruitier."

I laughed. I hadn't used my Vanilla shampoo this morning and I sprayed my new perfume on me. "Don't forget floral." I grinned. "My mom went crazy today and we went on a shopping spree. Two for one Honey Suckle Breeze perfume at Victoria's Secret."

I saw him raise an eyebrow. I sighed. "They sell more than just lingerie there you know." I sounded just like my mom.

Kennley was silent for a moment. It was like we were having our unofficial staring contest again. "I didn't just bring you here for the sunset…I wanted to talk to you."

"What about?" I didn't blink.

"Well really, I wanted to tell you something."

I didn't say anything waiting. I knew it was going to happen sooner or later. We were on the brink of a fight… it was only a matter of time before—,"

"I love you," he said.

I blinked.

He grabbed my hand and put it in his. "…More than that, I'm *in* love with you. I know we've only known each other for two months and been going out for only a month, but I am. I'm in love with you."

I gulped. I was sure that the hand he was holding

was now sweating buckets. Sure I loved Kennley, but was I *in* love with him?

I thought about my eighth grade year. My friend Braden and I had all of our morning classes together. We became really good friends over that semester. Braden told me that he liked someone. I asked him who and he said he actually liked two people. He told me the first person was Emma...go figure. But when I asked him who the second person was he said, "You". I all about fell over in my chair and fainted. I wondered what happened to a simple note, do you like me, check yes or no. I didn't expect him to tell me to my face. I didn't want to hurt his feelings. Then I wasn't sure if he was just joking around. I stood there staring at Braden like an idiot. I have no idea where it came from but I said, "I don't believe you". It was possibly the stupidest answer ever but for the next week he spent his time talking to Emma so she could convince me that he was telling me the truth. I guess I kind of knew the truth the whole time...but I didn't like him. We were friends. I didn't want to ruin that.

I sat there the same way staring at Kennley. I couldn't say, "I don't believe you" in this situation. But what could I say? I didn't know if I felt the same. It disgusted me when a couple would go out for a day or so and say, 'I love you so much!' all the time. I wondered if they really were in love with each other. It didn't seem like some word to be thrown around as if it was nothing. Being in love with someone was special...it was unique. I finally got what Emma had said to me during the Junior Beach Party.

"Not that kind of love. That's the kind of love you're born with. You have no control over that. And yeah, I love you but that kind of love isn't as unique either."

My mouth was slightly open as I searched for the

right words to respond back with. I tried to force myself to say it…but I couldn't.

"I…I don't exactly know if I should say it back because I'm not sure if I'll mean it. I don't really know what being in love feels like so how can I know when I'm actually *in* it?" I was talking so fast I could barely understand what I was saying.

He sighed. He didn't seem angry or hurt, his face was blank. "When you love someone you just know. It's not something you have to figure out if you're feeling."

I looked away from him and back at the sky. The sun had completely set and the moon was slowly appearing. "I'm sorry," I practically whispered.

He threw me a little grin. "Kahlen, for what? You have nothing to be sorry for. I'd rather you say that you aren't sure than lie to me. And besides, I wasn't expecting anything back. I just wanted to get my feelings out in the open."

He didn't hide it as well this time. His face was no longer blank and I could see the tiny bit of hurt touch his green eyes. Maybe he wasn't expecting an answer, but I knew he was hoping. I hugged him. "Just for the record, I do love you."

What a sad consolation prize. "I know," he said.

"*It's not the same Kahlen*," she said.

I stumbled into my room not really watching where I was going. I didn't care. I was too deep in thought to see my desk in front of me. I banged into it hard and it hurt. The desk shook and my jewelry box lying on top of it fell to the ground. I put my hand to my aching knee and bend down on the ground put all of my things back into the box. I grabbed a handful of necklaces and earrings that were all linked together. I realized that I was really unorganized. There was still one necklace in my hand. I absentmindedly tried to shake it off until I snapped back into reality and realized it was hooked around my finger. I looked down at my hand and all my thoughts about Kennley disappeared. It was the locket. The golden heart shaped locket, broken clasp and all.

I missed the days when my eyes felt eternally dry... when there were still barriers. I felt like such a wreck. The tears started spilling out and I tried to stop them. I tried to open the locket but it wouldn't budge. I felt like in the back of my mind I *knew* what was inside of it... but I couldn't quite grasp it. I remembered Emma telling me something about it but I didn't know what she had said. I knew if I thought about it too hard it would make my head hurt.

I threw the locket into the box and slammed the top down. I was so sick of being sad and feeling like this big empty gap inside of me as a result of something that had been ripped from my body. It hurt so badly and I was tired of it. I couldn't stand that she was gone. I couldn't stand a lot of things. It wasn't fair to me or to her that she wasn't here for me to tell her all about tonight. She was the one that dreamed of love... having someone being in love with her. I didn't. She was supposed to be here to help me, to create tons of pros and con lists about Kennley. She would have helped me figure this whole mess out.

I had made up my mind that I was done. I was done with pretending that everything was okay and that I wasn't mad and confused. I hated that he was hiding things from me. I hated being confused all the time. It was like I was on a rollercoaster ride with no end. I knew what I had to do. As much as I didn't want to hurt Kennley I had to. Any longer of this and I was going to go insane. It was for the improvement of my mental health. I knew I should have listened to myself that night. I should have waited to talk myself out of it. I was right…boys complicated things. The last thing I needed was an even more complicated life.

"*You always were such a scaredy cat,*" she said.

I ignored it. I wasn't scared. I knew that it was going to come to an end at sometime. I didn't expect us to last forever. I knew that in the end someone was going to get hurt…one person always falls harder than the other. I was killing two birds with one stone. I could protect myself from being hurt and make my life less complicated at the same time.

Another tear spilled from my eye, down my cheek, and to the floor. I hated how she wasn't here. She would never be here again…ever. I tried to be angry. It was so much easier to feel than sadness. If I hated Emma this would be so much easier. I walked over to my bed and plopped down on it hard. My guitar fell out of my closet and to the ground. It startled me and I gasped.

Something clicked in my head. I looked around frantically for some type of writing utensil in my room. I finally found a pen lying on the floor. I grabbed a piece of paper on my desk that actually last week's math homework and scribbled down all of my thoughts:

I almost hate you…
For leaving me here to cry
With no one here to wipe the tears from my eyes.
Why'd you have to go?
And leave me here all alone
Now it's over, right as it begun, when we
Were having fun.

I grabbed my guitar and began to play the melody I had been playing but I added the words. They seemed to fit. I just needed to get rid of the things in my life that didn't fit. I tried to look on the bright side…at least now I could stop lying to Bradley.

When Monday finally came around I was having doubts. I knew that if I thought about it too long I would talk myself out of it. I was an awful person. What kind of horrible person breaks up with some one after they tell you they love you? What if I waited a couple of weeks so I wouldn't hurt him so badly? I shook off all of those thoughts as I pressed harder on the gas pedal of my mom's car. I didn't want things to be awkward with him driving me to school after breaking up. I had it all planned out. I had gone over in my mind all the different scenarios. I imagined Kennley sad, mad, and indifferent. I was prepared on how to deal with everything.

I took a deep breath and took my first step out of the car. I walked onto the grass and down the path to the creek that seemed much more like a river surrounded by trees.

"*Kahlen, don't,*" she said.

I took another deep breath. Hurting Kennley was going to kill both me and him, but I had to do it. I had made up my mind and there was no changing it. I saw him sitting by the water…I wondered how he always beat me here. I tried to focus on other things besides him as I walked closer. If I looked at him for too long… if he smiled at me, anything, I would give in to my subconscious. I just needed to come right out and say it. I didn't even sit down when I finally got to him. I just stood there breathing harder and louder than normal.

"Hey," he said.

I could hear the smile in his voice. I didn't look down, just straight ahead. I took another deep breath.

"Are you okay?" he asked.

"*Don't,*" she said.

I shook my head no…both at my subconscious and Kennley.

"Well...what's wrong? Sit down, and we can talk about if you want."

I shook my head no again. I took my last deep breath. I continued to look straight over his head and said, "Kennley, I want to break up."

I heard him stand up. I caught a quick glimpse of his face. I felt my knees wobble. I looked down at the grass under my feet. I could feel him studying my face.

"No," he said.

Out of all the scenarios I had gone through in my head, this one was not on the list. I was completely taken aback. It was totally unexpected.

I still looked down at the grass. "Um...Excuse me?" I asked.

He gently put his hand underneath my chin and lifted it up so I had to look at him. I wanted to close my eyes but it was too late. Those green eyes were staring back at my brown ones and I could already feel myself losing the battle.

"You heard me," he said. "No."

I opened my mouth to protest but nothing came out. I thought about all the things I had gone through my mind on Saturday. I thought about what he was hiding from me, about how he deserved to be with someone who actually loved him back, and I thought about how I was sick of pretending things were perfectly alright with us.

"You can't—,"

"You're doing this because you're scared. You're scared of me...scared of us."

"*You're scared you might actually be in love him,*" she said.

He dropped his hand from my face. "So no...I'm not going to let you do this."

He was so close to my face I had nowhere to look

except for his eyes. "Well…" I started to say. "It's not entirely you're decision to make."

"No not entirely. But give me one good reason Kahlen."

I had plenty of reasons but none that I could remember at the moment. I tried to focus but I couldn't.

He kissed me practically sweeping me off of my feet. It was not supposed to be going this way. I pulled back and stepped backwards quite dazed and disoriented trying to gather my thoughts.

"No," I had to catch my breath. "I can't do this anymore. I'm so tired of pretending that you're not hiding anything. Why are you always so secretive?" I started pacing. "What am I supposed to think Kennley?" I waited for him to respond but he didn't. "Let's face it, we don't fit…and I'm done trying to."

I stopped pacing and looked at him. He still wasn't saying anything.

"And you don't have to worry about driving me," I continued. "I borrowed my mom's car."

I started to walk away but I heard his voice in the distance. "What? You mean there's no let's just be friends speech?"

I ignored him and walked faster away.

13. Confessions (2)

I walked into art class and sat next to Jenny. I was too off into space to even say hi to her. I felt awful… It was only fitting, I was an awful person. There was no way I could be friends with Kennley now because things would be too awkward. I had screwed everything up between us. I wished we would have just stayed friends so things would have been so much easier. I tried not to focus on everything that had happened this morning. So I concentrated hard on my artwork. We didn't have a specific project this week. Since the end of the year was quickly approaching our teacher gave us free reign. Our only rule was to make something… anything. I had decided to draw the creek at night. It actually didn't look half bad which surprised me. I was just trying my best not to screw it up now…like I did with everything else in my life. I sighed.

"So what's wrong?" Jenny asked. "I figure it has to do with Kennley considering you haven't said a word about him today." Jenny put down her pencil. She was doing a self portrait. She was a much better artist than me. The picture looked exactly like her—her caramel skin, short hair and brown eyes…it looked more like a photograph than a drawing.

"There *is* no more Kennley." I said flatly.

"He died?" She tilted her head to the side.

I was in no mood for her sarcasm. "You know what I mean."

"Okay," she said. "But why?"

I had to think about for a second. "Well…he told me he was in love with me and—,"

Her jaw dropped. "He told you he loved you and then you broke up with him? What kind of cruel, heartless monster—," she stopped her sentence short. "Sorry."

I didn't take offense by it. She was right. I knew what I was. "What makes you think *I* broke up with him?" I asked.

"Well the guy has been head over heels for you for awhile…you're the only one in this entire school that hasn't noticed."

I rolled my eyes. "*Anyways*…I couldn't say that I loved him back. I figured one of us was going to get hurt sooner or later and besides, the whole secrecy and mysterious thing wasn't working for me."

I was trying very hard to believe my own words. It wasn't like I had expected Kennley and I to last for long anyhow. He was just my distraction.

"This doesn't make any sense. You and Kennley are like a peanut butter and jelly sandwich. I personally think that a just peanut butter sandwich or a just jelly sandwich would be nasty…but together, it's perfect."

I sighed. "Kennley and I are not edible, Jenny." I knew I was completely ignoring her point but I didn't care nor did I want to discuss this anymore. It was my decision and it had already been made.

Jenny looked away from me and back at her picture and starting to work on it again slowly like there were so many things going through her mind that she wanted to share but instead kept her lips sealed. She started working on it again. I was waiting for her respond but she didn't. I usually liked the silence but now it was killing me.

"What?" I said.

"I just…I think it's kind of stupid," she finally said. She still wasn't looking at me focusing on her work. "All those reasons you listed…it seems like things you could work out if you wanted it to…not just give up."

I thought about something to say back but I couldn't. Everything I came up with in my mind would come out as too defensive. She didn't say anything either. We sat in our silence.

I wanted to switch lockers. I couldn't take it. Kennley wouldn't even look at me. He had a good poker face so I couldn't tell how he was feeling. He was emotionless. It wasn't like before when we weren't talking…this was worse. There was no slamming of lockers. This time we both pretended as if the other didn't exist.

By the end of school our silence was almost unbearable. I knew Kennley felt the same because when I shut my locker he was standing there beside me looking desperate.

"Kahlen, hear me out okay? I need to talk to you."

I sighed. "Kennley I—,"

"I will *stand* outside your bedroom window if I have to and serenade you if need be." His face completely serious.

I fought back a smile.

"Please," he said. I had never seen him this desperate before. "Just come with me to ICC and we can talk."

I stared at him for a long second. I was somewhat apprehensive. I knew how easily he might be able to sway me…he always had that effect, just like how he was swaying me now. Here he was in front of me pleading and although I was fighting to say no, I actually said, "Fine."

He smiled. "Okay. I'll meet you at my car." He

grabbed his stuff and disappeared out the big double doors.

I picked up my backpack off the ground and swung it around my back and sighed. I forgot my math book. I dropped my backpack hard to the ground and put in my combination to my locker quickly. I didn't see my math book anywhere in my locker. I looked up and saw it in the top compartment and sighed again heavily. I didn't remember putting it up there…but then again I never did.

Of course Bradley just happened to be lurking around. Without saying a word he came and towered over me to get the book.

"Thanks." I muttered.

He smiled. "So is Kennley giving you a ride home?"

I wondered why it even mattered to him. "Not exactly. We're going to ICC."

Bradley's face sunk and he almost looked… angry. "Listen Kahlen, you really need to know something—,"

"Can it wait till later Bradley? Kennley's waiting for—,"

"What do you see in that guy? Really, please, enlighten me." The tone in his voice changed. "He's no good for you anyhow." He handed me my book finally but when he did his hand lingered on mine for a second. I moved my hand away quickly. "I don't see how you two are broken up if you keep spending so much time together. He's just trying to manipulate you into getting back with him. Then again if you're stupid enough to let him maybe I should let you. Don't you see how Kennley is all wrong for you…or are you too blind to notice."

I recoiled at his words. "You know what Bradley…I

don't see how me and Kennley's business is any of *yours*," I snapped.

I didn't bother putting the book in my backpack. I walked off out the double doors and to the parking lot. There was something about Bradley that always put me into a bad mood. And that ridiculous bright shade on top of his head always hurt my eyes. I could hear his footsteps coming after me. It didn't matter how quickly I walked away, his long strides kept up with me.

"I have tried to stay out of this as long as I could," he said.

I slowed my paced. There was no use in trying to get away from him.

"I'm trying to be a good friend and—,"

Bradley always meant well. He was just the friendly geek that would always try too hard, or talk too much. He just didn't know when to stop and right now…he needed to stop. I knew it was wrong but I snapped again. "*Friend*? Bradley…we haven't said a word to each other all year until suddenly you decided to start bothering me a couple of months ago. Maybe you and I hold the definition of *friend* a bit differently. But a real friend would butt out and mind their own business!"

I heard his footsteps stop. I didn't bother turning around at all. I walked quickly to Kennley's car. He was there waiting for me leaning against it in his usual stance waiting to open the door for me. I stomped past him, opened the door for myself pushing him off to the side and slamming it behind me. I could feel his confused glare on me but I ignored it. He walked to his side of the car and got in slowly examining my expression.

He exhaled. "If looks could kill…" He muttered.-

His beautiful BMW purred to life and before I knew it we were out of the parking lot.

In between driving I could see him staring at me out of the corner of his eye. When we got to a red light he looked at me and then quickly turned away for the hundredth time.

Finally I said, "What?"

He didn't answer at first. "Well…I'm trying to figure out a way to ask you what's wrong without you possibly biting my head off."

I tried to relax. I was so angry at everything. It was one of those bad mood days where somehow even the innocent grass finds a way to bother you. I knew I was mostly in a bad mood about what Jenny and Bradley had said, and then everything with Kennley but I was sick of the permanent frown on my face. I closed my eyes and sighed.

"Have you ever had one of those days where it seems like life is just taking its entire wrath out on you?"

"Try one of those years…" he said sourly.

I allowed a tiny grin to spread on my face. "That too."

When we walked into ICC the familiar smell of candy, ice cream, and food filled my nostrils with satisfaction. I hadn't been here in a while. I loved the old fashioned booths and stools and the collage of old pictures of everything from old Hollywood to disco balls hung on the walls. It all seems so corny but it was accepted. I guess you could have called it the hot spot for teens.

We went up the counter to order. I ordered a strawberry milkshake and Kennley ordered a banana split…but with only vanilla ice cream. The lady at the counter tried not to give him a weird look like the one I had. He wanted the banana and the fudge and everything else that came with a banana split…but *only* vanilla ice cream. I wasn't a big fan of vanilla myself.

It seemed so plain and ordinary. I remember what he had said the last time we were here. Could it have been just last month? It felt like last year. He had said, 'can't beat the classics'.

We took our seats at a booth. I waited for him to start talking but he didn't. He looked like he was waiting for me to do the same.

"Well you said you wanted to talk so talk," I urged.

He still just stared at me but he was smiling.

I wasn't over my bad mood yet so I put my head in my hand and waited impatiently.

He was still smiling not saying anything, almost laughing.

The waitress came and brought us our ice cream and walked away. Finally Kennley's smile faded as he dug into his ice cream.

"I don't exactly know where to begin." He sighed. "I don't blame you for breaking up with me. I haven't just been a pretty crappy boyfriend lately but a crappy friend." He paused. "I uh—well…let's just say there is a lot you don't know about me, that a lot of people don't know about me. And I knew that I've been kind of snapping at you at lot lately and that's not fair to you."

He stopped talking for a minute to eat his ice cream. I hadn't even touched my shake, waiting for him to continue. I could tell he didn't want to tell me whatever it was that he was going to tell me.

"Such as…" I encouraged.

"Well, for starters…I'm adopted. I moved in with the parents I have now when I was about six."

I raised an eyebrow at him shocked.

"When I was fifteen I begged my parents if I could try to find my birth mom. They were reluctant at first and then they finally let me go. It wasn't hard to find her. She lived in the same place she had when she gave me away. She was willing to see me and answer all of my questions. I had plenty of memories from when I was little and was with her but they had faded some," he continued.

"Seeing her was a complete disappointment. She was a drunk, stumbling around the house. If my parents were there they probably would have dragged me out but I convinced them not to come. When I first looked at Layla I could see my face in hers. We have the same green eyes, the same kind of nose and lips. She spilled all of her guts to me about everything that had happened...about my biological father."

His hands clutched into fists as he continued. "When Layla was twenty-two one of her friends pushed her into going to a college party. Of course the party ended up getting out of hand. Some stupid drunk jerk raped her."

My eyes widen as realization hit. Kennley wasn't looking at me anymore as he stared off into the distance. He relaxed his fist a little and continued. "Thank God she had more morals than to just get an abortion... although no one would have blamed her if she did. The plan was to give me up for adoption but as soon as she had me in her arms for the first time plans changed. She kept me....but then things got harder. I remember that look in her face that she always had around me. I was young still, but it was kind of hard to forget a look like that. The look she gave me would send chills up my spine. It was hard enough dealing with the fact that she had been raped, but then dealing with a child too... Looking into my face knowing that that sick jerk is in there. It didn't help any that she was completely broke living on her own, and her family was angry with her for not pressing charges. She gave me up for adoption at six and not too long after Dena and Conner adopted me, and then Jimmy."

"Like I said earlier, at fifteen I convinced Dena to let me go find my birthmother. I had so many questions I wanted to be answered. So eventually I found her. She lived in Chicago. When Layla saw me it was that same look. She was drunk and told me all of this about the party, about how she barely even knew my father and didn't want to press charges. Needless to say, it kind of messed me up hearing all of that...Knowing that I wasn't even a love child, just the consequence of a crime that no one wanted."

"I started getting into all sorts of trouble. And once you've been expelled from enough schools you learn that it gets harder for any other ones to accept you. We moved here when I was sixteen. I fell in with the wrong people I guess. At the time I had refused to go to school. Dena then— as hard as it was for her— threatened to throw me out if I didn't start going again. She gave me a long lecture about college education and my future. So I started going back again but then I ended up getting expelled from Crest Moore and I transferred here. And now we have made a complete circle." He drew a circle in the air with his fingers.

I was amazed how he could say all of this with such an even voice while my fingers underneath the table were somewhat trembling. I stared at him incredulously. My mouth was open and I was pretty sure that at any moment the drool would start pouring out of my mouth. I couldn't even begin to process everything I had just heard. I could tell he was waiting for me to say something but I didn't. I could feel the color fading in my skin. I wasn't even sure if I was breathing.

"Are you okay?" He looked like he wanted to reach

across the table and touch my hand but he didn't... probably knowing I would have pulled it away. So instead he finished up his ice cream.

I didn't answer at first. I had never felt so disoriented in my life.

"Y-y-yeah...I'm fine. Just give me a second to process all of that."

I couldn't imagine how I would feel if I were Kennley. What an awful situation.

"What is your family like?" I tried to steady my voice.

"Well there are my siblings, Jimmy and Carrie. Jimmy is adopted just like me. It was just me and him for a while until I was eleven and we all got a surprise. Dena had been trying to have a child for years but she couldn't so that's why she adopted Jimmy and me. Then all of a sudden she's pregnant out of nowhere! She calls Carrie the miracle child." He grimaced. "Don't get me wrong, I love her and all but she is a *nightmare*. But, Jimmy's fourteen and Carrie's six. I already told you about Carrie, but Jimmy is sort of the opposite of her." I watched as his expression stiffened slightly. "Everyone says he's just like *me*, except quieter. He usually stays up in his room and reads all day. Then my dad, Conner and my mom Dena are possibly the oddest couple I have ever come across. They are so extremely different that it puts new meaning of opposites attract. Conner hates football; Dena would rob a bank if it meant she could go to the Superbowl. Conner could live off of snickers candy bars and Dena hates chocolate...the list could go on and on. They have absolutely nothing in common whatsoever. I still don't understand their relationship to this day."

I smiled slightly playing with the straw inside my

shake. I was happy that despite his crappy situation he had a good family now.

"Kennley..." I hesitated. "Earlier you said you fell in with the wrong people. Are those wrong people your friends now?"

I saw his body stiffen. "Some, yes."

"So, is that the real reason you wouldn't introduce me to them that night?" I asked slowly.

He sighed. "Kahlen, I told you...I just don't think that they are your kind of people."

I rolled my eyes. "Why?" I demanded. "If they're not my kind of people then doesn't that put *you* in that same category?"

This threw him for a second. "It's not the same." He paused. "I'm not the same as I used to be. I hang out with them a lot but I don't do what they do."

"Well what *do* they do?"

He sighed again. "They get into trouble a lot. Let's just leave it at that. I don't even like hanging out with them as much anymore."

We both didn't say anything for a while. I watched as he looked at me quickly and then down at his empty bowl. "So..." he began. "About this morning..."

I took a deep breath. "What about it?"

I knew he we were eventually going to have this conversation. I felt bad enough already without having to sit here and look at the pain touch those deep green eyes again...the pain that I caused. I knew without a doubt I still had feelings for Kennley and he did for me. But did that mean I was willing to change my mind about things so quickly? I tried to go over all the reasons in my head and I remembered what Jenny had said earlier.

"All those reasons you listed...it seems like things

you could work out if you wanted it to…not just give up."

I tried to tell myself that she was wrong…that I wasn't giving up although I knew deep down I was.

"Kahlen, I can tell you that I'm sorry…but I don't think that exactly solves things between us. I think there's something else."

I didn't say anything, waiting for him to continue.

"I think you're scared. I think that me saying that I loved you—," Just him saying it now sent a chill down my spine— "scared you…that maybe you might love me back…that you might end up getting hurt."

"No," I protested a little too quickly.

He grinned. "I won't hurt you. I promise you that if I do you can punch me in the face as hard as you want."

"I'll hold you to that." I smirked. I realized what my words could be construed as. "Not that anything's changed…" I said quickly.

"I know. But I just don't want to lose you…"

"Kennley—,"

"Not just that…I meant as a friend," he said.

I didn't know if Kennley and I could be friends without it being awkward. I knew it would be inevitable and I didn't want to spend my time pretending like it wasn't. I looked down at the table avoiding making eye contact.

"I don't know." I managed to get out. "I don't think its best."

He nodded. "I understand."

I looked up from the table shocked. It was completely out of Kennley's character to give up so easily. I was waiting for him to say something more but he didn't. I narrowed my eyes…he had to have something up his sleeve.

The waitress came to our table and took away Kennley's empty bowl. I looked down at my milkshake that I hadn't touched. Abruptly I took a sip of my shake. It was smooth and cold going down my throat and sent shivers down my spine. I had gotten through half of it by the time I got a huge brain freeze. I winced and grabbed my head. It wasn't long before I heard Kennley laughing. I wanted to say something but it would only make it worse…it was by far the longest brain freeze had ever had.

"Try pressing your tongue to the roof of your mouth," he suggested.

I did as told and saw he was still smiling amused. The pain in my head disappeared slowly.

"It worked." I said shocked.

"See," he said. "What would you do without me?"

I sighed. "The same thing I was doing before I tripped and rolled into your leg."

He smiled briefly before his face was serious. "Kahlen, I'm done hiding things from you, I promise." He reached over and put my hand in his. "Don't throw two months down the drain."

I looked away from him. I knew that if I looked him in the eyes I might change my mind. I slowly slid my hand away from his and into my lap.

"I think I should go home now."

All he did was look at me and smile like he was enjoying some private joke. It reminded me of how he had been smiling earlier when we had first gotten here.

"What are you smiling about?" I asked truly curious.

He started laughing now.

"I can't tell you that…not now anyways." He stood

up from our booth and I followed his lead confused. "You'll find out tomorrow."

I sighed. "Well what were you smiling about earlier?"

He smiled again just thinking about it. "I don't think you want to know."

I grew more curious. "Are you *hiding* something?" I challenged.

He sighed almost blushing. "Earlier…you were angry. And I thought that you looked…cute with that little scowl on your face that only grew wider as I smiled more."

I grimaced as my cheeks burned red. He was right…I didn't want to know. I knew that no matter what, he was going to try and make breaking up harder than it had to be.

"You never did tell me what you were angry at beside's life's wrath," he said.

We got up out of the booth and when we got to the door he held it open for me and I tried not to make anything out of this simple gesture. He was just so persistent.

"It was just some things Bradley was saying." I said.

Kennley groaned as we got into his car. "*What is his problem*?" He turned the key in the ignition hard. "What did he say to you?" he demanded.

I looked at him with my eyes wide. I could only think of one other time I had seen him this angry before. "He said a lot of things. He told me that you were trying to manipulate me into getting back with you and that you weren't good for me. He said that he wanted to talk to me about some things but I left before he could."

He sighed. "He just doesn't let things go does he? I should have known as much."

I watched confused as he gripped the steering wheel tighter.

"Ugh." He sighed. "What is it with blackmailing these days?" he vented. He looked over at me and his eyes were apologetic once he saw the puzzled look on my face. "Bradley's been blackmailing me. On my first day of school when I told the principal he ditched me I didn't know that Bradley was going to get in trouble or anything. The principal called him in the office to talk with him. It was just all too convenient for Bradley that my file was sitting on the desk when the principal had to leave the office for a second. Bradley saw all the trouble I had been in. The next day out of nowhere he came up to me and asked if I liked you. Before I could even answer he told me to stay away from you or he'd tell you everything he knew."

My jaw dropped. A couple of weeks ago I would have never believed this. I'd always ignored his behavior. My only reason for it was...Bradley would be Bradley.

"He was satisfied with us just being friends...and then thrilled for those couple of weeks when we weren't talking. I thought he had told you everything about me then and I was surprised you'd believe a stupid rumor from Bradley...no matter how true it was," he continued.

I put my hand to my face shocked. "I don't understand this. Bradley and I barely talk. It doesn't make sense for him to want you to stay away from me."

Bradley and I had barely been acquaintances throughout all three years of high school. We had had a couple of classes with each other, friendly waves and hellos in the hallways but nothing more. I remembered freshman year he helped me understand the inner workings of Shakespeare's mind through *Romeo and*

Juliet, and then sophomore year when he kept me focused on not passing out while dissecting a frog.

Before I knew it, we were in the school parking lot beside my mom's car.

He snorted. "You wouldn't understand…it's a guy thing. We tend to have territorial issues."

I rolled my eyes. That stupid Y chromosome had as many benefits as it did disadvantages.

"Ha! Like girls aren't territorial when it comes to guys…but you don't see us peeing on trees and fire hydrants to mark our territory. We have different ways."

Kennley chuckled. "Last time I checked I wasn't peeing on fire hydrants or trees.

"Duly noted." I smiled and he smiled back.

I fought to compose my face. I didn't want to be friends with Kennley…I knew I would be weak and give in. I wanted things to go back to the way they were before I met him.

"*Do you really*?" She said.

I started to unbuckle my seat belt. I reached for the car door and he reached for my arm. It wasn't like the other times when Bradley and Sean had grabbed my arm. His hand was firm around my wrist and yet somehow gentle…relaxed.

"Wait," he said. "Will I see you tomorrow?"

I knew he was referring to the creek. "Kennley I—," I stopped my sentence short. One look at those eyes made me want to make him happy. "I…" I looked away from his eyes and out the window. "Yes. You will see me tomorrow…at *school*— locker neighbor."

He let go of me and that same wicked smile crossed his face. I didn't even bother asking why.

"See you then," he said as I stepped out of the car. I walked over to my mom's car and sat down.

He didn't pull off yet waiting for me to leave first. I ignored him and reached in my pocket to pull out my keys which I had shoved in there earlier. My heart sank quickly to my stomach as I realized my pockets were empty.

Kennley silently held the ring of keys dangling from his index finger waiting for me to turn and notice. I got back out of my car and snatched the keys away from him.

"They fell out of your pocket." he said innocently. "Just like I fell for you."

I put my hand to my face as I hopped back into the car fighting back a smile.

He grinned. "It's okay. You can laugh. I was aiming for corny actually." He shrugged. "Although my favorite pick up line is: Did you have Campbell's soup today? Because you're looking mmm…mmm …good."

I sighed turning the key in the ignition. "Could you at least pretend to be somewhat rational for five seconds?" I had to admit that I was still fighting back a smile.

He scrunched up his face. "You know…it's not really my style."

Not wanting to prolong the conversation I pulled out of the parking lot leaving Kennley there without so much as a goodbye.

"*I give you a week,*" she said.

I sighed. I'd give me a week too.

14. Gifts

It seemed like any time I closed my eyes for a long period of time my reoccurring nightmare would appear. It was the same horrible dream, the one with me in the hospital. It was all I could really remember from everything that had happened. I didn't dare try to remember anything else so I wasn't sure if I could.

I remembered how those slightly off-white walls were driving me away from my sanity. Just the anxiety of waiting was enough to make me sick to my stomach. It didn't matter how many times I told everyone that I was fine, they all treated me like I had two broken legs and four broken ribs. I wasn't really aware of all that had happened. I remembered hitting my head pretty hard and having a really big headache.

I tried to think of something else while I lay in my bed restless. I opened my eyes. There was no use in sleeping anyhow. I was surrounded by the darkness unable to see anything accept the moonlit sky outside my window. This was how I was spending most of my nights...lying in my bed not sleeping. I tried, I prayed to dream or think about something else but I couldn't. It was the never ending nightmare. As much as I wanted to escape it there was no way out. I considered closing my eyes and letting the nightmare finish and take its course but then quickly changed my mind. I hated nighttime. I was so edgy and restive as I sat staring up at my white ceiling that I couldn't see because of the darkness. As much as I loved how pretty the Creek was at nighttime, I was too lazy to climb out of my window and leave.

So I was forced to lay for about four more hours in the darkness and think. If I wasn't thinking about the hospital and everything else that had to do with that, then I was thinking about Kennley.

I hated him…or at least I wanted to hate him. It reminded me of the movie *Ten Things I Hate About You* …which made me want to hate him more. It wasn't fair that he made me smile when I didn't want to and that he had a way of cheering me up when I was focused on loathing him. He had a way of seeming so immature at one point and then completely different at the next. I sighed. I didn't want to think about him either. I was trying to convince myself that I didn't have feelings for him…that I never did. It was such a lie, even I knew that. I knew this whole thing was stupid. Our break-up barely made any sense. All the time something in the back of my head was nagging at me about it and I didn't need the silence now to remind me of it.

I rubbed my sleepy eyes with my hands. I wanted the school day to come sooner so I didn't have to sit here and stew in the dark. I closed my eyes and tried to dream happy dreams. I would have settled for something like ponies flying on clouds or jumping over rainbows at this point but I wasn't so lucky. I tried to force images into my mind about stuff I wanted to dream about but nothing worked. I sighed and lifted my hands up and slammed them down hard beside me. I was so frustrated. I wanted to sleep. I was so incredibly tired but I knew that just like every other night, I wasn't going to.

If I wasn't going to get a new car, then the least my parents could do was put a TV into my room so I'd have something to do at night. I had to accept it. This was my life now. There was no use in trying to change it because sometimes it was just easier to settle.

"But you don't have to settle," she said.

My eyes were beginning to ache. I didn't care anymore about what I dreamed. The sleepiness was overwhelming. My heavy eyelids shut and didn't open again until I saw the sun peeking out over the clouds in the sky. It wasn't my alarm that woke me up but the birds chirping annoyingly outside my window.

I showered and dressed slowly. I was still so extremely tired that I couldn't move faster if I tried. I went down the stairs at snail speed and ate my breakfast slowly also. It was then that I realized that something was wrong. I looked around and peeked around the corner to look up the stairs. I made the small revelation that I was alone here. I looked at the clock panicked that I might be late for school. My heartbeat slowed with relief as I realized I still had plenty of time before school. But I was alone. Neither one of my parents were here which was odd. I hadn't even heard them get up this morning.

I felt stupid once I saw the big neon piece of paper hanging on the refrigerator.

Sweetie,

I figured you weren't paying attention last night when I told you that both I and your father had to go to work early. Guessing you still don't need to borrow my car so you'll ride with Kennley.

-Mom.

I crumbled up the stupid note in my hands and threw it in the trash. I would rather walk to school than ride with Kennley. I had no idea on how I was supposed to get to school. I pondered on not going there at all and maybe I could just stay at home, blast music all day, and dance to *Old Time Rock and Roll* in my underwear. It wasn't like my parents would have found out. I could easily lie and say I was sick if they did. What other choice did I have besides Kennley anyhow? For a very brief second I considered calling Marissa and then quickly shook it off.

I went outside with my backpack and sat on the porch looking out onto the street. There was really no point in me sitting out here but it gave me something to do. I thought about going to the Creek but I wouldn't dare in fear of seeing him there.

Out of nowhere, maybe out of my imagination, a dark BMW came into view. I squinted trying to see if it was really there in front of me. I was just so groggy that I was sure if I was daydreaming or not. The BMW pulled into my driveway and stopped. I stood up and started to walk down the porch stairs. I was blinded by the sun's rays and completely missed the next step in front of me. Before I knew it my balance was gone and I was tripping over both my feet. I fell down the tiny steps and landed hard to the ground. I didn't move, hoping I was dead. A tiny groan escaped my mouth as I put my hand to my head. I heard a car door open and footsteps running over to me. I opened my eyes and I could see a long shadow cast over me. I didn't dare look up at him.

"Kahlen?" he said. "Are you okay?"

I was positive my cheeks were bright red and I patiently waited for his laughter to begin but it didn't. I rolled over on my back so that I was looking up into the sky. My eyes still didn't meet his. He sat down beside me and lay down in the same position I was in.

"You are so..." He paused looking for the right word.

"So...*weird*. You have no idea how many hours of the day I spend trying to figure you out."

"You mean that whole puzzle thing?" I said thinking about one of our previous conversations.

"Yes, exactly. You never do what I expect you to do and it can be so frustrating."

"So you prefer to be around predictable people?"

"No," he answered quickly. "If everything in life were predictable then wouldn't things just be extremely boring?"

"Sometimes boring is good. It's easier that way. If life were predictable then we'd know which way to turn to dodge a bullet. We'd known how to get ourselves out of crummy situations."

"But sometimes bad situations are good. Sometimes life forces us into a change or a learning experience," he said. "Just because it seems bad at the surface, doesn't mean there can't be more lurking beneath."

I sighed. "What are we really talking about here because you just lost me in this semi-hypothetical conversation of ours?"

He chuckled. "I don't know...I think I'm lost too."

A couple of seconds went by before I said, "I fell. And it hurt. And then you didn't laugh...and now we are still on the ground," I said recapping everything that had just happened. Stating the obvious.

"I'll admit it was somewhat funny but I stifled my laughter. I thought I'd show you my sensitive and compassionate side...just so you can know all of what you're giving up."

I sighed. "Kennley—,"

"So do you need a ride to school? I was sitting at your creek—not waiting for you or anything, I already figured you wouldn't show—and then I saw your mom's car go by with her in it."

"Didn't you think I might borrow my dad's car then?"

"I did for a second, but I wasn't going to pass up the opportunity anyway."

I thought about if I had gone to the creek today. Kennley and I would be laying the same position staring up into the sky.

"You know if we don't leave soon we're gonna be late," he said. I got up from the ground very slowly. Kennley was already to the car by the time I had gotten my backpack off the porch. As I got into the car he said, "Can I ask you something?"

"Yeah, but it doesn't mean I'll answer.

"Fair enough," he shrugged pulling out of the driveway. "It seems like lately you avoid making eye contact with me. Why is that?"

I crossed my arms over my chest and stared out the window still avoiding eye contact. "You're very observant."

He grinned. "It seemed like an easy question to me."

I smiled. "Never mind then. You're not as observant as I thought you were."

That threw him for a second. "I have another question."

I waited anxiously for him to continue.

"Did someone punch you in the eye?"

I sighed. I had tried my best to use make-up to cover up the very dark circles underneath my eyes.

"I don't really sleep much."

"That's unfortunate."

I yawned and nodded still staring out the window.

For the rest of the ride it was pretty much embarrassing because every five seconds I would involuntarily yawn yet another time.

Kennley sighed. "If you're so sleepy then why didn't you just stay home and sleep in a little?"

He had no idea how hard sleeping actually was. "Well I was thinking about staying home until you showed up."

He grinned. "Yeah, well I have a way of changing people's minds."

"*You* didn't change my mind. I'm too stubborn for someone to change my mind. And besides…I couldn't afford to miss a day of school anyways. I have a lot of work to do before exams next week. We all can't skip school occasionally like you do."

"I don't skip school all the time…Just periodically. Everything is so predictable and routine. And I have good grades. I could probably fail all of my exams and still pass most of my classes."

I just sat there gawking at him. He was unbelievable. Of course someone like him could pull off good grades just to fit in with life's unfair pattern.

"How is that possibly possible? No one transfers school half way through the semester and isn't stressed about exams."

He shrugged. "School just comes easy to me I guess."

"Well my grades could probably be better if I made an effort to pay attention. I think my main problem is that I'm too stubborn. I don't have enough will power to force myself to listen. But mostly I have to be worried about English. I'm doing so awful in that class."

He didn't answer right away. I hated when he did that because I could tell he was thinking about something and it drove me crazy. He would always take his time, leaving me anxious.

"You know, Kahlen, this seems to be a pretty friendly conversation we're having here. I didn't forget about what you said yesterday but I think we could still manage to be friends at the very least."

I looked over at his face quickly and then back out the window wishing he would drive faster.

"...And maybe I could help you with English if you want," he said.

I shut my eyes closed and sighed. This was so stupid. I should have been able to be friends with him but I couldn't. I didn't want to deal with the awkwardness. I wanted to be stubborn and I wasn't going to let him change my mind.

Almost on cue we arrived at school. I was all too eager to jump out of the car and get away from him. Kennley and I both got out of his car and started to walk towards the school.

"By the way," he said. "I'm stubborn too you know. That's why it's usually easy to change peoples' minds."

I grinned a little. "Then I guess you've met your match."

"Yeah, I know." He sighed. "I'm starting to have my doubts on this one too."

We continued to walk towards the school in silence until it was suddenly interrupted. I scowled as one of the she-devils started walking our way. Kennley noticed my reaction but didn't say anything. She walked over by us and actually bumped me out of the way. I just looked at her shocked. I thought it was the kind of thing that only happened in movies, not in real life. While I was pushed off to the side I rolled my eyes at her mini skirt and tight pink tank top. I guess Marissa and Bradley had done their job well with spreading the word that we were broken up although Marissa still thought we were secretly together.

I quickened my pace to get further away from her...

but not without glancing back at the two of them. She had her arm linked around his while gazing up at him. As much as I didn't want to be, I was happy that Kennley didn't really seem to be paying attention to her.

"Kennley Morgan!" she squeaked.

"Hi, Megan," he said flatly.

"I feel like I haven't talked to you in forever. But anyways, with our big chapter test coming up on Friday I was wondering if you could tutor me. I'm so bad at calculus and you're a genius so...?"

I walked away quicker not wanting to hear his response. When I no longer heard their footsteps behind me, I couldn't stop myself from taking one more glance back at them. They had stopped walking and she was smiling and had her hand on his bicep. Kennley seemed indifferent...not that I cared. I didn't care what Kennley did. He was no longer any of my business so that she-devil could have him if she wanted.

When I got to my locker I slammed it open...not that I was angry at all. Inside of my locker was a little light blue box with a dark blue bow on the top. Extremely curious I held the box gently in my hands. There had to be a mistake. Someone probably had the wrong locker. I turned the box softly in my hand and saw my name written on the other side. It said, *from Kennley*. I put the box back in my locker and slammed it shut as if I was making some big point.

I didn't understand why he even tried. Maybe he only wanted me because I was a challenge to him. He had said it himself that I was unpredictable. It felt like a game he was trying to win. I couldn't see myself as desirable anyhow. I was damaged goods. I couldn't even have a guy tell me he loved me without breaking up with him the next day.

I sighed as I realized I still had to get my books out

of my locker. I put in the combination and opened it again. I unzipped my backpack to put the box in it. I was shocked when I saw another little box with dark blue ribbon on top. I was incredulous. How did he get into my locker and my backpack without me even knowing? It was all craziness. I snatched the first box from my locker and shoved in my backpack with the second.

It wasn't long before I saw Kennley walking in with Megan not too far behind. She waved goodbye to him and took off down the hall, but not before giving me a dirty look. I didn't even understand why she hated me. I had done nothing do her. Up until today I didn't even know her name.

Kennley walked to his locker and opened it with ease. I looked at him, waiting for him to say something about the little boxes that kept appearing out of nowhere. But he didn't. He put his books into his backpack slowly while whistling a random tune. He was enjoying this ...that much was obvious. I suddenly understood what he meant when he had said yesterday: *"I can't tell you that...not now anyways." "You'll find out tomorrow."*

He walked over to me and leaned against the locker. I watched as he peeked in it quickly looking to see if the box was still there.

"You know..." he said. "You're very entertaining to watch when you're *jealous*.

I sighed. I tried to think of something to say back but I couldn't. As much as I didn't want to admit it, I was a tiny bit jealous. No girl truly wants their ex-boyfriend to move on. We all secretly hope that they'll still pine from afar. So I stood there looking at him with my mouth half open like I was about to say something.

"I..." I started to say. "You're..." I watched as his smile grew bigger. I could not think of one comeback. I decided I didn't care what Kennley thought. I slammed my locker closed. "Ugh!" I said through my teeth before stomping off away from him.

It didn't take long for me to realize that my back felt really light. I walked back to my locker and picked up my backpack off the ground. Kennley was still leaning in his same position, looking amused.

"Oh..." I said. "And I'm not jealous by the way." I was acting like I was five. "I just think that you could do better than Megan...heck, anyone could do better than her."

"Well if not Megan than *who*?" he raised an eyebrow. "Did you happen to have anyone in mind?"

He was so ridiculous. I should have known he wasn't going to give up so easily...but it didn't mean I was going to give in.

"You are impossible," I said slowly before walking off to my first class.

I sat down in my usual chair in the back of the room waiting for class to start. I tried to think of something else besides Kennley...anything else. I was tempted to open the two boxes but I fought myself on it. I needed to stay strong. Looking at whatever was in those boxes wouldn't help my trying to get over him.

I hated English class. Not because of the people in the actual class but because of Mr. Simmons. He was the so called hot twenty something teacher. Every other girl in his class would be swooning as soon as they saw him. I preferred sticking to boys my own age or no boys at all. Mr. Simmons would still always give me that same stupid pity look. It had faded somewhat over the weeks but it was still there, permanently on his face.

Before I knew it class was over in a blur and I couldn't recall anything that had happened in the last forty five minutes. I was so angry at myself. I needed to do well in this class. I knew it would probably be best to ask Mr. Simmons for extra credit before final exams next week. It would be somewhat embarrassing to ask him because of the last time we had spoken privately. I had been rude to him and things had kind of been awkward since then but I didn't have a choice now. I had to ask.

As everyone filed out of the classroom I was hesitant to ask but I did. I walked slowly towards his desk. "Mr. Simmons." I said in my sweetest, most innocent, teacher's pet voice I could.

He looked up at me surprised.

"I was wondering if I could do some kind of extra credit to help boost my grade," I continued.

He grinned slightly. "I don't really have any extra credit work available. But…if you wanted to take up my offer from before, you could make up that test that you got a zero on."

I hated him. "There has to be something else I could do. I mean…that test was from two or three chapters ago!" I really and truly hated this man.

"Exactly…that way it will be good review for exams."

I sighed giving up. "When should I come in to take it?"

"Thursday. Seven-thirty."

Just like Kennley, he was enjoying this.

"Thank you."

I walked out of his classroom. I was appreciative for the extra credit but I felt like I was losing some kind of secret war. And I hated losing.

I walked back to my locker and saw another little box, blue bow on top, set neatly in my locker. I sighed. I had no idea how he was even breaking into my locker.

It was all so ridiculous. I took the other two boxes out of my backpack and put them back with the others. Maybe Kennley was under the misconception that I wanted his presents and that I was opening them. If I left them all in the locker he might get the idea that I didn't want them.

After I had gone to my locker a couple more times throughout the day I was convinced they had stopped. When I walked into the cafeteria I was unsuspecting that Marissa would hand me a little box with blue ribbon on top. She told me that Kennley wanted her to give it to me. She looked at me anxiously waiting for me to open it. But I shoved it into my backpack and Jenny cracked a smile. I had explained to her about all the gifts earlier today in art and of course she thought it was sweet and romantic. I didn't see it that way. It seemed like he was trying to prove a point...win a game.

I was almost positive that the gifts would stop by the end of the day when I finally went back to my locker. I let out a sigh of relief when there wasn't a little box propped neatly on the rest of my books. Bradley walked over to me and towered like he always did.

A bad mood washed over me. Bradley had that affect. I was contemplating on slamming my locker in his face and stomping away.

"I know you hate me and all, but I just wanted to say I'm sorry." He said. "I sort of crossed the line yesterday and it wasn't right. I just didn't want to see you get hurt and I honestly thought I was trying to help. You're a good person so I should trust your judgment in guys... but beyond that, I still think there's really something you should know." He said.

"Kennley already told me everything if that's what you're getting at. And it doesn't really matter to me.

We're still broken up not that it's any of your business but I appreciate your apology just the same."

His attention was distracted to something at the top of my locker that I couldn't see. He reached up in the top compartment and pulled out a tiny box with a blue bow and handed it to me.

I repressed a sigh. "You know, I think that they only made those top compartments for people like you who are six foot two to put us medium height people to shame."

He shrugged. "Actually it's about six foot three these days."

I put all of the boxes in my backpack and Bradley just looked at me eyes wide.

"He really doesn't give up, does he?" he said.

"No." I zipped up my backpack. "He doesn't."

After a second of standing there awkwardly, Bradley took me into a tight hug as if to make the apology official. As soon as I was out of sight, I shuddered. I never wanted to be forced into a hug by Bradley ever again.

On my way out to the parking lot I saw Jenny running up to me smiling. But I wasn't…not when I saw what was in her hand. She handed the box to me amused.

"Are you ever going to open these?"

I shrugged and put it with the rest of the boxes. I continued to walk towards Kennley's car which he was leaning against waiting for me with a smug smile on his face. I sighed as I walked closer. I walked past him quickly and opened the door for myself to make a point, figuring he would try and open it for me. I was about to sit down when I saw another box sitting on my seat. I ignored his glare on my forehead and put the box with the rest. He sighed and walked around to the other side of the car and got in.

"So how was your day?" he asked casually.

"Very...very...*blue*." I answered.

"Oh, and why is that?" he said with such innocent eyes.

"I don't know," I played along. "It just kind of seemed to be *following* me."

He just nodded.

The rest of the ride home was silent until we made it to my house. Before I got out of the car he placed a little box with a big red bow on top. I raised both my eyebrows.

"Doesn't this mean anything to you," he asked. "... that you're not easy to give up and I won't without a fight?"

I had nothing to say to him. I gave him a weak smile and thanked him for the ride before I walked into my house. He was making this so much harder than it had to be. I didn't want to hurt him, but it seemed like every time I was with him I could see the pain touch those green eyes. I went upstairs to my bedroom and dumped all of the boxes out my backpack. The red one was so conspicuous against all the blues. I decided to save that one for last. As much as I knew that opening the boxes would do anything but help with the goal I was trying to accomplish, I couldn't help my curiosity anyway.

I realized that on the bottom the boxes there were numbers. I opened box number one and saw a little note folded inside. I opened the note quickly.

Kahlen,

Once upon a time you told me you told me that you didn't have a favorite color. I have a hard time believing that considering most of your clothes are blue. So if you're wondering why most of these are blue...there's your answer. And if you haven't figured it out yet, look in the bottom of the box before you move on to the rest.

I looked at the bottom on the box underneath the tissue paper and saw a red puzzle piece. I took out the puzzle piece and placed it on my bed.

I moved on to box number two.

Kahlen,

I don't care if you're afraid of getting hurt, or that you can be so incredibly stubborn half of the time. I don't care…and I'm hoping that you won't either.

I pulled another red puzzle piece from the bottom of the box and put it by the first one before moving onto box number three.

Kahlen,

When I think about that beautiful girl in the black dress tumbling down the hill it makes me laugh every time. After that day I wouldn't have thought that you'd ever give me the time of day at all.

I kept up with the pattern and took out the puzzle piece and set it with the others before moving onto box number four.

Kahlen,

After getting to know you for a couple of weeks, I knew that I didn't want to be just your friend. I was incredibly unsure of your feelings which only made things frustrating

I quickly put the next puzzle piece with the other and moved onto the last blue box, number five.

Kahlen,

…but then out of nowhere, that kiss. I can't even begin to explain how confused I was. You acted like you hated me one moment, but then the next we were standing together in the rain. I realized something that day: Life without confusion was overrated.

I appraised the box with the red bow before I opened it. I was very curious as to why this one was red and all the other ones were blue.

Dean,

As you can see this one is a little bit different from the others. You may be wondering why that is. Well besides that the fact that blue is your unofficial favorite color; these two colors should remind you of a favorite something else of yours. Are you thinking about what red and blue reminds you of yet…? Spiderman. Despite my disapproval of the originality of being bitten by a stupid spider, I don't judge you for it. In case you haven't noticed, I love you. If you think I wasn't serious about standing outside your window and serenading you then you obviously know nothing about me.

Now I am finished, this is my last attempt to try and talk some sense into you. If I have possibly changed your mind at all, you know where to find me tonight; I get off of work at six. I promise that after tonight I'll leave you alone if you want…the decision is up to you. I've given you the puzzle pieces to my heart, I'm only asking for you to do the same.

Kennley

I sighed before digging in the bottom for the puzzle piece. I felt something strange by the puzzle piece underneath the tissue paper. I took the tissue paper out completely. The puzzle piece was blue with a keyhole in it. Beside it was a necklace with a tiny golden key hanging off of it that looked expensive. I put the puzzle pieces together and it formed a tiny red heart with a blue center. Kennley had given me his heart…and the key. I held the necklace in my hands for a long second. It was actually really pretty.

I couldn't understand why Kennley cared so much. I was beginning to feel overwhelmed that he did all of this for me. I didn't deserve it at the very least. Kennley could do better than me. He deserved someone who he wouldn't have to beg to be with him and someone that wasn't a heartless monster...someone who wasn't scared about every action they made before they made it. I really couldn't comprehend why he liked me so much. It didn't seem logical, reasonable...or even rational.

"*You always were extremely stupid sometimes. You never see anything clearly, including yourself*," she said.

I looked at my clock. I had a couple of hours before six. I was debating on even going to the creek or not. Maybe it was best if I didn't. Then he would move on just like I was trying to. I kept trying to convince myself that this was a mistake while at the same time I was contemplating on all the things to do to keep myself busy until six. I didn't have either of my parents here at the very least to sit and watch mind numbing TV with. My dad was *always* working these days and my mom spent most of her time at the office in her usual Hyde form.

I got ready as slowly as I could to help the time go by and then I went downstairs. I still had plenty of time left so I decided to make dinner. I actually knew how to cook very well to make up for my mom's lacking skills. I made baked chicken with mashed potatoes and steamed vegetables. That really helped the time fly by. I was practically rushing to get out the door when six came. I had the golden necklace in the pocket of my dark blue hoodie and speed-walked my way to the creek.

When I finally got there Kennley was of course sitting waiting like he always did...always beating me there. He smiled when he saw me which made my stomach feel uneasy. He stood up as I walked closer to him. I still hadn't made up in my mind why I had come here in the first place.

"Why?" I yelled taking the necklace out of my pocket. "Why did you do this? You shouldn't be the one trying to get me back; I should be trying to get you back. What I did earlier this week was stupid. I really didn't even have a good reason. And you're right...I am scared. After what happened earlier last month it seemed like it would be easier to push people away than get close to someone and end up losing them. I'm damaged goods. And it doesn't make sense Kennley! We don't make sense, were so different from each other. I was awful to you. Most of the time I have been, but you never stop! Why?" My voice cracked.

I didn't know why I was here. I was sure if this was me giving in or simply too curious to stay away. Either way, when Kennley stood up and slowly walked towards me my heart raced and slowed at the same time.

He took the necklace out of my hand and wordlessly put it around my neck. "I've already told you why. To tell you the truth I was a little unsure about us at first myself...then I realized that not everything has to make sense. I already told you about Dena and Conner, they're happily married. And think about corn starch and water. When you mix them together you get this nasty, watery goop. But then when you ball it up in your fist it's suddenly almost as hard as rock. Then when you release it, it goes back to the watery goop. It doesn't make sense and yet scientists are taking advantage of it for the world to make progress."

My breathing was crazy along with my rapid heartbeat. I felt like I had just run a mile.

"I honestly can't figure out why you like me. Even from the first time that we—,"

It took me a couple of seconds to realize he was kissing me. I could barely think now, let alone breathe. We were slowly moving backwards until my back was against the perfect shade tree. I could feel his fingers in my hair. I had completely lost my train of thought. The only thing I could think about was that Kennley had incredible lungs, but I didn't. I put my hands on his chest and pushed him away. I was so unbelievably disoriented that it took me a second to realize where I was. Kennley seemed content. He must have been able to see the surrender in my face. His face was still only inches from mine as he gave me room to breathe.

"Why..." I gasped. "...Are you so impulsive? You think you could let a person finish a sentence every now and again."

"Sometimes you have to be impulsive because if you think about it too long you'll talk yourself out of it." He was breathing hard too.

It didn't take long before his lips were on mine again. If my mind wasn't made up about Kennley and me when I got here, it was now.

"I have a confession to make," he murmured on my cheek while catching his breath.

"What—," I started to say before he interrupted me again. I couldn't focus on anything else but him at the moment. Multitasking was out of the picture.

"I lied."

I pulled back so I could stare at his face. His lips were red like mine probably were right now.

"In box number three or four…or maybe six, I said that if you didn't come here tonight that I would leave you alone. That was a lie. I probably still would have bothered you."

I nodded still disorientated and before I knew it, my back being pressed against the tree again. I didn't care anymore. At least if I did end up getting hurt, I would have lots of memories like these to look back on.

"I have a confession to make too," I gasped.

He didn't say anything waiting for me to explain.

"In first grade Peter Collins pulled down my shorts on a dare so I was left standing there in my underwear in front of everyone. I cried and ran out of the room but when I finally came back I drew my arm back and with all my might I punched that stupid jerk in the face. I actually made his nose bleed pretty badly. I can still punch pretty hard and I learned how to break a guy's nose from the movie *Miss Congeniality*."

It took him a second to understand how this story was at all relevant.

"I'm not going to hurt you Kahlen. I may disappoint you, but I won't hurt you. And besides, I said you could punch me in the face, not break my nose."

"Ha! As if I would need your permission, yesterday all you were giving me was a suggestion."

"Fine…I don't need to argue about this with you anyways because you're never going to need to punch me," he said.

"Never say never."

He kissed me quickly. "But it so much *fun*. It definitely makes my top words list."

I smiled.

"Oh and by the way I'm not tutoring Megan."

I shrugged…it wasn't like I actually cared about them in the first place.

"Is lying to yourself as fun as you make it seem?" she said.

He chuckled. I knew he wasn't buying my I-don't-care shrug. "When I saw that look you gave her and then the way she pushed you out of the way I realized that maybe I could use the situation to my advantage. You're actually quite entertaining when you jealous." He repeated.

I sighed. "How many times do I have to say I wasn't jealous?"

"Enough until you actually start believing that lie yourself." He grinned.

I sighed. "I should get home. My parents should be there soon and they'll be wondering where I am."

Our faces were still only inches from each other and Kennley seemed reluctant in moving back away from me. I slipped out his grasp and stumbled my way off of the grass still disoriented. Things had changed so much in only a matter of minutes...although I knew that it took less than that to completely turn your life around.

I heard his footsteps coming closer behind me. "You might not want to go back like that though," he said.

Before I could ask why, he reached and pulled a piece of bark from the tree out of my hair.

I smiled at him briefly and started to walk away but he was walking with me.

"How about I walk you home?" he said. "For safety precautions of course... It's getting late and the buddy system always prevails."

But it wasn't a question. We started to walk off in the opposite direction of the creek towards my house.

I smiled. "Yes... for safety precautions."

15. Ambushed

Flabbergasted didn't exactly describe how I felt sitting in Kennley's house. It was huge. I couldn't even wrap my mind around how big it was. He was obviously loaded...that was evident. He lived in a very prestigious neighborhood just outside of Crest Moore where all the houses were as big as his. I wouldn't have been surprised if I saw maids and butlers scrambling around but I didn't...not that I didn't think they had enough money to. They even had an indoor pool and hot tub. I was completely speechless. The only other time I had seen houses like this was on *Cribs*. I finally understood why Kennley had such a nice car. Kennley didn't really seem to notice my reaction to his mansion. He seemed more focused on his siblings than anything else.

Carrie was forever running down the spiral staircase or throwing mini marshmallows at Kennley's head. I understood what he meant when he said that she treated annoying him like a part-time job. Every five seconds he was apologizing to me for all the distractions.

I had no idea what I was getting myself into when Kennley suggested a study date at his house while he was babysitting. I needed to study anyhow although I didn't really think I could focus. It wasn't until I got to his massive house that I realized that Kennley and I didn't have any of the same classes...his were all honors courses. He wasn't really studying himself, he was helping *me* study. I didn't want to focus on school anyhow. Even if Carrie wasn't bothering Kennley, I still wouldn't have been able to focus. Kennley all by himself was distracting.

"Okay." I said. "Um...first kiss." I had no idea how long Kennley and I had been asking each other random questions.

"Oh gosh..." he grimaced. "I think it was sometime in middle school. My friends dared me at a party to kiss Rose Johnson. They only picked her because they knew she had a crush on me." He grimaced again. "It was *awful*."

I sighed. "What is it with boys and dares? And besides, it couldn't have been *that* awful."

"You just can't back down from a dare...it's a macho thing. And it was awful because she was sick so when I kissed her I caught it. I had the stomach flu for a week." He winced. "You?"

"Peter Collins." I said his name slowly. He was that same stupid jerk who pulled down my pants in first grade. "I never did understand that one. Out of nowhere he just planted one on me...it was probably a *dare*."

"At least the guy had guts," he said shrugging. "But... funniest thing you've ever done."

It didn't take me long to decide what was the funniest. When I looked back on all of my funniest moments they were with Emma. I knew Kennley could see the expression change on my face. Emma had always been a kind of a taboo subject with us. He knew not to bring it up and I tried not to think about it.

"One time Emma and I had this crazy paint war...and it was inside the house too. We got paint everywhere. I had to shower for a good hour or so before I finally got all of it out of my hair. My clothes were completely ruined...and the walls were very *colorful*." I felt the usual twist in my stomach but it wasn't so bad this time. It was bittersweet. "What about you?"

"Well it wasn't a paint war, it was a water war. It lasted the whole day. It was so stupid. I don't even know how it got started. And then, the next thing I know my friends and I were chasing each other down the street with water guns. It was pretty hardcore," he said. "Craziest thing you've ever done?"

The craziest thing I had ever done was probably going on a rollercoaster or using the *spicy* cinnamon toothpaste in the morning... I had never done anything insane or wild. "Nothing," I said. Kennley should have known better than to think I could even answer that question.

"Come on, there has to be something."

"I over think things. There is no way I'd ever let loose and do something wild." It was the pathetic truth.

"I can change that." He was smug.

I smiled. "You changed my mind *once*; don't expect to do it again."

"Is that a challenge?" he asked. "Because if so, I'll gladly accept."

"Ha!" I snorted. "Fine, let's make it a bet," I offered.

He nodded. "If I get you to do something wild and crazy, in return, you have to give me whatever I want."

"Okay...I'm giving you a month, and if you don't by then, you have to give me whatever *I* want."

We shook on it.

He raised an eyebrow. "Well what do you want?"

"I haven't decided yet," I said. "What do you want?"

He grinned. "I have some ideas."

"Like..."

"Don't worry. You'll find out *soon*."

He was really very arrogant about this. Changing my stubborn mind wasn't as easy as he wanted to make it seem.

"I think you're a tad bit over confident."

He shrugged. "Most embarrassing thing that's happened to you recently."

The only thing that came to mind was when I was crying at the creek and Kennley came over and hugged me. That was beyond embarrassing.

"Next," I said.

"Oh come on, I'm sure it's not that bad."

"First love," I changed the subject.

I didn't really know what to expect for an answer. I immediately regretted it as soon as it came out of my mouth. At first I had assumed that maybe it would be me, but there was still a lot I didn't know about Kennley. I anxiously waited for his answer.

"Next."

"What?" I said. "Who?"

He shook his head no. I scooted closer to him on the couch in the front room. I put my hand on his arm and slid it down to his hand. "Just tell me…please?" My curiosity was getting the better of me.

He sighed. "If you can pass then why can't I?"

"Well if you won't tell me then I'll go ask Carrie. She seems to know all of your business. I bet she's probably eavesdropping on our conversation right now."

To show I wasn't bluffing I started to get up off the couch. He put his hand on my waist and I stopped.

"Fine." He said. "But you have to tell me your most embarrassing first."

I sighed. My cheeks were burning red just thinking about it. "Well…for starters, you were there. That day at the creek, I thought you had left but you hadn't. And I was standing there bawling my eyes out. I could barely even see you come up and hug me because everything was such a blur. *That* was extremely embarrassing."

"How is that embarrassing? You had every right to be upset.

I didn't want to think about it anymore. I shook my head. "Your turn."

He sighed. "Do you remember Hannah Andrews?"

I flinched at the name. I was hoping it would be someone I didn't know. I knew I needed to keep a good poker face but I was struggling.

"We um..." he said. "We used to date, for awhile."

"How long ago did you break up?" There was not one ounce of jealousy or spite in my voice...or at least I hoped there wasn't.

He put his head back on the white couch and looked up at the tall ceiling. "Does it matter?"

"I'm just curious that's all."

"About three months ago."

I tried not to grimace. Three months ago had only been one month before he met me and I was trying very hard to convince myself that I wasn't some kind of rebound from his stupid first love."Why?" I asked.

"She uh...things just didn't work out okay?"

I couldn't hold my poker face for much longer. Kennley was smarter than to believe that there was no storm brewing beneath the calm exterior. I didn't know Hannah really but he had just given me another reason to hate her. I hated her.

"Weirdest combination of food you've tried," I said, obviously not wanting to know anymore about his past relationship.

He looked at me shocked that I hadn't hounded him with more questions. He smiled. "Trust me, you don't want to know. I've done a lot of dares in my day."

Ugh...I could only imagine. "Dares are so stupid.

That's where guys are different from girls. We don't have to do stupid dares to prove ourselves."

He grinned. "I happen to think that guys are different from girls in a lot of other ways..." He filled in the tiny bit of room between us. "...Ways I could illustrate if you want."

He was so impossibly distracting. I sighed. "You do realize that it's your fault that I have been here an hour and we still haven't gotten any studying done."

All of my books were still sitting in my backpack like they had been since we first got here. Every time I brought up studying he would find some way to get me to drift away from it. I hadn't even realized what he was doing until I was knee deep.

"I already know all of this stuff," he said.

Kennley was a genius. Of course he didn't need to study. "*You* do. *I* however still need to study and you're not helping."

"Okay," he said. "What can I do to help?" He seemed faintly serious.

"Well..." I grabbed my backpack and slid my math book out of it and placed it on my lap. "I flipped the pages until I found what I was looking for. "I can't remember how to solve this problem."

He was trying to point out something to me in the math book, but he leaned over—closer than necessary, and laid his warm hand on mine gently with his other hand on the page of the book. I wasn't even listening to what he was saying. Studying was useless with him around. He went through everything on how to solve it but as he was talking he moved closer towards my face. I couldn't remember a thing he had just said. He was only millimeters away waiting for me to come that last centimeter.

"...Maybe this was a bad idea." I closed my math

book as he moved away. "I should probably study alone where it will be easier to focus. I can't afford to screw up exams." I zipped up my backpack.

"Okay. I'm sorry. I'll behave." He moved away from me on the couch. "Two foot distance." He got my math book and opened it back up for me.

I sighed. As much as I was saying that I wanted to study I didn't have the will power to. We started studying and I was already starting to feel overwhelmed by boredom. It hadn't even been that long and I was already sick of it. I had read once that when you put student and dying together...you get studying. It rang truth with every syllable. My brain was going into overdrive and it was going to melt.

"It's been five minutes and I'm already sick of studying." I whined. "I'll study when I get home. But for now...got any suggestions?"

He grinned. "I can think of a couple."

I should have known that he'd move closer and kiss—

"Good arvo, blokes!"

The front door swung open and the guy named Ben I had met before stepped in and then stopped abruptly. He saw Kennley and I down the hall sitting on the long white couch caught right in the act.

"Oh um...I'm such a *drongo*...I should have knocked first or at least rang the doorbell." He was speaking in what sounded like bad English or Australian accent. Ben walked closer toward us and Kennley and I were still in an awkward position.

Kennley stood up shocked. "What are you doing here? How did you even get in, the door was locked... and you're a *what*?"

Before Ben could answer someone else stepped

through the door. It was one of the other people I had seen at the movie theater that night but I didn't know.

"He stole your house key months ago and made copies." The guy said as he dangled the keys from his hand. "Oh and he said he's a drongo. That's Aussie slang for complete moron."

Kennley looked completely bewildered. He looked from me to his friends.

Someone else walked through the door. "Not one of those things again..." he said. "Jordan why do you even bother with these stupid games, you know Ben's not gonna back down."

I figured that Jordan was the second one that had come through the door with the darker skin and brown eyes while Ben was the one with the brown hair that looked like it had been cut since the last time I'd seen him. The last one that I wasn't sure of his name almost looked frightening. There was a tattoo of an elaborate cross on his right muscular arm. He looked just about as tall as Bradley just not as lanky and friendly with his short black hair.

I sat there on the couch uncomfortably alone while Kennley looked like he was staring at aliens.

"Are you kidding me?" Kennley said. "You guys are like clowns getting out of a tiny car..."

Hannah stepped through the door and leaned against the wall. "And were not finished yet,"

Kennley looked like he was about to have a heart attack as he put his head in his hands and sighed.

Ben turned to the rest of his friends. "We were kind of interrupting something here mates," he said in his accent.

Hannah went and stood by the one with the short black hair and tattoo. I assumed it was Ross. The image of Hannah at the mall with another guy flashed through my mind. It was obvious she was cheating on him. I wondered if she had done the same with Kennley. Just thinking of their relationship made my blood boil.

Ross sighed. "How long do you have to talk in that stupid accent for and say words like, *G'day*."

Jordan looked at his watch and shrugged. "He only has five more minutes."

Ben plopped next to me along with Jordan while Ross and Hannah still stood off to the side.

"Kennley," Ben said. "Are you all right there, bloke? You look *bloody* awful."

He did look pretty awful, almost pale for his regularly tanned skin. He looked at me and then at Ben and gave him a dirty look.

"Relax mate." Ben said. "We're only dropping by. We didn't know you had *company*." He turned to look and me. Suddenly the large couch was feeling very small. "Ross wanted to talk to you for a few, no need to be cranky. So you go talk, and Jordan and I will get to know beaut lass over here." He put his arm around me and shook me a little.

I felt my jaw drop a tiny bit at Ben's gesture but mostly in the back of my mind I wondered why Ross would have to make house calls just to talk to someone.

Kennley started to walk back over by me. "Benjamin, I swear—,"

"Ah don't worry, old bloke. We won't crack onto her."

Kennley just scowled at him. "What is that suppose to mean?"

Jordan on the other side of me opened a tiny book labeled Aussie Slang and flipped through it frantically. "Did you say crack a fat or crack onto? Because if you said crack a fat I don't think Kennley's going to be too happy."

Ben raised an eyebrow. "I said crack onto, but what does crack a fat mean?" He leaned over across my lap at the book Jordan had on the other side of me.

Jordan moved the book away from him. "I don't think I should say the meaning out loud. There are ladies present. But crack *onto* means to hit on someone or pursue them romantically," he read.

Kennley's lips were pressed into a tight line. "Listen I—,"

"Kennley," We all looked over at Ross who was standing against the wall with Hannah. He motioned for him to come over. "We need to talk…in private." His voice was deep and full of authority.

I watched confused as Kennley obediently followed Ross into a different room like a little puppy dog. It was easy to see who the alpha dog was.

I was so extremely confused. I was even more disoriented than I was yesterday at the creek.

Jordan held his watch to his face. "Three…two…one."

Ben sighed. "Finally!" he said in a normal accent. "I was getting so sick of that stupid accent and saying *mate* every other word. Although I did want to use bloody hell in a sentence again…it's pretty fun to say."

Hannah rolled her eyes and left out of the room. It was obvious that they had all been here before since they knew their way around.

Jordan threw his tiny book on a chair nearby. "Now we need a new game to play…" he sighed.

"Ping pong table?" Ben said.

Jordan smiled. "You know it!"

I smiled as they ran off like five year olds into another unknown room. So I sat there awkwardly alone on the big white couch in the center of the room…all by myself. I couldn't process half of the thoughts that were crossing my mind. Before I could even try Hannah interrupted all of that by walking back into the room and glaring at me. It was like she hated me as much as I hated her. I crossed my arms over my chest and stared straight ahead.

"So...Katie is it?" Hannah said. Her arms were crossed just like mine.

"It's Kahlen." Was there some kind of unknown curse on my name?

She slowly walked towards me and sat down as far away as she could on the couch next to me. "Ben said we were interrupting something with you and Kennley. I guess that's typical. *I* know how *handsy* he can get."

It was almost impossible to ignore her jab. I looked over at her unable to hide my frustration.

"So how serious are you two anyway? You two aren't *too* handsy I hope?" she continued.

I wanted to cut off all of that blond hair and shove it down her throat.

"How is that *any* of your business?" I spat.

She examined her dark red nail polish. "Oh it's not. But that's not something that would stop me from asking anyhow. And besides, I should have already known the answer. You look so *innocent*...like a new born lamb."

I didn't know whether to take offense to that or not. "And you're not *innocent*?"

She laughed. "I guess that depends on your definition of the word. I'm guessing that being the good boyfriend he is Kennley told you that the two of us have history. You should ask him how innocent I am...maybe that will answer how innocent he is too."

I knew I shouldn't have let her bother me but she did.

She sighed. "These double-meaning conversation bore me." She stood up off the couch. "Ross!" she yelled. "Hurry up!" She turned back to me and smiled. "Kennley's going through a phase. I guess he's looking for girls with *virtue* these days. Hmph, what a change... So hold on to him tight while you can...a phase can only last for so long. Oh and I guess he likes brunettes too in this little phase of his. Usually he dates blondes. You know what they say... my kind have more fun."

"What kind of *fun*?" I asked.

"Does it matter?" She chuckled, "Wow, Kennley was right on the dot when he told me about you. He also said that you were going through a really hard time about that friend of yours. Emily, was it? I guess that's what makes you such a good *rebound*. You know...the vulnerable type. That's always is an attractive quality with guys like him...very easily manipulated."

I had never dealt with someone being so mean without coming out and saying a whole bunch of horrible things. She was almost secretively mean. I just glowered at her speechlessly. Ross came out slowly with Kennley following behind. I couldn't believe that she had actually brought Emma into this without even saying her name. As much as I didn't want them to, I could feel the tears brimming at my eyes.

She was still smiling at me. "Word of advice Katie; if you want to hang with the big boys...you gotta be a big girl," she whispered to me.

I watched as she walked the invisible runway over to Ross and slipped in his arms.

She had both her hands on his chest. "I'm hungry babe. Let's go get something to eat."

Ross looked like he was enchanted by her spell. "Jordan, Ben, come on or I'm leaving you!" he yelled.

It didn't take long before what sounded like elephants

stampeding up the stairs was actually Ben and Jordan following their master…their alpha dog, Ross.

I walked over to Kennley who was off to the side avoiding me. I didn't understand how Kennley could date someone that was just so…awful. And was I just a phase like he might be? Was he just as unsure of us as I was? I tried not to let the evil blonde influence me but it was so hard. I crossed my arms over my chest and looked into his eyes as I spoke trying to keep my voice even. "I want to go home." I said quietly, not wanting Hannah to hear.

He looked at me, his green eyes sad. "Jimmy's gone so I can't leave Carrie here by herself…She'd probably burn the house down."

I looked back at Hannah. She was glaring at me and I was sure that at any moment a hole was going to burn through my head.

"Can't you bring her with you?" I begged. "Just please take me home."

His expression changed as he heard the strain in my voice. I was just thankful to God that my tears hadn't spilled over. I was such a wimp. I wasn't used to dealing with mean girls besides the she-devils in art class. All that Hannah had implied about Kennley was overwhelming.

He nodded and then ran up the spiral staircase after Carrie. Feeling extremely uncomfortable with Jordan, Ben, and Hannah looking at me as I stood off to the side alone now, I started to head towards the front door. Ross wasn't staring at me though. His dark eyes seemed to be looking off into the distance at something that I couldn't see. He looked lost in space or his own world…but either way his face was intense.

Ben smiled at me. "It was nice meeting you Kahlen… for the second time."

I smiled weakly at him but when I turned back around Hannah was standing in front of me. She scared me half to death and I was left catching my breath.

She smiled. "It looks like it's time for some growing up." Then she actually winked at me.

I walked past her quickly and stood by Kennley's car waiting. I was so upset with myself. She didn't deserve the satisfaction of getting to me. It wasn't long before the rest of them filed out pulled out of the long driveway. Kennley came out practically dragging Carrie out the door. He got in the car and Carrie climbed into the backseat. I could feel him looking at me but I just stared out the window.

He sighed. "What's wrong?"

I didn't answer.

A little voice squeaked from the backseat. "Change the radio station, I hate this one." Carrie said.

We slowed to a red light. Kennley left the station as it was and ignored Carrie.

He reached over and put my hand in his. I didn't pull it away but I left it there limp. "What's wrong?" he repeated.

I turned away from the window and looked at him. "You could warn me next time you leave me in a room with vultures."

It took him a second to realize what I meant then he swore and put his head in his hands.

Carrie giggled. "Mom said you're not supposed to say that word around me. When I tell her you're going to be in trouble."

"Yeah and she also said that you should mind your own business and stop acting like such a *brat*!"

She stuck her tongue out at him.

"Kennley—," she said.

"What Carrie?" He was obviously annoyed.

"The light's green."

He whipped his head around and swore again. He pressed his foot on the gas and the car accelerated forward. "By vultures I don't think you're talking about Jordan and Ben, are you?" he asked.

I shook my head no. "They left to go play ping pong."

We both left it at that for what I thought was because there was a kindergartener in the backseat. A whole bunch of images of Hannah and Kennley were being forced in my head. I didn't think it was possible to hate her anymore than I had before but I was wrong. I guess I was wrong about a lot of things.

When we finally got to my house, I expected him to stay in the car but he followed me inside, yelling at Carrie to stay in the car.

We both looked at each other silently trying to figure all of it out. I should have expected that someone like Hannah would come to put a wedge between Kennley and I sooner or later. It seemed like nothing could go right with us…right when things were going good we'd been ambushed by something else.

"Listen Kahlen," he began. "I know that Hannah probably said a lot of crap about a lot of things back there. But she is so bitter and hateful and I must have been so blind that I could not see all of her evilness when we were dating."

I nodded like I understood, but I didn't.

"What exactly did she say to you?" he asked.

I really didn't want to relive the conversation. "She talked mostly about you, and her, she even brought up Emma briefly. 'The more vulnerable the easier to manipulate'…" My face sunk just thinking about it… thinking about how below the belt she had actually hit with that one. Bringing up Emma was just so completely uncalled for. I could even feel the tears brimming at the thought of it...and I was sure Kennley could see them. He sighed heavily and I had never seen him this stressed before. His face was even turning red with anger. "She's heartless. She doesn't care about anything or anyone. I swear one minute she's out to ruin me and the next she's trying to get back with me. She is so bitter about our break up that she can't let go."

His face was slowly turning back to the shade of his original color. He put both his hands on my shoulders so I was forced to look at him. "She's a serial cheater...she cheated on me, she's cheating on Ross. It's just another thing from my past that I don't want to relive. I'm sure that whatever she said to you about us was probably lies." He let go of me and ran his fingers through his hair. "I gotta get home so I'll see you tomorrow okay?" He kissed me softly before opening up the door and heading back to his car.

I stood there by the door staring at it still shocked by everything that had just happened. I couldn't process it. With so many thoughts that had just been put in my head there was no way studying was going to be easy tonight. My hand flew to my face as I gasped.

I swung open the front door just at the right time. Kennley was about to pull out of the driveway but stopped when he saw me. I ran over to the car and he let the window down.

"I have my test tomorrow and I left my backpack at your house. And I really need to study." I said.

He sighed briefly. "Are you telling me we drove all the way over here for nothing?"

I didn't answer.

He grinned slightly although I knew he was frustrated. "You owe me."

I got into the car. "Leaving me alone with Satan herself…I'd say were *almost* even."

Carrie sat up in her seat so she was closer to the front. "I thought you were leaving," she said to me.

"So did I," I said.

Kennley sighed. "Carrie, sit back."

She reluctantly landed back with a hard thud. "So," she said. "By vulture did you mean Hannah?" She asked.-

I chuckled. "Very perceptive."

"I don't like her," she said.

I looked back at her and smiled. "Yeah, neither do I."

She smiled too. "Is it because she wants Kennley back?"

Kennley gripped his hands tighter on the wheel. "Why are you out on a mission to make my life harder than it has to be?"

Carrie stuck out her tongue again and I smiled. She was your typical cute little kid. "So is it because she's trying to steal him from you?" she asked me again.

"Um…No. Not exactly..." I answered. "…Although that is definitely something to think about."

She nodded.

"H-how old are you again," I asked.

Kennley muttered, "Six going on sixteen."

"Wanna know something about Kennley?" she asked me suddenly and her face glowed.

I raised an eyebrow. "Yeah, sure—,"

"Carrie, if you keep quiet for the rest of the ride home I'll go swimming with you tonight like you asked me to earlier."

She pondered on this for a second while I was left wondering what she was going to tell me that Kennley didn't want me to know. It was actually pretty entertaining to watch both of them have their sibling rivalries.

"Do you promise?" she asked. "Because you always promise and then end up leaving to go meet up with your friends. And besides, I'm not so sure that I want to go swimming tonight anyways."

I smiled. "So what were to saying about Kennley?"

"Do you know his real name?"

My brows furrowed. "Real name?" But I wasn't saying it to Carrie as much as I was asking Kennley.

"Remind me to *thank* you later Carrie," he sighed,

"Your sarcasm gets old you know," she shot back.

I smiled. "Real name?" I asked again. I stared at him, waiting for an answer.

"Kennley is a nickname. It's short for my real name," he explained.

Carrie laughed. "I think she knows what a nickname is, stupid."

Kennley smiled. "Ha! You just screwed yourself over, brat. I'm not supposed to cuss in front of you just like you're not allowed to say stupid. We're even now."

I smiled. I remembered when I was little and words like stupid, and shut up were considered inappropriate by my mother. If I said them, they were usually followed by the speech, "if you've got nothing nice to say, then don't say it at all".

Carrie crossed her arms over her tiny chest and didn't say a word the whole rest of the drive there which Kennley seemed content with.

"Real name?" I asked.

He sighed again.

"Oh come on, is it really that bad?"

"Yes and no."

I looked at him waiting.

"I have two first names. My full name is Kenneth

Bradley Lawrence Morgan. If you haven't figured it out the Kenneth and Bradley got combined into Kennley. After a while it just kind of stuck."

I tried my very best not to smile...I really did, but it wasn't working. "I guess you and Bradley have one thing in common." Stifling my laughter wasn't working either.

He didn't laugh, or even give a tiny grin. He kept his eyes on road with his lips in a permanent frown.

I sighed. "Come on cranky, lighten up."

He turned to look at me. "That's funny, less than ten minutes ago you didn't seem to be in the best of moods either."

I shrugged a little. It was easy to be in a good mood now. If anything Carrie cheered me up for helping me learn more about Kenneth Bradley. I almost cracked another smile just thinking about it.

"I wasn't," I said. "But then I decided something."

He waited for me to explain.

"I decided that I didn't care about what happened. I don't want to let something petty put a wedge between us again. Last time I did that I almost gave up a best friend and a boyfriend all in one."

He smiled. I guess that made him happy. "You were wrong before about Bradley by the way," he said. "We have two things in common. I was wrong before when I said he didn't have feelings for you."

I grimaced. I could only be friends with Bradley... and even that was a stretch. I couldn't imagine anything more between us. I couldn't imagine anything more than friends with any guy besides Kennley. No one had really interested me over the years...mostly because I was never looking.

All I could manage to get out after several seconds was, "Ew."

Kennley smiled, pleased at my reaction.

I knew I was going into the lions' den with this one but I was too curious not to ask. "I saw Hannah at the mall with another guy last week…does um, does Ross know she's cheating on him?"

His smile faded. I expected him to say something like, "let's not talk about them", or, "it doesn't really matter", but he surprised me.

"He knows to some degree. Anyone with eyes willing to see knows that. But I don't think he really cares. Him and Hannah don't really care for each other as much as they like fooling around and—," He stopped his sentence short and looked back at the young eyes and ears sitting and listening intently to our conversation. "—and by fooling around I mean that they aren't committed to a serious relationship."

I smiled at his cover up.

"Ben, Jordan, and I don't really care what they do as long as we don't have to watch them make a public display of it. The only thing I can't stand is when he drags her along to wherever we go like some little harmless Chihuahua." He was talking slowly and choosing his words carefully for Carrie's listening ears.

I thought about me and Hannah's conversation. "About them fooling around—and by that I mean being uncommitted to a serious relationship…she kind of insinuated some things about the two of you earlier today."

"Figures," he mumbled. He turned the corner into his big neighborhood.

"And I was wondering if you two were…uncommitted to a serious relationship also."

As we got closer to his house I knew he was waiting until Carrie was out of the car. As we pulled into the driveway he ordered her to go inside while the two of us sat in the car.

He sighed. "One of us was."

I hated evasiveness. "Which one...she said you were kind of handsy."

"Not *overly* handsy." He said.-

I smiled content. "I happen to think that you're not as handsy as she let on. I observed that you tend to be when *studying*, or when trying to distract me from something."

"Oh yeah...?" He grinned as he unbuckled his belt and then put his hand on my waist and leaned in closer. The usual butterflies fluttered and the blood began to pump through my veins as his lips were on mine. "Which one is it now?"

I stared at him still mesmerized by his green eyes. I was waiting for him to get angry enough to turn into the incredible hulk at any second.

He didn't give me time to answer as the butterflies fluttered in my stomach again. Out of nowhere I got the image of these same lips on Hannah Andrews... his *first* love. I wondered if there were any other girls I didn't know about. I thought about what Satan had said earlier about how he usually goes to blondes. More images flooded my mind with him with a whole bunch of other girls...blondes. My mouth stopped moving as I thought about all the girlfriends I didn't know about. It was irrational for me to be angry, but jealously wasn't supposed to be rational...not that I was jealous.

He pulled back to stare at me for a second. I blushed as I saw Carrie sitting on the porch steps looking at us.

"What's wrong?" he asked.

"Nothing, beside's Carrie's glare." I told him half of

the truth. I wondered how long the image of him and Hannah would be stuck in my head.

He opened up the car door and stuck his head out the window. "Why are you sitting out here? I told you to go inside." He asked.

"You're not the boss of me you know. And besides, the door is locked and you have the key," she yelled back.

Kenneth Bradley sighed. "Jimmy should be back from baseball practice by now. Did you consider ringing the doorbell?" He slammed the car door shut and looked back at me.

"Second love," I said.

He stared at me smiling slightly. "Kahlen, when I said that Hannah was my first love, we didn't really go into specifics. I mean, I loved Hannah...a lot. And love was really and truly *very* blind, but I wasn't *in* love with her...Not really anyway."

I fought back a smile. "Second love." I repeated.

He smiled. "She doesn't exist."

I tilted my head at him confused. "But you said earlier that—,"

"Screw what I said earlier. Seeing Hannah today just made me realize how much I couldn't stand her when we were dating. Love is blind; I could somehow manage to deal with her then, but now..."

I still kept my head slightly cocked.

He smiled at me, amused. "Kahlen, you are my one, and my only love."

I wished I could say the same. It seemed like Kennley should have had a hard time saying 'I love you' like most guys would. But then again he wasn't like most guys. A wide smile spread across my face. "Are you sure you're not blind?"

He shrugged. "Even if I am, ignorance is bliss. But I think I am seeing very clearly these days."

I sighed. I wanted to be in love with him back. When I said I loved him it wasn't the same kind of love with my family and with Emma. It was different.

16. Yearbooks

There were no clouds in the sky and I couldn't even see the sun. It was depressing in a way that the sky was so empty and blank. I missed staring up into the sky trying to figure out what each cloud looked like. My imagination would always get the better of me and I'd somehow see clouds that looked like bats, hands, or daisies. Kennley easily got frustrated when he couldn't see the same thing. He was convinced I was insane or something along those lines. I'd have to try and point out to him where each of the fingers on the hand were, but he could never see them. Mostly he didn't understand the flowers I saw in the clouds. He didn't understand how I saw daisies from sunflowers, or roses from lilacs.

We wouldn't discuss clouds today at the creek because there were none. I was more disappointed than I should have been.

I looked over at Kennley and smiled. I couldn't get over his name…Kenneth Bradley. I liked it; it had a nice ring to it. It made me think about how much more I didn't know about him. It was like he had this whole secret life that I didn't know about and my curiosity was driving me crazy.

I put my hand to the key on my necklace and played with it in my fingers. I was beginning to grow very fond of the tiny golden key. The only time I took it off was when I was showering. I thought about Wednesday night when I had gone back to Kennley's house to get my backpack. I felt like I had been thrown into a trap once I walked inside the house. Dena had made it home and was very overly excited to see me. Before I even had time to think, she had gripped me in an awkward but friendly hug. She acted as if I was an old friend instead of a stranger. When she invited me to dinner, I didn't really have a choice but to say yes. Dena was a tiny woman with honey blond hair like Carrie. She was welcoming and extremely compassionate. It seemed like every word she said rang with sincerity.

Of course I had felt uncomfortable sitting with Kennley's family but it was hard to after awhile. They all kept having fun at Kennley's expense by telling embarrassing stories and showing baby pictures. After dinner he all but grabbed my collar and dragged me out to his car.

After dinner I had said to Dena, "Well it was nice meeting you."

"Oh, and you too Kahlen," she smiled. "You're welcome to come back any—,"

Kennley had grabbed my arm and started towing me toward the door. "We really oughta be going now. Don't you have to study for a test tomorrow?"

This is where Carrie chimed in. "No she doesn't. You two spent the whole afternoon studying didn't you....or were you two not really *studying* but—,"

Kennley and I were to the door now and all I could manage to say was, "Thanks for dinner Mrs. Morgan."

But during dinner Dena had commented on my necklace and asked where I had gotten it. I tried not to seem amused as Kennley's cheeks flushed. I told her that Kennley had given it to me which was followed by a long "Awww," from Carrie and then a sudden, "Ouch someone kicked me." I had a guess of who had kicked her from underneath the table.

I now understood what Kennley had meant about Jimmy. Although technically they weren't brothers... they looked somewhat alike with the same type of hair. The only difference I could find in them was that Jimmy had these piercing blue eyes that I was sure you could see from miles away because they were just so...blue, while Kennley's eyes were of course green. But from what I had seen at the dinner table they acted alike too, same mannerisms and all. It was like watching a little Kennley...except so much quieter...although Kennley was plenty quiet at the dinner table, mostly from his embarrassment.

I finally understood what Kennley had meant when he said that Dena and Conner were complete opposites. They argued over everything from Pepsi or Coke to Chinese food or Mexican. It was pretty interesting to watch though...almost like a TV show.

Now, as a gentle breeze went by, I looked over at Kennley who seemed to be enjoying the cloudless sky while I just found it depressing. I sighed knowing that the school day would begin shortly and I wanted nothing more than to stay here with him, even if it was for an eternity.

"Okay Kenneth, we better get to school before we end up being late."

He shrugged. "What's so bad about being late? I don't happen to have a problem with it."

"Well...we all can't be *bad* boys like you. And besides, being late equals detentions, which equals no thanks." I stood up off of the ground and waited for him to follow but he didn't.

"Who said anything about getting a detention?" he asked. "I'm late for class all the time and yet I've never gotten a detention…it's all about the people you know."

I looked at him incredulously. "And who exactly *do* you know."

"Show up late with me and you'll find out." He grinned.

I narrowed my eyes at him. "Hmm…it depends. Could this be classified as wild and or crazy?" I said referring to our bet.

"For you it might, but for anyone else I don't think it'd be such a big deal."

"Just tell me who your connections are." I acted like I was three and stamped my foot down on the ground while crossing my arms over my chest.

"I'm gonna win the bet you know…Sooner or later."

"I'm thinking later."

Kennley sighed and enjoyed the heat from the sun on his skin as he lay down on the ground ignoring me. He couldn't force me to be late. I was contemplating on reaching into his pockets quickly to grab his car keys. I always did want to drive his BMW but he would never let me. The alluring sound of his car purring to life put my old stupid truck to shame. What I wouldn't give just to hop in the driver's set for five minutes... And besides, you always want what you can't have more…Kennley would *never* let me drive his car, ever.

I sighed. "*Brad,* come on."

"Alessa, make me."

Kennley had forced me to tell him my middle name because I kept calling him Kenneth; he wanted to even it up.

I couldn't believe he had just said "make me". If he wanted to act like he was five…So would I. I reached down and grabbed his arm before attempting to drag him across the grass. At first his body wouldn't budge and then slowly but surely his body slowly began to inch forward.

"Are you seriously *trying* to drag me?" he asked.

"Trying but not succeeding." I dropped his arm and gave up. "How much do you weigh?" I had my hands on my knees trying to catch my breath. I felt so out of shape.

He shrugged. "I don't know. Somewhere around a hundred eighty."

My eyes wandered to his biceps…muscle weighs more than fat after all.

He stood up off the ground and reluctantly started walking towards his car.

"Can I drive?" I asked.

"No." His tone was reproachful. "That's the tenth time you've asked me that today."

"Well why not?"

"You've asked me *that* several times too."

He opened my car door for me like he usually did before going to the other side to get in.

He reached to put the key in the ignition but I covered it with my hand. "Please?"

It had been awhile since I drove a car considering mine had died. My dad said that there was no fixing it unless we bought a whole bunch of new parts which would be the equivalent expense to buying a new car. Kennley's car would always taunt and tease me. It was like it was saying, "Drive me! Drive me…nope never mind"!

"No." He said again. "Especially when you can't refer to it as its name instead of…'the *car*'…it's degrading."

"Sorry if I forget to refer to an inanimate object by name. Can I please drive *Eddie*?"

He sighed. "Kahlen…babe, Eddie means more to

me than you. It's my top priority. And I've seen the way you drive. You're an accident waiting to happen. It's nothing personal really. I'm the only one that drives Eddie...*ever.*" He reached over and tucked my hair behind my ear.

I narrowed my eyes at him but it didn't fade his smile at all. I moved my hand away from the ignition and sat back in my seat with a thud.

"Put on your seat belt," he ordered.

"Why do you care? Apparently I mean nothing compared to *the car.*"

He shrugged. "Think about it. Say some crazy driver—like you— hits us. I don't want blood getting on the seats."

My jaw dropped. "You are impossible." I put my seat belt on.

I made it my mission not to talk to him for the whole ride. When in doubt the silent treatment always worked.

When we were half way there he said, "I know what you're doing and you can't do it forever."

I tried to think of the longest time I had lasted with the silent treatment. This probably beat my last record. I could never really last for long. I always convinced myself that there was something really important that I wanted to say and I broke my silence. When we got to school I got out of the car and started to walk away until he gently grabbed my wrist and pulled me back. I was against the car now and I was tempted to say something but I didn't. This acting like a five year old thing was fun. No wonder Carrie took so much joy out of bothering Kennley.

We stared at each other for a long second before he quickly kissed me which took me by surprise although I knew it shouldn't have.

I opened my mouth and inhaled like I was about to say something but stopped right before sound came out. Kennley grinned.

"Kahlen, doing that to Eddie would be extremely awkward. You don't come in first, but you definitely make top five…First runner up even."

I shrugged. "I guess it really doesn't matter anyhow. I'll get to drive it in a month…I can wait."

He took my hand as we walked off towards the school. "Never gonna happen," he said slowly.

I just smiled. "We'll see."

I speed walked all the rest of the way to my locker. I had only a couple of minutes to get to my locker and then to my first class. It was all Kennley's fault. If I got a detention I was blaming him.

"What's your secret Kennley Morgan? Why don't you get detentions?" I asked swinging my locker open.

He narrowed his eyes. I knew he was going to be difficult about this.

I sighed. "If you tell me I'll do anything you want. I promise." I wondered if he could tell I was lying.

He smiled taking the things out of his locker slowly not caring about being late. "The ladies in the nurse's office love me. No one in this school ever gets sick or hurts themselves so it's pretty much abandoned. The only nurses in there are far beyond senior citizens. I helped them carry a couple of boxes one day. They've helped me out ever since. I stop by often and we'll sit and chat. They give me passes so I won't get in trouble."

My jaw dropped and I looked at him shocked. "So are you telling me you practically con old ladies?"

He shrugged. "It's their choice. I sent them a fruit basket once though. Millie said that she didn't get enough fruit in her diet."

I shook my head to myself as I slammed my locker shut and waved goodbye as I headed off to class.

For the first time in a long time I actually paid attention in Mr. Simmons's class. It was pretty boring and annoying as all of my underage female classmates gazed lovingly into his hazel eyes. It almost made me want to gag. I was beginning to realize why I had never paid much attention in the first place. As if I didn't already have enough things going through my mind, it was impossible to focus sitting in the back row. While all the girls seemed to be paying attention—just not to what Mr. Simmons was saying— the boys in the class would make little doodles on their paper of stick figures and rocket ships. And then the few girls that weren't interested in the middle aged teacher were passing notes back and forth and I couldn't stop my eyes from looking at their notebooks as they wrote. Apparently Chris might have a thing for Claire but Justin asked Nick who knows Chris and he said that he went out with Ally yesterday. My head was spinning just thinking about it.

Pay attention, pay attention! I willed myself but my mind kept drifting. In the last five minutes the only thing I had got out of *whatever* he was talking about, was something about Charles Dickens and final exams.

I stared at the clock insipidly and packed away all my things quickly as class was coming to an end. When the bell rang I was all prepared to speed walk out of the classroom and probably be the first one to go, but when I got to the doors Mr. Simmons stopped me on my way out.

"Kaitlyn, I wanted to talk to you about your test yesterday morning."

I let the Kaitlyn thing slide and looked at him anxiously waiting for him to say more. He took a couple of steps to his desk quickly and went through some papers. He handed me my test and my jaw all about dropped to the ground.

"Ninety-seven percent?" I gawked.

He was smiling. "Do you see how a little effort can go a long ways? I wanted to prove that to you. I knew you could do better than what you've been doing. Your first semester grades told me that."

He was right. First semester this was my best class and it had dropped to my worst.

I looked up from my test still shocked. I couldn't stop a smile from spreading over my face.

"Now," he said. "All you have to do is keep this up for Monday's test and you'll be fine come final exams on Tuesday."

I finally came back to reality off of the cloud I was on. Everyone in class had left and it was just him and I left in the room. I started to walk towards the door. "Well I better get to class."

He nodded, still grinning.

"Oh and Mr. Simmons…thanks." Hmm…he did have nice hazel eyes.

When lunch time finally rolled around I was all but tackled by Marissa. Her long and wavy red hair bounced its way to our table and she sat down with a smile. She threw her thick yearbook at me—yes actually threw. It almost landed in the little bit of food I had—and then a red glittery pen to sign it with.

Jenny sighed. "I knew I was forgetting something this morning in art. I was going to have you sign my yearbook," she said to me.

Marissa frowned. "Where's *your* yearbook?" She asked me-

I shrugged. "I guess I forgot to pick it up in the gym this morning. I had to practically sprint to my first class so I wouldn't be late."

Jenny took a bite from her apple. "The yearbooks are really nice this year."

I didn't think it was possible but Marissa's smile widened. "I'll take that as I compliment considering *I'm* the co-editor of the yearbook committee."

I looked through Marissa's yearbook seeing lots of, " LOVE YOU TONS MARISSA!!! HAVE A GREAT SUMMER!!" written in insanely large letters. I was surprised by the people that took it upon themselves to take up an entire page to write some long speech. I looked at my picture in the yearbook. My hair was shorter then; just shoulder length. Now it was at least two or more inches longer. I passed Emma's picture and couldn't help lingering on it for a long second. Unlike me, her hair was longer then and of course her picture was gorgeous. She couldn't help looking like a model every second of her life. The twist in my stomach began and I turned the page quickly. Towards the back of the book there was a whole bunch of random, candid photos of students. It took me off guard when one page was dedicated to the most popular best friends of the school. In the top right hand corner was a picture of me giving Emma a piggy back ride. I didn't even remember that picture being taken. I continued flipping and saw a black and white photo of the student body all packed in the gym with candles all around with a big picture of Emma on a huge projector. I knew I wasn't in this picture because I had stayed home from school to avoid things like this. Not like it didn't follow me later when Marissa gave me a CD of the slideshow that I crushed. In white letters at the bottom of the page it said:

In Memory of Emma Bryant

A Very Loved and Missed Daughter, Student and Friend.

May We Always Carry A Piece of Her In Our Hearts.

1990-2008

I closed my eyes and held them shut until the urge to break out in sobs subsided. It was days like this that I wished that our school didn't have different lunch periods or at the very least that I was in Kennley's lunch. If I was with Kennley right now I wouldn't have been looking through Marissa's yearbook. Although that thought was irrational because sooner or later I would have gone through my yearbook. But all the same, I wished Kennley were here.

I sighed. "Marissa, I'm no good with these things. I never have any clue of what to say. And besides, all your pages are so full that there's barely any room to sign it."

The most I could think of to say was "have a great summer"—yeah, that was original and rang sincerity—, or just signing my name.

She reached over the table and took the yearbook out of my hands. She flipped through some pages and then stopped and smiled.

"Hmm…I thought I reserved a place for you. See there's plenty of room right here. And I don't care what you say. It's the thought that counts right?"

I smiled weakly taking the book back from her. "Right."

I stared at the empty space for awhile before I actually wrote something.

You are amazingly nice.
Thanks for trying to be there for me,
~Kahlen.

Everything that I had said was true, but there was no need to mention how appreciative I was exactly for her trying to be there for me. Sometimes I still wished that it was just Jenny and I sitting at this table. I closed the book and handed it over to her.

"So…" Marissa started. "Are you guys going to

graduation tonight? You already know I am because of my sister."

"My brother," Jenny said.

"Only child," I said.

Jenny shrugged. "Sometimes I wish I was an only child. This is going to be my third graduation and then next month I have to go to my sister's college graduation. By the end of next school year I'll be so sick of graduations that I probably won't even show for ours."

Marissa flipped back that gorgeous dark red hair of hers. I always envied it. I knew *I* would look horrible as a red head but Marissa's hair looked almost velvety in a way.

She rested her chin on her hand. "Well Kay, you should come tonight too. I mean, you have to know some of the seniors. But then afterwards, Kelly, Alaina, Mark, Chris, Matt, Megan..." She was counting out the people on her hand. "I'm not gonna name all of them, but a lot of people are going to The T.J. Club after to hang out. You should come and bring the beau, she turned to Jenny. "And of course you're welcome to come too.

Jenny shook her head. "Sorry, I can't. I already told Maggie that I'd study with her for final exams tonight."

Marissa frowned slightly and then turned back to me waiting. I had winced at the name Megan. But besides that I didn't know any of the names she had mentioned. I was so socially inept. I tried to think of a good excuse in my head for saying no. I couldn't say I was sick and there was no way I could pull off a straight face and say I needed to study. Maybe I could have lied and said I had a date with Kennley and—

She sighed. "Kay, I have a confession to make." Marissa looked like some sad little girl who had eaten a cookie *before* dinner and felt guilty about it. "I kind of saw you and Kennley kiss this morning in the junior parking lot and so I figured that you guys weren't incognito anymore. So when I saw him in the hallway today and I asked him if he wanted to come and he said that you guys didn't have any plans. So now everyone else kind of knows that you two are together. You guys aren't still '*broken up*' are you?"

It took me a second to process it all. I had almost forgotten about us keeping our relationship under wraps. When I thought about everyone talking about us, and the buzzing in halls whenever we were seen together, I honestly didn't care anymore. It didn't matter. I was still a little shocked by my new attitude on matter myself.

I sighed. "No. We are not still *broken up*."

She smiled. "Perfect. So I'll see you tonight. But you don't have to go to the graduation if you don't want to. Since the graduation is in the gym, you can meet us there. Instead of us all driving an extra block to get to T.J.'s we're all just gonna walk. So be here around eight."

My eyes widened. I didn't remember ever saying yes to Marissa during our whole conversation.

"*You're not going to pass this up Kahlen. Live a little. Get to know some new people. At least you'll be with Kennley*," she said.

I sighed, "See you then."

"Can't wait," Marissa smiled.

I had been impatiently waiting for as long as I had known Marissa for her to say something that didn't sound sincere…and I waited. And I was *still* waiting.

I stood up and threw away the food I hadn't even touched. I was thankful that Jenny and Marissa stopped looking at me like I was anorexic or something every day when I didn't eat lunch. It was plain and simple. I wasn't hungry. I ate breakfast and dinner. Skipping one meal in each day doesn't classify me with mental issues.

I held up my wrist to see what time it was and kind of chuckled to myself. I didn't wear a watch but it seemed like the kind of thing that someone did when they wanted to know what time it was. I had never worn a watch. They always bothered me one way or another and yet me looking at my invisible watch on my wrist never ceased. Even though I didn't have a watch and too many heads were blocking my view of the big clock hanging on the wall, I knew that the end of lunch was approaching. Once everyone started to get up and throw away their food everyone knew that within five minutes lunch would be over.

I picked up my backpack off the ground. "I have my last and final meeting with Mrs. Kraft soon so I'm gonna go stop by my locker first."

I started to walk away out of the lunch room but I heard footsteps coming up behind me.

"You have Mrs. Kraft too?" Marissa asked.

I thought about the day I had seen her sitting in the office with her eyes red and puffy and then the folder that had fell off of Mrs. Kraft's desk.

"Yeah..."

"Cool, so do I. Isn't she the best? She's helped me out so much this semester."

I stared at her, studying her perky little face. I nodded quickly and continued walking off.

I basically barged into Mrs. Kraft's office and took my seat quickly. Before she could even react to my abrupt entrance I was talking a mile a minute.

"Why do you see Marissa?" I asked.

"Kahlen—,"

"No. Really...why? It just doesn't make sense. Her life is *perfect*. She is absurdly popular but it's impossible to hate her because she's too nice. You can't even be mad at her...ever. And it's so annoying—,"

"Kahlen I—,"

"I just don't understand. Does she drop by every so often to offer some homemade chocolate chip cookies on her way to go read to the children at the orphanage? Why?" I stopped talking and sat back in my seat.

"I can't tell you why Kahlen. It's confidential information."

I tipped my head back in my seat. "Oh come on, it's not like I'm going to tell anyone. I promise."

She actually started laughing at me. "Not only could I lose my license by not keeping that confidential, but it's not my business to tell. If you're really that curious then why don't you just ask Marissa yourself? She seems very fond of you."

My jaw dropped. "What? Does she talk about me in here or something?"

She didn't answer right away. "I talked to all of your teachers recently. They all said that you were doing better in class, that you had even made the extra step to start participating. And I'm proud of you for that. In a short amount of time you've actually raised all of you grades to some degree."

I shrugged. "It all depends on what I put my mind to."

She smiled. "Perseverance, persistence, those are all good qualities to have."

"It's mostly just stubborn..." I trailed off. She was just like Kennley. She had completely veered me off from Marissa to grades. I hadn't even realized she had done it until now. I sighed. "Mrs. Kraft, can I ask you something?" I tried to sound as innocent as I possibly could.

"Yes, of course, anything." Her face was immediately concerned and sympathetic.

"Why does Marissa see you?" I asked and she sighed.

"Please, at least give me something." I begged.

"Kahlen…all I'm going to say is that you and Marissa have more in common than you think. You should give her a chance to let her prove it to you herself."

I stared at her blankly trying to decipher what she had just said.

The rest of the session had gone by smoothly. I didn't ask anymore about Marissa. She kept asking me questions about my summer plans, and Kennley. We never did talk about Emma much which was ironic in a way considering it was the reason I was here in the first place.

The rest of the school day had gone by quickly too. It wasn't until after school that things started to get really interesting. When I walked to my locker after school there was a group of girls standing in the way blocking it. Over their heads I could just barely make out the dark, chocolate-y brown hair I knew so well.

"Kennley?" I tried to say over all the girls' heads.

He sighed. "Hold on. Honestly people do you think I can do them all at once?" He almost sounded coquettish.

I stood off to the side uncomfortably waiting for the obstacles in front of my locker to dissolve.

"Kennley what are you—,"

The giggling girls were driving me crazy. Half of them looked too young to be juniors as they crowded Kennley even more.

"Patience people. I promise I'll get to all of them.

And if I run out of time today there's always Monday." He sounded like a smug celebrity signing autographs. It took me a second to realize that all of the girls had yearbooks in their hands.

"*Kenneth*?" I tried.

I couldn't help but start to laugh. That seemed to get his attention. He stepped out of the crowd of girls who didn't look too happy to see me. I really couldn't believe I was watching this right now. It looked like a couple of juniors were in the mix of sophomores and it all seemed downright ridiculous. I laughed even harder when I saw that he was wearing sunglasses. He definitely thought he was a rock star. I didn't even know where he had gotten those from. He was so amazingly full of himself that I couldn't help but sit back and watch the show.

"Heeyy...Kahlen," he said slowly as if I had just caught him with his hand in the cookie jar.

A leggy blond with shorts that were too short, and a top that was too low came up to Kennley and put her yearbook up against his chest.

"You promised me you'd sign it today in science, Kenny," she said. It sounded like she really wanted to say, "Kenny, you promised me I could have your children".

Kennley looked away from me to her quickly. "That I did." He took her book and she gladly offered her back and a hard surface to write on.

Once Kennley handed her the book back she clutched him in a tight hug that lasted a bit too long. After the blond walked away Kennley sent the other fans away promising to sign their books later.

I just looked at him incredulously. He slid off his sunglasses and placed them in his locker.

"Hola, Mr. Popularity," I said opening my locker.

"Don't tell me you're jealous?"

I smiled. "Of what? The popularity or the girls?"

"Both."

I chuckled. "Hardly." I was barely jealous of some lower classmen and their adolescent crushes. The only one that really got to me was the blonde. I could hear Hannah's voice in the back of my head talking about how Kennley usually goes for blondes. "But then again, that depends...should I be?" I raised an eyebrow.

Kennley took a step closer to me and gently lifted the necklace that was underneath my shirt over on top of it so the key was visible. "Not really," He grinned.

After we were both finished at our lockers we walked out the doors to the parking lot towards his car. I was half afraid that there would be more girls at his car but there weren't. When we got inside and I asked to see his yearbook I understood why there were no more girls at his car. His yearbook was packed with signatures. It seemed like the majority of the girls had gotten to him earlier today. I couldn't believe half of the things I was reading inside of his book.

I gasped. "Have you looked at what these people are *saying* to you?" I asked.

He shrugged pulling out of the lot. "No." He sounded indifferent.

I began to read some of them out loud. "Hey Kennley—Then she put a little smiley face—this year's been fun, I just wish you could have been here the whole time. You're my favorite bad boy. We should totally hang out this summer. Love you, Megan." I pretended to gag.

"Which one. Megan B. or Megan G.?" He asked.

I missed his indifference. "She didn't say." I rolled my eyes. "Oh my gosh, listen to this one: Hey Cutie. I wanted you to know that you ruined my entire day when you told me you have a girlfriend. I think I can somehow manage to forgive you for it though. So call me so we can hang out. Insert smiley face here, Lexis."

We pulled up to a red light. "Okay, I think I'll take that back now." He reached for his yearbook but I backed away.

"No," I said. "This is just getting interesting." I flipped the page. "Hey Lover-Boy—insert fifty exclamations marks here—I am eternally grateful to you for helping me out in honors English. I wouldn't be passing that class if it weren't for you. Call me so I can make it up to you somehow. Yours truly, Kate. And she underlined the *yours truly.*"

He sighed. "Are you done now?"

I had the book over my face. I pulled it down so I could see him. He was looking at me while driving. "Pay attention to the road." I demanded. "And you said my driving was bad..." I turned to the back of the book when finally something in red, glittery pen caught my eye. I didn't read it out loud. It said:

Hey Kennley,

I'm so happy you came this year...better late than ever.

You make Kahlen happy, so that makes me happy.

You better not hurt her or I'll come looking for you...LOL!—but seriously, don't break her heart.

You rock, love you,

~Marissa

Kennley sighed heavily again at my silence. "What is it now?"

Maybe Marissa did deserve a chance. I stared at the page blankly until Kennley smacked my knee with his hand to get my attention. I closed the book and put in the backseat. I had known Marissa for a really long time and when I thought about it...I didn't have a legitimate excuse not to like her. Sure sometimes she was overly perky, but besides that she had always been out for my best interest. I thought about at lunch how she said that she had *reserved* a place in her yearbook for me. There wasn't a phony bone in her body...always sincere.

Kennley tapped me again and I snapped back to reality. "What was it this time?" He asked. "If this is about Anna then—,"

I smiled. "No this isn't about *Anna*. But what about her?"

He didn't respond right away and I enjoyed watching him squirm.

"So do you still want to drive Eddie?" He asked.

He was completely bluffing. I smacked his arm with my hand. "Oh don't tease me with your distractions. I don't care about whatever it is about Anna anyway. I don't care about any of your admirers as long as Lexis wasn't the only one you reminded that you have a girlfriend."

When we pulled up to my house I grabbed my backpack from the backseat and tried to steal his yearbook along with it.

"You know..." He said. "I don't mind a little jealously. It's flattering in a way."

"Kennley I'm not—,"

He kissed me goodbye but it wasn't a quick goodbye kiss like all the others.

I pulled back. "Do you realize that you are completely full of yourself rock star?" I joked.

He shrugged. "Not completely. I'll pick you up tonight at around seven-thirtyish."

I got out of the car and shut it. I was about to walk away when I heard the window rolling down.

"Oh, and Kahlen..." He sighed, "...leave the book."

I shook my head and walked to the front door.

"What? Are you going to break into my house and steal it back if I don't? I'll give it back to you later tonight. I've got some reading to do."

He reluctantly pulled out of the driveway shaking his head at me.

When Kennley came to pick me up I all about keeled over and died. Unfortunately my mom was home and she actually went through the whole interrogate the date thing.

When I saw his car parked in the driveway I ran down the stairs and tried to go out the door quickly. My mom stopped me so Kennley would actually have to come to the door. My heart dropped to my stomach as the doorbell rang. It was times like these that I wished I still had that stupid truck so I could drive myself. I opened the door slowly and Kennley was standing there in a black leather jacket with a dark blue t-shirt underneath and jeans. He looked like he had just showered so his hair was wet and slightly spiky.

"So are you ready to go?" he asked grinning.

I winced. "Not exactly. But do you happen to have a gun on you?" I tried to whisper but my mom and her super hearing heard me.

"Don't be dramatic, Honey. Invite him in," she said.

I ignored her. "And I only need *one* bullet."

Kennley smiled and invited himself in. He took a step in and greeted my mother. I knew he wanted revenge from when I had dinner over at his house.

I sighed. "Mom, don't you have work to do? Aren't you still working on the Berlin house?"

"Unlike your father I find it nice to take a break every once in a while. Ever since that whole investigation's been underway about drug dealing downtown he practically lives at the station."

She had a point. My dad had been pretty busy with work lately. But my mom had been busy too. I rarely saw them around the house anymore but I didn't mind so much. Sometimes I liked having the house all to myself. And plus, the more my mom wasn't here, the more I didn't have to witness her in full fledged Hyde form.

"Well mom, we really should get going." I stood up but neither one of them followed. Awkwardly I sat back down with a thump.

"So Kennley..." my mom started. "There so much I don't know about you. And since Kahlen had dinner with your family I was thinking—"

"Mom!" I interrupted. "Really, we should get going if we don't want to be late."

She sighed, "Honestly pumpkin, you're acting as if it's the end of the world."

It was times like these that I wished she would simply use the name she'd given me instead of food items. She was right. It wasn't the end of the world... it was the end of *my* world. I could already picture it in my head: All four of us sitting in the fancy dining room that we very rarely used. Kennley would sit there sickly enjoying every second of my discomfort. It was so incredibly awkward just sitting here now. I couldn't imagine sitting and talking for longer than an hour.

For the first time in the couple of minutes we'd been sitting here talking, I looked over at Kennley. He was laid back in what was designated as my father's chair relaxed.

He grinned, "I wouldn't mind coming to—,"

I don't know where all of my strength came from but all of a sudden I stood up quickly and yanked Kennley out of the chair and pulled him to the door.

"Sounds great, mom." I slammed the door behind us after yelling, "Bye."

We were standing on the porch while I was catching my breath.

Kennley was looking at me shaking his head. "Am I that bad?"

I studied his face. I wasn't sure if he was serious or not. I didn't how he could ever think he was. "It's not you, it's them." I gestured towards the front door. "My dad sometimes walks around the house in dress socks and my mom's pink slippers with rolled up sweatpants and a Rolling Stones T-shirt. It doesn't get much more embarrassing than that."

"Ahh...the cop." He put his arm around me and turned me to the direction of his car.

"Do you have a problem with him being a cop?" I asked getting into the car.

He sighed shutting the door behind him as he got in. "I never said I had a problem with it...I'm just not too fond of cops that's all."

"May I ask why?"

He grinned slightly although I could see something else lingering that was causing a sudden darkness in his eyes. "If I said no would that stop you anyway?"

I deliberated a second before answering. As much as I didn't want to possibly get into a fight with Kennley, I could help but ask, "Have you ever been arrested?" I avoided eye contact with him and looked straight ahead.

"Define arrested," he said slowly.

I sighed. "You know the whole hands behind your back, handcuffs, being in a police car, that type of thing."

"Oh *that*...no, I've never been arrested."

I sighed again. I knew he was hiding something...

just like he was always hiding something from me. I never understood why. It was like he told me everything piece by piece waiting for me to connect all of the dots.

"Why does everything have to be twenty questions with you?" I asked curtly. "Why can't you ever just tell me the whole truth instead of leaving me wondering and guessing?"

I didn't expect him to give me a straight answer, of course. But what I didn't expect was for him not to answer me at all. After a couple of seconds went by I turned to look at him but his eyes were on the road. He knew I was waiting for his answer. That much was evident.

"Because," he finally said. "I'm scared, Dean. I'm scared that if you find out who the real me is that you won't like him very much."

He still wasn't looking at me...not even a quick glance. I stared at him trying to think of something to say but no words were forming in my head. I let the topic drop and neither one of us said a word until we pulled up to the school. Kennley didn't bother taking my hand into his or putting his arm around me as we walked closer to the gym. All I could think of was the irony of it all. Usually I was the one making stupid decisions because I was scared, not him.

Our school gym was massive. It was absurdly large for just a regular high school gym but that's what made it convenient. All dances and other important functions were held in the gym...including graduation. The big gym doors were open. From the looks of it, it looked like graduation was far from over. I peeked my head through the door a tiny bit to see how far along exactly they were.

I didn't expect a wave of emotions to be flying

through me right now but they did. I saw all the seniors sitting down in their caps and gowns and it finally hit me that I would be sitting in their place next year... but without Emma. It all seemed so surreal when I thought about going to college and moving away. Then someday maybe getting married and starting my own family. Despite my being cynical, I wondered if Kennley would be a part of that family. Part of me told me that we wouldn't last forever. But then again, I didn't know the future so how could I know?

A girl whose gown was different from everyone else's walked up to the front of the stage that had been set up in the gym and she stood at the podium.

She cleared her throat before speaking into the microphone. "As we take this step into the next chapter of our lives I was forced with a question that I couldn't answer right away. Who am I? I could easily say that I'm a daughter, a sister, a friend, a student. I'm Hannah Graver. But it's bigger than that. Not just who am I in general. But who am I as a person. Who am I really?"

"I think that this is a question that we should all spend a little bit of each day meditating on. I believe that in mine and other's eyes I am smart, persistent, and sometimes a little goofy...but even beyond that. Who am I? What are my flaws, my talents, the things that aren't so easily seen at the surface? After sitting in my bedroom last night, still trying to finish writing this speech I found the answers to those questions. The answer is...I don't know.

"Then another question was brought to my attention. Who do I want to be? I think we can all agree the American dream is to be successful and happy. I know that I want to be successful and happy but not by the world's standards but my own. I dream of having a family of my own one day and a good job and head on my shoulders. I want to be happy.

"This brings me back to my first question. Who am I? I realized that these questions coincide. I have to know who I am and what I have to do in order to make the jump to who I want to be. And it's okay that I don't know who I am yet because I am still learning. Each and every day, if we pay close attention we will learn more about ourselves. Sometimes we get so caught up on everything else going on around us that we forget those two questions. I may not be able to answer that first question thoroughly but I can answer it enough. I am happy. I'm a good person and I know that the every person in this room has helped shape the person I am today and the person I will be. As long as I am those two things I'm satisfied."

"So now my fellow classmates, teachers, friends and family, I've asked myself these questions and now I encourage you to do the same. Who are you? Who will you be? It is scary to close one door in life and open the next. But I've found that the more we know about ourselves, the more confidence we gain, and the easier it is to take that next step. So ask yourselves those questions, gain that self-assurance, and take it. Take that next step...because you never know where life will lead you or how soon your opportunities will be cut short. As I ponder on my life, I think of the untimely death of a student in the junior class, Emma Bryant, and most of you know who I'm talking about. She was one year younger than me and thinking about her, I think about how many things I want to do with my life that I haven't yet.

So as each of us move on with our lives, let us find the strength to live up to our full potential...and the first step to that, is knowing who we are as a person. Take that next step. Take it for me, take it for Emma, take it for yourself." She looked somewhat teary eyed as she stepped down off the stage and took her place with the rest of her class.

I stared down at my shoes forced to ask myself those same questions she had just went through. Maybe I did know the answer to some extent a couple of months ago, but now I didn't know. After something terrible happens that makes you question your own purpose and existence it's reasonable to be confused. Of course I knew who I wanted to be. I didn't know specifics career wise but I wanted to be a happy person like she had said in her speech. But who am I now, today? I couldn't even begin to answer that question. I was waiting for life to give me that answer.

It took me awhile to realize that Kennley wasn't standing by me. I stuck my head back out of the gym and looked around. I saw him sitting on a bench staring at the ground in between the gym and the main building. I couldn't understand him these days. Maybe it was better if I was in the dark about the other aspects of his life. He looked somewhat sad, somewhat bored as he stared aimlessly at the ground.

I sighed as I walked over by him and sat down beside him. He looked up at me unsmiling and we both stared at each other not blinking. I looked away and slid my hand into his.

"I'm not going anywhere," I promised. "So there is no sense in you being afraid. That's my job remember?" I nudged him. "And besides, we'll *both* never know the truth if you don't tell me."

I took myself by surprise just then. I wasn't used to being the encouraging one. I was the pessimist. But maybe that side in me was fading. Just as Kennley was scared, so was I. He was scaring me. I knew he had a not so perfect past. I had realized that when we went to ICC that he hadn't gone into much detail when he said he got into a lot of trouble. I knew the police weren't out to get him or anything. He didn't really seem like the troublesome type yet I could see the dark side of him lurking beneath.

He didn't say anything back. He just squeezed my hand tighter as I leaned my head over on his shoulder. He obviously didn't believe me about what I had said. I wasn't so sure if I believed myself so much either. Only time will tell...

17. Secrets

"Would you just relax?" he begged. "You've been like this all day."

"I *am* relaxed," I snapped.

"You call this relaxed?" He gestured towards my tense body...my hands were shaking slightly. "You're stressed."

"No I'm not. When I'm stressed...I pace. I'm not pacing, I'm sitting."

Kennley gave up the fight, realizing there was no use in arguing with me. I knew he was right although I was too stubborn to admit it. It was Monday...Monday meaning the Monday before exams. I had to do well on exams if I wanted to raise my grades. All the tests I was about to take could make or break my grade. I had a good reason for being stressed.

All day he had been trying to calm me down because I was doing a poor job of pretending like everything was fine. He had invited me over to his house for a movie night to which I very reluctantly agreed to. My parents were overjoyed that I was at his house. They were sick of my frantic studying also. I had been cramming all weekend and the only daylight I had seen was the light coming from my bedroom window. I had even stopped going to the Creek in the mornings because I was too tried to get up early. I hardly ever saw Kennley outside of school anymore which he wasn't so happy about. My mom gladly let me borrow her car to go to

Kennley's. I knew she was worried that my brain was going to explode and it was evident that Kennley was also. I took a deep breath. I needed to relax.

He reached over and pulled my tense body closer to his. "Do you ever wonder why you're so jumpy all the time? Stress and anxiety coincide you know. Maybe—,"

"Thanks, Dr. Phil."

"I've seen snapping turtles snap less than you," she said.

He sighed. "You know how when I told you about the whole nurse's office thing, you said that in return I could have anything I want. Well want you to *relax*."

I knew Kennley didn't mind my constant snapping. He found it amusing actually which just put me more on edge. I didn't understand him half of the time. It didn't make sense that when I was mad…even if I was mad at him, he found it amusing. It was like I was putting on a show for him.

He grabbed the DVD remote and pressed play. We had decided to have a superhero movies marathon. By my request we had started out with Spiderman three because it was my favorite of the trio. By the time we were five minutes into the movie I could already feel my muscles relaxing and my mind drifting from everything involving exams. It helped that I was in his arms and the sound of his heart beating slowed mine.

I still couldn't get over how loaded Kennley was. I was tempted to ask why he had so much money but it wasn't the type of thing you asked people. Besides an indoor pool, hot tub, and game room, he also had a home theater which was where we were right now.

My heart was beating at a normal pace finally, but it all came to an end when Ben came flying through the door and I practically jumped through the roof. It was somewhat embarrassing that I flew to the other side of the couch.

Hannah was the next one through the door, "No… don't move off of each other for our account," she said flatly.

I took deep breaths trying to steady myself while I glowered at Hannah as she did the same to me. Kennley seemed to be scowling at Ben who was the only one that realized Hannah and I were three seconds from slitting each other's throats. Jordan and Ross filed in shortly after. Kennley paused the movie and stood up off the couch. I stopped glaring at Hannah long enough to notice that Mount Kennley was about to blow.

Ben backed away closer to the door. "Maybe we should have called first. Not that it would have mattered because you never answer your phone anymore."

Kennley sighed putting his hand over his face. "Keys." He held out his hand.

Jordan moved closer to Kennley. "We didn't use the keys to get in. Conner opened the door—,"

"Keys." He repeated.

Ben dug in his pockets and finally placed a silver key in his hand.

Kennley grinned briefly. "And the extras."

Jordan dug in his pocket this time and handed him three silver keys.

Hannah made herself welcome by brushing past Kennley gently and plopping down on the couch beside me. I scooted over until I was as far away from her as possible sitting on the couch. Hannah did the same to the other end of the couch. Ross followed after his little Chihuahua and sat down in between us. I was beginning to feel extremely awkward. Ross somewhat frightened me. Everything about him just seemed so dark. At first glance it almost looked like his eyes were black just like his hair.

Kennley turned to Ben. I figured it was because he was the easiest one to get stuff out of. "For the last couple of days it seems like you guys have perfect timing lately when it comes to showing up at my house uninvited. Why is that?" He narrowed his eyes.

Ben did the same. "Did I ever tell you how happy I am that I don't have a little sister...?"

He sighed heavily dropping his head slightly. "My cell phone right?"

Ben nodded.

I fought back a smile. Carrie really was a devious little sister.

Ben walked past Kennley and Jordan followed. They both sat down in chairs as Ben pressed play on the DVD remote and then paused it right back again.

Ben looked at Kennley holding up both of his hands. "Hey K, where are the snacks man? How do you expect us to have a movie marathon without snacks? I mean if you're gonna do something at least do it thoroughly.

Kennley sighed again.

"You know Kennley," Jordan started. "You really should be used to us showing up uninvited by now. We've been doing this for a long time and usually you're anger subsides after ten minutes or so."

Ben announced he was going to get snacks after Kennley refused to. Before he left though, he and Hannah had an argument about how much butter he was going to put in the popcorn.

Hannah eyes almost never left my face and I couldn't take it much longer. I didn't understand what I had ever done to deserve a stare like that. What had I done to offend her...sure I was with her ex, but she couldn't have been that bitter could she? I didn't want to spend another second in that room with her. I didn't understand what I had done to Hannah to make her hate me so much besides interfering with a relationship that ended three months ago.

"Maybe Ben might need some help downstairs." I stood up quickly and left before anyone could say anything.

Ben wasn't too far ahead of me. He slowed his pace so I could catch up to him walking down the many hallways. When I was finally walking beside him he looked down at me and smiled.

"Don't let her bother you," he said.

It didn't take me anytime to realize who and what we were talking about.

"In a way I'm a little happy that she hates you."

I looked up at him shocked. "Why?"

He grinned. "I swear every month she picks a new person to hate and ruin their life. Last month, I was her target. In April she brought her dog over to my house. Her dog ended up peeing on all of my old *Teenage Mutant Ninja Turtles* tapes. It was awful. I mean those were like antiques. I swear she convinced that mutt to do it."

Of course someone like Ben would have *Teenage Mutant Ninja Turtle* tapes.

I sighed. "And now she's moved on to me."

"And with motive this time too. She's the ex-girlfriend. She has a reason to hate you. That just makes it all the more worse."

It was only the beginning of June. I could have cried at the fact that I had a whole month to go.

Ben and I walked into the kitchen and I watched as he moved around going through cabinets grabbing popcorn and candy. He had enough food for twenty people lying on the counter for us to bring back upstairs.

My heart sunk to my stomach when Hannah sauntered into the kitchen. I noticed that she had added some dark streaks to her blond hair to make it dirty blond...which was only fitting.

Hannah reached her hand into the bowl of popcorn and put a single piece into her mouth. "Benjamin, how much butter did you put into the popcorn?"

He brushed past her and put a whole handful of popcorn into his mouth. "What is it girls and carbs and fats? I don't get it personally. As long as you don't look like a fat cow, no one cares if you gain a couple of pounds from eating chocolate cake...*or* overly buttered popcorn."

Hannah rolled her eyes. "I'm not worried about my weight, genius. Not only is all this butter disgusting and greasy but it's bad for your heart."

"Cry me a river..." Ben popped a marshmallow into his mouth.

I didn't know my heart could sink any deeper but it did once Hannah moved her glare from Ben to me making me feel incredibly uncomfortable.

"So, how are you and Kennley doing?" she asked moving over to the cabinets to grab a bag of popcorn to stick in the microwave.

"Fine." I said curtly.

She raised her eyebrows. "Why not spectacular?"

"Why do you care? Don't you have a boyfriend you should be worrying about instead of mine?"

Ben chuckled to himself quietly before exiting out of the kitchen with bowls of food. I looked at him panicked. I couldn't believe he was leaving me alone with her.

Hannah seemed to be a little thrown by what I had said. I guess I struck some kind of nerve. "You know...when I was going out with Kennley, we shared everything with each other. We didn't have any secrets. We didn't want a relationship based on lies. Is it the same for you two?"

I didn't answer right away.

The microwave went off and I jumped back. Maybe Kennley was right. I was really stressed and that was making me anxious.

She laughed at me before the glare returned. "When in doubt, Google is a good place to start."

I tried to ignore everything she had just said. I grabbed the package of cookies Ben had put on the counter but forgot to bring up. I quickly hurried out of the kitchen and made the long trip back up the stairs. My calves and thighs were burning when I finally got there. The door was cracked and I stopped to catch my breath before going in.

I heard Ben laughing. "Hell hath no fury..."

"Ben," Kennley said and his was voice reproachful. "I was kind of counting on you to be the peacemaker down there. Where's Kahlen?"

"Probably tied to a stick roasting over open flames right now."

Kennley sighed.

Ben chuckled. "Well dude, what did you expect? Did you think being the kind of person Hannah is that she'd forget how you publicly humiliated her by dumping her and yelling at her about being a slut and a cheater and then—,"

Jordan was laughing now. "Ha, I forgot about that. That was hilarious. And it was in front of like half the school too. I even think someone filmed it on their cell phone."

As much joy as I got out of the image of Kennley publicly dumping her it didn't really seem like he would do that sort of thing. Something else must have happened for him to do that. And then I almost felt bad for Hannah...almost. I couldn't imagine the embarrassment of all of that.

I heard Kennley sigh heavily. "I said I was sorry, didn't I?

Jordan laughed. "Dude, girls are like elephants, they never forget.

I didn't like being compared to an elephant.

I could see Ben setting the bowl on the table through the crack in the door. "All I'm saying is you need to check your women. We already have enough drama without another love triangle with another girl running to Ross—,"

"Enough," Ross's deep voice said and I was amazed at how there wasn't another sound in the room.

"Maybe I should go downstairs and—," Kennley broke the silence.

"No," Ben said. "Maybe we should let them duke this out. I mean it might be entertaining to see a catfight. And do you think your parents would let us fill the hot tub with mud...nope, that's too much work. I guess water would do just fine. But who do you think would win?"

"Hannah," Ben and Jordan both said at the same time before laughing.

Kennley grabbed a pillow and chucked it at Ben. "Man shut up."

I heard Hannah's footsteps coming up the stairs so I figured now would be a good time to go in instead of being caught eavesdropping. I opened the door further. It was funny that all the guys except Ross jumped back and looked guilty. I wasn't sure if I was seeing things but I could have sworn that Ross looked at me and smiled.

I didn't have to look at my clock to know that it was three in the morning. I woke up with my head pounding. I knew I shouldn't be wasting the precious time I had to sleep or at the very least, if I wasn't going to sleep I could have been studying. But there was something in the back of my head that I couldn't let go. It was the evil, menacing voice of Hannah Andrews. There was something that she had implied to me earlier that I had ignored. *"When in doubt, Google is a good place to start."*

It suddenly clicked in my head. I got out of my bed abruptly and the sudden movement didn't help my head any. I knew I should try to go back to sleep. It would have been the smart thing to do instead of risking being sleepy or actually falling asleep during exams. But then again, if I did try to go back to sleep I would have been wide away anyhow...especially with something like this nagging me in the back of my head.

I went over to my dresser and turned on the laptop I hadn't used in a while. When my desktop came up I was happy that I had changed it from a picture with Emma and me to one with me lying on the beach with sunglasses on. You could even see the reflection of the sky and clouds on my glasses. I got online quickly and went to Google. I sighed as I typed in: Kennley Morgan.

I half expected...and hoped that nothing would come up. But hopes aren't reality and I learned that as soon as many websites came up with the name Kennley Morgan. I scanned down the page quickly and clicked on the first website. An article in the newspaper from 2005 came up.

Skipping

"Fifteen year old Kennley Morgan was expelled. Why you ask? Because of skipping. At Rigley High, showing up late to class, or not showing up at all earns you a detention. The freshman Kennley Morgan however did not step up to the rules. Some of you may be thinking, "Expulsion, that's a bit harsh." But some might argue otherwise. Also at Rigley High there is a limit to how many detentions one student can get per school year before getting put on academic probation. And if you get a detention and don't serve it, you get more detentions including Saturday detentions. If a student still does not attend, suspension is involved. But how many times can a student be suspended? Well let's just say Kennley Morgan passed his limit gaining him expulsion. What I found interesting was that despite the amount of time he actually spent at school, he is at the top of his class grade wise. I'm sure the principal took that into account before his final decision which it was officially made last week Tuesday."

I wasn't too alarmed by reading this. Kennley had said that he had been expelled a lot even though he didn't go into great detail about it. It wasn't until I got to other articles about him that my heart began to seem frail. I found other articles about him being expelled for fighting and drinking. I even came across a video of him fighting someone else. I couldn't imagine him doing either. It said that he had been caught drunk on campus and he had been getting into fights. I found another article labeled: Cheating Scandal and Crest Moore High, Four Students Involved, One Expelled.

A video from YouTube came up. I clicked on and

was truly surprised that it was Ross and not Kennley from 2006. The video was from the news.

"Junior Ross Hopkins at Crest Moore High has found himself in tons of trouble. Look at these before and after pictures of Dan Abbott's home that was broken into on Friday night."

I winced at the after picture. The inside of the house was completely destroyed. They didn't leave one lamp unbroken.

"Although expected that Ross Hopkins wasn't alone in this act, the rest of the people along with him had gotten away before the police had gotten there leaving Ross to take the blame. The one question that Ross Hopkins refuses to answer is, why? No one is sure of the motive especially because Dan Abbott doesn't even live in town."

The screen changed to Dan Abbott in his home.

Dan put his hand to his face. *"I just don't understand why anyone would do this. They didn't even steal anything; all they did was wreck everything. I'm very confused as to why someone would do this. I can't really think back to any enemies I've made over the years. I'm just happy that my five year old daughter, my baby boy, and my wife and I were out of town at the time and we have good neighbors that called the police."*

The screen went back to the anchor woman. *"Ross Hopkins will be facing fines to fix the house and many hours of community service. He is lucky that he is just shy of being of age so he will not be facing jail time. Once again, police suspect that others might have been involved in this act but Ross was the only one at the scene of the crime."*

I looked at the screen incredulously. I couldn't understand why Ross would do something like that. But other questions were being brought to the surface in my mind...Ross wasn't alone and I had a guess who could have been with him.

It didn't fit though. The Kennley I know, and the Kennley I had learned so much about tonight didn't match. They were like two completely different people. If it weren't for the pictures along with the articles I would have thought they were talking about a different Kennley. There was a lot that he had left out in telling me about himself. I knew what he meant when he had said that he was afraid for me to know the real him. But I already did know the real him, the one who was nice and funny and impulsive. That was the real him. The person I was reading about tonight wasn't the real him...but maybe it used to be.

There were articles on different Kennley Morgan's but mainly the one I knew just popping up again and again, and now I was realizing just how popular my boyfriend was, and it wasn't in a good way. There was even something in the newspaper about him driving drunk at some point and with every piece of news my heart sunk to a new level.

I understood why Hannah had done this. Maybe Ben was wrong. Maybe Hannah wasn't out to ruin my life. She was out to ruin Kennley's life and she was trying to do it through me. She wanted me to know the truth about Kennley. She's trying to drive another wedge between us. I had to give it to her though...She was an absolute genius, an evil genius.

I didn't know what I was going to do now. Could I just pretend like I didn't know about all the things Kennley had done? Would he ever tell me all of these things himself? It was all so frustrating. My head began to pound more. I turned off my laptop not wanting to see more. I had already seen enough to keep me awake for the rest of the night.

I was so shocked that I didn't think I had blinked in the last couple of minutes. I opened my bedroom door deciding to eat something while I was up. There was a thick book lying on the floor with a note on top. It was a yearbook. I picked it up curiously and continued walking down the stairs. When I got into the kitchen I quickly turned the light on so I could see. The note on top of the book was from my mother.

Honey,
Marissa stopped by while you were at Kennley's house.
She said that she got your yearbook for you.
`Mom

I hadn't had much time to talk to my parents. As soon as I got home from Kennley's, I went upstairs, showered, then went to bed. I didn't even remember saying hi to them when I walked through the door. I was still very tired although my mind was completely wired right now. I had been studying like crazy and I hoped that it would be enough for tomorrow. I was happy that I had my English and math exams first so I could get them out of the way.

I opened up my yearbook and was surprised that there were signatures. I couldn't believe that Marissa would go through the trouble of actually having people sign it. I would have gotten my book earlier today if I would have gone to lunch. I decided to skip it and go to the library to study. It wasn't like I was missing out on anything.

I was actually growing a new appreciation for Marissa Harrison which surprised me. The night at The T.J. Club she hadn't even seemed annoying to me. I had actually had a good time.

I flipped through my yearbook and lots of people that I didn't know had signed it. In the mix of people I didn't know I saw Kennley's handwriting.

Dean,

I don't really understand this whole signing yearbooks thing. I mean, what's the point in writing a page long speech talking about things I could say right to your face? I guess it's about memories and telling people how you feel about them so ten years from now we have something to look back on. Well you already know how I feel about you so is there really any need for me to write about it? I'll keep this short. This has been an interesting two and a half months

Love you,

Kenneth Bradley

I smiled and then sighed. I was beginning to feel so torn. How was I supposed to act like I didn't know? What if I just told him that I knew everything? I wondered if he would be mad at me. There was another question in the back of my mind...was I *okay* with it all? After a while of staring out into space I came to a conclusion. Half of the things I had learned about Kennley weren't really him. I remembered him saying at ICC that he wasn't the same as he used to be. If that was the truth about him then I could live with that. But I still had a ton of questions that needed to be answered.

18. The Moon

I hated grocery stores. No, more than that, I loathed grocery stores, despised them even. They were always cold and my arms would be covered with goose bumps as soon as I stepped through those automatic doors. It seemed like everyone was always at the grocery store at the same time which made it incredibly crowded and the big squeaky shopping carts didn't help. Unfortunately I had been dragged here by my mother.

Thomas Designs had been a business started by my mother around two years ago. Their two year anniversary was today and we were throwing an enormous party at our house tonight. My mom was almost as big a procrastinator as I was. She had all but poured water on my face to wake me up this morning to do some last minute shopping for the party. I unwillingly stumbled out of bed with an attitude. I was realizing that it was easier for me to sleep during the day than it was for me to sleep at night and my mother had interrupted my much needed rest.

It was more than a relief, a gift from God himself that school had been canceled today. There had been a big storm early this morning that caused a lot of accidents on the express way. Tree branches had fallen down all over the streets and everything. I was used to having snow days...but never *rain* days. It was somewhat amusing that the storm was over now. It seemed to end right after school was announced canceled. Now the sun was peeking its way through the clouds in the blue sky.

When my mom had asked me to go to the store with her, it wasn't exactly a question. It was terribly wrong of her to force me to go. She knew how much I hated grocery stores. Heck, anyone with ears to listen knew how much I hated grocery stores. My parents thought that it was irrational but I thought just the opposite. Most of the time, people bothered me. That was part of the reason why I never really had any other friends besides Emma.

Today in particular, I truly detested the grocery store. Not only was I tired from my sleepless night but there was a woman behind us that I could have sworn was following us. I turn around every so often to scowl at her hoping she would get a hint. She was a woman with light brown hair that seemed so tiny with her frail frame; I couldn't believe she had five kids. I tried to imagine her pregnant. I got the image of her holding her protruding stomach and then toppling over on top of it.

I sighed heavily as my mother debated on regular Ranch dressing or Cucumber Ranch. It seemed so pointless to spend countless seconds deciding on something that hardly mattered. I also sighed because behind me two of the five kids were sitting inside of the shopping cart crying and the other three who were old enough to walk were fighting. I didn't understand why it was mandatory that the woman bring her annoying children with her to the store. I considered the fact that maybe she didn't have anywhere else for them to go but at the very least she should have been able to keep them under control. The two oldest kids were as bad as my mother arguing about which cereal to buy.

I couldn't take much more of this without completely losing my mind.

"Mom," I said curtly over the crying. "What other things do you need on the list?" I needed an escape.

"I need paper towels and—,"

I knew that paper towels were on the other side of the store. I could see freedom, almost smell it. "Perfect. I'll go get them."

I practically ran away from the annoying woman and her kids. I soon as they were out of sight I slowed my pace. I walked as slowly as possible to the other side of the store to stall going back. I wasn't really paying attention to where I was going as I studied the square patterns on the floor that were running together in my mind.

Kennley couldn't leave my mind. Not even for a second could I escape constant thoughts about him. I knew I couldn't go forever acting like I didn't know everything he had been hiding. And in the pit of my stomach it hurt to some degree. He had promised me that he was done hiding things. I wondered had he lied to me about anything. I could feel the trust in our relationship beginning to fade. I thought about Dan Abbott. His beautiful home was destroyed and I couldn't understand why Ross or Kennley might do something like that to a stranger and his family. Nothing made sense these days and it wasn't helping my constant headaches.

I should have expected to run into something eventually because I wasn't paying attention to where I was going. But if anything, I expected to run into a pole and embarrass myself. I didn't expect to run in to something frail and then hear something crash as it hit the ground.

I looked up and saw an old lady with a cane looking

at me like I was to blame for all the bad in my generation. She had been carrying a can of chicken noodle soup which had fell to the ground and been dented because of me. I picked up the can and handed it to her. My cheeks flushed and I apologized to her at least twenty times in three seconds. I started backing up in the other direction as I keep apologizing frantically. If I had of been paying attention instead of thinking about Kennley I wouldn't have practically injured a senior citizen. This was all his fault. I still wasn't paying very much attention as I backed up and rammed into something hard. But it wasn't a pole, it felt like something muscular and tall. I turned around quickly and believe it or not Ross was standing in front of me. I actually had to wipe my eyes because I wasn't sure if I was seeing things or not.

I suppressed a scream that was dying to be released from my mouth. Ross was so *dark*. I didn't know how to describe him in any other way but that. He seemed to be amused. It seem like it wasn't because I had ran into him but because I had ran into an old lady who was now giving me the stink eye.

We both stared at each other for a long while. I was breathing extra hard trying to catch my breath and steady my heart beat.

"Hi." I managed to get out. I looked around him waiting for the other clowns to get out of the car, as Kennley had put it. "Where are the others?" I asked stupidly.

His eyebrows furrowed. "What others?"

I realized that I had never said so much as one word to Ross. But it was strange. I felt incredibly uncomfortable standing in front of him and yet so at ease at the same time. The feeling didn't make much sense.

I blushed. "I'm sorry. I was just kind of under the impression that your kind traveled in packs of fours."

He grinned so briefly that I wasn't even sure if I had seen it cross his face. "Well, it used to be fives."

I sighed. "No thanks to me I guess."

He shrugged. "It's not *entirely* your fault although you do play a role."

I couldn't believe I was talking to Ross. I was actually having a conversation with him. I hadn't even heard him speak more than a couple of sentences.

"Why are you here?" I wanted to hit myself over the head for such a stupid question.

His face was suddenly serious, if that was even possible for it to be more serious than before. "Well this is kind of a secret and all so I don't know if I should say."

It was like he spoke fear into my heart. I gulped. "O-oh," I stuttered.

"But I don't know...you seem trustworthy enough." He was speaking in a hushed tone drawing me in closer. "So the real reason why I'm here is because... well, I'm actually buying groceries. *Scandalous* isn't it?"

I couldn't help but laugh. I was so stupid. I almost couldn't believe it myself but he was laughing too. I didn't know someone so dark could have a sense of humor.

"But shouldn't you be at school?" I wasn't sure if Crest Moore had a rain day too or if he was just skipping.

"I'm a senior so I'm out of school already. And we didn't have school today anyway so I was over at Hannah's house. My mom wanted me to go grocery shopping on my way home so here I am."

I nodded. "Here you are."

An awkward second passed quickly.

"So why are *you* here?" He asked.

I stood there like an idiot not answering. I honestly couldn't remember why I was here or even where I was. I noticed that Ross's eyes were actually blue. They didn't seem as dark as they did before but there was still a weird presence about him.

"Um…I'm shopping for a party. My mom has a big work thing tonight and I volunteered to get the paper towels."

He looked down at my arms that looked fragile and lanky compared to his. "…And yet your hands are empty."

"Well I was on my way to get them but I kinda bumped into something." I winced just thinking about it.

"*Two* somethings actually," he corrected.

I smiled sheepishly. "Sorry about that by the way."

He shrugged. "Why don't you make it up to me then? Some friends of mine are throwing a huge party to kick off the summer. You should come. It's Friday night at nine."

I couldn't have been more surprised if someone would have come behind me and hit me in the head with a bat. Was he only inviting me, or was that an extended invitation for Kennley too? Surely Kennley already knew about the party anyhow.

"Actually I think Kennley's working Friday night."

He grinned slightly. "I didn't say anything about Kennley coming. And besides, he's busy most days anyhow. He never even answers his phone anymore. I think the last time I called him and he actually answered was about two and a half months ago when Ben was—," He paused. "—Well Ben was being stupid and I needed his help. After that he got so sick of us bothering him that in protest he actually smashed his phone to the ground. Dude's got a temper. He didn't have another phone for a couple of weeks so he used mine for some reason and ever since some of his admirers were calling me asking for him. I'm just happy they've stopped now."

I turned tomato red and I ducked my head down a little so Ross wouldn't notice. He was wrong. It wasn't admirers that were calling him, just one. I had embarrassingly been that one.

"But..." he continued. "You're not busy Friday night are you?"

I just looked at him shocked. I couldn't believe it was the same person I had seen yesterday. And it almost sounded like he was asking me out although I knew that he wasn't. He had a girlfriend and I had a boyfriend. There was no reason at all that he would be interested in me.

"*Didn't Kennley tell you that they're in a very open relationship?*" she said.

"I don't know. Parties aren't really my scene."

He grinned. "Well what *is* your scene?"

I shrugged. "Probably something along the lines of a nice quiet evening curled up in front of the TV with a bowl of cereal." It didn't sound as pathetic in my head.

I was still shocked that I was standing in front of Ross...the bad alpha dog himself.

"What TV shows?" he asked.

This threw me off guard. "Mostly reality shows or re-runs of *Gilmore Girls* and *The Fresh Prince of Bel-Air*." That didn't sound as pathetic in my head either as it did actually coming out.

I wasn't sure if he disapproved of my TV choice or not because all he did was nod once.

As if I wasn't pathetic enough, my mother came walking down the same aisle Ross and I were standing in. She didn't see us at first and I stood frozen in fear of her actually seeing me. I saw realization flicker in her eyes as she pushed the basket quickly towards me.

"Sweetie, I decided to get both the cucumber and the regular. I even got Zesty Italian. I want people to have their options..." She trailed off as she saw the tall, frightening young man standing in front of me looking amused. Not only was I grocery shopping on my day off, but I was grocery shopping with my mother. It shouldn't have been embarrassing yet I wanted to run away and hide. "Honey, who is this?" She gestured towards Ross.

I tried to see my mother through Ross's eyes. For the most part, we looked a lot like each other with the same features except her hair was lighter, shorter than mine, and wavy.

"Um...This is my—," I cut my sentence short. Ross wasn't my anything. I wasn't really sure if we were friends or not although we were having a very friendly conversation. "This is my...this is Kennley's friend."

He stuck out his hand. "Ross."

My mother took his hand and shook it. I could tell that she thought he was frightening also. She turned from Ross to me. "Well I see you haven't gotten the paper towels, so I'll go get them and you can go meet me over there."

I nodded as she walked off looking back at me suspiciously. I turned back to Ross. "I guess I better go." I started to walk off in the direction my mom had gone in.

"Wait," he said when I had walked a couple of steps. "By the way, I think that you would win in the fight."

I stared at him puzzled for a second. I thought about

when I had been eavesdropping at the door yesterday at Kennley's.

He smiled. "You're not as sneaky as you think you are. The door was cracked and I could see you standing out there listening to us."

"Oh." My cheeks burned red. "But I'm not so sure I'd win."

"We'll see."

I shook my head no. "Very unlikely. Fighting someone doesn't exactly fit in with a quiet evening with TV and cereal."

He didn't seem so dark anymore…more like dim. "No, I guess it doesn't."

{space}

I was officially sick of the business party. It had been dragging on all evening and I wanted everyone to leave so the house could be peaceful again. My dad and I were more like caterers than guest. We were responsible for refilling the trays of foods to keep everyone satisfied. Everyone was now just walking around mingling so I hid out of the back porch looking up into the sky.

I wished I could see more stars. The city had its limitations when it came to nature. I could see the bright moon lighting up the sky and a few stars as accessories along with it.

I sighed. I still couldn't stop thinking about Kennley. It was like a bad omen had washed over me and I was fighting the inevitable. I could feel that something bad was going to happen. I was trying to plan out in my head of all the ways to confront him about my new found knowledge. I knew it the back of my head that he would be mad at me. He would be mad at me for being stupid enough to listen to Hannah and then possibly jumping to conclusions. But I had a right to be mad at him also. He hadn't told me the whole truth…isn't that considered a lie of omission?

I thought about how easy life was as a kid. Everything was so simple and anything but complex. The biggest worry in the world was getting a time out or the chicken pox. As a child I lived a sheltered life with not too many cares or worries. Everything was headache free. It didn't seem fair that as I got older I'd have to face the hardships of puberty, more responsibilities, and tough life decisions. It seemed like as I got older, everything got harder. I still shuddered at the thought of college which was rapidly approaching. I kept waiting for myself to finally get a grip on life and then as soon as I started to get that first hand on the steering wheel, the whole thing was ripped from me. It felt like I was freefalling…always trying to catch my breath. It wasn't fair. As much as I knew that fact, it still seemed like something should be able to go my way. I wanted to get through this storm of mine so badly. I wanted to fast forward so I didn't have to go through every miserable day waiting for it to be over.

It seemed like Kennley was the moon in my starless night. It was the only thing that gave me a little bit of hope and light. But I needed stars. I wanted stars. I couldn't be satisfied with just the moon forever. But I wasn't willing to give Kennley up…not just yet.

My father opened the screen door behind me and sat down on the porch beside me. He smiled at me briefly before putting his arm around me and pulling me closer to him. I leaned my head against his shoulder and sighed heavily.

"You know…" He said. "It's nothing like this when I go camping. You can hardly see the dark blue because of the star filled sky. You should come with me sometime so you can see for yourself."

"Dad, you know how I feel about the outdoors."

He grinned. "Didn't you hear Kido? Being high maintenance is out of style these days. It's time you rough it up a little. There's nothing like sleeping in a tent and peeing on the ground."

"Oh, well when you put it like that..." I said sarcastically.

"Really Kido, it's not that bad. I think you'd actually like it if you gave it a fair shot."

Just the thought of sleeping on the cold hard ground with nothing but a tent, a fire, and a sleeping bag to keep me warm made me feel uncomfortable. I'd much rather sleep in my comfy bed or a nearby hotel than camp with my dad.

He released my shoulder and tilted his head up to the sky. "So are you just out here hiding out from the party or is there something more on your mind?"

I sighed. "Dad, do you ever wish that you could be young again, so everything wouldn't be so hard."

He chuckled. "Kido, you are young. And being young *is* hard. Everything is so confusing that half of the time you don't know right from left. But it passes. It may not seem like it now, but it does."

I didn't believe him for a second.

He stood up on the porch from beside me. "Well I gotta get to work before I'm late."

I turned to look at him. "Work? It's nine o'clock. You need a vacation before you work yourself into an early grave." My voice cracked.

I couldn't imagine what I would do without my dad. I figured that he would pass before I would but I hoped it wouldn't be soon. I wasn't sure how I could possibly manage to stay sane if that happened.

He heard the strain in my voice and sighed. "You know good and well that I'm not going anywhere anytime soon. Don't waste your time worrying about me. You mother does that enough for all three of us."

I nodded.

He leaned down to press his lips to the top of my head quickly before heading towards the screen door that lead into the kitchen. "Oh, and Kahlen..."

I looked up. Just by saying my actual name he had my attention.

"Try to get some rest tonight okay?" He continued.-

I knew he must have heard me up last night. I nodded again before he left.

No sooner than my dad left, Cece came and sat down next to me cheerfully. It had been a while since I had last seen her but she was still the same, beautiful and quirky with her short blond hair.

"Hey BD," she said. She was wearing a long khaki skirt and lavender top.

It took me a second to remember that BD stood for boss's daughter. "Hey Cece." I tried to sound equally as cheerful but it came out as flat.

"So are you out here hiding from the party, or are you just naturally anti-social?"

I smiled weakly. "Anti-social actually."

She nodded. "That's understandable. Only children can be that way sometimes I think. Before I decided that I wanted to go into interior design, I did psychology for a little bit. I like helping people."

I couldn't help but smile at that. Cece didn't look like the therapist type.

"But besides being anti-social you seem sad. Is something wrong? I bet it's about a guy isn't it. Your boyfriend maybe?"

I sighed. My life didn't revolve around Kennley. He

wasn't the center of my universe. "That's part of it," I answered.

"Well what's all of it?"

"Life," I said sourly.

"Life sucks some times. Being a teenager definitely sucks. But try being a teenager with cancer."

"What?"

"Ka Duh." She hit her hand against her forehead. "I'm sorry, that's right...you probably have no idea of what I'm talking about do you?" She reached to her neck and lifted up her necklace with a silver heart at the bottom. I leaned in closer to see what was engraved on the heart. It said: Survivor.

"My parents got it made for me a while back. I was diagnosed with cancer at fifteen. It's in remission now. But during the beginning of it I was so terrified of dying. It didn't seem fair that I had this whole life ahead of me only to be taken away by a stupid disease. I wrote in my journal everyday so when I died the people I loved would have something else to remember me by. I was inspired by Ann Frank in a way. But the weird thing is that before cancer I was the shiest person you would ever meet. I know it's hard to believe but it's true. But after, I was so happy that I was going to live that it seemed pointless to spend life tucked away in my shell. I even got a new hairstyle of out it. I used to have long hair but then when I had to grow my hair all back again I realized that I kind of liked it short."

I just looked at her shocked. "That must have been really hard for you."

She shrugged. "It's definitely something that I wouldn't want to re-visit in my life but I don't regret it." She smiled, "It's all about making good out of bad experiences."

She was so incredibly optimistic.

"I can't believe you used to be shy." I shook my head in amazement.

"Holy mother of sugar, I know. It was mostly because I was scared. I'm not exactly sure what I was afraid of…I guess of living. But as soon as living was slowly being taken away as one of my options…things changed. Don't tell Laura I said this, but that's the reason why she doesn't have a boyfriend. She's afraid to fall in love. She'll never admit it but she is. It's kind of sad actually. The way I see it, I'd rather have had a great life and die at fifteen than live a boring shy life and die at eighty. Love is a risk but a risk worth taking."

"Have you ever been in love?" I asked.

"Once…and it was absolutely *terrifying*. And yet it was some of the best days of my life. I ended up getting hurt in the end but I've never regretted it. I'd do it all over again if I had the chance," she said. "Have you?"

"I don't know. But I think I'm coming close," I admitted, more to myself than Cece.

She smiled. "Are you terrified?"

"*Without a doubt*," she said.

"Most definitely," I answered

"Well then maybe you're closer than you think."

I looked up into the sky. It had gotten darker so more stars were visible but still not too many more than before. Mostly just the moon lit up the night.

I sighed. "Maybe."

You can't be satisfied with just the moon forever…

19. Changes

Exams were finally over and I actually felt confident about all of my tests. Despite that being the one good thing going on in my life, everything else had been its usual bad. I had been avoiding seeing Kennley all week. The only time I had talked to him was on the phone which had been short and to the point conversations.

"Hey, how are you?" He would ask after finally answering on the fourth ring.

"Good," I'd lie.

"So um, listen, work's been crazy lately. I'm sorry I haven't been able to spend much time with you."

"No. It's fine. I've been busy too." Another lie.

Then he would curse and yell something in the background to Carrie and I'd probably hear a crash of some sort in the background.

"Uh…is everything okay over there?" I'd ask.

He'd sigh. "Yeah. It's fine. Things have just been… hectic, that's all." His voice would sound strained causing me to pretend like I wasn't worried.

Then there would be another crash, or something else that would cause him to say, "Sorry Kahlen. I gotta go. Love you alright, bye."

I would say bye but by the time I had, he would have already hung up. I keep chickening out whenever I'd talk to him. I was trying to find an easy way in my mind to tell him all that I knew about him. But there was no easy way.

I walked to Dean's Creek half suspecting that Kennley might be there. We hadn't agreed to meet each other but I couldn't avoid him forever. It was hard to miss seeing someone and trying to avoid them at the same time. I missed those green eyes, and his smile, even his smell.

I saw him against the grass with his eyes shut sun bathing shirtless. There was only one time before that I had seen Kennley without a shirt on. It seemed like forever ago when he had been teaching me the art of distraction. I still couldn't believe he had jumped into the water. The water looked fresh but I still didn't trust its cleanliness. I kind of chuckled to myself at the fact that we both spent most of our time at an old abandoned creek. It didn't make sense.

I walked slowly over to him hoping to scare him like he often did to me. Maybe I could prove that I wasn't the only jumpy person on this planet. I came up behind him tip-toeing. I tried to stick to the task at hand but I couldn't stop my wandering eyes from appraising him a moment before I plopped down beside him quickly.

His eyes opened slowly. I hadn't startled him whatsoever. "Next time don't step on a branch. It totally ruins your cover."

He wasn't smiling, or even giving a little grin like he usually was when he saw me. His face looked blank which for him always meant he was either in deep thought, or upset. He sat up off the ground slowly and grabbed his nearby gray shirt and put it on.

"You look upset. What wrong?" I asked observing the slight frown on his face.

He sighed. "I'm not really in the best of moods and to only make matters worse I didn't get very much sleep last night."

"Well why not?" I prodded.

"Does it matter?" he snapped.

I looked at him shocked. "No...I just thought that maybe if you wanted to talk about it—,"

"You never want to talk about what happened over spring break with you and Emma I respect that. I pretend like nothing ever happened just like you do. Why can't you do the same for me?"

I felt my stomach flip flop inside of me.

I recoiled as if he'd slapped me. I backed away and got to my feet on instinct. "I'm...I'm sorry." I didn't know exactly why I was apologizing. It was partly because I was so stunned that he'd actually say something like that. It was like he was purposefully trying to hurt me.

He sighed heavily before standing up and facing me. "No Kahlen, stop. Don't apologize. I should be the one saying sorry. You didn't deserve that."

He looked truly apologetic as his green eyes stared back into my brown ones. I didn't have a choice but to forgive him. It was impossible to resist surrendering.

"I'm kind of having one of those days when life is taking its entire wrath out on me and it sucks. But that doesn't justify me snapping at you like that."

I smiled half heartedly. "Well what can I do to cheer you up?"

He took a step closer to me and wrapped his hand around mine and placed it around the back of his neck. He grabbed my other hand and did the same so they were wrapped around his neck.

"Kiss and make-up."

I was completely chickening out. I wasn't supposed to be kissing him... I was supposed to be finding out the truth. I didn't want to risk a fight...and right now we were doing anything but fighting. But I knew I couldn't avoid it forever. And it didn't help that Kennley distracted me every chance he got.

I pulled back. "Make-up or make-out?"

He still wasn't smiling. He wasn't scowling either but his face was blank. "I don't really see the difference."

I wanted to cheer him up. It was my mission and I didn't want to stop until it was accomplished. I wouldn't be satisfied until I saw the usual sparkle his eyes had when the corners of his mouth would reach upward happily.

"You're working tonight right?" I asked. I wondered if going to the party would cheer him up.

He narrowed his eyes at me. "No, why?"

I titled my head slightly. "Well Ross said—,"

He backed away from me. "Ross? Since when are you and Ross talking?" he said curtly.

I didn't understand why he was going so hot and cold on me. It felt like I had just struck a nerve with him. "I-I bumped into him earlier this week. He invited me to a party tonight and said that you couldn't come because you had to work. I thought maybe a party would cheer you up."

I could tell that something was really bothering him and it just went into overdrive when I mentioned Ross.

"Are you sure you want to go? I mean these kinds of things get really out of hand sometimes.

Are you sure that's really your kind of scene?"

I sighed. "That's *so* irrelevant. And besides, this way I still don't lose the bet. You're not getting me to do something crazy, I am."

I could tell that Kennley wanted to go but he was hesitant. I figured that a lot of his old friends would be at the party so maybe that would make him happy.

"Are you sure you want to go?" he asked again.

"Eighty-three percent sure."

It was a relief that he grinned briefly. "What about the other seventeen?"

The other seventeen percent of me wanted to talk to him about everything I knew. My boyfriend was practically an ex-con…or at least I hoped he was an *ex*-con.

I smiled. "The other seventeen percent of me wants to finish making-up." I lied.

Kennley wasn't the only one who was good at distractions.

What exactly does one wear to a party? I kept asking myself that question over and over again as I stared into my closet. I had been staring at it for a long time now and still nothing popped out to me that said *party*. I finally settled with a blue v-neck shirt with a black tank top underneath.

I saw Kennley waiting in his BMW across the street. I didn't want to have to deal with him coming inside to be interrogated by my parents so I figured this way was easier. I told them that I was leaving but I never said where. The beauty of it though- was that they didn't ask where I was going. If they would have known I was going to a party at someone's house that I had never even met before with a whole bunch of other people I didn't know, plus no parental supervision… things would have gone badly. I sort of implied I was going to the creek with Kennley although I never said the exact words. My parents trusted me. They trusted me to be home at a good hour and not to do anything stupid. I trusted myself too…but it didn't mean I wasn't scared to get thrown into the lion's den.

I ran out the door and across the street to Kennley's car. I told him to wait before he pulled off. My parents weren't the brightest bulbs in the auditorium but they would have been a little suspicious if they heard a car pulling off when I'm supposed to be walking in the opposite direction to the creek.

It took us awhile to get to the party considering it was all the way in Crest Moore and I was beginning to get anxious. I was trying to prepare myself for all the wild things I was about to see. From what had been implied earlier I assumed it would be like the ones I had never seen in real life but only in the movies. There would be dirty dancing, alcohol, drugs, sex, and maybe even police. I gulped. I was possibly the stupidest person on earth…I wasn't just walking into the lion's den…I was leaping—jumping even.

When we finally got to the party, Kennley noticed how tense I was. We were walking on the sidewalk to the house with the millions of people inside and the music blasting. I knew the neighbors couldn't be happy with the noise level. I got the image of my dad coming to bust up the party, uniform, gun and all, and then sees me standing there like a deer in headlights. I shuddered.

Kennley grabbed my hand and squeezed it gently. "Promise me you won't leave my side tonight."

"I won't," I promised.

There was no way I wanted him farther than three feet away from me. The door to big house was already open and as soon as I stepped in, the music was making my ear drums pound. It didn't take us long to spot Ross and the others. They were sitting on a couch off in the corner of the room away from everyone else. As Ben and Jordan greeted Kennley, I was still holding onto his hand tightly. I was completely taken by surprise when Ben stood up and gave me a big bear hug. I was beginning to realize that these things were to be expected from Ben...randomness.

"Um...Hi." I said once he let go of me,

"Kahlen my friend, you're right on time. I apologize though because I have to speak in rhyme." He said in a bad accent.

"And an Irish accent." Jordan added.

I just nodded.

So much for three feet away...Kennley walked to Ross who had summoned him over. Ross whispered something to him that sounded like, "It's happening tonight."

My heart started beating loudly as if it were about to pop out of my chest. I couldn't go on pretending like I didn't know anything for much longer. I was scared it might change things between us. I convinced myself that I hadn't heard anything Ross had just said and I wasn't going to let it bother me.

Hannah looked bored with her arm propped up on Ross's shoulder. "Babe, go get me a drink, will ya?"

Ross nodded and stood of the couch. It was amazing how one moment Ross is the alpha, and the next he's a little slave. I figured that the drink Hannah wanted didn't happen to be juice, soda, or water. Ross returned quickly with the drink in a big red cup and Hannah chugged it down with ease. I glowered at her. From the last time I had saw her she had added some black and red streaks to her hair.

Jordan and Ben left to the other side of the room discussing something petty while Hannah moved her hand to Ross's back and started making circles with her hand.

"Babe, let's go dance."

Ross turned to her. "No."

I turned to him shocked. I had never heard him say

no to her before and he didn't look like he was about to change his mind. He always seemed so disinterested in everything around him, including Hannah…and yet sometimes it seemed like she was his kryptonite. He had a way of talking where you couldn't argue with him. His voice rang with authority…like he was someone not to be messed with.

Her hand stopped moving around his back and she folded both of her arms over her chest making a, *hmph* sound.

I couldn't stop the smile from spreading over my face. Ross noticed and for a flicker of a second his expression changed from his permanent scowl. Hannah glared at me before getting up and going across the room to get another drink. I had no idea how she had gotten over there that fast. It looked like it was impossible to push through the big crowd of people. I saw someone pushing through the insane amount of people to come our direction. When he was finally out, he was breathing hard trying to catch his breath.

"Kenny, my boy!" he threw up his hands and said. "I thought I saw you somewhere around here…and with an accessory I see." He looked over at me and I smiled weakly.

Kennley's smile was bigger as he reunited with an old friend.

"Kahlen, Vinny—Vinny, Kahlen," Kennley introduced us.

Vinny was a little shorter than Kennley with dirty blond hair and blue eyes.

Vinny smiled. "Well I guess that new school of yours hasn't been completely bad to you."

"No, not completely." Kennley put my hand back in his.

Vinny's smile faded. "The rest of the school year

was so boring without you. And next year it's gonna be awful without having you around for a senior prank."

Kennley shrugged, "You'll live."

After a couple of minutes the conversation between them fizzled out and Vinny fought his way back across the room. By the time Hannah had come back across the room she was stumbling. She didn't seem fully drunk yet, just somewhat buzzed.

The noise level in the room was beginning to become unbearable. Kennley suggested we go out on the back porch and I gladly followed. We sat looking up into the sky while I lay in his arms. It surprised me that no one else was out here. It was just me and him. For some odd reason I started having a montage of flashbacks of all the times Kennley and I were together. I thought about all the times he had made me smile and laugh and how I got butterflies around him. I thought about how stubborn the both of us were and yet somehow he had managed to always get his way. I thought about the necklace he'd given me that I very rarely took off. I had the key to his heart while he was patiently waiting for mine. With the big montage going through my head I started laughing at the memories.

He looked down at me. "What?"

I smiled. "Remember when you practically stood me up at the Creek. I was *so* mad at you."

He grinned. "I got there late, I didn't stand you up."

"Yeah well remember how you promised to make it up to me, whatever I wanted. You said that you were up to challenges. But I never did think of anything I wanted, I wonder if my wish/favor has expired."

He wrapped his arm around me tighter. "Those types of things don't expire, although I had almost forgotten about that too."

I thought about all of the bad things that happened

with Kennley and me. I thought about all the times when we acted like five year olds, slamming lockers and stomping away. I thought about how all of those bad things ended...time after time again, I would be the one yelling or pacing and it would end up with my heart accelerating and then slowing while the butterflies fluttered in my stomach. He was always so impulsive thinking that a kiss could solve anything, which it usually did. I hated that whenever I tried to hate him, he'd always love me more, or when I wanted to be mad, he somehow make me smile. He had confused and amused me at the same time. It was like I was having some kind of epiphany in the silence of the sun setting below the clouds. I was in love with Kennley. I had no idea how long I had been but it was like some memo had just been sent to my brain. Kennley was right, when you're in love someone, you just know.

I knew that now would have been the perfect time to tell him but when I opened my mouth, something else came out. "Can I ask you something?"

"If I said no would that stop you anyway?"

I was hesitant. "Who's Dan Abbott?"

I regretted the words as soon as they came out.

Kennley slowly let go of me. I watched as his expression slowly changed. "What?"

I sighed. There was no use in backing down now. "Hannah told me to search you online and I was wondering who is Dan Abbott."

His face was blank so I couldn't decipher his emotion. "What does it matter who Dan Abbott is? What does any of my past matter? I've told that I don't exactly have the best history, why can't you let that go? Why can't you move on? I don't hound you with questions about your past!"

I couldn't believe he was actually yelling at me.

"Well I'm not a criminal, Kennley! And maybe if you didn't keep me in the dark half the time then I wouldn't have go online to get answers about you. I wouldn't care about your past if you weren't so secretive about it. You acting this way just makes me think you have something to hide."

He sighed heavily. "I can't even say I love you without you breaking up with me. I guess it might be silly of me to think that telling you I've been too drunk to spell my own name, in fights through most of my freshman year, and almost arrested multiple times might make you break up with me again. Maybe if you weren't so afraid of everything it would be easier to be honest with you. And I don't think you're scared because of what happened with Emma, I think you've been afraid your whole life!"

He stood up and went to the door. "Dan Abbott's my biological father by the way." He slammed the door as he left which made me jump.

Speechless, I stood up from the porch and went back inside the house. I expected my eyes to well up with tears but they didn't. I pushed through the crowd and I was beginning to feel dizzy. There was too much chaos around and I was almost positive I was going into shock. I took deep breaths in and out. I had never been claustrophobic before but I was beginning to feel that way with everyone so crowed and pressed against each other. I needed to sit down and think everything through. I was so confused and hurt. I couldn't believe that Kennley would stoop so low as to bring up Emma.

My life was beginning to feel so surreal. It felt like a movie and I was on the edge of my seat watching rather than actually experiencing it. I was so sick of being confused. And I was sick of being scared. The realization hit that I wasn't afraid anymore and it felt somewhat exhilarating in a way.

I saw stairs on the other side of the room which was my escape to someplace possibly peaceful. It took me longer than I expected to get to the other side of the room…Especially when some creep tried to offer me a glass of beer. I almost puked just from the smell of it. I had never tried beer but the smell was always nauseating. I didn't understand how anyone could even drink that stuff. When I finally got up all the stairs to the second floor I thought the tears might finally begin but they didn't and I still felt dizzy. I saw a whole bunch of doors to which I assumed was leading to bedrooms. I needed some place where I could be alone. I opened up one of the doors and a couple was in there making out and I shut it quickly. The next door was the bathroom. It went in and splashed some water on my face and wiped it off with a towel. The girl I saw in the mirror I recognized but at the same time she looked so unfamiliar. I saw the same brown hair and eyes that I saw everyday but something was different. Slowly but surely I was changing from the person I used to be. I was putting down those careful barriers I had once put up.

I stepped out of the bathroom and opened a door down the hall. At first I thought it was empty because the door was partially open. I moved the door with my hand quietly. It was hard to see if anybody was there in the dark and then red streaks popped out to me. I saw Hannah sitting on the bed kissing someone I couldn't see but I figured it wasn't Ross. I was about to leave when I realized the guy was Kennley.

I swear I could have fainted then but I tried to keep calm. I thought about all the hundreds of movies where the main character catches their boyfriend kissing another girl and then as soon as the main character runs away mad is exactly when the boyfriend pushes the girl off him. So I stayed and waited. I waited for Kennley to push Hannah off of him and explain to her that he had a girlfriend and she was kissing him and not the other way around. I stood there motionless waiting with only the sound of their lips against each other in the room.

The tears finally spilled over as the realization sunk in. There was a vacant bedroom across the hall that I ran into. The darkness was blurry from my tears and I was almost in hysterics. It felt like someone had kicked me in the stomach leaving me to catch my breath. I couldn't believe my eyes although it was impossible not to. Maybe I had the wrong guy. Maybe it wasn't Kennley I had seen. Maybe it was just someone with dark brown hair, green eyes, and the same jacket Kennley had been wearing.

I wanted to hate him so badly but I didn't, I couldn't. I loved that stupid jerk and I had thought up until a second ago that he loved me. The golden key around my neck was suddenly beginning to feel very heavy. I had gotten my wish. I was alone in the dark with the only sound being the hum of the music downstairs. But I wasn't alone for much longer. Someone walked into the room and I immediately stood up off of the bed. I thought it was a stranger until I recognized the short black hair.

"Kahlen?" his deep voice said.

I only replied with my sniffles. I sat back on the bed and put my head in my hands. I couldn't stop my tears even if I tried.

I expected Ross to walk back out of the room but he didn't. He came and sat next to me on the bed.

"Kennley is stupid. He's known for messing up a good thing when he has it," he whispered to me.

I figured he knew what was happening next door. I didn't surprise me that he didn't care. It seemed like him and Hannah were in a very open relationship. I couldn't really comprehend what was happening next door. I couldn't understand why he would do this to me. I thought about what he had said to me at the movie theater when he told me that he would never do anything like that to me or anyone else. Then again he had also told me that he would never hurt me, that he loved me. It was all foolish lies I should have never believed.

I wiped the tears away from my eyes and looked at him. "Why are you in here?" I asked.

"Because my ear drums were about to explode and plus you look like you could use some company."

I didn't say anything as the tears kept falling uncontrollably. I wanted to hate Kennley so badly.

"I don't understand why he would do that to you," he said. "You're not like the other girls I know. You're classy and smart...nothing like Hannah."

I didn't understand why he was trying to comfort me. "I'm *innocent*." I sobbed.

He reached over and put his hand on my cheek. He slowly moved it up and wiped a tear away. "That's not always a bad thing. A pleasant change actually."

I just looked at him shocked as he closed in the space between us and put his lips to mine. I was so confused and frustrated that the tears kept falling while he kissed me. I was prepared to push him off of me and leave but I wanted to get back at Kennley. I wanted him to hurt just like I was. I started kissing Ross back with absolutely no spark flying between us. He wasn't Kennley, this wasn't right. I thought about Hannah and him in the other room and I brought my body closer to his. This was my attempt at revenge.

Ross pulled back to look at me for a second and then crushed his lips into mine harder. He slowly moved me back so that my head was on the pillow and he was on top of me. My heart was beating so fast that I was afraid it was going to pop out of my chest. I slid my hands to his chest and tried to push him off but he didn't seem to notice. He was so much stronger than me which didn't help. I pushed harder and he must have known I was trying to get up. I felt him put down his body against mine harder. He put both of his hands out over my sides creating a cage making it impossible to escape. Ross pulled back for air giving us both room to breathe.

"Ross, I can't do this." I gasped. "What about Hannah?"

I could barely make out his face through my tears but it looked like he was grinning.

"What about her?"

He was kissing me again but I wasn't kissing him back. I tried to push him off of me but it wasn't working. I turned my head to the side away from him.

"I can't do this." I repeated. "Let me go."

He pretended like he hadn't heard me. I felt like I was in a wrestling match and I was losing.

"Please," I begged. "Get off." Suddenly fear washed over me like a ocean during a hurricane.

He continued kissing me but his lips were angry this time that I wasn't kissing him back. He managed to use one hand to undo the belt around his jeans while keeping me trapped. I took advantage of it and wiggled one hand up to slap him hard enough that put his other hand to his face. I squirmed out of the bed quickly and I ran to the door. Ross had gotten hold on my arm and tried to pull me back. I shook it off hard and sprinted out the door tripping into someone standing in the hall.

The tears were falling harder than before as I realized what had almost happened. The person I had tripped into grabbed my waist so that I didn't stumble to the ground. I looked up to see it was Kennley who had caught me...but he wasn't looking back at me. He was looking at Ross standing behind me with his jeans unzipped.

I was panting now and the tears fell. "Don't touch me!" I yelled at Kennley.

He looked at me confused for a second and then as the realization struck he let me go. As soon as he let go I realized that he had been supporting my weight. I fell to the ground and put my knees to my chest bawling.

There was even more commotion going on upstairs now than there was downstairs. Kennley looked from me to Ross and many profanities followed after.

"What is wrong with you?!" Kennley yelled.

I wiped the tears from my eyes so I could see clearly.

"I could ask you the same question. Where's Hannah?" Ross said zipping back up his pants and fixing the belt.

Kennley stared at him for a long second before he threw the first punch sending Ross backwards a step. After that it was all pretty much a blur between them. I flew up to my feet with my back pressed against the wall. They were both on the ground now with Ross on top of Kennley punching him in the face. I screamed for them to stop but neither one of them listened to me. Kennley pushed Ross off of him and I saw that Ross's lip was bleeding. I couldn't keep track of who was punching who as they rolled on the ground by my feet.

I heard lots of people running up the stairs to see the fight while I was still somewhat in the middle of it.

"Stop!" I yelled. "Kennley, please stop!" My voice was lost in the chanting of the crowd that had been formed.

Before I even saw how it happened Ben and Jordan pushed through the crowd and dragged them both off of each other.

"Are you two crazy!" Ben yelled in a normal accent.

Kennley and Ross were still staring at each other like tigers ready to attack.

Ross wiped the blood from his lip. "You owe me man!" He yelled over the crowd. "You wouldn't be standing where you are right now if it wasn't for me. You probably wouldn't have even been in this state right now. I took the blame for you that night. You owe me!"

"So that justifies you trying to sleep with my girlfriend? I used to owe you Ross but I don't now. Not anymore," Kennley yelled. "You're on your own tonight." Kennley shook Ben off of him. The crowd of people left because the fight was over, and they all moved back down the stairs. Jordan let go of Ross, and him and Kennley looked at each other for an immeasurable moment of time.

Ross wiped his bloody hand off on his shirt. "As of right now, you're dead to me." He brushed past Kennley and looked at me shooting a chill down my spine before moving down the stairs.

I was still pressed against the wall with my tears finally stopping. Kennley hadn't moved from where he was and neither had Jordan or Ben. It was like time had frozen leaving us all stuck in our own misery. Ben turned and looked at me. I knew I must have looked awful. My eyes were red, my cheeks wet, my shirt was slightly twisted, and my jeans were unbuttoned. I was two seconds away from being in the fetal position.

"Are you alright, Kahlen?" he asked.

I realized then that I was breathing extremely hard. Kennley looked over at me too and my eyes didn't leave his face. I could feel the tears welling up again but I blinked them back.

I could feel Ben and Jordan looking at me but I didn't respond. The only thing I could think about saying was, "yeah I'm fine. It's not an ordinary day if I'm not almost raped and cheated on".

Despite all of it, I still loved him. It was stupid and insane but part of me wanted to work this out. My eyes still didn't leave his face but those green eyes didn't work the magic they usually did.

My throat was dry and I could barely speak. "Take me home." It came out as a little less than a whisper.

Kennley walked closer to me and I started walking down the stairs with him following behind me. Hannah was at the bottom of the stairs leaning against the wall like she was waiting for us.

She stopped in front of the stairs and was looking past my head at Kennley.

"We need to talk," she said.

I curled up my fist to stop from slapping her.

"No, I think we talked enough Hannah," he muttered.

I pushed past her and started walking towards the door. She grabbed my arm and yanked me back. Pretty soon I was going to have a big bruise there from everybody doing that.

"Looks like you've still got some growing up to if you want to be a big girl." she said-

She was obviously drunk and her breath smelled

awful. I shook her hand off of me and took a step closer. I heard everyone gathering as if another fight was going to take place.

"Big girl?!" I asked. "Is that what you are Hannah?"

Kennley tried to push us back from each other. I ignored him and took another step closer to Hannah so that our faces were only inches from each other.

"Because to me," I continued. "You're nothing but a big, bitter, slut!"

I couldn't help but smile slightly. Emma would have been proud of me for that one.

She scowled. "Get out of my face!" She spat.

I grinned evilly. "Gladly."

I stomped my way to the door and walked quickly to Kennley's car. He wasn't too far behind as he quickly unlocked the door and hopped in. He didn't start the car right away waiting for my wrath. I didn't say anything. I couldn't. I was speechless. The silence in car only made the long drive to my house that much longer. I could see Kennley out of the corner of my eye looking at me periodically seeing if my permanent expression had changed but it hadn't. My face was stuck this way... emotionless.

When we finally got to my house it took me a second to realize that we had stopped and were in my driveway.

"Kahlen," he sighed.

I unbuckled my seat belt and just stared at him waiting.

"Say something."

I sighed. "What do you want me to say? Do you want me to yell and scream and cry? Because newsflash, I've already done all of that. Do you want me to dump you and then stomp my way inside my house? Is that what you want?"

"Don't you want an explanation?" he asked.

"I'd rather not relive it if you don't mind."

"Well I'm sorry anyhow," he seemed sincere. "I was angry and I went to go yell at Hannah and she told me that she still loved me and if I gave her one kiss she'd leave me alone. Before I could say anything she kissed me...I just didn't push her off right away, and I'm sorry. But I know that's not an excuse."

I chuckled darkly. "You wanna know what the really sick thing about it is? It's that in the mist of all of this *crap* I realize I'm in love with you...and I'm not scared anymore. And then I see you in the room with *her* and I wasn't even mad, I was just hurt. It was strange actually. As much as I wanted to hate you, I still didn't. The only thing I was feeling was pain, just like I am now. Then Ross walks in and tries to comfort me. Then next thing I know I'm kissing him and still all I could think about was you, loving you. Kennley, I know I'm supposed to be mad right now but the only thing I'm concerned about is you. I don't want to lose you, especially to Hannah. I think we can work this out."

Kennley just stared at the steering wheel not saying anything. It was like he was having an epiphany of his own. He shook his head. "You could have been raped... just like Layla and it would have been my fault, and all you can think about is losing *me*?" He sighed. "This isn't right. Kahlen I can't do this anymore."

I stared at him incredulously. My phone began to vibrate but I ignored it.

"Maybe you were right, maybe we don't make sense," he said.

He looked at me waiting for me to say something.

"Has anyone ever said anything to you about your eyes?" I asked.

He looked at me confused. "Kahlen, what does that have to do with anything?"

"At first when you look at them it doesn't seem like they fit with everything else about you, especially your hair, but then after you look harder you realize they match perfectly. And we both don't know what Ross would have done tonight…maybe he would have stopped."

He shook his head slowly. "No. This just isn't working out."

I knew the water works would begin shortly. "Not everything has to make sense Kennley! If anything you taught me that!"

"Yes. Considering my life I am the perfect person to be taking advice from!"

"You know what Kennley…" A single tear dropped down to my chin. "You're wrong. I wasn't right about anything. I had it all messed up…Just not what I thought I'd be wrong about!" My phone started to vibrate again and I took it out quickly so I could hit ignore. It was my mother calling and apparently she had been trying to reach me for a while. I answered my phone.

"Kahlen, I've been trying to call you. Where are you?" she yelled.

I looked at the time. It wasn't past curfew yet. Her frantic voice was scaring me. "I'm at home mom," I looked and saw that all the lights were off in the house. "Where are you?"

She sobbed. "I'm at the hospital."

"W-what? Why?" I asked scared.

"Your father's been shot," she cried. "Just…just meet me at the hospital downtown right away."

Just like my heart, the line went dead.

Part III

Character cannot be developed in ease and quiet. Only through experiences of trial and suffering can the soul be strengthened, vision cleared, ambition inspired, and success achieved.

-Helen Keller

20. Screw Up

Being at the hospital was making me remember. I still couldn't remember much of what happened before we got to the hospital that night though. I could only remember what had happened right before the accident. I was daydreaming now but I could see it clearly in my head. I could see the elevator doors closing in front of my face and my dad as he dragged me back into my room. I remembered a conversation the doctor had had with me before he gave me the bad news.

"Kaleen," the doctor had said pronouncing my name wrong. "Because of your concussion you probably won't remember much of what happened but if you experience any other memory loss make sure you come back to get that checked out. And also, you will probably have some bad headaches every now and again but they should pass eventually. Again, if they don't, get it checked out so we know for sure nothing is wrong." He paused and smiled at me gently. "You're very lucky you know—not just for surviving, but because most people are somewhat traumatized from accidents. But you don't remember so you won't be traumatized."

He then moved on to tell me the bad news about Emma. I already knew the news but it hurt hearing it just the same. It's an odd feeling actually. In my head it felt like my whole world was falling apart and yet when I'd open my eyes everything was at ease.

I rocked back and forth in my seat remembering. My head hurt now but that was because I was stressed. I had plenty reason to be. I didn't know so many bad things could happen in one night.

I had a complete disdain for hospitals and yet here I was again...but this time I wasn't the patient. I was the one sitting in the waiting room at the edge of my seat. Surprisingly Kennley was sitting there right next to me as anxious as I was. It was weird actually, seeing him anxious. He was always so laidback. I figured that he would just drop me off and leave but just because he was my ex-boyfriend now didn't mean he wouldn't care about the happenings of my life. It was bittersweet about my dad. I was happy that I had something to focus on beside Kennley, but I'd rather he not be in the hospital.

I didn't really know any of the details of what had happened to him. My mom was somewhere running all over the hospital either finding coffee, or asking nurses the same questions that they couldn't answer. All I knew was what my mother had told me. She said that they were at home and my dad got a call to go downtown and the next thing she knew she was getting a call from the hospital.

My eyes were still red and wet from when I was going into hysterics. When we had been sitting in the car after my mom called me I all about fainted. I had stopped breathing and the color was fading in my skin. When I told Kennley that I needed to go to the hospital his face was as pale as mine thinking that there was something wrong with me. It was almost flattering in a way that he would be so worried about me. But I was calmer now though—as calm as someone could be in this situation. But I was taking deep breaths every couple of seconds to steady my heart beat.

"Kahlen, I'm sure everything is going to be fine," Kennley assured me.

I ignored him staring into space as I took another deep breath. I didn't want to talk to him, I couldn't talk to him. I hadn't the slightest clue of what to say. I was so angry at him. He had cheated on me, and then broken up with me. Neither of those things sounded like something Kennley would do. I thought about the bad mood he had been in earlier. Something had happened that I didn't know about.

I had made up in my mind that I wasn't talking to Kennley anymore. It wasn't like before when I was giving him the silent treatment; I actually had a good reason this time. Technically I had cheated on him too but it was different. I felt wrong in justifying my behavior but not wrong enough not to.

I saw my mother walking towards me. She had on black sweatpants, a gray top, and her hair was pulled into a messy bun. I stood up and walked over to her quickly.

"Mom, where have you been?"

{remove space]Her hands looked like they were shaking. "Around," she said. "I don't understand how you can sit there calmly. I figured you'd be pacing or something like you always do. Your face actually looks somewhat composed." Her face was anything but composed. She was sweating and she looked like she was on the verge of tears.

"Did you find out anything?" I asked.

She sighed. "Everyone around here seems to think I'm crazy and won't tell me anything. But he's in surgery right now. The bullet was shot through his back. Luckily it passed his spine but they're afraid it's moving toward his heart."

I took a deep breath. I could feel my heartbeat

accelerating as the blood pumped quickly through my veins. My mother was taking deep breaths too but she sounded like she was having a panic attack. I pulled her over to some chairs that were purposefully far away from Kennley. We sat down, and she broke down.

{remove space}"Kahlen I can't take it. I commend you for how you handled everything with Emma. I don't know what I would do without your father. I don't know if I can take it." Her tears were flowing uncontrollably down her cheeks. I wasn't used to seeing her like this. I had seen her sad and crying, but never to this extent. "And I felt so badly for you. I could see you going through this great pain and I couldn't take it away. As a mother I'm suppose to able to protect you and I couldn't. I couldn't stop your pain. I felt so sad, so badly for you."

I thought about that same pity look. I thought about if we lost my dad and how that face would return again as soon as it was finally going away. I shook off those thoughts quickly. I reached over and hugged my mom. It was contagious watching people cry. I couldn't keep my face composed like before.

"But that's just it mom, don't you see? I don't need you to be sorry for me…I need you to be strong for me."

We were still hugging tightly and I didn't care that she was cracking my spine because I was doing the same to hers. I didn't know how long we stayed this way but when we finally released I had a hard time getting myself back together.

My mother's phone rang and she walked off quickly to some place quieter. I watched as Kennley got up and walked over to me. He sat down in the seat beside me. I turned my head away from him like a three year old.

"Are you okay?" he asked.

My eyes were still wet and very red. I knew I must have looked terrible but I didn't respond. Wordlessly I got up from my seat and walked off. I heard Kennley sigh before I heard his footsteps following behind mine quickly.

"Kahlen," he said.

I walked quicker. I didn't even know where I was going but I just kept walking.

"Kahlen stop."

If I walked any quicker I would have been running. I saw it then. I saw my escape as two doors opened slowly. I stepped into the elevator and pressed the close button several times but it was too late. I was trapped in the elevator with Kennley.

"Kahlen," he breathed trying to catch his breath. "Don't hate me okay?"

"Hate you?" I looked into his green eyes. I was still mesmerized but it didn't stifle my anger. "I'm mad at you...so extremely and terribly mad at you, but I don't hate you, Kennley. I can't hate you. I've tried many times before and failed. I don't think this time is going to be any different."

He sighed. "I'm sorry."

I knew he meant it, that much was clear but all it did was infuriate me more. I pressed the first floor button with all my might trying to release some anger. "For what? For cheating on me? Breaking up with me out of nowhere? Or shutting me out of your life every chance you get? What really surprises me is that I don't *care* about everything's that's happened in your past. The only thing I care about is the fact that you won't open up to me. You don't trust me enough to let me into your life...not completely anyways. You know me better than I know myself and yet I can't say the same for you, can I? I don't ask for much Kennley..."

He didn't respond running his fingers through his chocolate hair.

I softened my tone. "Something happened today... and I know it's bothering you. I assume you still won't tell me because you never do. So here," I unclasped the necklace and let it fold in my hand. I grabbed his hand that was so big compared to mine. I opened it slowly and placed the necklace it in. "Take this back. You never really gave me the key to anything anyways."

My neck felt naked but I tried to ignore it. It felt like something was missing now which made me uncomfortable. I knew this was a big step. Giving him the necklace spoke finality. It wasn't like before when I could look into his eyes and feel the doubt of us being broken up for much longer. But this time I knew that things would stay this way. It hurt so much that I tried to focus all of my emotions on being angry. It was so much easier.

Kennley looked at the necklace for a while in his hand lying there with the key on top. I did the same. I had the urge to put my hand to my neck so it wouldn't feel so empty but I fought myself on it.

His green eyes looked back up at me. He seemed angry now and hurt, just like I was. "Fine," he said loudly. "You wanna know the truth? I screw up everything. Everything I touch, I ruin! This morning, Jimmy, my *fourteen* year old brother found drugs in my room and got caught with them at school. My parents are pissed at me and him but mostly at me because they think they're *mine*! But they're not and they won't believe me because I'm a screw up. I don't even know how the drugs got there but my best guess is Ross left his crap in my room."

I blinked once and my lip quivered from every heavy emotion that was causing me to go on this never ending rollercoaster. I didn't say anything and Kennley continued.

"My ex-best friend is a drug dealer and for the last couple of years I've been trapped with him because of guilt. That night I talked him into going to Dan Abbott's house because I was so angry with myself...and with the world. I needed to take it out on someone. The neighbors called the police and there was enough time for only one of us to go through the window to escape before we got caught. He took the blame, he let me go. Ever since then, I've owed him. And then he steals Hannah, gets me into doing things I don't want to do because of guilt, and then he tries to steal you too!"

I had pressed my back against the wall. I wasn't used to him yelling like this. I looked at his red eyes. He wasn't crying but it looked like it could be a possibility. I had never seen him like this before. I knew if he was this upset that it had to be something big. I felt immediately concerned. I reached my hand out to touch his arm.

"Kennley..." I said softly.

He backed away. My hand hadn't yet touched him. "Everything is always my fault Kahlen, everything! And I can never make up for it. No matter how much I try... And then I come to this new school hoping to start fresh, to be better, and to actually make my parents proud for once. Then I find a girl that I like, a lot actually, and it's nice that she doesn't know anything about me so there's nothing to judge but the present. I just wanted to make that *last*, Kahlen. I didn't want another person judging me or being disappointed in me. But I guess it doesn't matter anyway because of course I'd screw it up...like I do with everything else in my life... especially you."

I didn't know what to say to that...or to any of what he had said. Before I even got the chance his cell phone rang to Barbie Girl but neither of us laughed. The elevator stopped and the doors opened. Both of us still stayed where we were.

"What?" He snapped when he answered his phone. He paused for a second. "N-no." he stammered.

{remove space}A whole crowd full of people were coming to get on the elevator. We were on the main floor now and before I knew it Kennley had pressed through the crowd and was heading for the doors to the parking lot.

"Kennley wait!" I pressed through the crowd running to catch up with him.

It was raining outside and we had both walked outside the doors now getting soaked by spring's immense moisture. Kennley was looking at me now as intensely as I was him. We didn't say anything. The vision of the time before that we had been standing in the rain flashed across my mind. I couldn't believe it was over between us. I let the tears fall freely now. He couldn't tell if I was crying or not in the rain.

"It's my fault…" He yelled. But it seemed like he was talking more to himself than to me. "He wanted me to go with him."

Before I could even begin to ask him what he was talking about he looked at me intensely for a fraction of a second before abruptly—so abruptly I didn't see it coming— crushing his lips into mine. I pushed my confusion aside and kissed him back with all the strength I could muster. He pulled back slowly leaving us both breathless.

I couldn't even begin to fathom all of this. But this didn't seem like a reuniting kiss at the very least…more like an official *goodbye*. I reached my hand up to wipe the tears and the rain that was dripping down my face. He reached over and put his hands in mine.

"I'm sorry, Kahlen." I could barely hear his voice over the rain. Then he was gone. I couldn't make out his blurry figure running into the long winding parking lot to his car.

I looked down in my hand and in it was the little golden key attached to the necklace.

Finally my dad was out of surgery. He was in his room still knocked out. My mother and I both stayed there by his bed kind of hovering around him. The doctors said the surgery had gone well which was good. But it was so hard sitting there thinking about the person that shot my dad. If he had better aim...I don't know if I could go on. But I had already thought it had been the end of the world once before and lived. So I figured I could live through this too, but not easily.

"That phone call earlier was the police station," my mom told me in a hushed tone. It was silly that she was whispering. My dad was a heavy sleeper anyhow and plus they had him on drugs to knock him out. "They seem to know more on the situation than anyone here does," she continued. "They said that there was a home downtown that they were suspicious of illegal drugs being stored and used. They knew the people who lived there weren't getting the drugs on their own. Someone else had to be involved. Your father and some others went down to arrest the people but someone had a gun. The guy got scared and shot him. But he didn't get away. Another police officer shot him in the leg and arrested him. Despite everything that happened, I kind of feel bad for the guy. He's just a teenager. He just graduated this year and now his whole life is down the drain."

I took a deep breath trying to convince myself that I was wrong. I tried to convince myself that same person

I had been kissing only hours before now, wasn't the same person who had shot my father...almost killing him. I felt repulsed.

"Did they say the name?" I asked unsteadily.

"Yes but I wasn't really paying attention to that part. But I think it was something Hopkins."

The room was now spinning from my dizziness.

Her brows furrowed. "Are you okay? You look sick. Honey, you're turning *green*."

I gulped. "Nope. I'm fine. I'm just tired that's all."

"Well if you want you can take my car home. I'm probably going to stay the night anyway. So you could just come back in the morning if you want."

I stared off into space blankly. I finally got what Kennley had been talking about early. He had said, *"It's my fault, he wanted me to go with him."* I understood now. Ross wanted Kennley to go with him downtown. Maybe if Ross would have had backup, he wouldn't have shot my dad. Kennley thought it was his fault.

She dug her keys out of her purse and I took them gladly. It was about one in the morning right now so I knew I needed to get some sleep. But I wasn't sure if I would be able to or not. My mind was too wired for any type of rest to seem feasible.

21. Moving On

I was finally treading water rather than drowning in it. I had accepted that Kennley was no longer in my life. After the first week apart I still had my doubts about how long this break up would last. Now I was done soaking in my own misery. I was sick of keeping myself locked up in my room all the time and falling asleep to my radio. Or if I wasn't listening to the radio I was playing my guitar.

My parents were beginning to worry about me as always. I eavesdropped on them talking about me saying that I had returned to the person I was roughly three months ago. I had to admit that even I was getting tired of me. My necklace had gotten shoved away with all of the other phases of my life in my closet. Originally I had laid it on my desk but it had gotten old quickly when I had to stare at it every day.

I sighed. I needed another distraction. Although I moved my necklace, Emma's locket still laid in the open. I could see the light bulb slowly flicker to life above my head. I remembered my Mom telling me about Julie calling and she wanted to talk to me. I had purposefully never gone. I knew it was wrong to be angry with Julie but I needed someone to blame for something. Surprisingly, Julie had never called back after that last time to remind to come.

Above my dresser was my mirror and I could see my awful reflection looking back at me. I looked like I had been punched because of the dark circles underneath my eyes, my lips were cracked and my hair was a borderline haystack. I couldn't believe that in only two weeks I had let myself get this bad. It was ridiculous that a boy could have this much power over someone. It didn't make sense that I should be so upset, but I was. I needed to move on. In the back of my mind I was sure Kennley had moved on since he was the one that broke it off but it didn't make sense that he gave me back the necklace. If anything, it was just something else to keep me up in the middle of the night, around three o'clock, to think about...and then that kiss, it was enough to leave me breathless even now, but really, more confused than anything else.

I ran my fingers through my tangled hair trying to comb it out. I felt like I had been in a coma and had finally woken up. My room was a mess just like me. I couldn't stand one more second of this. Abruptly I threw the covers off of me and onto the floor. I took a long shower cleansing myself of all worries and concerns with my vanilla shampoo. By the time I was finished getting myself and my room back together three hours had gone by. I felt so much more refreshed now.

I put on the most convincing smile I could as I walked down the stairs to face my parents. It was your average boring Saturday. My mom was being completely overprotective of my father. He was perfectly fine now. He was sore, but fine, alive at least. My mom treated him like a newborn baby. My dad milked the getting-waited-on-hand-and-foot thing for a while before it started to get old. We both figured that my mother would return to her regular self sooner or later but none of us were really the same after that night. My dad could now consider my mom's worrying as tolerable and I didn't even mind being called Kido anymore. Near death experiences tend to give people more perspective on things.

Although my mom tried to hide it, I could tell that she was surprised by my neatly brushed hair, clothes beside pajamas, and I had even went the extra step by putting on fruit passion lip gloss.

"Can I borrow the car?" I asked.

She studied my face. "Um…of course…But where are you going?"

I knew she suspected Kennley was involved. I didn't really have to tell either of them what had happened between us, they had both figured it out on their own… along with the rest of the hospital that had heard us yelling.

"Ms. Bryant's house…finally."

{remove space} Her eyes widened. "Oh, I had almost forgotten that she had called. But did you call the house first to make sure she's home?"

"No." I shrugged. "I don't really care if she's there or not. I just really want to get out the house."

My dad snorted. "It's about time. I was wondering if this place was feeling as much as a prison to you as it is to me." He looked comfortable on his chair, stretched out.

My mom sighed. "This house is not a prison. You just need to learn to take a break every once in awhile. You're not the Energizer Bunny you know."

I smiled at the look my dad gave my mother and then quickly grabbed the keys and headed out the door and to the car. It wasn't a long drive to the same blue house I remembered. Luckily Julie was home and was overjoyed to see me. I almost didn't recognize the woman I had known over all the years. She had cut her waist long blond hair into a fashionable bob an inch above her shoulders. For anyone else the hairdo might not have worked but Julie had an angular type of face that matched perfectly.

It took Macy two barks until she recognized me and practically tackled me to the ground. I didn't have to fake a smile anymore. Seeing Macy truly did make me happy. It was strange that I didn't realize how much I really missed her until she was licking my face.

Before I had time to wipe the slobber off me, Julie had gripped me into a spine crushing hug.

"Kahlen, you came!" she said releasing me.

"Yeah, sorry I didn't get around to it sooner. I just had a lot of things on my plate."

She shook her head and her new hairdo moved along with it. "Perfectly fine. I've been quite busy myself too...I finally realized that it was time to make some changes in my life."

{remove space}I examined the house. Everything was much cleaner than the last time I had been here a couple of months ago, which was a huge relief. I shuddered at the memory of the last time I had been here. I remembered the harsh words that were said, all the memories that had passed through my head, Julie passed out in my old truck, and it was all overwhelming.

She walked over to the small brown leather couch in the other room and gestured for me to follow. "Well," she began as we sat down. "First and foremost I wanted to apologize. I know I said some horrible things to you. When you came before I was still in a really bad place. I wasn't exactly dealing with anything. I know that's still no excuse for everything that happened and I'm really and truly sorry you had to deal with that."

I tried not to wince at the memory of her stumbling up the stairs drunk. "It's okay. I'm just happy that things appear to be better now."

She sighed. "Nothing like death to give you a clear perspective of things. I just wish that I could have figured everything out sooner."

I smiled half-heartedly. "Story of my life..."

"Well Kahlen, I was going to take Macy for a walk but since you're here, are you up taking care of some unfinished business? I still haven't touched anything in her room and I can't leave it like this forever. As much as a part of me wants to it seems like that would be sort of sick in a way."

I took in a deep breath. So many emotions were flooding through me. I tried to keep my thoughts clear. "You mean you haven't taken care of it already?"

She shook her head. "Of course not. I didn't feel right to do it without you. And plus I need all the help I can get. Emma was a pack rat just like me." As much as she tried to hide it I could see the pain in her face. "So you're not busy are you? Your mother told me you have a boyfriend now and I know how you teenagers can be. Relationships are the top priority."

I tried to keep my face blank. "Nope, I'm not busy." There was no need to give her all of the gory details.

We walked up the stairs to the second floor and the same door with the splattered paint sent a certain chill down my spine. I closed my eyes and took another deep breath before twisting the door knob slowly. Still nothing had been touched in her cluttered room. It still looked like she had been sleeping in the bed this morning which already made my eyes well up with tears. I blinked them back and turned to Julie. She had some boxes behind her all set to be filled. She started to walk towards the closet.

"Wait," I said quickly. "Do you have a camera? I want to take pictures of it before we move anything."

She nodded quickly before walking back out of the

room. I took in every aspect of the room and tried to pull myself together. But it wasn't easy...the room even smelled like her. It was impossible not to feel the twist in my stomach as I tried to fight back the overwhelming emotions.

Julie came back and handed me her digital camera. I took several pictures of every little object of the room to make sure I would have something to help me remember it perfectly. Finally I set the camera aside and looked at Julie who looked just as distraught as me.

"Are you ready?" she asked.

"No," I shook my head. "And I never will be. But that doesn't mean I can't get the job done."

She nodded. "I know exactly how you feel."

I started by taking all of the many pictures documenting Emma's life off of the walls. I figured with as many pictures as she took that she wanted to be a photographer but she was fascinated with interior designing just like my mother. I pulled all of the photos into a big box and set it off to the side. It had taken me at least an hour to take down all of the pictures and now the room looked naked without them.

Julie was working on folding all of her clothes neatly to send to charity. I started working on all of the many things stacked on the desk and dresser still fighting away tears every second. As I put away all of the magazines and lotions, a tiny notebook that looked too familiar popped out to me. It was my notebook that I was under the impression had still been under my possession. It was hard to fight a smile from spreading across my face. The notebook was labeled *fortune cookie*. Not too long ago I had started carrying a tiny pocket sized notebook with me to write down every fortune cookie-like thing Emma said. She was always so annoyed at me for that which just made it all the more fun. I was surprised she had stolen it from me. I didn't bother opening it because I knew that if I did I wouldn't be able to keep my eyes dry for much longer. I placed it in my pocket and continued to pack away my best friend's things.

I could see the daylight fading in the sky as we neared the end of emptying out the room. It looked truly naked now. I had finished most of the room while Julie mostly worked on packing away all of the many clothes Emma had. There were enough clothes to fill a store in her room.

"Kahlen," Julie said. I was appreciative that she was one of the few people that actually called me by my name.

I stood up from the piles of boxes I was surrounded by and looked at her waiting.

She pulled a purse out from the closet. "The hospital gave this to me and at the time I just threw it in the closet but I found this inside of it." She pulled out a cell phone that was too very familiar. "I know this isn't hers. Do you know whose this is?"

{remove space}I smiled. I had the faint memory of asking Emma to hold onto my cell phone for me. I couldn't wait to go rub this in my mother's face. I never really lost my cell phone. It wasn't my fault I had a concussion and couldn't remember...heck, I could hardly remember anything. It was a miracle after the accident that I could remember my own name.

{remove space}"Yeah, that's mine." It was barely a whisper as I looked at it in awe.

I took the cell phone from her and examined it. It was exactly how I remembered, not that I expected it to change. It even had the pink heart drawn in nail polish, compliments of Emma. I put the cell phone in my other pocket and looked around the near naked room and the moon now slowly rising outside the window.

A soft sob came from Julie. I looked over at her immediately. The tears were streaming down her face silently as she looked at the ground. "She's really gone isn't she?"

I closed my eyes to try and stop my tears that were stinging my eyes. "It seems like no matter how much time goes by it still feels so surreal. I have a hard time believing it most days myself," I said.

{remove space} She wiped away her tears and we both stood facing the bed that still hadn't been touched. I couldn't force myself to lay one finger on the bed. We both had nothing else to do except take care of it. We stood staring at it for an immeasurable moment of time.

I broke the silence. "One more picture." I walked over to the corner of the room where the camera had been set. I slowly took the picture before dropping the camera and my hands beside my body.

"Are you ready?" I asked still staring at the bed.

"Not even close." She shook her head. "I just wish..." Her tears started again. "I-I wish that I could have been the type of mother she deserved. It wasn't beyond me to shirk my responsibilities as a parent sometimes. And yet amazingly she turned out fine." She lifted her head up and smiled at me briefly. "I blame you for that."

I released one tear to drop from my eye quickly. "I wouldn't go that far."

"Really? Because I would."

Still neither one of us moved from our positions at the foot of the bed. My feet felt planted in cement. It seemed like we could potentially be here until tomorrow morning.

"You know Kahlen, I'm thinking of moving," she said

slowly. "I kind of want to get a fresh start someplace else and I'm miserable half of the time because this place holds too many memories." She was hesitant to continue. "I was thinking about moving to Chicago and I've already gotten a job offer there."

I looked at her shocked. "Wow," I managed to get out.

She chuckled lightly. "Yes, I know it's not exactly a ten minute drive."

I wasn't sure how I felt about her moving. "Well when would you leave?"

"I don't know...Either the end of this month or towards the middle of July."

My jaw dropped. "That's only a couple of weeks away!"

She nodded. "Your mother already has the going away party planned. She's known for awhile but I told her I wanted to tell you myself."

"Wow," I repeated quietly.

She sighed. "I think a move is what I need most right now. I need some place to start new."

"Can't you start new in a house around the corner?"

She ignored my question. "But there's something else I wanted to tell you...or ask you rather."

I waited for her to continue anxiously.

"I know how your mother feels about dogs...but I really think it would be best if you took Macy. I mean, it's hard enough taking care of myself these days let alone someone who can't even get themselves food and water. I was wondering if you would be willing to take Macy...indefinitely."

I looked outside the open door. Sitting outside in the hallway panting was the dark lab I had grown to love over the years. I smiled at Macy and within seconds she had made it past the boxes to me. I reached down and ran my fingers through her dark hair. I didn't have to think about my answer long.

"Of course."

Julie let out a sigh of relief. "Perfect. How about we go pack up her stuff."

I looked from Macy, to Julie, to the untouched bed.

"You know Kahlen, I don't really have the heart to do it and I don't think you do either…so let's call it a night." She reached and took my hand in hers before giving it a tight squeeze and then releasing it.

I nodded slowly, looking at the bed. "Agreed."

We gathered all of Macy's things. She almost had more things than me and we actually had to pack them away in a suitcase. I couldn't believe that Macy was coming with me. So many different emotions were going through me. I was somewhat sad about Julie leaving. I couldn't imagine someone else living in this house. Just the thought of it made me feel uncomfortable. I was happy about Macy coming. It felt like this way I would have a piece of Emma with me and plus I missed seeing Macy at *least* once a week like before. I was sad that the once colorful and lively room was now bare, but despite all of those feeling still a part of Kennley ached inside of me. It was a different kind of pain that I hadn't yet experienced and none of it made sense. I was infuriated but at the same time I longed to see him. This was the longest we had been apart in three months.

As I rolled the suitcase to the front door with Macy following in behind, Julie stopped me. She walked over and gripped me in another tight hug. This was so unlike the woman I had once known before. I could have sworn it was a completely different person. When she released me, she kissed my forehead.

"Every girl deserves a friend like you," she said.

I couldn't even begin to tell her how wrong I thought she was.

She then looked down at Macy and dropped down to her knees. She sighed. "I know you must think I'm awful for shipping Macy off with you after all of these years. But I know she'll be better off with you. I know that leaving her will make her happier than if she stayed with me." She held Macy's face so that her brown eyes were looking back into Julie's blue ones. "I know you'll be better off this way Macy. Don't hate me for abandoning you."

Macy's only response was a nice wet lick on the nose.

"I love you girl," she said giving Macy's head a little shake. "Be good for me." She rose back to her feet and looked at me for a second before waving goodbye as we headed out the door.

When I got home both my parents eyes almost popped out of their heads. My dad was of course thrilled but my mom on the other hand...

"I'm gonna kill Julie," she kept repeating. "I'll kill her." It was unlike my mother to be homicidal.

I sighed. "I don't understand why you have such a problem with dogs. It's not like Macy's going to be any trouble."

"Pumpkin, if you can't take care of a phone, how can you take care of a dog?"

She was never going to let that go was she? I dug in my pocket and pulled out my old cell phone. "I never lost it actually. My hands were full and I handed it to Emma...she just never got the chance to give it back to me. It's hard remembering those little details with a concussion and all."

The conversation ended there. There was nothing

else my mother could possibly say to that. Of course she knew the reason why Emma had never given it back to me. My eyes stung more just from the thought.

I unpacked all of Macy's many things and got everything set up for her. The day had gone by pretty quickly and it was almost midnight. My parents were already in the bed while I searched through my room frantically for the charger to my old phone. Macy seemed to be amused lying in her brown fluffy dog bed on the floor beside my bed as I walked back and forth shutting things as soon as I opened them. In the place I never expected to find the charger...lo and behold it was underneath my bed. I plugged up my phone, satisfied, and pulled the tiny notebook out of my pocket. I flipped to a random page.

The funny thing about love is that it's so irrational. I've never been in love but I've observed that people hate the person they love for the same reason they're head over heels for them. But that's the beauty of it...something being so irrational and rational at the same time. It's practically magic...

I remembered this being one of the longer fortune cookie sayings. It was mostly the last part that was somewhat profound. *But that's the beauty of it... something being so irrational and rational at the same time. It's practically magic...*

I slammed the book closed and threw it on my desk. What I had just read was somewhat spooky. It was too fitting to my current situation.

I lay back in my bed and turned on my radio and turned off my lamp. I was actually tired enough to sleep tonight. No longer than five seconds of lying in the bed in silence was all interrupted by Macy jumping into the bed with me and sleeping by my feet. I sat up quickly and Macy lifted her head up to look at me and cocked it to the side.

"Macy…" I groaned. "You have your bed, and I have mine. I think you may have gotten that confused."

In protest she put her head back down on my leg hard and let out a deep breath through her nose. I sighed and put my head back down on my pillow. Surprisingly the extra warmth by my feet was comfortable and before I knew it, I was asleep.

Kennley had told me that he wanted to talk to me. As much as I didn't want to be, I was thrilled. I had practically ran to the creek and waited for him to show up. He didn't get there much longer after me.

"Kahlen," he said my name with relief…almost as if he thought I wouldn't show.

I stood up off the ground and looked so see where he was. He was over to my right about ten feet away.

"Kahlen, I'm sorry. I'm sorry for everything that happened."

I smiled. "I'm sorry too."

"And I miss you. I'm sick of being apart."

"I know. So am I." I missed everything about him, even the stuff I hated.

Quickly he closed in the space between us and—

I woke up to chaos. Everything happened so fast. Macy jumped out of the bed and barked, Jenny screamed, and then I screamed, which made Marissa scream also. I caught my breath and screamed again. My eyes and my mind couldn't make sense of what was happening. It was all so disconcerting.

"What are you guys doing here?!" I yelled, wiping the sleepiness from my eyes.

Jenny was catching her breath also. "You have a dog?!"

Marissa was the calmest of all of us. "It's not hers. It's—…it's Macy."

Macy ran over to Marissa and jumped up on her happily. I rubbed my eyes quickly. Maybe I was still dreaming except my dream had taken a horrible turn. I was so confused.

"How do you know Macy?" I asked Marissa.

She ignored me. "Why are you still asleep at one in the afternoon?"

Jenny being the moderator put her hands out between both of us like she was breaking up a fight. "Okay, so obviously a lot of questions need to be answered here…and they can be answered later. But for now, we are on a mission that hasn't yet been accomplished."

"Which is?" I asked curtly.

Marissa smiled. "Oh, we're kidnapping you."

I narrowed my eyes in shock. "Why—,"

Marissa quickly gave Jenny a look before a loud whistle blew. Macy barked and I jumped back.

"What—,"

The whistle blew again, interrupting me.

Jenny let the whistle drop back around her neck. "We figured you might be somewhat difficult and even brought ducted tape in case you continue to struggle."

Marissa nodded. "We're doing this for your own good Kay. So get dressed into something hot and meet us downstairs…and don't even think about climbing out the window."

I narrowed my eyes as they left my room in silence and Macy followed Marissa out the door. I sat in my bed, still underneath the covers, possibly more confused than I had ever been in my life which was really saying something. I did as told and got dressed. I put on a pair of jeans and a t-shirt. As soon as I opened up my door Marissa was standing there which scared me half to death.

"I said something *hot*," she examined my outfit.

She walked into my room and to my closet. She pulled out a tight red short sleeved shirt and a mini skirt. Both of these things I didn't wear often…I wasn't even sure why I had them. Marissa looked down at my feet.

"Change into these, the flip-flops can stay," she ordered.

I wasn't used to seeing such a demanding side of Marissa. I figured it would be pointless to argue her on this. I knew that all of my questions would eventually be answered so it was best to do as told for now. I changed into the items she had picked out and because I was being a good prisoner I was allowed to brush my teeth and my hair alone before going down the stairs. Jenny and Marissa were both sitting on the couch comfortably watching TV.

Jenny looked back, saw me and gave a praising whistle with two fingers in her mouth. I always wondered how people did that. I would try to do it myself and just look like an idiot. We walked out to Marissa's car and I was forced into the backseat harshly.

"Can I at least know where you're forcibly taking me?"

Jenny shook her head no. "Sorry."

I sighed heavily to truly express my annoyance. But I wasn't as annoyed as I had led on. I was actually somewhat excited about all of this. I hadn't seen either of my friends in a while and it was nice seeing them now. Although I was completely and totally happy that school was out, I did miss art class and lunch. I was still in shock at my new found appreciation for Marissa. Ever since that night at The T.J. Club I realized I really had nothing against her after all.

It was a quiet drive to wherever we were going. Jenny and Marissa would occasionally start talking in code which I would sigh loudly to express my utter contempt. When we pulled into the parking lot to Rocco's, I contemplated jumping out of the window and making a run for it.

"Listen Kay," Marissa started. "I know about what happened between you and Kennley. My family went out to eat here yesterday and he was our waiter. I asked him how you were doing and he didn't respond right away. So I made him tell me what was going on. He said you two broke up. Then when I asked him who broke up with who, the look on his face was answering enough—,"

"No!" I protested loudly. "I am not going in there... just no!"

Jenny sighed. "Just think about it. We go in there to eat, we don't even know if he'll be our waiter, but maybe he sees you and once he gets a good look at you he'll know exactly what he's giving up."

I shook my head quickly. "There is no way I'm going in there."

"Kay, don't you even want to see him...just a tiny bit?" Marissa urged.

I did want to see him...but I didn't want to see him. I didn't know how I would handle that exactly. It hurt enough just thinking about him, I had no idea what seeing him would do to me. "That's irrelevant." I sighed crossing my arms against my chest.

"It is completely and entirely relevant." Jenny said.

I narrowed my eyes at the both of them. "Fine." I opened the car door and they followed. But as they started heading in the direction of the restaurant, I was heading towards the sidewalk. "I'll walk home. It should only take me an hour or so." Although there was sarcasm in my tone, I kept walking towards the sidewalk so they would know I wasn't bluffing.

I didn't get very far before they ran over to me blocking my path in the middle of the parking lot.

"Plan B?" Jenny said to Marissa.

Marissa nodded. "I figured we'd get to plan B soon anyway. I knew bringing her here would be a long shot."

"What plan B?" I asked.

They ignored me.

I swear time started moving very slowly when I saw the restaurant doors open and Kennley walked out. I figured his shift was over now. He didn't see me at first but then, I saw his head turn quickly in our direction. I knew he hadn't seen me...or at least didn't recognize me because he didn't make eye contact. But then before he took his next step he stopped dead in his tracks and turned his head again in our direction. His eyes met mine and it felt like our gaze was impossible to break. His mouth was opened slightly just like mine and we both didn't move from where we were.

This was ridiculous. We had been friends before, it didn't make sense that we couldn't now. We were acting like idiots but neither of us caved. I blinked quickly and looked down to the ground. Marissa and Jenny hadn't noticed anything while they discussed possibly moving on to plan C instead. When I had finally gotten the nerve to look back up, he was gone. I knew he felt guilty. I knew I should have gone over there to tell him I didn't blame him for what Ross did and he shouldn't blame himself either. But I couldn't. My feet felt glued to the ground.

They had finally decided on Plan B. We were back at my house now after picking up ice cream, candy, and magazines. We were spread out across my bedroom floor with a bowl of popcorn between us.

"So," Jenny said. "Tell us everything that happened. Play by play."

I took a sip of my soda. "I will, as soon as you guys answer all of my questions."

"Okay, shoot." Marissa said.

"Are you guys out of your minds or did you just wake up this morning and think, 'Kahlen's life is too boring. Let's spice it up a little!'?"

Jenny looked up from her magazine and smiled at me. "We're your friends. You're obviously hurting. Need I say more? I know this time isn't like the last time you broke up. That was different. But this time...I mean you're not even wearing the necklace he gave you."

Instinctively I place my hand to my neck and then dropped is slowly and my cheeks flushed a dark red.

"Kay, as soon as I found out, I called Jenny and we planned this whole thing. We figured you'd need time to wallow, or at least find someone to beat Kennley up for you."

I couldn't help but laugh. I couldn't picture kind hearted Marissa finding a hit man. They both started laughing too.

"Okay...so play by play...What happened?" Jenny asked.

I buried my head in my pillow to hide myself away from their anxious eyes. I didn't want to think about everything that happened that night...let alone discuss it.

"—and don't even say it's a long story," she added.

I sighed. "As my friends, I am going to expect that

you two will respect the fact that I don't want to talk about it."

They groaned.

"Seriously..." I said. "The story is so long I could write a novel about it. So...starting a new topic, how have your summers been so far?"

"Uneventful," Jenny said.

"I just got back from Hawaii," Marissa said.

{remove}I just looked at her. I wanted to hate her so much. I looked at Jenny who was giving her the same look. I smiled. I actually had friends now. I wasn't alone like before and it was a good feeling. Although I preferred not to be woken up so abruptly, it was nice to have people that had your back when you needed them. I had almost forgotten what that had felt like. I smiled glad I had successfully sidetracked them.

"Think about it this way..." Jenny said. "If you tell us what happened maybe we can figure this whole mess out somehow. I feel like there's something here I'm missing. This break up really doesn't make sense."

I rolled my eyes. Maybe I hadn't completely sidetracked them after all. She wasn't the only one who felt like she was missing something. Reluctantly I decided to tell them...but an *edited* version of course.

"He had been acting strange all day. And I had thought everything was okay until we went to a party and we got into a fight—,"

Marissa placed her hand under her chin listening intently. "What kind of a fight...like on a scale of one to ten."

"Um...probably and eight and a half, possibly nine."

She grimaced.

"Continue." Jenny urged.

"But we basically ended up stalking in different

directions and..." I stopped my sentence short. I wasn't sure how I was going to edit everything that happened after because it was all vital information to the breakup. "Then...then um...he took me home and broke up with me."

Marissa's jaw dropped. "Kay, I'm so sorry!" she said it like she was the one who had hurt me instead of him. "I can't believe he did that. It doesn't even make sense!"

"Well what was the fight about?" Jenny asked.

I tried to pretend like I hadn't heard her. "Yeah well you guys already know about my dad and the hospital." I continued. Everything that had happened downtown had been on the news nonstop for the first week after. I was just happy that my mom seemed so concerned with everything else that she didn't recognize the person she had met at the grocery store was the picture being flashed on the screen. "But Kennley was really upset about some things that happened with his family and I think that's why he was acting so strangely. I was so angry with him that I gave him back the necklace...but when he was about to leave he gave it back to me."

All three of us were silent after that.

"Well..." Jenny said, finally creating sound in the quiet. "It seems like you two have some unfinished business."

I sighed. I didn't want to have unfinished business. I wanted to move on from the rut I was in. I knew exactly what I needed to do before finally moving on. As much as I loved him, maybe my life would be better, less complicated without Kennley. Then suddenly something clicked together in my head. It was like I could see the dots connecting.

"I think that he hurt me intentionally so he wouldn't have to hurt me." I said slowly, still thinking it all through. I thought about all the stuff he had said at the hospital that night about screwing things up. It was like everything was coming together in my mind.

"What?" Marissa finally said. "That doesn't make any sense."

"I think it's kind of like he took himself out of the game...so he wouldn't have to lose."

"You mean he ended things with you so you couldn't break up with him first?" Jenny asked.

I knew neither of them had the slightest idea of what I was talking about but I didn't feel like explaining.

"No, I think he broke his promise to keep his promise. He hurt me so he wouldn't hurt me. He didn't want to screw things up any further.

"But—," Marissa said.

Jenny stopped her. "Shh...I think she's having an epiphany or something."

I was staring off into space now, almost oblivious to everything that was going on around me.

"Or something..." I said quietly.

22. Coming Around

I locked myself away in my room fighting what I knew I had to do to officially move on. I had too much baggage with me for closure. To distract myself from my many thoughts I was playing my guitar. I had added on to the song I had been composing. I added a second verse…

I need you now.

I wish you could be here somehow.

You were my hope, my faith, my love.

Sent to me like a dove.

And then the same chorus, which was really just the melody to the song.

La la la

La de dah dah dah dah

La de dah dah dah dah

La de dah dah dah ah ah ah

I stopped singing abruptly when I heard a car outside my window. Neither of my parents were home. My mom had let the prisoner— my father— go hang out with his friends to watch some sports game and my mother was at work. I didn't see either of their cars in the drive way and I went back to my bed figuring I was being paranoid.

I sighed and struck a random chord hard. There was only so long I could stall doing this. I took a shower, got dressed and ate breakfast...which was really a late lunch. When I was all set to go, stupidly I hadn't realized that I had no means of transportation. I didn't have a car, and both of my parents were gone. At this point I would have gotten down on my knees and begged for my old stupid car back. As if life didn't suck enough already...no car during the summer time with two busy parents is a whole new level of suck-age.

If it wasn't a sign, then I didn't know what it was besides perfect timing that my dad pulled into our driveway. I was happy and sad at the same time. I was secretly hoping I had a reason not to go do what I was about to do.

My dad slumped out of the car slowly. I assumed he was still sore.

"Dad I need a car," I whined.

"It needs gas." He handed me his keys. "Where are you going because your mom wants you to stop by the office around five?"

"I have some unfinished business that I need to take care of." I sighed. "But I don't just need a car now...I need a car in general."

He chuckled. "Need or want?"

I rolled my eyes. "You know sometimes if a want is great enough it can become a need."

He started to walk slowly to the front steps. "You know Kido...Most kids your age get summer jobs so they can raise enough money for a car," he yelled back at me.

I ignored him and got into the car. I wondered why

Kennley had a job. It's not like he really needed the money. From the looks of his house he had all the money in the world.

As I pulled out of the driveway, I cranked the radio up loudly to distract my constant thoughts. When I really looked back over the past couple of months... music was the only thing that made sense. It was the only thing I could count on to be consistent. Music could be anything I wanted it to be...it all depended on what song I was listening to. It was hard to understand everything that was happening in my life, especially lately, and it was nice to have something to connect with at the end of the day. Music never let me down.

As I started to go out of my neighborhood...another option was presented to me. I could go straight towards Kennley's house, or I could turn and go to the creek. The light changed and I made my decision...I knew I was stalling but procrastination doesn't mean you don't eventually get things done. The creek was as beautiful as ever except with one major, humungous, colossal flaw. The sign that said Dean's Creek had been taken down and now laid next to another sign that said:

Winnie's Convenient Store.

Coming Soon.

Construction Starts July 11th.

I could have passed out right then. It seemed almost unethical to chop down all of these gorgeous trees for a very unnecessary store. If I wasn't sure if God hated me or not before... I was now. I was absolutely sure that nothing in my life was fair at all. I was almost brought to tears when I thought about how many memories had been made at this creek. The rhythmic sound of the rippling waters didn't calm me like they usually did. I was so completely disturbed at the thought of all that surrounded me being gone. Without the creek…I wouldn't be so helplessly in love. These past couple of months would have been so entirely different. I had no right to be surprised that whoever this Winnie was wanted to crush my heart further so it was completely grounded into dust. It only made sense that something else would go wrong in this so-called life of mine.

Feeling that the tears might come I stomped off to the car and drove away quickly.

It wasn't a long drive to Kennley's house because as anxious as I was, I pushed the speed limits the whole way there. I sat in their driveway for a couple of seconds trying to catch my uneven breath. I slowly stepped out of the car and walked to the door. I reached my hand up to push the doorbell but before my finger got there the front door swung open. Of course as anxious as I was…and stressed, I screamed startled and almost went flying down the stairs until someone steadied my balance with a hug.

"Kahlen, I've missed you." Carrie released her hold on me. "Why don't you come over anymore?" She asked as sweetly as she could.

Still flustered I couldn't answer at first.

She sighed. "I know you guys broke up."

"Um…then why did you ask?"

She shrugged. "I was curious what your answer would be."

I formed an O with my lips.

She had left the door open and I looked inside the house, my eyes searching for Kennley. "Why did you guys break up?" she asked.

"Um…" I paused.

"You say um a lot," she noted. "Did you guys break up because of Hannah? Kennley says Ross put the drugs in his room but I think it was Hannah. She seems like she would do something evil like that."

Disconcerted I asked, "Is Kennley home?"

She nodded quickly. "Yeah, he is. He was downstairs lifting weights but when I told him I saw you pull up in the driveway he ran upstairs to change and put on some cologne because he—,"

I hadn't even seen where Kennley had come from but he was holding his hand over Carrie's mouth. He yanked his hand away quickly.

"Did you just lick me?" he yelled before wiping his hand off on Carrie's blond hair.

I guess Kennley hadn't finished changing because he was standing in a pair of jeans and only and black muscle shirt. I sighed heavily. Maybe I could come back later when he was fully clothed. It would make concentrating on the right things a lot easier.

It was extremely awkward for a second with Carrie and I standing on the porch and Kennley standing at the door. Carrie was in between us as I ignored Kennley's glare looking at the ground. He sent Carrie off quickly by suggesting she go watch SpongeBob. It was just us now standing in silence.

"You can come in," Kennley said slowly.

Reluctantly I stepped inside the house still looking at the ground.

"Um…hi." I grimaced to myself. I did say um a lot.

"Hi," He said after a second.

"So um…I need to talk to you."

He waited for me to continue but I didn't, still looking at the ground.

"About…" he urged as we walked into a different room farther away from Carrie's listening ears.

Kennley's face was blank and emotionless. I couldn't tell what he was feeling or thinking which was driving me insane. My right pocket felt suddenly heavy. The necklace was in there ready to be brought back to its rightful owner but as I stuck my hand in my pocket…it didn't come back out. I couldn't force my hand to grab a hold of it and place it in his hand. I was chickening out.

"I went to the creek today and they're chopping it down and replacing it with a convenience store, I said sourly."

For a second I could see the pain and shock cross his face before the poker face returned. "I guess that's… convenient. You know if you ever had a craving for a candy bar or something it's not that far away."

I tried to keep my face as blank as his although if anything he had just infuriated me with such an indifferent response.

"So is that all you wanted to say?" he asked.

I looked up into his green indifferent eyes. I felt desensitized by them now. "Yeah," I lied.

I slowly started to head off into the other direction. Like so many people had done before, he got hold on my wrist, but gently, and pulled me back slowly.

"Kahlen, how's your dad doing?"

"Better."

"And…" He was hesitant. "How are you doing?"

"Better." I sighed. "And you?"

It was strange that we were both being so formal. "Well things have been going better around here. My parents at least believe me about the drugs now…and Jimmy's…*repentant* I guess."

I was surprised that he had offered as much information as he did. I could see his blank face slowly fading away.

I nodded. "That's good."

It felt like fifty pounds could have been in my pocket

now. I knew I couldn't prolong it for much longer. I couldn't run away from my problems forever. Moving on was harder than I had imagined. As much as I wanted to forget about Kennley, he was always in the back of my mind lingering there. Our break up didn't make sense and I needed closure more than anything.

I broke the silence. "W-why did you break up with me?" I didn't mean for it to come out as a whisper as I looked back to the ground. "I just—," I sighed. "If there's any chance of me moving on at all, I just need some closure, and you giving me the necklace back doesn't exactly help...So why?"

He sighed too, looking away from me. "I don't know...a lot of reasons."

I didn't think it was possible but I hung my head lower. It felt like at that moment my heart had been stung with rejection.

"No," he said quickly. "That came out wrong. They're not bad reasons...not about you anyway. You know I love you...regardless of anything that's happened. That's why I gave you back the necklace."

A compelling feeling was coming over me to touch him. It didn't make sense that suddenly I wanted to hug him or touch his arm. It was probably because you always want what you can't have. I thought about the times when he had been so impulsive in kissing me. I pondered over that wondering if it would work now. I struggled against myself to stand still and not move closer to him.

I sighed. "You're still not helping with the whole closure thing here...What were the reasons?"

"Dena and Conner were going to send me to boarding school in Glen Arbor, Michigan because of the whole Jimmy thing. It's still in state but it's not exactly the shortest drive and I'm not really a fan of long distance relationships. And besides all of that, I'm not really the best influence. If you don't believe me, Jimmy's living proof. You shouldn't be hanging around me anyways."

I shook my head. "You're not a bad guy Kennley. I know that for a fact. You may have done some bad things...but that doesn't make you a bad person." I thought about the mini epiphany I had earlier. "Are you sure this isn't just about you taking yourself out of the game...so you don't have to lose...you don't have to hurt me?"

"I like to keep my promises."

"Well..." I sighed. "You have a funny way of showing it."

He grinned very slightly. "My face is still open to punching."

I grinned too. Ha, like I needed his permission. "An eye for an eyes makes the whole world blind right?"

He shrugged. "Eyesight is overrated."

I smiled at him briefly before walking towards the front door. "I don't blame you, Kennley. I...I know you feel guilty about everything that happened with Ross, but you shouldn't. I'm happy you didn't go with him that night. If you did you'd be in that jail cell with him."

"Kahlen—,"

"You didn't pull the trigger...he did."

I walked out the door to the car. I just sat there for a second trying to get a grip...on myself and my life. I didn't have the creek anymore and I didn't have Kennley anymore. The sooner I let both of those things go, the easier my life would be.

Another car pulled into the driveway with Ben inside. Surprisingly there were no other clowns to get out of the car with him. It seemed like since their fearless leader had been taken away, the pack split up. Ben waved to me when he got out of the car and walked up to the porch. I watched as he rang the doorbell and patiently waited for someone to come to the door. I guess he didn't have any more copies of the house keys…or they changed the locks. Kennley opened the door.

"Hey Ken—,"

The door slammed in Ben's face. My eyes widened in shock. Ben stood at the closed door for a second before slowly turning around on his heels.

He nodded to himself. "He hates me."

I stuck my head out the car window. "Ben I'm sure he doesn't—,"

"No…he hates me. He hates all of us. The only person he doesn't hate is you."

I sighed. "He broke up with me."

"That's not hate. That called stupidity."

I smiled at him weakly before putting the key in the ignition. The car came to life for a second before dying. Incredulous I turned the key again…it did the same thing.

"You have got to kidding me!" I yelled. Maybe there was some curse on me or something.

Ben stuck his head inside the car. "You're out of gas."

I threw my head back on the seat. I remembered my dad saying the car needed gas but I wasn't paying attention to him.

"Great. Now what am I supposed to do? I have to be somewhere in fifteen minutes." Ugh…I was going to be in so much trouble. Why couldn't I just remember to get gas? I put my head in my hands soaking…no drowning in my own misery.

"I can drive you."

I looked up. "What?"

"To wherever you need to go…I can drive you."

I mulled over it for a second. "But I can't just leave the car here."

"Well, go explain to Kennley why there's an extra car in his driveway and then get it towed later."

That idea might actually work. I cocked my head to the side and looked at him. "Since when did you become so…" I couldn't think if the right word.

"Rational?" he offered. "I don't know. I think losing all of your closest friends does that to you."

All I managed to say was, "Oh." I got out of the car and walked to the front door. I rang the doorbell and it opened in a matter of seconds abruptly.

"What part of leave me alone don't you—," Kennley stopped once he saw it was me. "Kahlen?"

"Listen…I'm sorry—,"

"Sorry? You have nothing to be sorry for. I'm the one who messed this whole thing up between us. That's why I figured it was best that we stay apart."

I let what he said hang out in the air for a second.

"…I'm sorry that I have to leave my car in your driveway because the tank is empty…"

His face was blank again. "Oh."

"I'll try to get it taken care of as soon as possible." I promised.

"Well do you need a ride home or—,"

"Ben's taking me. I just thought you might want to know why an extra car would be sitting there."

This was possibly the most awkward conversation I had ever had. He just nodded before waving goodbye. I sighed heavily. I really wanted to tell him how stupid I thought this break up was but I couldn't force myself to turn around. I guess that made me just as stupid as him.

I got into Ben's black SUV and we pulled out of the

driveway with Kennley watching before he left and shut the front door behind him.

"Is it just me or does everyone have a car except me?"

Ben chuckled. "This is my mom's car."

"Oh," I said. "So...why does Kennley supposedly hate you?"

"Well no one else had the money to bail Ross out. So I called and asked Kennley to...I-I didn't know that he shot..." He cut his sentence short. "How is your dad doing by the way?"

"He's doing well now, recovering. But if you didn't know then why don't you tell Kennley that?"

"Yeah...well if you haven't noticed he isn't exactly talking to me. He isn't talking to any of us. The only bright side to all of this is that Hannah's gone AWOL."

I wasn't used to seeing this side of Ben. He wasn't his normal jovial self. "Ugh...please don't say that name around me." I grimaced.

"What happened that night anyway? I mean, I know Kennley and Ross had a lot of bottled up feelings so a fight was bound to happen sooner or later. Like when Kennley caught Ross and Hannah I thought it was going to be a fight right then and there but surprisingly, all Kennley did was yell at the both of them, publicly dump Hannah, and walked away. But I guess that tells you who he cares about more. He fought over you."

"Yeah...after kissing Hannah," I said sourly.

"Really? That...that doesn't sound like him. I know he had been really upset earlier that day about something but I really think Hannah is more to blame than he is."

I tried to picture it in my head. I couldn't see Jordan or Ben drug dealings. They didn't seem like those kinds of people. "Have...have any of you ever dealt drugs?" I asked hesitantly.

"No…Never. That's just Ross. I mean there's a difference between pulling pranks at school and drinking a couple of beers every now and again, and then dealing drugs…" He shook his head.

"Well why does he do it?" It sounded like a stupid question once it came out.

"Ross like any other person does it for the money. His mom's been laid off for a while. The money's tight… but I don't think it really justifies drug dealing. We've all tried to stop him but he never listens. Like about three months ago he was going to a really bad part of town and it didn't seem safe. I told Jordan I was going down there to try and stop him. Jordan told Ross…and Ross told Kennley. And before I had even gotten there Kennley had made me pull over. I don't even know how he got to me so quickly…I think it was because he was at some creek. I guess it wouldn't have mattered if I went anyway…he had taken a few safety precautions. I don't even know where he got a gun."

I remembered that first day I had met Kennley at the creek. I remembered him angry and running down the street. I had almost forgotten about that until now.

"Wait…how long ago did you say that was?" I asked.

"April-ish I think."

I chuckled. "I think that was the first time Kennley and I met. I was at Dean's Creek and I kind of rolled into him."

He raised an eyebrow. "Rolled?"

I shrugged. "I lost my balance…and rolled."

Ben sighed. "He'll come around."

"What?" I asked.

"He'll come to his senses eventually. What I've learned about Kennley is sometimes he can… Well, he'll have his Kennley moments where he shuts out the rest of the world. But he eventually comes around. You just got to give him some room to cool off."

I sighed. "And how long exactly does it take him to… come around?"

"For my situation…I don't know, maybe a week or so. But for you, I think a little push in the right direction might help."

My eyes widened. "I have a hard enough time pushing myself as it is. How am I supposed to push someone else?"

"I'd say I'd talk to him for you but we're not exactly on speaking terms."

"He'll come around," I said it although I didn't believe it myself.

I showed him the way to Thomas Designs and when we finally got there you could see Cece and Laura through the glass windows sitting in their usual positions. Laura was doing Sudoku while Cece had a magazine by the phone.

"Thanks for the ride Ben." I said getting out of the car.

"No problem." He wasn't looking at me while he was gazing at something through the glass windows. "How about I walk you in?"

We were parked ten feet away from the door. I stared at him suspiciously. I walked to the door and he followed me but his gaze never left whatever he was looking at.

"Hey BD!" Cece greeted me.

Laura sighed. "Cece…her name really isn't that hard to remember."

"Laura I told you I'm no good with names, you know that. And if you're so good with names then what's BD's?" Cece said.

Laura looked up at me and smirked. "Hi Kahlen."

I gave her a greeting smile. "Is my mom in her office?"

Cece nodded. "But before you go...who is this behind you. Is this the boyfriend?"

Before I could respond Ben walked over to Cece and smiled. "This is the boyfriend's single friend actually."

I was happy he didn't throw the ex in there. It was embarrassing enough being dumped without having the whole world know.

Cece smiled. "Well does boyfriend's single friend have a name?"

"Ben," he smiled.

"Ben...I like that, it's simple. I think I can remember it." She stuck out her hand offering a hand shake. Ben took her hand and shook it. "I'm Cece." She smiled.

Laura and I both just stood there looking at the two of them with our mouths open wide. But when I really thought about it, Ben and Cece were perfect for each other. I chuckled to myself before walking into my mom's office. She was flustered as always, sitting in her big comfy chair with a billion papers on her desk.

"Hey, mom," I said shutting her door behind me.

She looked up at me and let out a sigh of relief. "Oh sweetie, finally you're here. Can you believe Louisa took the day off? I've been so busy today that it's almost been unbearable without an assistant...and I remember a certain someone promising to help me. But what took you so long to get here? Your father told you right? He's at home right now isn't he? He needs to rest and—,"

"Mom!" I said stopping her. She was talking a million words a second. I could barely understand what she was saying. "Calm down."

She took a deep breath. "Why are you late?"

I grimaced. "We need to call someone to tow dad's

car…it's completely out of gas. I left it at Kennley's house."

"Then how did you get here?" she asked. "You know what? Never mind I don't want to know…about any of it. So I'm just going to pretend I didn't hear any of that because I'm under enough stress as it is."

I smiled. "I can live with that."

She smiled too. "You're not off the hook; you're just off my hook. I assume you must have known to get gas and forgot so you can go call your father and have him deal with it. And hurry back because I need your opinion on a couple of things."

I sighed and walked out of her office. I reluctantly pulled out my cell phone and called my dad. The phone rang for a while. I assumed Dad was stretched out on his reclining chair. I imagined him taking his slow time walking to the phone. He was using being in the hospital as an excuse for a forty five year old man to act seventy.

"Hello?" he said.

"Dad I—,"

"Kido…do you mind telling me why my car just magically appeared in the driveway without you in it?

It took me a while to respond. "What? I don't know how it got there. I kind of forgot to get gas and I got a ride from a friend to the office." My brows furrowed. I wondered who would have… "Dad I'll call you back, bye." I closed my phone.

I didn't understand Kennley these days. He was sending me so many mixed messages. Maybe it was just a friendly gesture. As much as I wanted to call him to thank him…I couldn't force myself to open my phone back up. I walked to the front by Cece and Laura…and Ben.

I stood a couple of feet back still amused by this

emerging relationship. There was just one tiny little problem the two of them had to face...

"So how old are you?" Cece asked.

"Seventeen."

The look on Cece face was classic. Laura and I both burst out laughing at the same time. Tears were practically streaming down my face.

"Woah, woah, and woah! Back up, rewind, jail time, no thanks." She said before putting her head in her hands.

Ben looked so confused. I walked over closer to Ben trying to stifle my laughter.

"Geez Cece!" Laura said still laughing. "Pick on someone your own age...or flirt rather."

"It's only a five year difference," she said in a hushed tone.

"Almost six, your birthday's next month!" Laura said.

"No it's not." Ben chimed in. "I mean...it would still be five years...I turn eighteen in three weeks."

Cece wrote something down quickly on a tiny piece of paper. "Oh sugar apples...I can't believe I'm doing this," she said handing Ben the piece of paper with her number. "Call me in three weeks and not a second before."

Ben smiled. "Gladly." He took the number and put it in his pocket. He started walking towards the door. "Kahlen, can I talk to you for a minute?" he said gesturing towards his car.

"Sure," I said as my eyes narrowed.

I followed him out to his car. We walked behind it so we weren't seen through the glass windows.

"Ben what did you want to talk—,"

He gripped me into a bear hug and I couldn't breathe. "I love you," he said once he let go of me. "I just met my potential soul mate…and I blame you." He grinned. "You know what else I blame you for?" He asked. He didn't give me time to answer. "Kennley called me a couple of minutes ago and he actually doesn't hate me. I got a chance to explain to him, and he's finally cooled off."

"How am I to blame for that second part?" I asked confused.

"He called me because of you. He wanted me to tell you that the whole car thing is taken care of. It gave me a chance to explain to him about everything that happened."

It was hard to be happy for Ben when I was still sad myself. "Why couldn't he just call me himself?"

It took him a second to answer almost like he was hiding something. "He'll come around."

I spent my whole Tuesday night at Thomas Designs until around eight o'clock when we finally got home. I still couldn't get over my dad's tan Toyota Camry sitting in our drive way with the keys sitting in the ignition. I didn't know how Kennley got the keys. I figured they probably fell out of my pocket like they always did. I knew I should carry a purse so I could keep track of things like cell phones and keys…but for some reason purses annoyed me. I hated having something to hold on to all the time.

I felt like I should thank Kennley. But if he couldn't even call me to tell me himself…why should I?

23. The Stars

Being the helpful daughter that I was, I made breakfast. Not just the good old cereal in a bowl…I did the whole shebang. I made, scrambled eggs, bacon, sausage, toast, and I even cut up some fruit and put it in a bowl. I was starting a new chapter of my life as of today and I wanted to start it off right. I was sick of being sad and confused. I decided I wanted to be a new Kahlen…the one who doesn't depend on anyone, the one who can push her own self in the right direction. Just the thought of it felt empowering. I had my doubts on how long this new chapter would last but I was trying not to be a pessimist about it. The old Kahlen was a pessimist; the new Kahlen was optimistic, or at least trying to be.

Both my parents ate their breakfast silently while looking at me suspiciously every now and again. I knew they were both waiting for me to say what I wanted. They knew that I wouldn't have just made breakfast… just because. The old Kahlen would never do that. It was somewhat irritating how they both chewed slowly, looking at me out of the corners of their eyes.

My dad cut a piece of sausage with the side of his fork and stared at it for a long second suspiciously.

"Is there something wrong with the food?" I asked curtly.

He put the sausage in his mouth and chewed little by little. "No…not with the food."

I sighed. "I hope you know it's insulting that when

someone does something nice that you expect that they have an ulterior motive."

"So I expect wrong?" he said, highly doubtful.

"There is no ulterior motive. You already know what I want. So there's no need to butter you guys up first before I ask you."

"Honey, and what is it you want?" she asked.

"The same thing I've been asking for, for over a month now. It hasn't changed. But that's not what this breakfast is about. Like I said...I was just doing something nice."

My dad sighed. "Kido, if you can't even remember to put gas in the car—,"

"I had a lot on my mind that day. They're chopping down Dean's Creek and putting in a convenience store. I was going to get gas but then my thoughts were so cluttered that I forgot one measly time."

They were both silent for a moment thinking. I grinned. Maybe I was getting somewhere with this.

I grinned at the thought of victory. "It doesn't have to be a fancy car....just a car. They say there's no car like a used car. I'll take one as cheap as they come as long as it doesn't break down on me." I really hoped they wouldn't go out and buy me a piece of junk despite what I had just said.

"We'll think about it sweetie. After all, your birthday is coming up."

My birthday? I had almost forgotten that existed. I barely remembered what day my birthday was on. I never cared much for my birthday. It was always just another year, another party. It never really seemed to matter to me. But still my mother would go out of her way to throw a huge party with family and friends. My dad would barbeque and no one would leave my house until about midnight so being the good host I was, I was forced to endure it.

"Got any ideas of what you want to do for your birthday this year? It is the big one-eight." My father asked.

Eighteen...big whoop. "Mom, I spent my sweet sixteen watching movies with Emma." But even then, the next day she threw a big party for me despite my wishes. "Do you think I really care about my eighteenth birthday? How about we do something simple like go out for dinner? I'll even comply and let you tell waitress it's my birthday so they can sing and bring me a free dessert."

"But where's the fun in that?" she asked, truly not understanding why someone could be so passive about their birthday. We had the same discussion every year. I didn't know why she wasn't used to it by now.

I could see I was getting nowhere with this. "You know what mom...You can do whatever you want for my birthday. You can even have a parade if you want. Surprise me."

She sighed. "...More like your father everyday..."

My dad smiled. He wasn't big on birthdays either. He ate the rest of his breakfast and patted his stomach appreciatively. "Well I'm gonna go to the outdoor equipment store while the sale is still going on. I'm going to go camping this weekend...that is if can have early parole?"

She sighed and her lips moved into a slight scowl. "For the last time, this house is *not* a prison. I just thought it'd be best for you to rest instead of trying to go right back to work."

He chuckled to himself in disagreement. "Well any of you two high maintenance ladies care to come with me?" He was already walking away from the table, knowing both of our answers.

"Sure," I said.

They both looked at me incredulously.

"I mean why not? I'm up to new experiences. You can't knock it till you've tried it, right?" I was so optimistic I was scaring myself. By the look on their faces I was scaring them too. Great, now they probably thought I was high or something.

"Uh-um..." he stammered. "Okay...Why don't you come with me to the store then so we can get you some hiking boots?"

I nodded getting up from the table. "Mom you should come too so you won't be here alone all weekend."

She rolled her eyes. "Not only does Julie need help packing and I have to plan a birthday party and a going away party that happen to be on the same day...it seems like your father's insanity is contagious. So you two have fun," she said. "Somehow I'll manage to go on without you." Heavy sarcasm.

As I put on my shoes at the front door I could hear her mumbling, "...More like her father everyday...if I hadn't been there when she was born I'd have my doubts she was mine."

I chuckled. "I heard that," I yelled before shutting the door behind me.

I never knew there were so many different types of sleeping bags and tents. Some tents looked more like houses instead of portable shelters. While I gawked in amazement at the whole camping world, my dad was off somewhere gazing at fishing rods. I walked over to him with my new hiking boots in hand, trying to grasp the excitement he felt for a stick with a string attached.

He looked like he could have cried. "Do you know

what this is?" He asked me. He gently took a very fancy looking stick and string down and held in his hands like it was a newborn lamb instead of a fishing rod.

I tried to think of something nice to say about the rod that he thought was baby Jesus but I couldn't. If you can't say anything nice, then don't say it at all…so I didn't. I just shook my head no.

"Kahlen…this is the Shimano's Cumara. It has received the Best of the Best award for spinning rods from *Field and Stream Magazine* not to mention a 2008 Best Value award from *TackleTour.com*." He was borderline obsessive.

"Um, wow," I said.

He took a moment of silence before he put it back with the other rods.

He grinned still looking at it. "The boys and I call it Excalibur."

I stifled my laughter. I didn't even bother asking who the boys were. "Well why don't you buy it then, Dad?"

He snorted. "Hah! You think your mother would let me spend over hundred dollars on a fishing pole when I already have a perfectly fine one?"

"Have you seen mom shop? Hundreds of dollars are wasted per shopping trip on things she doesn't need. Splurge a little. Indulge yourself in…*Excalibur*." I acted like I was a model on a game show and put my hands out presenting the stick and string. I watched as he fidgeted with his hands over what he was going to do. "Tempting, isn't it?"

He took the rod into his hands again. "Maybe you're right…"

"That seems to be the case most of the time," I agreed.

He gripped it tighter in his hands and walked over

triumphantly to the cash register. "Ricky," he said to the cashier. "I'm doing it."

Ricky looked like the camping type. He was rugged and looked like he wasn't afraid to get down and dirty. "You're doing it?" Ricky said with the same amount of incomprehensible enthusiasm. "Bobby! Get over here! Bill's buying Excalibur."

I had a guess that these were the boys he was talking about. Bobby walked over from the other cash register and it took me at least ten long seconds to realize they were twins.

"You know we get the G. Loomis Bronzeback in next week." Bobby said.

Ricky smiled. "The King Arthur himself, baby."

My dad's jaw dropped. "Isn't that one over 250 dollars?"

{removed space}"And worth every cent," Ricky said. "But come on...being the loyal costumer that you are, we could probably get you a discount."

My dad closed his eyes in pain as if he was torn between the two. "No," he finally said, and his voice was strained as if the decision was causing him pain. I tried really hard not to roll my eyes. "I'll just stick with the Cumara."

"I would say it's your loss but you can't go wrong with Excalibur," Bobby said before walking away.

I just stood off to the side pretending to be uninterested in the conversation. Their excitement was truly unfathomable.

When we finally got back home I tried to pack light for my weekend trip which was surprisingly, fairly easy. By morning I had an uneasy feeling about what I was about to do. I couldn't believe I was going camping. That sentence alone sounded so wrong.

We woke up bright and early to put all of the camping

gear in the car that would barely fit. I sighed heavily before sitting in the passenger's seat and watched as my dad drove to my ultimate doom. I tried to stifle my inner pessimist.

It was about an hour drive to where we were going. I could tell we were getting closer once we were surrounded by the woods. There wasn't a fast food place in sight. I saw lots of cottages as we drove by.

"Why do people like to live in the middle of nowhere?" I asked.

"It's actually a pretty popular area out here, actually."

"Don't people wonder if bears will come wandering in their houses."

My dad just looked at me and laughed. "There aren't too many bears out here."

I looked at him for a long moment...Thinking back to weeks ago when I thought I might have lost him. Just the fear of that happening again someday was part of the reason I had agreed to come with him. "Dad...?"

"Yeah Kido?"

I looked out into the open road. "Why weren't you wearing a bulletproof vest?"

He sighed. "I...I was in a hurry. I didn't think that I'd need it. Maybe I am a little deserving of your mother's worry prison."

I smiled weakly. "Maybe."

I was thankful that my mom didn't seem to remember Ross and my dad had never met him really. If they did, I didn't think they'd really approve of Kennley...not that there was anything to approve of now.

This sky was somewhat salmon colored as the sun set beneath the clouds. Maybe it just seemed that way because I had fish on my mind. I hated fish. I had forgotten about that one little aspect of camping. Not expecting company, the only other food my dad brought was baked beans and potato chips. I put new meaning to the word *sucked* when it came to fishing. My father being the show-off that he was caught a whole buckets worth.

As optimistic as I was trying to be…I hated camping. I couldn't pitch a tent and I couldn't even light a match to start a fire. People like me who were not taught any survival skills were meant to stay indoors. I was so sick of mosquitoes treating me like a drive-thru. The whole right side of my body was puffy from the stupid bloodsuckers' many attacks.

I was so frustrated I could have cried while I grabbed another handful of potato chips. But my dad was thoroughly enjoying himself. He seemed to enjoy every aspect of camping. I was just happy we were going home tomorrow evening because I was two seconds from being in the fetal position.

"You really like it out here don't you?" I asked, looking at his beaming smile.

"Everything is so peaceful and quiet. What's not to like?"

I fought back a smile, envisioning myself whipping out a huge list to answer his question. But he was right in a way. It was ironic how you could hear the birds chirping constantly and the crickets and yet it never really seemed like noise. Still everything was serene in a way, but then it would be interrupted suddenly with me whacking off mosquitoes. My stupid bug repellant didn't work.

"I guess I understand what you mean…to some extent."

He sighed. "What do you think are the chances of your mother coming up here?"

"What do you think are the chances of the fish you're eating right now coming back to life," I chuckled. I looked back up at the sky. It was no longer salmon colored. The sun was setting further and night was quickly falling.

"Good point." He chuckled too. "But maybe someday she'll come around."

"And maybe I just saw your fish move on your plate."

He purposefully stuck his fork in his grilled fish hard and slowly put it in his mouth chewing loudly.

As the sky got even darker I was beginning to dread my next upcoming obstacle. I didn't want to sleep on the ground. Even though we had a big tent, sleeping bags and covers, I still imagined it cold and uncomfortable. I also didn't know how I was going to get through the night with my dad's snores. My mother thought I snored too but I found that highly unlikely. I almost loathed myself for agreeing to come to this hell on Earth.

"Kido, look up."

I did as told. I couldn't believe how quickly night had come. The sky was covered with thousands of stars as plentiful as the sand on the beach. I had to remind myself to breath while gazing at the beauty my eyes beheld. I had never seen anything like it. It was truly extraordinary.

"Nature's beauty at its best." He said.

I was speechless. I couldn't even begin to form words. I wasn't even sure if I was seeing right. It all seemed so surreal. I saw a shooting star fly across the sky. I could point out the big and little dipper for once. There were no helicopters or planes flying overhead. Nothing disturbed the amazing peace the stars created. It was really such a shame—a tragedy even, that the sky didn't look like this at home. It was far from fair.

Compared to the immense sky, I had never felt so insignificant in my life.

Life without love is like a starless sky— it was weird that out of all the fortune cookie-like things Emma had said to me, that was the one that really stuck. I fully understood it now. I knew what being in love felt like and what a star-filled sky looked like. I couldn't find the right words to describe it all. Each word I came up with just kept coming up short.

"Wow." I said.

"Just think about how this is over our heads every night but we can never see it…" he mused.

I didn't want this to be my last time seeing a sky like this but I also didn't want to go camping again. There had to be some compromise.

"Dad…what if there was a way to get mom up here?"

He raised his eyebrow. "Like…?"

"We passed a lot of cottages on the way. What if we bought one? Think about it, mom and I don't like the outdoors, you do. If we have a cottage you could still camp if you'd like or you can sleep under a nice wooden shelter. We'd still be in the woods…just with a bigger shelter over our heads."

He looked at me for a long second, his brows furrowing. "You know that just might work…that is if we had an extra hundred thousand dollars lying around."

I sighed. I hadn't thought about that. "Well maybe we could rent it out to people when we're not using it. That way it's like the cottage is paying for itself. And think about all the new business mom is getting."

"You're feeling very business woman-like today aren't you?" he asked. "You tried to sell me on buying you a car, buying Excalibur, and now a cottage? There's something that's just not normal about that. Shouldn't you be concerned with clothes and make up?"

My jaw dropped. There were so many things wrong with what he had said. "You don't have to buy me a new car. You can buy yourself a new car and give me your old one. You know, it's a miracle that you fit all of this camping gear in your car in the first place. Don't you think it would be better if you had a bigger car or cottage to store all of this stuff in?" I asked. "And I'm just going to ignore that last part about the clothes and make up completely."

He shook his head. "You are unbelievable. I'm starting to think you could make a lot of money as a sales woman."

"No, I'm just stubborn and can be inventive when it comes to getting what I want."

He rested his head on his chin. "A cottage…" He mused.

"A cottage that pays for itself… You yourself said that this was a popular area."

"A cottage…" he repeated again. He gave his head one last shake. "I'm going to call it a night."

I sighed. "Okay. But I'm going to stay out here and stargaze for a little bit."

He nodded. "Don't get eaten by any bears."

"I'll try my best."

24. Mixed Messages

"You bought a cottage?!"

My parents were fighting in their bedroom down the hall from mine. I could hear my mom yelling from down the hall like she was standing right by my ear. I flinched at her high pitched voice.

"...Because you don't just go out and buy something that cost THOUSANDS of dollars without telling your wife. At the very least a phone CALL would have been NICE!" she yelled.

I had successfully talked my dad into buying a cottage. On the way home we found a real estate building. We stopped in and they showed us the different cottages for sale. We finally settled on one that had two floors and a small basement, two bedrooms, and a view of the lake. It was beautiful. It almost reminded me of a big version of the creek. I knew my mom would love it once she saw it.

"Lisa!" my dad yelled over her voice. "Think of it this way, you can interior design it however you like. You have free reign. And we can rent it out to people and that alone should pay for the monthly payments."

It took a second before she responded. "This still isn't a decision you make with your seventeen year old daughter."

"Almost eighteen."

"That's not the point!"

"You said I needed to rest and relax more. When I go

camping I am relaxed. And nothing is permanent yet. Technically we bought the cottage but not all the papers have been signed. I wanted you to go see it first."

I smiled at the silence. I guess my mom seemed okay with that.

"A man named Ricky called," she said changing the subject.

"Oh?"

"He wanted me to tell you that the King Arthur arrived early and that Excalibur and King Arthur were meant to be together."

"Yeah..." he sighed. "I bought something else too..."

"Let me guess, a car, a yacht, something else that cost thousands of dollars?!"

Today was the last day the creek would belong to Dean before it was transformed into a tacky convenience store. Words could not express how frustrated I was just from the thought! As entertaining as my parents' fight was, it was getting annoying. I needed an escape from this house. I said goodbye to Macy who was laying down on my bed comfortably before opening my window as far up as it would go. I knew I could have used the front door but I still liked my window better. The creek was beautiful as always but something about it seemed different that I couldn't quite put my finger on. The wind whistled through the leaves and the lukewarm water rippled into the forest. The clouds still formed the strangest images that only someone like me could see, but still something was different. It wasn't the fact that I was alone here which I had rarely been over the last couple of months. It wasn't the fact that the Dean's Creek sign had vanished or that the Winnie's Convenience store sign had been taken down too. Then it finally hit me. There wasn't any physical difference, or at least not yet. The only difference was that the creek didn't feel like mine anymore. It was now some stranger's named Winnie which ate me up inside further. It didn't make sense to feel so attached to a piece of nature and yet I was and wasn't ashamed of it.

I let out a deep breath before sitting at the foot of the water looking at my reflection. It was strange looking at the image of someone I recognized but didn't at the same time. I could see that beyond the whole new optimistic leaf thing, I was changing. I wasn't the same girl I was months ago avoiding funerals. I wasn't so scared of life like I had been before. I was willing to take the risk to love. Just thinking about love made my heart feel like it was going to beat out of my chest. I fought back all of my thoughts about Kennley although it wasn't working. As much as I loved him, I wasn't sure if I wanted to anymore.

I should not have been surprised that Kennley sauntered his way around the perfect shade tree and sat by me, overfriendly. I got the image of the first time he had plopped down like this beside me the first time we met and forbid a smile from spreading across my face. I grimaced when I saw that he looked like a male model while I was dressed in a t-shirt and cut off shorts, not expecting company. I combed my fingers through my hair and looked off into the distance trying to avoid eye contact.

"It can't be just another coincidence that we're both here at the same time. There has to be some reason why...like the universe is throwing us together or something," I said quietly, not looking in his direction.

"Well I'm sorry. I didn't know that you preferred to be alone."

I fought myself on turning to him to see the expression on his face which was almost impossible to do.

"I didn't say that."

"Then what are you saying?"

I sighed, ignoring his question. "So is the universe throwing us together or is there another reason that you're here?" I turned to him and stopped breathing at the sight of the smile reaching up to those glistening eyes. My borderline obsession with his eyes didn't make much sense either.

"I'm here actually because I was looking for you. I stopped by your house and you weren't there so I figured this would be the next best place to look. But who knows…maybe the universe is throwing us together after all."

"Maybe," I said. "But why were you looking for me?" The curiosity was burning inside of me to the very core.

"I don't want to lose you Kahlen. I want us to be friends."

"Friends…" I repeated the word slowly leaning back on my hands. Right, because us being friends was completely feasible after I had found out how much trouble he really had been in, he cheated on me, I kissed his best friend who then tried to rape me, before he got into a fight with Ross, broke up with me, and his now ex-best friend shot my dad….yeah, being friends was completely comprehensible. The really sick thing about it all was that I still loved him…so where did that leave us now?

I knew that without a doubt being friends with Kennley would be awkward but I figured that would pass eventually. But I wasn't sure if I could be friends with Kennley…Just sitting next to him now I had that same burning desire to be as impulsive as he had been in the past.

"Kennley, what brought all of this on? I thought you said it was best if we were apart because you're a bad influence." I couldn't say the last part without making a face.

He shrugged. "I was being stupid and I'm sorry. But after you stopped by my house something clicked in my head I guess. I had gone to your house earlier that day though, I even heard you playing your guitar, but then I chickened out and went home"

My cheeks blushed. My mind began to race with thoughts about him hearing me singing and playing my guitar. "Oh," I said.

"You were good though. Really good actually," He assured me. "And that song you were singing…did you write that yourself?"

I tried to compose my chagrined face. "So you want to be friends?" I asked, ignoring his question.

"Acquaintances at the very least."

I sighed heavily. "As much as I still love you…I don't know if I can be friends. I know I told you that what happened at the party didn't matter to me but parts of it still eat me up inside. You know, forgive not forget."

He sighed too. I could see the expression change immediately on his face. "I should have never taken you to that party in the first place…I knew how wild it would be but I was being selfish…I just wanted an escape for a night, I guess. And I shouldn't have yelled at you the way I did and then walk out on you. I wish I had some excuse to justify my behavior but just the fact that I was in a really bad mood doesn't cut it for me." He shook his head to himself. "As soon as we got in that fight outside on the porch I was so angry with myself that I tried to go upstairs to get some peace and then Hannah walked in."

My jaw clenched just by the sound of her name. I wasn't sure if I wanted to hear much more of what happened after this point but I kept listening anyway.

"But when she started talking to me, she was acting like the Hannah I had once liked instead of the one I can't stand now. I wasn't expecting it but she kissed me…the problem was, I didn't push her off right away which I'm guessing is what you saw. But I did eventually push her off. I told her that I couldn't do that to you."

I shook my head. "But by that point you already had."

"And I'm sorry for that. Really and truly completely and entirely sorry. But that doesn't mean you're not at fault for anything either. What about you and Ross?"

I winced in disgust just thinking about him. "It's pretty much the same story you told I guess. But when I kissed him back…I didn't know he was going to try anything. I guess me kissing him was my version of punching you in the face."

He grimaced. "An eye for an eye makes the whole world blind I guess."

I chuckled. "Whatever happened to eyesight is overrated?"

"Things change," he grinned.

I couldn't help but sense that there was a double meaning behind his words but I ignored it."So…" he said. "Friends?" He stuck out his hand waiting for me to shake it.

"I think I can manage that." I sighed before extending my arm to put my hand in his and as soon as his warm hand was against my clammy one I felt the exact opposite. I looked away quickly and he dropped my hand.

"Do you realize we have nothing in common?" I said quickly to change the subject.

He sat there thinking for a second. "We have to have something in common."

"Well I guess we're both stubborn."

He laughed. "Yes, but somehow I always manage to get things my way when it comes to you."

I narrowed my eyes at him. I wanted to deny it and tell him he was wrong but the truth of the matter was he was right. Time after time again he would get his way. I gave him a look.

He shrugged. "It's not my fault you're so easy to convince."

I snorted. "More like distract..."

"Well maybe you should focus more."

"It's hard to focus around you." I admitted sheepishly wishing the words had never come from out of my mouth.

"And why is that?"

I sighed. "Because you're so spontaneous and impulsive that half of the time I have trouble keeping up with you...not that you make it any easier."

"Easiness is overrated."

"A lot of things are overrated."

"Like...?" He asked.

"Stubborness. I'm turning over a new leaf...a new optimistic leaf."

He chuckled. "I'll believe it when I see it."

I narrowed my eyes at him. "Am I really that much of a pessimist?"

"No. Sometimes you just tend to see the bad side of things."

I punched his arm as hard as I could but it didn't really seem like I did much damage. "Shut up!"

"You asked," he shrugged, smiling at my wimpy punch. "So..." he said. "What are you doing for your birthday?"

I looked at him surprised that he had brought that up.

"Yes, I do remember your birthday," he said. "July

11th. You're so young. It's about time you turned eighteen."

"Says the person that's like two minutes older than me."

"Yes, I can see how you can get two minutes confused with four months."

I gave him a dirty look. "But anyways…I don't know what I'm doing for my birthday exactly. My mom plans it every year despite my wishes."

"Well maybe she won't this year."

His green eyes looked away from mine and up into the sky. I looked up too. I could tell the sun would start to set soon. I knew I would have to leave before it got dark although I didn't want to. As much as I wanted to hate Kennley, I didn't. I wanted things to go back to normal and for right now, it seemed as if they were.

"I think I'd see a pig fly with a monkey dancing on top of its back before I see the year my mom doesn't plan a party. I'm pretty sure it will be the usual…barbeque in my backyard with people I haven't seen in years. You should stop by."

He smiled, "Will do."

I sighed while his green eyes worked their regular magic on me. "Kennley…I missed this."

"I've missed this too. See, this is living proof that exes can be friends after all."

"We spent one month as friends, two months in a relationship, a little less than a month apart…and now we are friends again. We have a made a complete circle." I drew a circle with the tips of my fingers.

"Hopefully we won't be going around and around. I really hate on and off again relationships. They're so annoying," he said this like he knew from experience.

"Well how many relationships have you been in? I

heard you only dated blondes." I tried my best not to come off as the jealous ex-girlfriend.

He looked at me, studying my face for a long moment. "I've been in four relationships including you...but only two of them were serious. And actually, I've been liking brunettes these days."

I was going to combust if he sent me anymore mixed messages. "Really? Because I want to dye my hair red but I'm not sure how it will look on me. What do you think?" I held my hair out over my face examining it.

"I'd pay good money to see that actually. It would be good for blackmail when I need it."

I smiled. I knew that I would look absolutely awful as a red head. "That bad huh?"

He nodded. "I'm not really thinking red is your color."

"Well what is my color?"

He smiled. "I think green in more your type."

I could tell he wasn't insinuating something because of his eyes. It was only my half obsession with them that made my eyes tense slightly.

"Great! Then I would match the grass. And you should dye your hair magenta." I laughed. This conversation had taken such a ridiculous turn.

"What's the difference between pink and magenta?" He asked.

I rolled my eyes. That was such a boy thing to say. "It's a different shade of pink. One's darker than the other."

I looked around the creek and sighed. Although it had only been a couple of months, I felt like I had grown up here. It seemed like everything around me was changing. I just wanted to keep one thing the same. I sigh heavily and focused on trying to keep my voice even. "I can't believe this place is going to be gone and replaced with a convenience store. I remember when I first found this place. My mom was practically hovering over me all the time after the accident and I needed some place to get away. I was just walking around... wandering aimlessly. Then I saw it...and I didn't care that it was abandoned because it felt like mine and I liked that. That's why I was so completely put off by you at first. You ruined the peace. You disturbed my safe haven. I borderline hated you for that."

He smiled. "Yeah, well I'm not going to apologize. You made my day actually...it's not very often that you see a girl's dress go flying up like that. If it would have went up a little higher..."

Ugh...Kennley had no shame. I grimaced. "It's not like I flashed you or anything. It didn't go past my thighs."

"It was close though."

I sighed. "Well I hope you enjoyed yourself." I thought about me and Ben's conversation the other day. "Why were you there that day anyway? Or were you just wandering aimlessly like me?"

It took him a second before he responded. "I don't know. I don't really remember. I remember why I left so abruptly. I was upset with Ross...but I think I was there for the same reasons that you found the creek. I was just driving around in Eddie for awhile. Haven't you ever just drove around...just for the fun of it?"

"Not recently...considering my current car issues. Thanks for earlier this week by the way. I'll pay you back—."

He stopped me. "No. Consider it an early birthday present. But you made things a lot easier by losing your keys like to always do."

Sitting here at the creek was just making me sadder thinking about how I wouldn't have it anymore.

"Strangely, I don't know what I'm going to do without this place. It's like it's become a part of me."

"Well, we both have our memories...isn't that what makes this place so special anyhow."

I chuckled. "Don't flatter yourself, Morgan. I loved this place before you."

"Regardless Dean...you have to admit I play some role in making this place special...no matter how tiny that role may be."

Millions of images flashed up in my head at all the moments we had spent here. I remembered him gently putting the necklace around me, my back being pressed up against the perfect shade tree, hugging him for the first time, and me trying to drag him to his car. All of these things had made the creek so unbelievably special.

"And do I have a role in your play?" I asked.

"Leading lady...regardless of anything that's happened."

I looked away from him and sighed although it came out more as a yawn. I was waiting for my body to self destruct with his stupid and confusing mixed messages. I didn't understand how he didn't want to be together but insinuate the complete opposite.

"Okay well...you at least have two lines in mine. There are no small roles though right? Only small actors."

"Whatever lies help you sleep at night..."

I sighed. "Okay fine. You have monopolized my life up until it came to a screeching halt last month." I regretted the words as soon as I said them.

He grinned. "I never liked monopoly anyway. I'm more of a checkers kind of a person."

He was being so incredibly immature and somehow

I still couldn't stop smiling. "I wasn't talking about board games... and I hate board games anyhow."

His jaw dropped. "Who doesn't like board games?"

I had unfortunately played many board games in my day. I was completely burned out on them. "You've never been to a Thomas Friday family fun night. I'm just glad that my parents haven't done another one since that awful movie my dad picked out. And besides... we've all been pretty busy lately which I am eternally grateful for."

"I never did come to the family dinner," he stated.

I was so incredibly thankful for that. "You know, when I think about it...maybe God doesn't hate me so much after all because I'm pretty sure I would have keeled over and died if I had to sit through a dinner with you and my parents."

"What happened to that new optimistic leaf you were talking about?" he challenged.

The sun was setting beneath the clouds now. It wasn't as pretty as I thought it had been before. Everything felt diminished after seeing the sky out in the woods.

"It's getting late. I should get home." But I didn't move from the spot I was in. I was happy that Kennley and I were at least friends again and I didn't want to leave but I knew my parents were probably wondering where I was.

"No wait...the sun's setting. Stay and watch it with me."

One look at his eyes and I gave in. I still remained unmoved next to him and we watched the sunset for the last time at Dean's Creek as my eyelids got heavier...

After I had finished rereading the same magazine for the fourth time I had time to stew with irritation. I stared off into the ocean looking at the waves gently crashing to the shore as the sun was almost finished setting. I rolled my eyes and sighed to try and release some of the frustration I felt. It felt like it had been hours since Emma left and never came back leaving me alone on a beach towel. I glowered out into the distance trying to think happy thoughts but inevitably the drifted back to Emma.

Finally I saw her walking through the sand towards me. She flipped her hair back and sent waves and smiles to everyone she crossed. She was so overly friendly sometimes that it drove me insane.

"Hey," she said sitting down next to me.

I looked at her briefly and then picked up the same magazine I had no interest in reading again. I flipped through the pages as I ignored her. She understood my anger immediately and sighed.

"I know you hate me and I'm sorry. I was talking to Marissa and..."

"And you forgot about me." I tried to keep my voice indifferent and I continued to fake read the magazine. "Don't worry, apology accepted."

"How many times do I have to say I'm sorry for you to forgive me?"

"I just forgave you didn't I?" I said flatly, flipping the page.

I could feel her glare on me before she grabbed my magazine and set it down.

I looked down at my empty hands. "Hey!" I yelled.

"You could have came and joined Marissa and I or talked to some other people besides me."

I grimaced. "You know how I feel about Marissa Harrison, Emma."

She sighed. "She's really not that bad once you give her a chance. Why do you think so many other people adore her?"

"Maybe they figure popularity's contagious."

"That is not the case and you know it. Kahlen look around. We are surrounded by at least one hundred people that we've known since middle school. You didn't have to sit here all by yourself waiting for me while reading stupid magazines."

I shook my head to myself. "Emma, I'm not good with other people. Don't you ever wonder why you're my only friend? I'm not charismatic like you. You're gorgeous, smart and talented—,"

"Stop!" she yelled. "Would you stop staying that? Geez Kahlen, you never see yourself clearly. You put me up on this pedestal and it's like you think I can do no wrong but then when I finally do, you can't take it. You say I'm gorgeous, smart and talented but the truth of the matter is you're at least ten times more of all those things. Sometimes I feel like you're always trying to live your life through me because you're afraid to live your own. I can't deal with the pressure of trying to live up to this perfect image you have of me."

My only response was silence. I finally looked up from the sand and her blue eyes were gazing intensely at my brown ones.

"I know that came out harsh..." she continued. "But it's the truth. You can't be dependent on me. And I'm sorry....again, for abandoning you for Danny and Marissa. And...for before that when I snapped at you for the whole locket thing."

I sighed. "I wasn't trying to invade your privacy or anything. I just know that the locket means a lot to you and I wanted to know why."

"If I tell you what's inside, will you forgive me."

I nodded although I already forgiven her.

"Well the locket's kind of old so it's hard to open sometimes. It used to belong to my grandmother. I have never met her though. She died when my dad was young."

I listened more intensely. Emma never really talked about her dad which I respected. Although I hadn't known from experience I knew death could be a touchy subject. All I knew about Emma's dad was that he died before her and Julie moved here when we were eleven.

"My dad was really only a father to me when it was convenient and I guess on my tenth birthday…it was convenient. He surprised me by showing up and then even more when he was actually sober for a change. He gave me the locket and inside is a picture of my grandmother and on the other side is a picture of my dad. I know it meant a lot to him to give it to me. It was the only thing he had left from her. After that day I never took it off. But after my birthday…little did I know that my dad was going to get drunk and be stupid enough to drive…I think you know where the story goes from there."

I felt so badly for Emma. Although her dad wasn't the best, it wasn't fair that he be taken away from her permanently. "I'm sorry Em…"

She nodded, staring off into the ocean. "So am I. Still sometimes even today I think….what if….or maybe if he didn't get drunk that night that he'd still be here today. But I know that living your life on maybes and what ifs is pointless. It demeans life to some extent in my opinion."

I smiled weakly. "You should write a book someday."

She smiled too. "You're already writing one for me

with that stupid little note pad you carry around and write down what I say."

I shrugged.

"So…" she said. "Does this mean you forgive me for so rudely abandoning you?"

I grinned. "You were forgiven like five minutes ago Em."

"Well that's good to know because I have good news."

"Like…?"

"Marissa and I met these guys and they were like fawning over us which was hilarious to watch. But they want to meet us later."

I rolled my eyes. "Well you and Marissa have fun."

She sighed. "Not Marissa and me…they want to meet me and *you*. You know that Marissa is the happiest single person to ever walk the face of the earth. So I told them about you."

"You know how I feel about relationships. I don't need any more complications in my life."

"Neither of them are cute. I just thought it would be fun to hang out with some new people."

I smiled, guessing that neither of these boy's name's started with a D too. I wasn't sure if Emma realized her obsession with boys whose names started with Ds. I found it funny.

She folded her hands together and adjusted herself so she was on her knees giving me a puppy dog look. "Please Kahlen…if you go with me I'll be you bestest friend forever."

I chuckled. "You already are."

"Good. So that means you'll come with me." She beamed.

I gave up the battle realizing that I wasn't going to win this argument.

25. Earthquake

In an uncomfortable position I rolled over onto my pillow that was harder and warmer than I had expected it to be...almost muscular. My eyes shot open at the speed of light. I was surrounded by trees, grass, water... and Kennley.

Already hyperventilating, I moved off of his chest and shook his body violently. He was an overly heavy sleeper so I had to practically assault him to get him to wake up. His eyes finally opened and he seemed just as disoriented as I had been. I was hyperventilating so much I thought I was going to pass out. I didn't even remember falling asleep.

"No," he said as he wiped his eyes with his hands.

I couldn't even form a sentence to express all of the thoughts that were going through my mind.

I started pacing. "What time is it?"

Still sitting on the ground, he pulled his cell phone and slammed it shut with a groan. "It's one o'clock."

I tried to steady my heart beat to keep from fainting. "In the morning?!"

He stood up and ran his fingers through his hair. "No, in the afternoon!" he snapped sarcastically, gesturing towards the darkness that surrounded us.

"Ugh! I have to get home, my mom is probably freaking out right now. My parents are going to kill me because of this." I was on the verge of tears. I could only imagine what was waiting for me at home.

"Yeah well I'd rather my parents kill me than send me to Glen Arbor!"

My uneven breathing was finally calming. "Kennley what happened?"

He sighed. "You fell asleep and I was going to wake you up but...but I guess I fell asleep too."

I buried my head in my hands. "Ugh! I'm so stupid... and because of it, I'm going to die, and you're going to Glen Arbor." I could feel the moisture being created at my eyes. "I don't want you to move to Glen Arbor. Can't you explain to your parents what happened?"

I could barely make out his face in the darkness but I could tell he was moving closer to me while I paced.

"Yes, I'll explain to them that I stayed out all night with you because we fell *asleep*."

I glowered at his sarcasm. "Okay, I know that sounds bad but it's the truth. I'm your ex-girlfriend remember, they shouldn't think that we did anything." I wished it was light enough to see his expression but I couldn't. I let out a big breath. "I don't want you to move to Glen Arbor." I repeated.

He took another step closer to me and I could see the torn expression on his face. "I don't even know how I'm supposed to get home."

I looked around for his car but I didn't see it anywhere. "How did you even get here?"

"Ben drove me. He said that your house was on the way to wherever he was going. I think he mentioned something about a soul mate."

Although it was the most inappropriate time to smile I did. It hadn't been three weeks yet and I wondered how Ben meeting up with Cece had gone.

"I need to get home," I said with my smile fading.

"You can go ahead on. I'll just call Ben and get him

to come pick me up. He's one of those people that stay up till three in morning every night."

I gave one final sigh before Kennley unexpectedly grabbed me into a hug. "Happy Birthday by the way... and I really am sorry...for everything."

"Thanks." I whispered to him as he released me.

I sprinted all the way home and ended up lying on the grass outside my window because I was exhausted. I felt so out of shape as I fought to catch my breath.

{removed}I got up slowly and climbed up the tree to my window. I opened it quietly and saw Macy sitting on my bed. She rose up her head and cocked it to the side and I thought she would bark. I motioned for her to stay, hoping she would keep quiet. As I stepped through the window, I lost my balance and went falling down hard and brought all the things on my dresser down with me.

All the lights in my house were off so I figured that my parents were sleeping. I was surprised that they weren't out looking for me. I was expecting to come home to wrath that would have me cringing in the corner.

I got up slowly hoping not to make any more noise and slowly picked up all of the things that fell off of my dresser. I picked up my old cell phone that was fully charged now. I wondered why my mother hadn't cancelled the service on my phone when I lost it. It didn't seem like the smartest choice on her part but maybe she always thought I would eventually find it. I accidentally hit a button on the phone with my finger and the screen lit up. It said I had two messages. With my burning curiosity I went to my voicemail and listened intently.

"Hey Kahlen, don't hate me okay? I'm sorry. I

completely forgot about you but I'm on my way to the other side of the beach as we speak."

It was her...it was Emma. It felt so surreal to be hearing her voice. I saved the message and replayed it over and over again before moving on to the next.

"Geez, what is the point of having a cell phone if you never answer. So I guess I'll have to tell you I'm sorry when I see you then...but you know I love you. Don't hate me. Bye."

Bye....that was the last word I had heard Emma Bryant say. I closed my phone and stared at it for a second before getting into my bed and lying there motionless with Macy's warm dark fur against my feet. Before I knew it, I was drifting off to sleep.

The two guys that we had met up with, whose names I had already forgotten had a silver Bentley that was absolutely beautiful. I had always wanted a Bentley but they were so expensive.

Of course the first thing that Emma said was, "Can we drive it?"

The two boys who were practically drooling over Emma nodded yes while they wiped the spit from their chins.

"Perfect!" she smiled. "We'll be right back I promise."

Whatever their names were...they were incredibly stupid to let two strangers drive their car. Emma jingled the keys in her hands as we walked over to the car.

"Emma, are you sure we should do this?" I asked.

She shrugged. "What's the worst that could happen? We're just driving a car."

"I don't know, I just have a like a premonition about this or something."

She sighed. "No, what you have is called scaredy-cat syndrome. Get in." She motioned towards the car door. I stood motionless outside the car. She sighed heavily again. "Think of this like diving."

Among the many sports Emma played, diving was included. "Diving?" I asked.

"Yes, diving. Diving is like life Kahlen. Once you climb those ladders and get up on the board you can't mull over everything that might happen. Sometimes you just have to jump and trust the water and yourself to catch your fall. You may not always win the gold. But losing is better than not trying at all."

I took out my note pad. "Wait…could you repeat that but say it a little bit slower.

She grabbed the pad out of my hand and put it in her purse. I looked at her with my jaw dropping. "Okay fine," she said. "It's like the hundred meter dash in track. When I'm getting into the blocks and I'm down on the ground waiting for the gun. My heart is about to beat out of my chest. I can feel my body tingling. All my worries are just piling up on top of each other. But as soon as that gun shoots it all goes away. When I'm running I don't think. I do. Nothing matters anymore. All I see is the finish line… nothing more. I don't hear anything. I don't feel anything. Then as soon as it's all over…It feels like such a rush…Like getting off a roller coaster."

"You sound like a druggy," I said.

"Yeah well you sound like a pessimist."

"Takes one to know one," I said childishly.

She smiled. "Likewise."

I sighed before getting into the car against my better judgment. I tried to remember everything she said so when I finally got my note pad back I could write it down. Emma turned the key in the ignition and the beautiful car purred to life.

Everything was a blur from that point on. I was suddenly in a hospital bed with my parents standing over me and my head pounding. Disoriented didn't even begin to explain how confused I was. There was only one logical reason I could come up with for why I was in a hospital bed...we must have gotten in an accident. I didn't really remember the accident, just the sounds of metal crashing hard against something else. I didn't know how it happened or why.

After hours had passed of unbearable waiting the doctor finally came and told us what happened. He explained how Emma had been in far worse condition than me and how everyone did all that they could. Seven words that he said really stuck out to me.

"Her heart just gave out on her."

Emma would never give up on anything no matter what the circumstances.

And then I felt it. I could feel the ground moving beneath me and everything around me quickly falling to the ground. The world was crumbling into nothing and all I could do was stand still and watch the earthquake consume everything that I once knew and loved. But then, when I opened my eyes I saw that everything was at ease. And it was surreal that as the war and the earthquake went on inside my head, everyone and everything else around me was completely fine. Then I realized that life had been moving on without me as time stood still in my mind. I realized that somehow, I would have to start moving on with time...with life.

26. Birthday Party

I woke up to the sounds of the birds chirping annoyingly out my window and my mother opening up my bedroom door. I winced, waiting to be yelled at and interrogated with questions but she looked relatively calm.

"Oh," she said surprised. "You're back already? I didn't even hear you come in?"

I rubbed my sleepy eyes. I had no idea what she was talking about.

She sighed. "You're in trouble."

I felt my heart sink to my stomach. "Mom, I'm sorry I just—,"

"I'll let it slide because it's your birthday but next time, do me a favor and call if you're going over a friend's house. Don't just leave without telling me. I was having a panic attack when I called Marissa and asked her if she knew where you were...then I felt like an idiot when she said that you were sleeping over at her house."

I couldn't believe it...Marissa had covered for me. "I'm sorry mom," I said, somewhat dazed. "But if you didn't think I was in here right now...why were you coming in my room?" I had always been curious if my mother snooped through my things when I wasn't around.

"Sweetie, relax, I was just coming to see where

Macy was...and I guess I found her. She seems to have taken a liking to your bed."

I chuckled. "I've noticed."

"Honey, I have some errands to run and your father is hanging out with some friends. We should both be back late this afternoon so we can have your birthday dinner then."

My eyes widened. "You mean you're not throwing me a party?" I was surprised by the hint of disappointment in my voice.

She smiled. "Isn't that what you wanted?" Then her face shifted to a slight frown. She looked like she was about to cry. "Happy eighteenth birthday Pumpkin....it seems like just yesterday you were running around in your underwear singing I'm a Little Teapot."

I grimaced. "Mom I was three."

She looked at me for a long moment still frowning before sighing while closing my door.

I plopped my head down hard on my pillow hoping to get at least two more hours of sleep even though it was already noon. Right when I was beginning to doze off my cell phone began to ring. I tried to ignore it but even when it finally stopped ringing...someone started calling again, and again. I got up out of the bed groggily and walked over to my cell phone.

"Hello?" I answered.

"KAHLEN THOMAS!!!!" she yelled.

"Marissa?" I asked.

"Where are you?!"

"Marissa, calm down. I'm at my house."

She exhaled loudly. "I almost had a heart attack last night because of you. And then I had to lie to your poor mother even though I wasn't sure if you were hurt, or kidnapped, or—,"

"Marissa, calm down," I repeated. "I'm fine. I was with Kennley—,"

"Oh my gosh…don't tell me you two—,"

I sighed. "We fell asleep…nothing more. And thank you for covering for me. You have no idea how big a hurricane I just avoided."

She seemed calmer now. "So are you two back together now?"

"I think we landed on friendship." All I heard on the other end was laughter. "What?" I asked.

She was still laughing. "I'll believe that when I see it."

I couldn't believe how truly tickled she was at the idea of Kennley and I being friends. "We were friends before weren't we?"

Unbelievably, she *still* laughing. It even sounded like she was crying. "Face it Kay, you two were never really friends to begin with. The whole school even knew that. The only person who didn't was you. You guys liked each other from the start."

I tried to deny it but my mouth wouldn't open.

She sighed as her laughter died out. "Okay, I'll talk to you later. Oh, and happy birthday Kay."

"Thanks. Bye."

I owed Marissa my life and my first born for covering for me. I got about an hour or so more of sleep before Macy was barking and my window was shaking. I sat up quickly and screamed quietly when I saw Kennley outside my window standing on the tree.

I stumbled over to my window and opened it and stood back as he stepped in.

"What are you doing here?!" I asked.

Macy jumped off of the bed and ran over to Kennley and started barking and sniffing at him.

"You got a dog?" he asked.

"That's beside the point. What are you doing here? And there's a front door you know!"

He shrugged. "I tried the front door but no one answered. So then I climbed up the tree."

I was so bewildered by everything that had just happened in only a matter of minutes. "What if I was changing in here or something?!"

He grinned. "But you weren't…and by the way you might want to get curtains or something. I'm sure the neighbors across the street have gotten an eyeful of you changing before."

I sighed, trying to calm myself. "Why are you here Kennley?"

"I wanted to talk to you."

I was a complete mess. I was still in the clothes I had been wearing yesterday, my hair was a mess, and for some reason my face was always really pale when I first woke up.

I frowned. "Oh no. You're not going to boarding school next year are you?" I asked, sitting on my bed.

He smiled. "No actually. When I didn't call Ben to come pick me back up before we went to sleep…he figured maybe…" He was struggling for words.

I rolled my eyes. "Let me guess….his head's in the gutter just like everyone else's."

He grinned. "Yeah, pretty much. But he called my parents and told them that I was staying at his house."

I laughed and Kennley looked at me confused. "Marissa did the same for me. So…is that all you came here to talk about?"

I was still trying to wrap my head around all that had just happened. One moment I was asleep off in dreamland and the next I'm letting Kennley through my window. It was hard to process and I felt disoriented.

"Actually…I didn't really come here to talk. I wanted to take you somewhere so get ready to go."

I narrowed my eyes at him. "Where?"

He walked towards my bedroom door. "Save the questions for later…but for now, get ready or we're going to be late."

I stared at him as he closed the door behind him. He was particularly smug about something.

Of course I had absolutely no idea of what was going on. But I had practice in being kidnapped. I knew that I should just go along with the flow and pretend to play along. And plus, I didn't mind so much about being kidnapped by Kennley. I got dressed quickly and hurriedly brushed my teeth and hair hoping I wasn't taking too long. I ran down the stairs and Kennley was sitting comfortably on the couch next to Macy.

"So where are you taking me?" I asked.

He just shrugged, following behind me out the door. I looked around but I didn't see his car anywhere."

"We're walking," he stated, looking at my puzzled face.

We started walking down the sidewalk while I studied his face in search for answers.

"Why are we going to the creek?" I asked finally figuring out where he was taking me. "Doesn't construction start today?"

Both his hands were in his pockets as we strolled along the sidewalk. "Not until later today."

I narrowed my eyes. "You are incredibly smug about something. What do you know that I don't know?"

He narrowed his eyes at me too. "Cotton."

I looked at him confused.

"Ten…nine…eight…"

I sighed. "Peanut butter." I knew he was trying to

distract me by playing random but I decided not to care…for now.

"Fire."

"Plants."

"Stickers."

We continued to play the random game until we got to the creek. As I looked beyond the trees and to the small meadow I saw my parents and friends, and food and decorations. I was completely speechless.

"Surprise," he whispered to me.

My breathing was becoming unsteady as I walked closer to everyone that had been anxiously waiting to greet me.

I was so completely shocked. "What about the construction and the stupid convenience store?" I asked.

He smiled and walked me over to a new sign planted in the ground. It read, Kahlen's Creek. "There isn't going to be any construction. I officially bought this piece of property and I'm giving it to you."

My hand flew to my mouth and I was afraid I would faint. My eyes widened with the uttermost shock. I couldn't even begin to fathom why he would do all of this. I didn't even want to think about how much money this must have cost him. I stretched up on my tippy toes to wrap my arms around his neck so tightly there was no way he could escape. It was everything I could do not to cry. I was so completely happy. I hadn't felt this way in so long.

He chuckled. "I'll take that as a thank you."

I still had my arms around him until I fought myself to let him go. I turned around and everyone was still smiling at me happily. I walked over to my parents and hugged them. I was in a hugging mood.

My mom shook her head. "So *he* can throw you parties and it's alright, but I can't."

"Wait..." I said. "Kennley did all of this?"

She nodded. "With a little bit of my help of course... but mainly him."

I felt like I was floating on a cloud. I even pinched myself to see if I was dreaming or not although usually I had nightmares and this was far from awful. Everything felt so completely surreal.

Everyone was here. Marissa and Jenny came up to talk to me, along with Cece and Laura, Ben and Jordan...even Bradley was here. I was guessing he and Kennley had made amends. All of Julie's friends were there also for her going away party. Julie came up and hugged me. But then she reached for my hand and placed a key inside of them.

"If I want to start completely new, it means getting rid of this car of mine also."

"Oh..." I said overwhelmed. "I don't know what to say." Thank you didn't really seem to express all the gratitude I felt at this moment.

"Kahlen you are like a daughter to me...you know that. I just wish I could have been a better mom."

I smiled and hugged her again. "I'm going to miss you."

She shrugged. "The train ride to Chicago is only a little more than an hour away."

"I'll keep that in mind."

It was like the creek had been transformed. Benches and even a swing set had been put up...and yet the creek still seemed exactly the same. Still majestic in its beauty.

I was feeling so completely overwhelmed once all the other presents started to come. I got a new guitar from my parents, money from both Ben and Jordan. I got a bracelet from Cece that had a heart on it just like her necklace. The bracelet said, Survivor, just like hers. She gave me a good wink when she handed me the tiny box. Laura gave me a Sudoku book and another tiny book with Cece's most amusing little phrases. Jenny gave me a picture she had painted of me which was absolutely amazing. I still didn't understand how so much talent could come from such a little person. Marissa gave me CDs of some of my favorite bands and another CD marked slideshow. I didn't know how she knew that the one she had given me earlier had been smashed to bits but I was appreciative of it. But still... out of all the wonderful gifts I had gotten, Kennley's was by far the best.

It felt like he was reading my mind when he asked me if we could go talk alone. I needed to get away from the party...I was so overwhelmed. We walked off over on the sidewalk away from the party and the music.

"Kennley...you really have no idea how much this means to me. I can't thank you enough. Really I can't." I was tempted to hug him again. "But still...I wish you wouldn't have spent that much money on me. I'm hardly worth it. I appreciate it, but really, you should get back whatever you spent for this place. How did you get the money anyway?"

{removed}He sighed. "That's not important."

"Kennley tell me," I demanded.

He was hesitant. "I...I sold Eddie."

My hands flew to my face as I sunk down slowly to the sidewalk and landed with a good thud. I could feel the tears welling up but they didn't spill over. "No! Kennley, you did not sell your car over me!" I was practically hyperventilating. "Why would you do that?! That car meant *everything* to you and then some and this is just a stupid creek!"

He sat down next to me. "I'll get a new car eventually."

"Why…why would you do that?!"

His voice was so much calmer compared to mine. "Because…that creek means a lot to you…It means a lot to *me* also. I had to do something."

I shook my head. "I'll help you…I'll help you get it back. I'll sell my new car if I have to."

"Kahlen," he sighed. "It was my decision. It's already made."

I shook my head again. "I still don't understand why…"

He grinned briefly. "We both hate dances."

I looked at him confused.

"The other day you said we don't have anything in common besides stubbornness. We both hate dances."

I knew he was trying to distract me but I let him. He was right. We both did hate dances. I smiled thinking about when he had asked me to prom and I said no. He was only asking me for my benefit of course.

"I still can't believe I got rejected by my own girlfriend…not that I'm complaining." He shook his head in disbelief.

I chuckled. "Okay so maybe laughing in your face was a little rude…but I'm not that big on dances and neither are you. So it worked out perfectly."

"Indeed it did." He grinned. "Favorite sport… I don't think we've done that one yet."

"Football…my dad used to be seriously obsessive. It kind of stuck."

"Ha. We now have three things in common."

"Do you play?" I asked curious.

"I used to…but they don't really let you play sports when you're on probation."

"Oh," I grimaced although I was happy he was openly talking about his past now.

"Funniest thing you've ever heard," he said leaning in his usual laidback position.

"We've done this one before," I said.

He shook his head no. "We did funniest thing you've ever seen…not heard."

I rolled my eyes. There was no use in arguing with him. I knew I would lose in the end. I started laughing at the memory of the funniest thing I'd ever heard. Tears were actually streaming down my eyes. "Okay…" I said trying to stifle my laughter although it wasn't working. "The funniest thing I've ever heard was when my mom was under the impression…"

"What?" he urged anxiously.

I could hardly talk because I was laughing so hard. "She thought I was pregnant with your baby. She clarified and said that it was only a quick moment of doubt but I still couldn't stop laughing."

Kennley started laughing too. "Pregnant…ha! It used to be whenever I'd touch you you'd flinch…so a pregnancy would be highly unlikely."

I glowered at him. "No, that was like the first week we were going out. And I wasn't flinching…I was just jumpy."

He sighed. "Do I make you nervous?"

"Sometimes yes, sometimes no."

"Why?" he asked.

"I've already told you…It's mostly just your impulsiveness. I told you that I have a hard time keeping track with you."

I sat looking at him, contemplating my own impulsiveness. Maybe if I mustered up enough strength I could…

"Yeah well I've been thinking things through more these days." He said looking down at the ground.

I tried to read his green eyes but he wouldn't look up at me. It seemed like he was thinking very hard about something. "Whatever happened to, 'if you think too much you'll talk yourself out of it'?"

You don't think…you do.

It wasn't Emma's voice I was hearing in my head but my own.

He sighed. "Well I—,"

I kissed him with as much strength and energy I could muster. I didn't care if after he would reject me or if in the end I would get hurt. I could feel him pulling his body closer to mine and his hand moving to the small of my back. That was anything but a rejection. I pulled myself closer to him as well until I was practically sitting on his lap with our lips moving in sync. I wrapped my arms around his neck and I wasn't sure if it was possible but I brought myself closer to him. I didn't want to stop. I wanted this moment to last forever. His lips were anything but gentle against mine as I felt his hand slide to my waist and lingered there.

He pulled back breathing hard looking at me with absolute confusion. After several seconds of us looking into each other's eyes, our faces only millimeters apart, he said, "Wow."

I couldn't respond still trying to catch my breath.

He moved back from me and stared at the ground again. It still didn't seem like rejection. He looked like he needed a minute to get over his utter shock.

"You've never kissed me like that before," he stated.

"I've never missed you this much before, and you've never bought me a creek." I sighed. "I know that getting back together would officially make us an on and off again relationship but—,"

"Third time's the charm right?" He said.

I smiled. "I believe I've heard that one before."

He kissed me except it was much shorter than the last.

"I love you," he whispered as he pulled back.

I couldn't help but laugh. "I had no idea how much until today. I still can't thank you enough for all of this." I could feel the tears welling up again just at the thought.

"You really don't have to thank me...you'd be surprised how much of a deal this place really was since it's abandoned and all. It didn't cost an arm and a leg...just an arm. So really, don't sweat it."

My smile widened. "You win the bet you know."

His brows furrowed. "How?"

"You got me to do something wild and crazy."

"Such as...?" He grinned.

"You got me to fall in love. Now you can get anything you want."

"You know...I think I've already got it," he said. "But your wish/favor hasn't expired."

I decided not to tell him that all along I wanted to drive Eddie considering it wasn't an option anymore. And as stubborn as I was, whether he liked it or not, I was helping him get another car.

"You know, Kenneth Bradley..." I smiled. "I think I've got everything I want too."

He smiled too. "I'm glad."

We both leaned in for another kiss when suddenly I had been sprayed in the face with water. I turned to see where it had come from. Jordan and Ben were standing in front of us with a bucket of water balloons. Kennley was the one who had really gotten hit. His entire head was soaked. I couldn't help but start to laugh.

"Kahlen, you know how some people do birthday hits or pinches for each year...well I do water balloons," Ben explained.

"Then why did you hit me?!" Kennley yelled. There was no hint of humor on his face as he wiped away the water from his eyes.

"I don't know...you looked so *hittable*," Ben smiled.

Jordan reached into the bucket and chucked another one at Kennley which he dodged. The balloon didn't pop so Kennley picked it up and clutched it in his hand so tightly I thought it would pop then.

Ben began to back up slowly. "Dude, we are so dead."

Jordan began to back up also. "Run!!"

All three of them took off running down the street and I watched amused as Kennley nailed Ben in the back of the head.

The rest of the evening was a blur...but a very eventful blur. Everyone had gotten into a full fledged water balloon war. It was craziness. It lasted for the whole rest of the party. I was the main target and ended up completely soaked. What got me the most soaked was the blow I took from Marissa...who knew the girl had such a good arm.

Somehow it ended with Marissa and me sitting on the porch of my house dripping wet. The boys were still somewhere running down the street while the rest of the adults were still having the going away party.

She sighed. "Is Macy inside? I haven't seen here in so long. I want to say hi."

My brows furrowed. "Marissa, how do you know Macy?" I asked.

She sighed again. "Kay, don't take this the wrong way but sometimes I think that you think you're the only one who was friends with Emma. Emma was friends with everyone. You're not the only person missing her. That's why I saw Mrs. Kraft sometimes. I needed help grieving just like you. I know I wasn't as close to her as you but I spent a lot of summers with her at camp and we'd hang out sometimes during the school year but you never went with us...So of course I know Macy."

All I could say was, "Oh."

"I hope you don't take offense to that in any way," she smiled weakly.

I smiled half-heartedly as well. Marissa Harrison didn't have a mean bone in her body.

"She was really one of a kind wasn't she?" I said.

"Yeah and the way she would somehow manage to make everything sound like it came straight out of a—,"

"—Fortune cookie." I grinned.

Before I knew it we were both laughing hysterically and I had no idea why. Tears were streaming down our eyes because we were laughing so hard. I tried to stop but I couldn't. My stomach was beginning to hurt so much that I had to.

"I miss her," I sighed as my laughter slowly subsided. "I miss her so much."

We both sat there watching the sunset while sitting on the porch. We sat in silence. Nothing else needed to be said. We had a whole lifetime of conversations ahead of us. There was no need to rush anything. I liked it that way. Things were going to get better. I had told myself that many times before but I had never had believed it until now. I had heard before that life's not about getting through the storm, it's about learning to dance in the rain. And I was finally dancing and I felt so free. Bad and terrible things happen in life but if we don't learn from them, we waste an experience and lesson. I had lost a lot of things this year but I also gained a lot also. Isn't that what life was about anyway? Making good out of a bad situation?

Emma would have been proud of me. I didn't need her anymore. I didn't need her to help me actually live my life. I was finally doing a good job of that myself. I wasn't afraid anymore. I wasn't afraid of the future and all of the consequences of the present. I was finally diving. I had nothing to be afraid of. I knew what it was like to feel like I had lost *everything* and lived. Nothing would stop me from living anymore. Nothing, not even the sky was the limit. I couldn't be satisfied with the sky now. I wanted something further than the clouds surrounded by the deep waves of blue. Further, further, further...I wanted stars.

Epilogue

I walked up to the gravestone with the key on my necklace swinging back and forth as I stepped through the snow. My cheeks were already red from the bitter coldness that surrounded me. It didn't make sense that there was snow in October. But if you lived in Michigan, it was only to be expected. I felt bad for all of the trick-or-treaters…and sadly Ben, Kennley, and Jordan were some of them. It didn't make sense that they were still going door to door in costumes begging for candy. They were all entirely too old…it was embarrassing. Ben was a going as a ballerina; Jordan was supposedly a business man with a briefcase and all who really looked more like someone in the mafia. Surprisingly Kennley's was the most disturbing of them all. He was a can of soup…yes, an actual can of soup, Campbell's tomato soup to be exact. I had even used that *Mmm… Mmm good* pickup line on him. I had no idea where he had found the costume. I was happy I had at least another week or so to try and talk them out of going. Kennley wasn't the only one always getting his way these days. I still had hope that I could persuade him.

I still pushed my way through the snow trying not to completely freak myself out with all the gravestones around me.

I took a deep breath. "Emma Christine Bryant… long time no see... unfortunately. I don't exactly know where to begin. You know sophomore year when you thought biology was hard or when you were learning to surf when you vacationed in Hawaii...well believe me I've faced a lot harder. I know I sound like broken record because I keep repeating this but it's not fair. You're supposed to be here Em. You're supposed to be standing beside me and it's not fair. I'm still a little confused as to why you instead of me. Survivor's guilt I guess. You were so much better than me in every way. I've never met someone as nice, charismatic, and optimistic as you. Someone like you deserves to still be one on this earth alive.

"Those first couple of days the pain was unbearable. I've never felt so depressed and useless in all of my life. And I was selfish really. I wasn't thinking about that you were gone, I was thinking about myself. I was thinking, 'What am I going to do without her? How am I supposed to go on living when she's not?' The first couple of months were so strange. I would hear your voice in my head most of the time. I guess I still felt that I needed you in a way.

"It's not the actual earthquake of the death that hurts the most, it's the aftershock. Anyone that says that childbirth is the worst pain in the world has obviously never lost someone... although I've never given birth."

"I'm sorry by the way. I should have gone to your funeral. It was just me being selfish again. I took me awhile to realize that it wasn't all about the closure. It's about remembering and celebrating someone's life and I missed that farewell party. But maybe it was fate that I missed it. If I wouldn't have, maybe these last seven months wouldn't have been the same. You know how you were always looking for love, it's also not fair that I wasn't looking and yet I rolled into it. I've found someone that loves me and I actually love him back.

"You would be proud of me if you were here. I'm

actually living my life like you always wanted me to. But it was easy to be satisfied watching you live your life when you were here. It was like watching a movie or reading a book. But once that was gone, I was miserable. I still can't fully comprehend that you're gone. It feels like you're on a long vacation although I know that's not true."

"I still can't fully explain to you how much it hurts. It's like this deep pain in the pit of my stomach that won't go away, but I don't want it to. Because if it goes away, if I don't hurt anymore, then it will feel like you're really gone. It's so bittersweet."

"When we said best friends forever, it means for eternity. You are my best friend and I will always love you and nothing can take that away from me, not even death."

"I always needed you. I was so dependent on you and it wasn't fair. I treated you as my crutch sometimes instead of my best friend. And I'm sorry for that. But I don't need anyone anymore…not you, not Kennley, or my parents. I'm doing fine on my own for once."

I pulled out a picture of Emma and I and placed it onto the snow along with a piece of paper with my finished song for her.

I almost hate you…
For leaving me here to cry
With no one hear to wipe the tears from my eyes.
Why'd you have to go?
And leave me here all alone
Now it's over, right as it begun, when we were having fun.

La la la.

La de dah dah dah dah

La de dah dah dah dah

La de dah dah dah ah ah ah

La la la

La de dah dah dah dah

La de dah dah dah dah

La de dah dah dah ah ah ah

I need you now.

I wish you could be here somehow
You were my hope my faith my love
Sent to me like a dove

La la la.

La de dah dah dah dah

La de dah dah dah dah

La de dah dah dah ah ah ah

La la la

La de dah dah dah dah

La de dah dah dah dah

I won't forget.
I won't replace.
You'll always fill this empty space…
Reminding me I have to be strong.
I won't forget.
I won't replace.
You'll always fill this empty space…
Reminding me I have to go on.

We'll meet again someday,
In heaven with the angels,
With you right beside me.
With you right beside me…

La la la.

La de dah dah dah dah

La de dah dah dah dah

La de dah dah dah ah ah ah

La la la

La de dah dah dah dah

La de dah dah dah dah

I almost hate you.
For leaving here to cry.
With no one here to wipe the tears from my eyes…
I miss you

I smiled briefly before saying the last word I had heard her say. "Bye."

ABOUT THE AUTHOR

Paige Agnew was born in Michigan. She wrote this book in 2007 as a result of a personal loss. Paige has enjoyed being her school newspaper editor and writing the theme poem for her graduation. Her compassion and sense of humor is in all of her writings. When Paige is not writing, she enjoys sports, dancing, singing, playing the piano, playing with her dog, spending time with family and friends, and of course reading. She is also actively involved in her church and community. Paige is currently in the process of publishing other books.

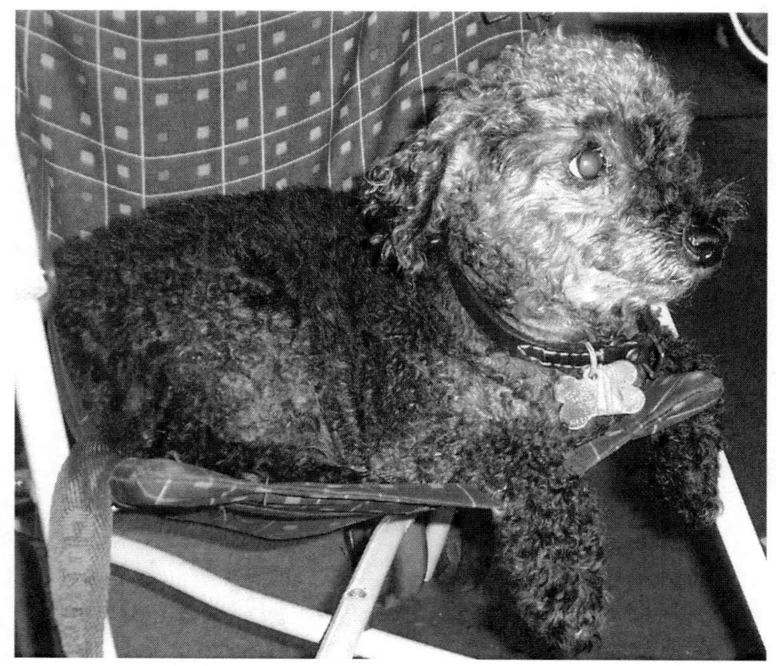